LOVE'S FIERY PRESCRIPTION

LOVE'S FIERY PRESCRIPTION

Flynn's Crossing Romantic Suspense Series
Book 9

Yvonne Kohano

K̶E

Nanokas Press

A Division of Kochanowski Enterprises

LOVE'S FIERY PRESCRIPTION
FLYNN'S CROSSING ROMANTIC SUSPENSE SERIES BOOK 9

Nanokas Press/KE Press books may be ordered through booksellers or by contacting:

Kochanowski Enterprises/Nanokas Press
PO Box 1274
Clackamas, OR 97015-9594
www.yvonnekohano.com
yvonne@yvonnekohano.com

ISBN: 978-1-940738-39-0 (sc)
       978-1-940738-85-7 (e)

Nanokas Press First Edition: 06-05-2016

Also by Yvonne Kohano

Love's Fiery Prescription, Book 9
(Noah and Nicolle)

Love's Fiery Resolution, Book 10
(Gideon and Danielle)

And more to come!
**Learn about upcoming releases at
www.YvonneKohano.com.**

Subscribe to Yvonne Kohano's enewsletter to be among the first to learn about new releases and special offers. Visit www.yvonnekohano.com for more information.

Follow Yvonne at www.yvonnekohano.com, on Facebook as Yvonne Kohano, and on Twitter @yvonnekohano to learn what tickles her about being a writer, and at www.GooseYourMuse.com for creativity tips.

LOVE'S FIERY PRESCRIPTION

Prologue – January

He strummed his fingers along with the song. That riff, the one leading into the chorus, was always the blazing hot part. Of course, it sounded best when the guitar player rocked it loud enough to deafen people in the next county. He and Gideon had tried to imitate it, the lyrics delivered in a wild screech, the guitar yowling and the drums' percussion strong enough to make rakes and shovels bang against the rack hanging on the garage's back wall.sad – "

Gideon, one of the reasons they left LA. The accidents he claimed were nothing more than that. Lives lost, lives Noah wasn't there to save.

His ease evaporated and he glanced up and down the aisle as he thought about the other big reason, the one he hoped he'd left behind. He noticed nothing obvious, but a threat could lurk anywhere, stalking his family. Even now, the tension never left him.

"Come on already, Char. Father is getting fidgety."

Noah swallowed the worry, realizing he wasn't living up to his promise to himself. Be in the moment. This time was about the girls. He used to be Daddy, or at least Dad. Elena decided those names were gauche. She wanted to call him Noah, but he had to draw the line. He was grateful his younger child didn't yet look at him as if he was an alien from another century, yet being the operative word.

Elena tapped her foot out of time with the overhead music and watched her sister with marked exasperation. Charlotte was having a hard time selecting a binder for school. In the last few months, his outgoing bundle of energy had developed numerous decision-making issues, from what to wear each day to which books she wanted to read. She'd become quiet, too quiet. The psychologist assured him it was a method of coping with upheaval from the divorce. Noah understood the why, but he didn't know how to fix it, another source of ongoing frustration.

"Would you like me to help you, sunshine?" He knelt next to Charlotte and examined the binders in their selection of styles and colors. His little girl smelled like her favorite lavender shampoo and bubblegum body wash. She leaned into his shoulder and he felt her nod as he inhaled with a pang. Up the aisle, Elena expelled another frustrated sigh and popped her gum. The popping accelerated as her eyes focused on her cell phone, her thumbs typing faster than her jaw could chew.

His daughters brought him immense joy. He wouldn't give up time with them for the world, which made him eternally grateful this job came along. It provided an opportunity to move the girls away from the less savory aspects of life in Los Angeles. He wasn't sure his kids felt the same way, but they'd come around. Or so he hoped. He hoped Gideon would come around too.

"Father," Elena popped to emphasize two elongated syllables, "why can't we study online at home? Lots of kids do it. Amelia goes to school online and then she can travel all over the world with her mother. If I'm going to be stuck in this effing hick town in the middle of effing nowhere, I should be able to go to school online so I can interact with people who are more my type."

"Elena, language." He sighed, knowing this was a futile reproof. It didn't matter how many times he asked her to watch her tendency to curse. He'd even taken away her cell phone for a week.

"It isn't like it's even a swear word. I mean, you say worse. I've heard you."

Yes, unfortunately, she had, on the phone with his ex-wife. Trying to be a good example, he set up a curse jar, and whoever said a bad word had to put in a quarter. He hadn't yet figured out what would happen to the money. Coins were beginning to accumulate.

"Char, honey, how about this binder? Will this work for you?" He tapped a white one at the beginning of the rainbow of choices, and his daughter nodded solemnly.

He grabbed two for good measure and stood, placing them in the shopping cart.

"Father, I cannot believe you picked white. Only morons get white. I mean, really." Elena stalked over to the cart and picked out the binders with two-fingered distain. "Charlotte needs appropriate colors, or she won't fit in."

Her irritation sent the message loud and clear. His eldest thought he was a clueless dork and therefore unfit to do something as straightforward as picking out the correct binders for school. Elena took over the job of helping Char, debating the merits and reasons why each color might or might not work, and Noah realized they'd be there for a while.

His daughters' heads bent together in intense conversation. He'd do anything to protect them. Slay any dragons and neutralize any threats. He just had to see them coming. He couldn't always be at his girls' sides. Horror could ambush them on any street corner, at any alley entrance, even in a pristine green park.

The piped-in music changed to a heavy metal classic delivered in show tune fashion more appropriate to a dentist's office, but despite its presentation, he bopped his head along with the rhythm. Music always soothed him, and today, he needed to restore his sense of calm. This move north to Flynn's Crossing made him almost as jittery and unsure as the girls. Unsure wasn't in his genes, or at least up until last summer, he didn't think it was.

He hadn't always been clueless either. In almost everything else in life, he was the bomb. Wait, did anyone say that anymore? He couldn't help nodding and bumping along to the beat. If that made him un-cool, so be it. He was a clueless embarrassment to his girls, who were sure they knew more than he did.

Swaying with an occasional snap of his fingers, he let his eyes roam the stacks of paper and dividers extending down the aisle. This early on a rainy Thursday morning, they had the place to themselves. His shoulders shook in a little shimmy when it came to the chorus. He grabbed a package of highlighters and pulled off a passable dip and dive with the fake microphone, mouthing the words to the music. As absorbed as they were, neither of the kids noticed. No one else would witness his rock and roll tribute.

Except for her.

He stopped bopping, his eyes snagged on the person at the end of the aisle. She wore a grin that said she'd seen the whole exchange. The song moved on to the next verse, and as if she was part of the band, she bobbed her head back and forth in a parody of a back-up singer. The movement made her braid of light red hair toss on her back. Her lips parted when it came to the chorus, and he found himself grinning and playing along. Together, they lip-synced the words until they were cut-off by an announcement paging any available associate to assist a customer by the printers.

The woman shrugged at their interruption but grinned, and his smile grew in return. She looked vaguely familiar. Was she someone he knew? From here, the expression on her face spelled fun and mischief. What color were her eyes? Even hidden by a tan jacket with a logo on the front, he could tell her body was fit. She was tall, but then, he wasn't, and she might have to lean down to kiss him.

Where the hell did that come from?

Did he need to put a quarter in the jar if he only thought the words?

It didn't matter. He hadn't kissed a woman in so long, he couldn't remember how long it had been. He kissed his daughters, and he kissed his mother on those rare occasions when she breezed in and out of their lives. He occasionally did a cheek buss with colleagues who were good friends. But kiss a woman, as in full lip-on-lip action?

"You aren't listening, Father. We're done. God, will you stop being such an embarrassment?"

"Quarter in the jar when we get home," he said to show he was listening.

"Charlotte is getting blue binders, because blue is cool. I, on the other hand, will have red, since red is my power color." Elena sashayed down the aisle as she delivered the information, already giggling and typing into her cell phone as she passed around the corner out of sight. Char followed on dragging feet, leaving dark heel scuffs on the off-white tile floor.

Noah knew how she felt. The last few months hadn't been a party for any of them, and through it all, he hadn't taken a break to breathe. Now he wanted to stay here and play rock and roll star with the intriguing singer at the other end of the aisle. Elena would never notice, and he'd be spared her derisive comments in front of the first woman to catch his eye in ages.

She stood where she'd been lip-syncing, that sunny smile still on her face as she examined his family with friendly curiosity. When his eyes met hers, she raised her hand and gave him an enthusiastic thumbs-up to go with the grin. A moment later, she disappeared toward the back of the store, as he stood motionless.

He felt a small hand on his and he turned his palm over automatically and closed his fingers, giving Charlotte a squeeze of recognition. When he looked down, her serious eyes filled her watchful expression. It hurt his heart to see her so silent and somber.

She shot a glance down the aisle, and her instant smile lit up his world. She leaned in and he leaned down, because whatever she said would always be important.

"Daddy," she whispered, "that lady looks like fun."

Chapter 1 – Mid-Spring

"You need to get back in the driver's seat where women are concerned, bro."

Noah Kinkead stopped toying with the wrapper from his straw long enough to give his older brother a hard glance. Gideon was a couple of inches taller and carried about twenty more pounds of solid muscle. Even so, he slouched in the cafeteria chair, legs sprawled in the aisle between tables. Noah sat up straight and barely avoided folding his hands on the scarred surface as a counterpoint. He guessed every pair of female eyes and some of the male ones were tracking Gid's every breath.

He decided to go on the offensive, at least hard enough to get his brother to lay off the dating advice.

"You look tired. Did you catch any breaks after the fires down south?"

Gideon shrugged, scanning the room with idle interest and occasionally giving a woman a small smile and nod of recognition. When he stretched his arms above his head, his abs rippled under his regulation t-shirt, and Noah swore a few female sighs echoed in the sudden silence. For Gideon, it was always like that.

He tried not to feel envious. Boy, did he try. When they were kids, Gid seemed to be stronger and faster and braver than anyone else, and Noah idolized him. He was every guy's buddy, and every girl carried a torch for him. None of that had changed. His big brother attracted friends and women faster than kids picked up colds and w th even greater frequency.

Across the table, Gideon raised an eyebrow and lifted his chin in the direction of three nurse aides. Their vigorous waves in return forced a breeze on the plants next to them. Giggles and whispers followed, and Noah didn't need to turn around to figure out they knew Gideon. Knew him as in the biblical sense, he'd bet.

"You never stop, do you?" Noah couldn't bank the disapproving tone in his voice. Gideon was a player, and yet women kept coming.

"Hey, I keep them happy. Ask any of those women if I disappointed them. They'll tell you I gave them a good time, and I never led them on with expectations. Good, healthy fun, and that's it." Gid focused on Noah with a questioning tilt to his head. "Don't you ever want to start dating again?"

Noah's thoughts flashed to the redhead from months ago. He'd replayed their mock-rock moment many times in his mind. He'd hoped to run into her again around town, but Flynn's Crossing wasn't cooperating. Who was he fooling? Even if he found her, he didn't have time.

"Don't you ever want to settle down?" Sickened by the sudden thought that the redhead could be another of his brother's conquests, Noah countered with more anger than he intended.

Gideon leaned in as if confiding a secret. "Why would I? Come out to the bar with me tonight. We'll pick up a couple of good-looking women and party. The place is hot. You know what kind of groupies we firedogs get. And you, a doctor? Geez, we'll have to fight them off."

Noah sighed, knowing this conversation would end up at a dead end. Gideon always wanted him to get out more. He never seemed to understand that Noah had responsibilities. He had children. He'd grown up. Gid never seemed to.

Gid sat forward and focused on Noah in sudden seriousness. He examined Noah closely as he said, "I'm glad we could get together today. It feels like the fire season never ended from last year. Four years of drought makes everything a hundred times worse. I'm sure we'll be called out nonstop over the next few months."

He shook his head and Noah joined him in sober reflection. Extreme heat over the last few summers escalated the danger. Not for the first time, he wished his brother had chosen a less risky profession. Wildland firefighting carried guaranteed hazards. Add to that people who refused to leave their homes, and Noah was the next one to see them injured or burned in his emergency department.

Even though he knew he probably shouldn't, Noah had to ask, "How are you handling it these days?"

Gideon stilled in a second, his face dropping into an expressionless mask as he shifted his gaze to the window. There was no need to clarify what 'it' was, a fire that led to a tragedy including the loss of a child. Gid had mentioned it only once, when he was completely shit faced and a disorganized tale involving a child burnt to a crisp poured out. That was right before he threw up the results of a binge and passed out on Noah's patio, face planted in his own vomit. It was enough to highlight his emotional pain from the incident. Noah often wondered if his brother's Gideon's soulless partying was a reaction to it.

Instead of answering, Gid rose, still watching the May sunshine in the hospital's garden courtyard. He crossed the room to stand in front of the window, and Noah had his answer. Gideon wasn't handling it. Perhaps this time, Noah would be the brave, strong one and find a way to help his brother. His fear lingered on the idea that this may be something outside of his control, no matter how hard he tried.

"I cannot wait to leave this town."

Elena's proclamation wasn't new. Since their mother confirmed her willingness to have the girls for the first two months of summer vacation, she uttered those words at least once a day. This too spiraled out of his control, and Noah had yet to figure out how best to deal with his older daughter's distain for their new home.

He continued to stir the sauce in the pan, wishing he understood what the attraction was in Orange County. Elena was a popular girl. She was growing into her mother's good looks, and when she applied herself, she proved to have inherited Noah's solid brain to match. Based on her social life here in Flynn's Crossing, she had made plenty of friends over the past few months. But all she ever talked about was the desire to return to the heat and smog.

"You say that every day, you know," Char observed. She didn't even bother to look up from her homework when her sister harrumphed in disgust.

"Just because you don't have a social life, little sister, doesn't mean the rest of us shouldn't either. Did I tell you Barbara has a Mercedes convertible now? It's going to be awesome to drive around in it."

Noah stirred faster, wishing the sauce would hurry up and simmer so he could feed the girls. He'd check their homework, and they would enjoy their favorite evening pastimes. Elena would text and message with her friends in the privacy of her room, and Char would draw in front of the TV as she watched children's programs recorded throughout the day. Char talked to him while she simultaneously copied pictures of cats and followed the show's storyline with its supposed hidden lesson.

Elena continued as she simultaneously thumbed her phone, "Barbara said we can take drives on PCH, hit the beaches, and go up to the coast. I can't wait."

He felt he should correct Elena, but it wasn't worth the battle. Besides, it seemed his ex was fine with their daughter calling her by her first name. In fact, she was fine with the girls calling her new husband by his first name too. James.

Noah stopped stirring, staring at the red sauce and willing it to bubble. When it didn't, he turned up the heat. He felt the wave of bitterness rise up and block his airway.

Barbara had little or no regard for how difficult it was to raise a responsible almost-teenager. She bribed the girls with clothes and shows on her weeks of custody. It didn't matter that they didn't need those things, or that the concerts and such weren't always appropriate for their ages. She did what she wanted and returned the over-amped and exhausted girls full of unrealistic expectations without so much as an apology.

And every time, Noah had to start over. Charlotte would come home silent and stressed, and weeks would pass before she regained her footing and turned into a semblance of a normal child again. Elena, on the other hand, tried to grow up too fast, acting older than her age and causing enough trouble to force consequences. Noah was still grateful to his colleague who shared a parenting tip with him. Don't take away the phone. Take away the phone charger. Elena straightened up fast after that episode, but that didn't mean the war ended.

"I'm going to eat my salad in my room, Father." Elena picked up her bowl off the table and scooped greens into it. With fork in hand, she turned for the kitchen door.

"That's all you're going to eat?" His stomach tightened as he felt the next skirmish begin. She was slender already, almost too skinny in his opinion. Since the plans for summer solidified, she'd been on a kick to lose weight she didn't carry.

Elena gave him a finger roll of dismissal as she waltzed out the kitchen door. Noah followed, even though he knew it was useless.

"You have to eat protein too, you know. Greens alone aren't going to keep you healthy. Elena? Put some chicken on it, or a hard-boiled egg."

In response, he heard the resounding click of her bedroom door. If he forced the issue, it would result in a fight, yelling, and ultimately, tears. The yelling would be hers. The tears, his.

"It's okay, Daddy. She ate tuna out of a can when we got home from school."

He turned back to Char, busy scribbling on notepaper. She'd covered sheets with her tight, precise handwriting. Thankfully, one of his kids still talked to him.

Crossing to her, he kissed the top of her head, inhaling the sweet flowery scent of her shampoo. Sometimes, he still got to brush her hair, but not very often anymore. His little girls weren't going to be little for much longer.

Char cuddled into his arms, still writing. His younger miracle always seemed to know exactly what he needed. For that, he was grateful.

"What are you writing, sunshine?"

She sat up and pulled the pages together, stacking them carefully so the corners lined up. She picked up the stack and gave it a couple of snaps against the table before handing them to him.

"It's a story, Daddy. It's about you and Uncle Gid, and how you both find beautiful ladies to love you. I don't want you to be lonely when I grow up, Daddy."

That did it. His throat felt too narrow, and without thinking, he hugged Char tight. His little girl had such a big heart, bigger than anyone else he knew. She saw too much and understood more than her years on the planet. His little old soul.

"Don't worry, Daddy. You'll find her. See, it's right here. You and Uncle Gid both find princesses, and you get to live happily ever after. Did you and Uncle Gid have fun at lunch today? I want to color now."

And just like that, she changed the subject with a skill most adults would envy. Disaster averted as she wiggled out of his arms. Maybe she had a future at the United Nations. Or President of the United States.

He pulled in a deep breath and pushed it out, wondering, not for the first time, how he and Barbara produced such different but remarkable daughters. They had married too young, worked too hard, and never truly connected as a couple, yet they managed not to completely screw up two miracles. Even if he and Elena currently rubbed each other in all the wrong ways, he hoped that too would pass.

"Uncle Gid is fine. He said to tell you he misses you. He's going to stop by before you go to see your mother, as long as a big fire doesn't take him into the field." Except for the fine part, all of that was true. Noah tried not to lie to his girls.

"Do you worry about him a lot, Daddy?" Char paused her coloring to regard him with solemn interest.

Noah found himself nodding. "Yes, I do, princess. He has a hard job, one that is very important but can be very scary too. Not everyone listens to firefighters, and sometimes, that makes a fire much worse. I worry that some day, when he's trying to save someone, he'll get hurt."

Char nodded in apparent acceptance. "I'm sure he tries to be careful, just like you do, Daddy. Can I tell you a secret?"

He nodded, intrigued with what she would share. She always seemed to have a surprise or two lurking in that overactive mind.

"When we lived down there," she pointed out the window in what he took to mean a vague southerly direction, "I was scared you'd get hurt at the hospital. You know, like when they bring in bad people with guns or people on drugs or something. I've seen it on TV. Doctors can get hurt too."

He needed to screen the shows she watched with a more careful eye, but what she said was true. Gang wars didn't stop at the emergency room door, and even a random teenager on PCP had physical strength beyond anything normal. He'd experienced those threats more times than he wanted to remember.

"Well, you don't have to be scared anymore, do you?" He added a smile, trying to reassure her.

Char nodded her head and grinned back. "I'm glad we moved here, Daddy, even if Elena isn't. I like it. And I wish I didn't have to go back this summer."

So did he, but there was no way he could tell her that.

Chapter 2

The squeak sounded with every stroke forward on the left handle of the elliptical machine. She really should grease it, but she forgot about doing it as soon as she got off the thing. Besides, after the first minute, she didn't hear it anymore.

"Will you please spray something on that arm?"

The disembodied voice from down the hall held frustration and a touch of pissiness. She changed her stride, trying to find the sweet spot where the sound disappeared. Then she floated faster again, and there it was.

"Nici? Now, please." Pissy turned to pleading.

Nicolle Trajan stopped, stepping off before Danielle would come looking for her and demand she fix it immediately. She couldn't blame her twin for feeling out of sorts. Just because Danielle made lieutenant in the sheriff's department didn't mean she could ease up on the competitive drive. She said she still had to prove herself, even as every man and woman under her command respected her, or so it appeared to Nicolle.

But the last few months hadn't been easy, not for Danielle, not for Nici and not for the people they worked with.

"Nicolle? I didn't mean you should stop altogether. You need to find the spray stuff and spray it, and then you need to work out. Even if the season hasn't officially started, that doesn't mean you shouldn't stay in shape."

Despite the message, Nici smiled. Neither one of them needed to worry about being in shape. When Nicolle decided to take up mixed martial arts a year ago, Danielle said it never hurt to learn another method to neutralize a threat and took the self-defense courses with her. When they sparred, they went all out. Some things were too important even for twins to tone down.

Nici dug through the drawers in the garage where they kept basic tools for household repairs. She thought she remembered a can of lubricant in here somewhere.

"Here, get it done, okay?"

She nearly slammed her finger in the closing drawer as Danielle's head popped around the doorway. As usual, it was like looking in a mirror. They'd played all the usual twin tricks when they were younger, like trading places, sometimes even with boys they didn't care about.

Lately, though, the stress of Danielle's job was aging her faster than it should have. Thicker lines spiraled out from the corners of her eyes, and a distinct crease connected her eyebrows when she frowned, which was often. When Nicolle asked her about it, Danielle assured her she faced less monstrous things than Nici had.

The handoff of the can took no more than a second, Danielle not even looking as she dropped the cylinder in Nici's outstretched palm. While they weren't perfect mind readers, they did have that twin connection. Nici felt Danielle's stress pounding through her. Danielle carried Nici's pain too.

A squirt, a few gliding steps, another squirt, and the elliptical stayed silent as she resumed her workout. Though officials hadn't called for an early start to the fire season, no one had told the sparks and flames. She'd been called out a dozen and a half times since the first of the year. Working side by side with the federal arson investigator, she'd examined every fire to ensure they cataloged and photographed anything of a suspicious nature. Fire behavior analysis wasn't only about how fires acted when they were raging. She needed to understand how they started too.

"Are you watching the time? I thought you had to be in the office by nine today."

Nici smiled at the bossy tone. Danielle needed to chill and in a major way. She was turning her eight minutes and thirty-eight seconds head start in the world into eighty years.

Climbing down and giving the elliptical an affectionate pat, Nici chugged water and wiped her face with a towel. She hated exercise, even though it was unavoidable in her profession. The only good part about it was when she was done.

"I said – " Danielle walked around the corner and ran into Nici. Both twins reached out to steady the other, Nicolle with a laugh and Danielle with a frown.

"I heard what you said. Damn, you have a tractor-trailer stuck up your butt today. What's eating you?"

Danielle's frown darkened further and she threw off Nici's grip on her arm with an angry shake.

"I do not have a tractor-trailer or any other vehicle stuck up my ass today. You're going to be late. I'm just reminding you."

Nici took another drink from the water glass and regarded her sister's back with more seriousness. Tension drew a tight bar between her shoulder blades, and Danielle's walk across the kitchen was more of a stalk than a glide. Her braided hair hung down her back and barely moved as she marched to the cabinet holding her gun safe.

This was the part Nicolle never got used to. Danielle twirled the combination and opened the safe, removing her personal weapon and checking it with routine ease. The cool cop attitude descended the minute she put it on. Nicolle had only seen it shaken twice in all the years since Danielle became a sheriff's deputy.

"Thank you for reminding me, though I did learn to read a clock at the fire academy. They're big on telling time there. It was right up there with learning how to squirt water on a fire to put it out."

The corner of Danielle's mouth twitched in response. It wasn't that her sister was without humor. Recently, they had scant time to relax. Stress was taking its toll on both of them in its own way.

"I'll pick up groceries on my way home, since it's my week to cook. Any requests?" Danielle twirled a pen in her hand and held a notepad in the other, sticking out a hip in a good approximation of a diner waitress ready to take an order. She even popped imaginary gum in her jaw.

"Something you can't burn would be good," Nici replied, knowing that would goad her sister into a wisecrack.

"Okay, the ever-popular cereal and yogurt it is."

Both women laughed, the tension easing for a moment. When they decided to buy a house together in Flynn's Crossing, home base for both of their jobs, their mother had doubts. She said they'd be stepping on each other's toes all the time, and they'd never have privacy for their boyfriends. Nici never planned to look for a boyfriend, and Danielle not only didn't care to but also never had time.

Nici thought fleetingly of that man in the store months ago. He'd seemed so carefree, singing away without worrying someone would judge him. She'd like to find someone like that, but her chances of that were zero. She could never trust her instincts again, and she envied the unseen woman lucky to be the mother of his daughters.

Tossing the pad and pen on the counter, Danielle said, "Be safe today," her expression sobering.

"Be safe today," Nici echoed, matching her twin's seriousness. The mantra had become a superstition for both of them, as if the words alone could defend them. They knew they wouldn't, but somehow, it always made them feel better.

The door closed with a soft clink, and Nici let her mind drift back to the dark place where the words hadn't worked.

>>>>>

Her office, such as it was, consisted of a corner cubicle with a table piled high with reports, maps, and resource books. The stacks left only enough space for her laptop and her favorite coffee mug, the one that read *'I'm a Firefighter. To save time, let's assume I'm never wrong'*. Danielle bought it for her when she got her first permanent posting. Who could have predicted how wrong she could have been at important times?

Today wasn't a good day to be thinking about that. No day was. She couldn't turn back time. As their mother always said, learn from mishaps and make sure you don't put yourself in their way again.

"Trajan? Trajan?"

Her squad leader's voice boomed through the small space. The others seated at their makeshift desks hunkered lower, unwilling to catch the eye of the captain. They expected his rampage. A string of arsonist-caused wildfires scorched acres last year. Nici hadn't been on those fires, but her recent promotion to head the fire behavior detail meant she'd reviewed every word of those reports. They'd even run through team training scenarios to determine how the fires might have been fought differently.

"Trajan?" The captain sounded like he'd flashover if she didn't appear in a second.

"Be right out." She slammed shut the laptop and unplugged it. As she did every time she left the cubicle, she tapped the nose of the little stuffed version of Smokey the Bear for luck. Firefighters needed a healthy dose of luck to supplement their training.

"Trajan, what the hell?"

It was a milder version of Cap's typical greeting. In the ranks, the tale went something like this. Cap had been parachuting into wildfires since they had to hitch rides on flying dinosaurs and used piss and spit to put out flames. He hadn't softened with time. This man knew everything about wildland firefighting, and what he didn't know, he could ascertain with accuracy in a nanosecond. People fought hard for the privilege of working with him.

"What the hell, Cap?" It was the only response Nici ever felt worked. Sometimes, it even brought the trace of a smile to the captain's creased face. That, or he had gas again.

"Slam the door, Trajan. Why didn't you tell me about this?" He waved a piece of paper like he felt a need to fan flames. Nici couldn't even read the stationary's logo with the speed of the fluttering. Taking in the handful of people staring after her from the bullpen with avid curiosity, she let the door whisper closed. Cap rarely shut the door.

"Tell you about what, sir?" She stood at parade rest even as he motioned to the only available chair.

"This – this – I don't know what the hell to call it. This travesty that is supposed to pass for justice in this country. Crap, the world is going to hell, the devils are burning it down, and we're the ones who are supposed to put out the fires."

He waved the paper harder, and Nicolle timed her grab for a downward movement, extending the wave and breaking the page free of Cap's meaty hand. The only reason it broke free was because Cap was missing the first two joints of his middle finger and had broken all the others so many times, their grip was no longer what it should have been. That missing middle finger was part of his legend too.

Nicolle steadied the page. She took in the logo first, freezing in place as it registered. Her eyes scanned the document quickly, returning to the second paragraph. She forced her hands to remain steady, even though she shook inside. Who would guess that the force of words alone could make her lose her cool so quickly?

"Why didn't you tell me, Nici?" This time, sympathy filled the question's delivery. Cap was the only one here who knew. She hadn't wanted to share it with anyone else in the squad. Other than her sister and their parents, no one else in town knew either.

Her legs hit the chair and she let her knees bend, even though she didn't want to show a single iota of weakness. Forcing herself to inhale a deep breath, count to ten, and let the air out with a slow hiss, she focused again on the typed page. The embossed logo screamed at her in gold and blue. The black of each inked letter seared into her eyes. The words flowed, running into each other. She tried to make them mean something else, but the message was still the same.

She would never feel safe.

Chapter 3

Large hands Noah knew to be incredibly agile and skilled wrapped around a coffee mug appearing too small. Soothing music played here in the cafeteria, punctuated only occasionally by stat announcements. Doctors, nurses and other staff mixed with loved ones taking a break. From the cheery colors on the walls to the courtyard garden outside, every effort had been made to turn this place into a refuge.

The deep chasm of contrast from what Noah had left behind wasn't lost on him. There, hospital staff ate in an interior room guarded by security, the choices limited to food dispensed by machines at prices everyone considered robbery. It was much better than leaving the building for something from a local grocery or snack shop, though, where the crime could be real and deadly.

Wise eyes behind no-rim glasses took in their surroundings, settling an indulgent smile on the young family feeding a baby in a stroller a couple of tables away. The African-American man's bulk had changed little since his college football days at USC, and Noah, like everyone who idolized him, had watched the tapes of his playing days. The man could have gone pro, but instead, he dedicated his life to the highly stressful world of emergency medicine.

Noah followed Dr. Marcus Dawson's gaze as the man grinned at the baby. In LA, Marcus stood out for his sheer size, but his commanding presence also flowed around him like a kingly mantle. Here in rural Flynn's Crossing, Marcus and his university professor wife Davinia sometimes stood out for a different reason.

The young mother gave Marcus an uncertain small smile in return, as if unsure how to act. Returning to the task of feeding the baby, she edged the stroller a few inches farther away, as if her unconscious fear couldn't be ignored.

Noah heard the brief exhale, almost a sigh. Marcus knew he stood out, and Noah hated the apparent reason for a man he called a friend as well as his mentor and boss. If only people knew what amazing things his sharp mind and practiced hands could accomplish, the lives he had saved when no one else would have been able to. Doctors who worked for his emergency medicine staffing service sang his praises until the man blushed, but he earned every accolade.

"How are the girls settling in, Noah?" Marcus's refined tone belied his rough upbringing, a man with nothing who now ran a company placing doctors in hospitals all over the country and around the world. He joked about his latest project, a winery, and how the best way to make a million dollars from it was to lose four million first.

Noah shifted his gaze back to Marcus, trying to keep anxiety out of his expression. "I'm not sure. Elena constantly texts and calls and video chats back home, as she puts it. She can't wait to visit her mother this summer, to goof off with those friends and ride around in a Mercedes."

Marcus huffed, a sound that carried understanding as well as disappointment in one tone. "And your younger one?"

"Charlotte's harder to read. She has a best friend now and a circle of girls she shares play dates and games with. But she's still too quiet. And with the maternal visit approaching, she's getting quieter again. Frankly, I'm worried." It was one of the many things that kept Noah up at night. Allowing the girls to venture back into unsafe territory left him shaky and uncertain. But the court had ruled. His ex had custody for the summer.

"She'll find her way, that one. I remember her as quite a little fireball. Kind of reminds me of my oldest." He took a sip of coffee. How he kept a cup going for an hour, Noah had never been sure, but he'd seen it time after time.

Noah had learned everything about emergency medicine that could never be taught from a book or on a rotation from this man. He'd seen him find miracles to hold on to lives that, by all accounts, should have been lost. Marcus, the legend in medicine, was also a great father based on the way his children turned out. When Noah felt adrift as a dad, he turned to the big man for advice on that as well.

He smiled at the indulgent tone Marcus used to describe his daughters, long grown. How could he stand to be so far away from them? One girl in Montana, and the other in Chicago. Noah didn't think he'd be so accommodating when the time came.

An overhead page for a fellow doctor made them both fall silent. The 'stat' didn't go unnoticed. Considering the person paged was a neurosurgeon, even worse.

Noah waited until the room settled again, and asked, "And your son?"

Again, Marcus shook his head with a chuckle. "Monty's transfer to Sacramento came through, and Davinia can't wait to have him close by. She wants him to find a nice girl and get married, but he's the intellectual type. Smart as all hell, but shy, and sees girls as a threat. He's a young man with secrets."

He fell silent and examined Noah with steady attention. In return, Noah fought the urge to fidget in impatience. The memory of the letter hidden under random medical papers in his desk at home rushed to mind. Threats came in many forms. While Noah's were more nebulous, that didn't mean they were any less frightening.

His tone falling quiet once more, Marcus asked, "How are you doing, Noah?"

How was he doing? He didn't often stop to ask himself the question. Over a year and a half had passed since

Barbara made her big announcement, moving out of the house before their angry words stopped echoing in the hallways. Twelve months since the incident, the one that caused him to question whether he should continue to think of himself as a healer of bodies. Five months since he'd sold the house, gotten rid of most of the furniture, and moved the girls to what Elena referred to as a cultural wasteland.

He shook his head in response, unable to formulate an answer that would make sense. Part of him was ashamed, because he was sure the man he admired saw through prevarications.

"You think it's easier to see trouble coming here." Marcus didn't bother to phrase it as a question, and Noah nodded with a new wave of shame. Marcus's gaze wandered to the young family again, his expression sadder but appearing resigned.

"Yes, unfortunately, the color of their skin might stand out here, but not the color of their money." Marcus turned a serious face to Noah, and in the harsh reality of his worried eyes, Noah felt a new wave of fear wash over him. "Someone who looks like you, Noah, you might never see coming."

The words felt like scalpels stabbing his heart. His children would never be safe. He didn't worry for himself, but for them. Elena and Charlotte were the top priority in his world, and he swore he'd protect them at all costs. He glanced at his hands, expecting to see blood there.

"Dr. Kinkead, stat. Dr. Kinkead, stat."

The page arrived at the same time as a buzz sounded from the cell phone on his hip. Noah rose, as did Marcus. Noah's quick glance caught the last vestige of worry on his boss's face before the man clapped a lunch plate sized hand on his shoulder.

"Put it out of your mind, Noah. You're safe here. Now, let's go see what we're dealing with."

>>>>>

Noah snapped the gloves off and pulled the paper gown free of his arms. Blood splattered across the front like red paint from the brush of an over-eager kindergartener. The boy the blood belonged to was lucky, luckier than he probably had a right to be. Luck had run out for the woman he ran into. Hers dyed the sets of gloves and gowns already in the barrel, and Noah hurled the colorful addition on top in a new surge of anger.

Shaking his head, he laced his fingers behind his neck and leaned into them. He hated days like this. A teenager not much older than Elena, high on prescription drugs he got from his parents' medicine cabinet and behind the wheel of a car he had no business driving at his age, much less in his condition. A petite well-coifed little woman, probably someone's grandmother, in the wrong place at the wrong time, crossing the street in the marked pedestrian walkway. A collision. Guess who made it out with only scrapes and bruises?

Death was never pretty and never easy when it was unexpected and completely avoidable. The boy's parents claimed he didn't know what he was doing because of his privileges. What the fuck was he doing behind the wheel of a car?

Quarter in the jar.

A timid knock sounded on the lounge door. Usually the hasty courtesy was followed by the door swinging in immediately, but not today. A few seconds later, the quiet knock sounded again, and this time, the door crept open a few inches.

"Dr. Kinkead?"

Noah took a deep breath. He was sure the staff knew he was bordering on fury. Losing a patient didn't sit well with him. Losing a patient who should never have been hurt in the first place crossed a line.

"Come in," he said, trying to control his voice.

The desk clerk peeked around the door. She was new. Tammy? Cammy? Something like that. This was her first day. Wide eyes filled the frames of her glasses as she tried to give him an apologetic but shaky smile. The kid may not have seen that much blood before.

"I'm sorry to bother you. A deputy needs to talk with you. He said it's important. I'm sorry."

It wasn't the girl's fault things hadn't gone well today. It wasn't right for him to take his bad mood out on her, and he pushed harder against his fingers, trying to gain control of his emotions.

"It's okay. No need to apologize. Give me a minute, then send him back here, okay?"

The girl nodded, looking a little surer of herself.

Noah nodded back. "Not the best first day for you. I'm sorry about that."

The girl started in surprise, giving him a more genuine smile. Shaking her head, she said, "Wow, they were right."

She confused him enough to distract his thoughts. "Who was right?"

She relaxed against the doorframe and her grin widened to show straight white teeth. He realized she was older than his first impression, probably in her later twenties.

"They said you're really nice. And you are. The last place I worked, the doctors had bad tempers and were stuck on themselves. You're not. Dr. Monica isn't. This is a nice place to work." Her face suddenly sobered, probably thinking about the case they'd just faced. "I mean, given the circumstances."

Noah realized the tension had drained away from him during their exchange. Yes, it was a good place to work on days when he could save a life or assure a loved one the emergency would have a happy ending. He couldn't imagine doing anything other than being an emergency room doctor and helping people.

He tried to ignore the sudden surge of memory, of that dark night when he contemplated whether he wanted to be a doctor at all. Tried, and failed. He'd lost patients. He'd had to explain horrible things to family members in such deep denial that even seeing the bodies of their loved ones didn't help them understand. But no night was as scary or as warped as that one. It still made his stomach clench with fear, hundreds of miles away.

'An eye for an eye, doc-man. I'm going to cut you like you cut him. You hear me?'

That voice, full of menace and rage. Noah needed some time alone, time to kick butt at the gym and work on his form. He'd become complaisant. How hard would it be for someone with the right connections to find out where he'd moved? He should ask the cop about that.

"Dr. Kinkead?"

He blinked at the soft voice. Cammy – that was her name – came back into focus. She watched him with pointed concern.

"Are you okay, Doctor?"

He nodded at her question, taking a deep breath and pushing away his disquiet.

"You can send the deputy back." He nodded and waved her off, and the young woman disappeared, closing the door quietly behind her and leaving him to force his memories to safer thoughts.

Flynn's Crossing's Armstrong Medical was damned better than the public hospital in Los Angeles, where the poorest used the emergency department as their personal medical clinic. Drive-bys shootings, substance abuse, domestic violence – he'd seen it all there. It taught him to appreciate his family and his life much more than he might have otherwise. It made him grateful his then-wife was an accountant, safe in an office in an upper-end car dealership rather than working in a riskier profession. At least, he had thought they were safe.

One abrupt thump on the door was all the warning he had before it swung fully open. A man in uniform marched in with a righteous scowl on his face. When he saw Noah, Sheriff's Deputy Jake Kermarrec shook his head in apparent disgust and didn't even bother with the formality of a greeting.

"I cannot fucking believe it. The parents are sending for their lawyer, saying the kid's rights are being violated because we want to ask him questions. How high is he yet, Noah? Because I have to say, he seems pretty damned normal to me."

"It depends on how his body metabolizes the drugs he ingested, but I'd say by now he has a good idea of what he did and the potential consequences."

Vehicular manslaughter. Noah shook his head, thinking about the injuries sustained by the old woman. She never stood a chance, even though the paramedics were around the corner and the trip to the hospital was less than two miles.

"So I can question him?" Jake flipped his notebook back and forth, making the pages ripple and the cover snap against his hand. His anger made the little room feel smaller.

"I'd wait a while. We'll keep him isolated in the exam room. I have no problem saying it's necessary to ensure he doesn't have a delayed adverse reaction to the drugs. We did a full blood panel at admission, but there's no doubt in my mind that he was high when he was transported. In another couple of hours, we'll give him another tox screen so there's proof, if the parents decide to lawyer up, that he knows what he's saying to you."

Jake nodded, still snapping the pages in time to rocking back on his heels. He sighed, his shoulders slumping. It almost looked like the deputy sniffed once.

"I still can't believe it. Miss Reed. You know, she was my high school English teacher. She retired about five years ago, I guess. Taught almost anyone under the age of fifty here in town. It's a damned shame. Miss Reed."

Shaking his head again, Jake turned, pausing with a hand on the door. He looked back at Noah, nodding again. "Thanks for everything you tried to do, doctor. The whole town appreciates it, you know. Fucking damn shame. Sometimes this job just sucks."

The door closed on hissing hinges, and Noah couldn't make his legs move. Yeah, sometimes this job just fucking damn sucked.

He needed to buy a couple of rolls of quarters.

Chapter 4

The butcher behind the counter waited without the usual gab. Everywhere Noah went this evening, people seemed subdued. Word spread fast in a small town. Miss Reed. It sucked.

Even the music playing in the grocery store sounded melancholy. This song had been a hit thirty years ago. He didn't feel inclined to bop to it, not so much as a head nod. Some days, he felt like Superman. Today, not so much.

"Take your time. I need to check on a couple of things in the back. Just ring the buzzer when you're ready and I'll come right out." The man was halfway through the swinging door when he stuck his head back out and said, "Hey Doc, thanks, you know, for Miss Reed. She was a nice lady. You tried, and that's what's important."

He nodded at the butcher without looking at the man, feeling the too-familiar rush of chill. He knew the signs. Stress. Overload. He needed to be somewhere quiet and process the day. Had he missed anything? Could he have done anything differently? On one level, his intellectual side knew he'd attempted every possibility to save the woman's life. Sometimes injuries were too much to overcome. His emotional side hated the fact he couldn't save her.

He stared into the glassy eyes of the fish in the cold case. He felt as cold inside as the ice the dead creatures lay on. He couldn't make a decision. Maybe he should buy a couple of pizzas and call it good. But then what kind of example was he giving his children?

A whoosh of air passed and settled as someone stopped next to him. A finger pushed the buzzer a little longer than necessary. He glanced over, then snapped his gaze back quickly.

Light red hair, a braid falling down her back. In profile, her face had a ski-jump nose and high cheekbones. Tight lines grooved the corners of her mouth as if she was displeased to have to wait for the butcher. She scanned the back, then turned and scanned the store behind them. Her eyes finally landed on him.

It was her. He hadn't forgotten the chance encounter in the office supplies store. It was the closest he'd gotten to a dance date in more than a decade. There had been something about the woman. Like Char said, she looked like she was fun.

Not now, though.

He found the first real reason to smile in hours. Look, here he was, sans kids, and here she was, shopping in the same place. What were the odds? Okay, this was Flynn's Crossing, population around seven thousand, with only two grocery stores. The odds were better than they would have been in LA.

She stared at him with a frigid expression on her face. Maybe she didn't recognize him. Maybe she was close to Miss Reed and blamed him. His smile wilted with the thought.

But he had to try. "The music's not that good today, is it? Certainly not bop-worthy." He waited for her to remember.

Her frown deepened, drawing a pronounced line between her eyebrows. Her stance shifted as if she balanced on the balls of her feet, and she settled the purse on her shoulder in the grocery cart at her side and rested her right hand on its opening.

The butcher came out of the back, staring at Noah expectantly.

"I'm not ready yet. She is, though." Noah gave a courtly wave to the redhead.

The butcher turned and gave a surprised jolt. "Hey, good to see you, T. Shame about Miss Reed, isn't it?"

The woman shifted her eyes without turning her head. "Don, I need two steaks."

Don's eyes dropped at her abrupt request. He pulled on gloves and grabbed thick beef out of the case, not saying anything else. He had the goods weighed and wrapped with fast movements, sliding the plastic bag with its contents across the counter in less than a minute.

The woman's eyes shifted back to Noah, and he felt distinctly uncomfortable. It had to be the same woman. He might have only seen her from a distance and for a few minutes, but he was sure. She, on the other hand, didn't seem to recognize him.

"Thanks Don." She grabbed the steaks, dropped them in the basket without looking down, and backed away, keeping the cart at her side and her eyes on him. Something pinged. As she slipped down the aisle, she pulled a cell phone from her pocket as she broke their stare.

On top of the day he'd had, this strange meeting left him feeling even emptier. Maybe he would have learned her name today. But then, Don seemed to know her.

"Who was that, Don?" Noah still gawked at the place where she'd disappeared, willing her to return.

The butcher didn't answer, and Noah turned back to find him shaking his head.

"Um, I'm not sure."

Don had called her 'T'.

A younger couple came up to the case, waiting to be noticed with barely concealed impatience. Don snapped on fresh gloves and turned to Noah.

"Now what can I get for you?"

"A name?"

The butcher looked momentarily confused before realizing what Noah was asking and shaking his head. "Can't help you."

Noah sighed, wondering if the day could get any worse.

>>>>>

It turns out it could. The call from the school proved it.

"You can't do this. I need my phone. I'm isolated without it. I have to talk to people, important people. We have to make plans."

Elena looked like she was about to burst into tears, but he'd had enough. He couldn't help but wonder if this was how it started for the parents of that boy.

"Elena, you left the school campus today without permission. You skipped classes. You have final exams coming up and you missed important course work. Which part of this do you think I should overlook?"

Because he couldn't overlook any of it. He'd witnessed, all too often, the results of inattentive parents or those willing to let things slide rather than fight to keep their kids on the right path.

"But Daddy, how will I charge my phone if you take away the cord? It'll run out of battery."

The 'daddy' almost did it. If she used it deliberately or she was that close to losing it altogether, he didn't know. He told himself to stay strong. It will be better for her in the long run, even if it hurt them both like hell now.

Quarter in the jar. He sighed and let his gaze fall to his shoes.

"All the kids do it, you know. Even the goodie-goodie ones. It was just coffee at the bakery. Geesh, it's not like I stole a car and hit someone or anything."

Noah's eyes shifted from his shoes to his daughter's suddenly stricken face. He couldn't say anything, not when his emotions were so mixed up. Anger, grief, disappointment. Aimed at Elena? Not completely. At today's tragedy, partly. At himself, mostly.

In a quieter voice, his daughter said, "I'm sorry, Father. I didn't mean it. About what happened at the hospital today, I mean. I know you did your best, and like, everyone knows it. You're a hero, like, everyday." She paused, taking her turn at examining the tile floor as if the pattern held the secrets of the universe. Then she continued, "It's just that, like, I'm not like these kids. I miss my friends. I want to go home."

It pained him to see her so miserable, but even Barbara had agreed this move was for the best. It wasn't only personal threats forcing the issue. Elena, and too soon, Char, would be in schools where being in a clique or a gang was what mattered. Even the quote-unquote good schools had problems in LA. Noah had seen it all. Poor kids with stab wounds or gunshots holes from gang fights. Rich kids overdosed on party drugs or sick with alcohol poisoning. The ones trying to be good and getting caught in the middle. Southern California wasn't where he wanted his daughters to grow up. But how could he explain this to a twelve-year-old who felt like her world had been upended?

He stepped closer to her with caution. Sometimes she was happy to have a father, and some days, she wanted to be treated like an adult, twelve going on forty. He wasn't always sure which day today might be.

"Honey, I know you miss your old friends. But you have new friends here. You're so busy, I need an extra calendar just to track your comings and goings." He took another step forward. Elena sniffed.

"I thought you were having fun with your friends. Maybe during next year, you'll feel like getting involved in other things. You know, like some of the cool clubs and after school stuff."

Elena sniffed again, but she didn't retreat as Noah advanced. He felt like he was stalking a timid prey, one prone to sudden bursts of flight. Finally, she looked up at him.

"Don't say cool, Father. It's so old-fashioned."

There she was. He stopped walking but couldn't help smiling.

"What? God, you are so strange." She glanced at the curse jar, but there was a smile on her face as she did it.

"Tell you what. I'll spot you the quarter this time, and add my own when I say, god, you are such an amazing person." He grinned as he dumped two quarters into the glass container, enjoying the tinkle for once.

"You are such a strange parent." But Elena smiled as she wiped her eyes.

He couldn't help but wrap his arms around her and felt a huge relief when she put her arms around his waist too. He said, "You know, it's just that I worry so much about you and Char. You're my world, you know? When you're not where you're supposed to be, I don't know how to find you, especially if you don't tell me. What if there was an emergency?"

He hated to guilt-trip the child, but she needed to understand these things could become serious, and fast. He didn't want to add his secret fear, that someday, someone would come looking for her, and they'd find her before Noah could.

Chapter 5

Securing her hands like a talisman around the bottle long grown warm, Nici waited with her head leaning against the sofa's soft back. She stared at the ceiling for a good fifteen minutes before shutting her eyes. No answers were written in the popcorn texturing they'd yet to scrape off. The unopened envelope lay in her lap. She'd wanted to put on fire retardant gloves to pull it out of the post office box. Its weight rested like a boulder on her thighs, and she tensed her muscles against the pain.

A key turned in the lock. Danielle's energy pulsed through the wood, warming Nici and reassuring her. How had she missed the rumble of her sister's truck? She should be hyper-alert, but instead, she failed to pick up this mundane sound. When the door banged into the wall, she kept her eyes closed and waited for the likely barrage of questions to come.

When no voice demanded explanations, she slid one eye open a slit and realized the sun was almost setting. She snapped that eye shut and concentrated on the scratch of upholstery against her neck to distract her. Cold hit her hands and forced her to release the empty beer with a gasp.

Danielle stood over her, a green grocery bag dangling from her shoulder and a carton of ice cream held out against the backs of Nicolle's hands. Her intense frown made the line between perfectly shaped eyebrows look like the American River Canyon, steep and unyielding. Before Nici could thank her for the emergency supply, Danielle turned away and dropped bags and purse on the small kitchen island. Nici let her eyes fall shut again in relief.

No questions. No third degree. No comments. Just the clatter of flatware before a handle nudged her fingers. They closed around a spoon, big enough to carry a quarter cup of crisis-mending cream to numb her emptiness.

Dropping on to the sofa next to her, Danielle popped open her own carton and began ladling in time to Nici. If she noted the letter on her twin's lap, she didn't comment. She merely scooped, slurped and swallowed in rhythm with Nici's movements.

The room darkened with dusk, and neither one of them shifted to turn on a light. Ice cream disappeared at a steady pace without words. When Nici stared into the bottom of the empty carton, she had a moment of regret. Not for the calories consumed, because she'd work those off easily with a longer morning run. No, it was because soon, words would be necessary. The simple act of stuffing one's face to deal with life's problems would no longer be enough.

Danielle leaned back and sighed with the same heaviness of spirit Nici felt. Dark filled the corners of the room. In a minute, it would be a scary darkness, but for this breath, it still felt comforting. Nici closed her eyes and slumped back as well.

Beside her, Danielle shrugged deeper into the cushions. She said, "How was your day?"

They'd just consumed rich pralines and vanilla bean ice cream at the rate of a quart apiece. Danielle knew how the day had gone. The only thing she didn't yet know was why. The letter burned through Nici's jeans once more with fiery intensity. She said nothing.

"Okay, I'll tell you about my day, other than the obvious. The county's budget can't support the addition of the six deputies I need to provide basic coverage without burning my people out. A new joint task force was formed to deal with the arson issues, but you probably know that already. Oh, and a kind of cute guy made a creepy pass at me at the meat counter."

Damn, yes, and wow. Talking about the guy seemed safest.

"A kind of cute guy? What kind of creepy pass? Like a leering, feel you up kind of pass, or did he simply smile at you?" Nici opened her eyes to watch her sister's reaction.

Danielle raised a very specific finger, but smiled. "If he'd felt me up, he would have had a surprise, now, wouldn't he? My weapon was in the back of my jeans."

"Seriously? In the back of your jeans? What are you now, an outlaw or something?" Nici retrieved the spoons and cartons and stood, marching to the wall and switching on lights as she went to the kitchen. Brightness brought a sense of normalcy. Trash dumped, she tossed the spoons in the sink and stared out the window. Outside, their trucks sat side by side in the driveway. Anyone could see when they were home.

"I still can't believe it," Danielle said, her eyes shut and her face frowning.

Since that damned white envelope mocked her from the floor, Nici had to ask. "Can't believe what?"

Her twin's eyes snapped open and stared at her in disbelief. "Miss Reed, of course. I thought that was why we needed comfort food."

Nici had forgotten about hearing the buzz surging through town like so many angry bees when she opened their post office box and found the same type of envelope Cap waved in her face that morning. Her eyes strayed to the envelope screaming at her from the beige Berber carpeting. She gripped her fingers together to stop their shaking.

"What did you think this was about? Hey, what's this? You didn't open this yet."

She didn't need to turn to know what her sister referred to. Behind her, she heard the rip of paper like a scream. She didn't want to know, was afraid to know. But she had to know, even as her limbs fought her brain's command to turn around and watch. She turned around anyway.

Danielle's elbows rested with casual ease on her knees as she pulled the multiple pages of paper from inside the white casing. Her frown returned, opening the canyon between her eyebrows. Vertebrae straightened one by one, moving her body from relaxed to alert bone by bone. Cop mode fell like a superhero cape over her twin's body. Nici knew that look, felt the surge of anger ringed with concern as her own. She appreciated Danielle's willingness to be her champion in this one place where she didn't feel strong enough to be her own.

"Fuck."

Expecting questions, Nici stood frozen at the sink. If Danielle reacted like this, the news couldn't be good. When her sister shook her head from side to side and a grunt of obvious disgust left her lips, Nici's heart rate leaped another few points.

"You need to read this," Danielle said continuing on to the second page as she held the first in Nici's direction.

"Tell me."

Danielle didn't bother looking up, merely shaking her head to deny the request. Nici's feet carried her forward without a conscious command, but she couldn't bring her hand up to take the page.

Danielle shook the page at her, still reading. She dropped page two to the floor and continued reading on to a third. Nici's fingers trembled as she reached out to retrieve the first page. The crinkle made her think of a spark right before it ignited into a blaze.

>>>>>

Nici tossed and turned, unable to settle, incapable of releasing the flood of memories. Sleep eluded her until an hour before her alarm sounded. Its blare woke her from a terrifying dream where she ran as fast as possible, but she couldn't escape the wall of flames at her back. Sweat soaked her sheets and her room felt suffocating, even with a cool breeze shifting the curtains over the window.

She'd left the window open last night out of habit, a habit she now felt compelled to change. Despite assurances her attacker remained a thousand miles away with his location monitored by law enforcement, she knew how these things worked. Budgets were tight, and the further from being a marked danger someone was, the easier it was for them to fall off the radar. She needed to be more careful.

Her morning routine accomplished by rote, she hit the road to work off the ice cream. Flynn's Crossing was a small town, but its streets fanned out to surround a downtown area and arteries feeding the freeway. The large footprint offered plenty of running options. She'd usually vote for the bike trail through cooling woods, but today, she wanted to be seen. More importantly, she wanted to see.

Her pace quickened with her thoughts as her eyes scanned the road from side to side in a sweep designed to identify any threats. It was a move her sister taught her. She wanted to see the attack coming. She hadn't seen it before.

The sounds of car and truck engines and occasional honks of recognition sounded as she ran. One ear bud dangled and hit her chest from time to time, a constant reminder to pay attention despite the music to keep her pace. She was faster now, stronger than she had been four years ago, and wiser in a way no woman should have to be. She had survived it, regained control of her life, and put the past where it belonged.

If only life would cooperate. That damned letter, as if these kinds of mistakes happened all the time. Assurances their mistake would be corrected. Declaration of their commitment to oversight and watchfulness. Empty words.

At mile five, she was back on Main Street. Her tempo dropped with her final mile, but her vigilance never lessened. Next time, she wanted to see trouble before it found her.

Chapter 6

The dull gray of the smoky sky matched the color of Nici's mood as she pushed open the door to the fire command post. The fire season had been in full swing before this early call for its official start. Dry lightning strikes started fires in inaccessible forests that might burn until the fall's rains. People trying to do the right thing, clearing defensible space on their property, ignited others. Carelessness from those who didn't think accounted for still more.

And then, there was the one that worried every man and woman among them most. Arson in the forests. Deliberate and consequential. Wildland firefighters took the brunt of these calls, but things escalated and even city forces had been needed on the last premeditated strike.

The white board at one end of the long bullpen noted current actions, marker ink color coded to indicate their status and forces deployed. Thankfully, their region was quiet this morning, but that didn't mean they could relax their vigilance.

"Hey Trajan, got a minute?" Cap waved her in his direction, and she veered off course only long enough to drop her backpack on her chair.

"Sit down, would you? God, can you believe how hot it's supposed to get? Over a hundred again by this weekend." He mopped at his forehead with a bandana that might have been new when he began fighting fires a few decades ago.

"I have an assignment for you. Joint task force to catch this summabitch firebug." He hissed out the wretched title with understandable venom.

She wanted to be on the front lines helping to fight the fires, and her natural inclination was to argue. With her fire behavior training, she felt she could be of more use in the field, helping her comrades in suppression understand what each monster was going to do next.

Except there was a bigger monster. Anyone who would purposefully light a fire in tinder dried to combustible sawdust was worse than a madman. She knew what a madman could be capable of. This one had to be stopped.

"I want you on point. You're a hell of an investigator, and if anyone stands a chance of catching the bastard starting these fires, it's you. I need you investigating the hell out of this."

She processed his request without moving. This was both high praise and a big letdown. She needed action, particularly after news becoming more deadly day-by-day. Anything to keep busy and avoid dwelling on the fact that bars no longer contained her attacker.

Cap leaned forward and squinted at her. "Anything going on I need to know about, Trajan?"

She shook her head, straightening her shoulders in an effort to push the thoughts out of her mind.

"Good. Another thing. I'm assigning you a partner."

"Cap, I'm used to working alone. I'm better off that way."

He didn't respond as he continued his stare. Compassion came a moment later, and he shook his head too.

"I'm assigning Kinkead to you. Two reasons. He's a hell of a firefighter, and he has a good nose for things that look suspicious."

Nici shifted again, leaning in this time. "I can understand you wanting another pair of eyes on this, but I can handle it better alone."

He continued as if she hadn't spoken. "Reason number two. Command thinks Kinkead's involved in some way, and while I don't want to believe that about a man who's dedicated his career to fighting wildfires, I can't discount the possible connection. It's been raining plastic red flowers around the suspicious starts and around Kinkead. Keep extra eyes and ears on him, Trajan. Tell me what you think."

She opened her mouth to argue, but a single direct glance from Cap was all it took. Countering his order would be useless.

She said, "You want me to babysit Kinkead and see if he could be involved in the arsons."

Cap nodded, shuffling papers on his desk as if searching for something. He extended a page with his marred hand. "Records request. Boxes should be waiting for you at command. Pick 'em up and come back here. I'll introduce you." He made a shooing motion with his remaining fingers.

"But Cap, I – "

"Now, Trajan. I expect you back by eleven-hundred."

Three hours to stew on this. She'd heard about Kinkead and his tendency to romance every woman who crossed his path. That wasn't what worried her, because she figured he was probably harmless. No, it wasn't that.

He would slow her down. They needed to find whoever started these fires, and she had a suspicion different from Cap's about who that might be. She pushed that thought away faster than she had Cap's command, but she had no better luck forgetting it than she had changing his mind.

Gideon Kinkead proved to be everything she'd heard about, and less. He didn't strike her as the firebug type, despite the red roses left near his squad, fire by fire. More to the point, in the two days since they were assigned to this investigation, he'd proven to be insightful and intelligent, and as angry as she was that the sources of these fires appeared to be deliberate.

Two days, and they'd made little progress. Nici flipped through the volume of pages, wondering if there was an end to the masses of suppositions, assumptions and random musings in this case. Tasked with the job of reviewing all suspicious fires in the region, wildland and urban, for the past year, hers were supposed to be the fresh set of eyes that found the link.

Across the desk from her, Gideon did the same. She reminded herself there was a reason he was here instead of on a fire line. She wasn't sure what to make of the man who had been too close to the arsons.

Periodically, he punctuated something he read with a curse or a disbelieving snort. At least they were on the same page about that. They argued about everything else. Or rather, she argued. He smiled as if he expected her to fall into his arms and drop her panties, which, as she understood it, is what most women he cast his eyes on seemed to do. And those roses. Why did they appear when he was on the fire line? Maybe the stories weren't true. Then again, smoke, meet fire.

"This doesn't make sense."

Gideon had been saying that often since the captain declared he and Nicolle were partners on this analysis.

"What now?" She heard the irritation in her voice.

"A different accelerant in each fire. A different combustible fuel. Varied structures. Geographically different locations. I'm not convinced it's a serial."

He looked up at her over the boots he insisted on propping on the table in the cramped room. Since fire command had no suitable spaces to dedicate to long-term use, Danielle gave them space in the sheriff's office, camped in a less-traveled supply room filled with items confiscated from various crimes and released from evidence but never claimed. The mix included firearms slated for legitimate sale, other weapons heading for meltdown, and handcuffs in various colors, including fuzzy pink. She didn't want to think about where those came from.

She supposed she could see the allure as she stared back at him. Women loved male firefighters. The average man's attraction to female firefighters was somewhat different. Strength, determination and dedication in men were turn-ons for women. Vice versa, not so much.

"You forget the common denominator, Kinkead." She waited for him to comment, and when all he did was return her intense stare, she added, "You."

She waited again, and still, he said nothing. His comment about this not looking like a serial could be intentional, designed to throw their investigation off track. Nici would keep an open mind, though, because investigations relied on evidence.

As if it would prove her point, she pulled out the case file for the first fire last summer, the one by a remote cabin near Desolation Lake. The wilderness area's popularity fell in the later fall and the cabin hadn't been rented to anyone. In fact, no one in that sector had pulled a permit for a campfire either. It wasn't accidental, though.

Flipping through the pages, she found the photo and passed it across the table. This time, Gideon put one worn brown boot in the floor. She examined the sole of the other as he scrutinized the page. It wasn't as if he hadn't stared at it for hours over the last few months, she was sure. She'd seen the stab of fear before he covered it.

She had it memorized. Every fire behaviorist and arson analyst in Northern California, southern Oregon and Idaho, and parts of Nevada had it memorized. The Feds called in profilers with no success. The manifesto.

'Justice will be mine. Punishment will be mine. Revenge will be mine.'

It ran a full page single-spaced, with little room for margins. Most of it was a rant, or so the psychologists and profilers said. The fact that made it scary, though, was that it had been delivered to Kinkead's squad, and it referenced that fire they fought with tragic consequences.

Gideon dropped his other boot to the floor, the resulting thud reverberating despite the carpet and clutter. He shook his head, disagreeing with her, but he didn't meet her eyes. His tanned skin turned a paler shade as he stared at the words.

"It could be a coincidence. We've been at many strange fires. You know, since we're the elite squad."

"That doesn't explain anything. It was in your gear the first time. A similar kind of plastic flower is near your gear every time. Why is that, Kinkead?"

The man rose, not in sharp movements, but with sudden animation. He wasn't much taller than her, but his bulk filled the room. He turned away without meeting her eyes and examined the wire cages holding firearms. Shifting without speaking, he slid to the shelves of other paraphernalia. One hand reached out and fondled the fuzzy handcuffs, selecting a pair in neon green from the box and bringing them out. He hung the pair at eye level as if weighing a purchase while keeping his back to her.

"Have you ever felt like you're being watched, Trajan? Like someone's drilling their eyes in your back, except when you turn around, you can't see them?"

Her blood chilled with his words. Yes, she knew that feeling. Four years ago, she should have listened to it. That same sensation had returned, though she convinced herself it was nerves more than reality. Much as she wanted to discount Kinkead's worry, it paralleled hers too closely.

She wanted to believe him. Despite his crazy tendencies, Kinkead seemed solid, the kind of wildland firefighter who would have your back and die alongside you rather than let you burn alone. His instincts were phenomenal, which was another reason he was sitting in this room with her instead of supporting his squad. A man like this didn't see danger in the shadows unless there was, in fact, danger in the shadows.

Unless. She didn't want to consider it, didn't want to waste time on ideas that could destroy a man's career.

Unless. He could be crazier than crazy. God knows some of the things they saw on the job would sicken anyone's mind.

Unless. She didn't know much about him. It wasn't unheard of for a first responder to snap under pressure.

Unless. He was their arsonist.

Chapter 7

Gideon's voicemail had been brief, only stating he was returning to the fire front tomorrow and he wanted to see Noah before he left. The timing couldn't be better. Noah had confessions of his own to share.

Noah blinked to locate his brother in the flickering bar light. Noise blared from a soccer game, whispered from the golf tourney, and surged from a national news feed. Flat screens lined the walls, the parts not filled by neon beer signs. Higher on the walls in the pub room, stuffed animal heads cast shadows in dimmer recesses. Wildlife seemed to be staring at him with malevolence in their glassy-eyed gazes.

"Noah, hey, over here."

He tore his gaze away from a particularly menacing bear to follow his brother's voice. Gideon sat in a dark corner, far away from the busy dartboards and screens. Jake occupied the other seat.

His brother kicked an available chair away from the table as he approached. A pitcher of beer sat in the middle of the table, and his brother's glass was on the emptier side of half full. Jake's glass held what appeared to be water. The pitcher was half-full. Was Gideon the only one drinking?

"Hey bro, glad you could make it. Girls get off okay?

Noah sat abruptly, the feeling of deflation taking his legs out from under him. He'd put Elena and Charlotte on a plane for LA this morning, with assurances from the flights attendants they'd only be released to their mother's care at the other end. Elena had rolled her eyes in apparent embarrassment as she flopped into a seat a few rows back.

Char crawled into the window seat in the first row and diligently fixed her seat belt in place.

The differences between his daughters could not be more marked. Char had given him a solemn kiss and patted his cheek, telling him to have a nice summer. She looked like she was going to cry, but she held it in. Elena was too busy texting and giggling over whatever her friends said to do more than give him a fly-by whisper of air on his skin.

"Noah? Everything okay?"

The question came not from Gid but from Jake. The cop's gaze carried a hint of wariness, as if he recognized something troubled Noah.

Shaking himself back to the present, Noah said, "Yes, I put the girls on a plane to spend the summer with their mother. I miss them already." He eyed the pitcher and the empty glass in front of him.

One beer. He didn't often get a night off from his children, followed by a day off from the hospital. In fact, since they'd come to town, he could count the times he'd been this unencumbered on one hand. He reached for the pitcher, and his movement coincided with his brother's shove of his now-empty glass toward him.

Noah met Gid's bleary, bloodshot eyes. Loose skin folded under those baby blues, and his face looked gray under his tan. It wasn't the first beer, and maybe not even the first pitcher. He looked tired, like he hadn't slept well in weeks. Maybe it was women. Maybe it was worries. It certainly wasn't work, since he hadn't been on the line.

As Noah tipped the used glass and filled it halfway, Gideon's eyebrows went up. He frowned and opened his mouth like he was going to argue. Noah tilted his clean glass and filled it, replacing the pitcher in the center and lifting one brow in response. If Gid wanted to drink himself into a stupor tonight, he'd have to do the heavy lifting. He did, reaching for the pitcher and filling his glass to its rim.

"Cheers," Gid said, and barely waited for responses and clinks before he put the glass to his lips and drank in a continuous stream. When he stopped, only a quarter of his pour remained.

Frowning in turn, Noah took a brief sip. If he had to drive his brother home tonight, this might be his last taste of the evening. Jake gave his own glass a silent unreadable stare. No one filled the silence, and Noah felt the pressure rise in direct proportion.

"Thanks for coming out tonight, guys, really, thanks. I wanted a sendoff. I can't tell you why. Just a feeling I have." Gideon drained his beer and reached for the pitcher, disappointment coloring his expression when he hefted its nearly empty shape over his glass.

Jake shifted his intent gaze in Gid's direction, and Noah pushed his nearly full glass farther away. Someone needed to keep a level head tonight, and it appeared it would be him. Recently, he wondered if Gid's dramatics were a plug for attention or a cry for help.

The cop asked, "What's eating you?"

Gideon's gaze darted around the room, as if he sought out the pub's darker corners looking for someone. He shifted in his seat, first sitting taller and scanning again, then sinking low enough to be in danger of slipping to the floor. He couldn't be that drunk already, could he? But Noah knew the answer to that. He could be. He probably was. His brother had never been a drunk before this past year.

Not for the first time, Noah wondered about the full story of what had happened last summer. He never knew what was real and what was bullshit when it came to his older brother. In fact, he wondered if he knew him at all.

"You are a serious drag, did you know that?"

Noah's hands tightened on the steering wheel at the taunt. He fought the temptation to wrap them around someone's neck and squeeze hard.

"I mean, the girls are gone, and you're a bachelor with no commitments. Those women were hot and they dug fire and blood. You know what I'm saying?" Gid reached across the front seat and slapped an open palm on Noah's shoulder to emphasize his slurred words.

Yes, they were good-looking women. Blonde, well endowed, chomping on gum as they sipped drinks in tall frosty glasses that came in the colors pink and blue. Those colors matched their fingernails. They fawned over Gideon, and when he introduced Noah as a doctor, hung all over him too.

They made him feel unclean. They were barely old enough to drink legally. Fuck, not only unclean, but ancient.

He was up to two dollars for the curse jar, and that was for the words he'd vocalized. He'd give himself a break on the ones only ringing in his mind.

"What time do you need to be up tomorrow?" Noah was going to set Gideon's alarm an hour before that. He suspected his brother would hit the snooze button – if he even heard the alarm – multiple times.

"Base by nine. Why don't you turn this buggy around? Plenty of time to romance a lady tonight."

Noah didn't say anything. He couldn't say the words on the tip of his tongue. He didn't want to think them. Then Gideon slapped him again, hard enough to make his arm sting.

"What the fuck is wrong with you?" The words burst out of Noah like a vessel rupture. He knew driving with these emotions was a mistake. His anger would take over and they'd be patients in the ER.

Gideon smiled as the minivan pulled to the gravel shoulder in a cloud of dust, as if he thought they were preparing to turn around. When Noah turned off the engine instead, he slumped in his seat and set his back to the door.

"What is wrong with you?" Repeating the question never hurt, not when Gideon was in this condition. He might not have heard the first time. Hell, he might not remember three seconds ago.

Noah turned too, feeling the door handle cut into his spine. The armrest with its seat heater switch poked his ribs. In this position, he could kick Gideon if he felt like it. He felt like it now.

"I asked you a serious question, Gid. I don't get what's going on. Do you know how bad this is for you? Your liver is probably a mess."

Gideon closed his eyes and leaned his head back. The pronounced thud of skull hitting glass sounded once, twice, three times. Six times in total, before Gid gave a hiccup that could have been a sob. In the shadows, wounded torture twisted his expression. Noah forgot about his anger. He could never ignore a person in pain.

Gid's voice was almost a whisper when he said, "Noah, I killed someone."

It stopped his heart for a moment. He probably forgot to breathe. It was like when that GSW came into his first ER rotation. The bullet lodged in the kid's lungs. Blood soaked the kid's clothing. Only a kid. A belligerent, high, teen-aged girl not much older than Elena was now. Noah still remembered the mother's face crumpling when he delivered the news. Her keening words, "Not my baby, please God, not my baby."

Breathe. Not his brother.

He turned forward, realizing his hand shook as it turned the key in the ignition. The clank of the plastic fob, something Elena made for him years ago before she decided she was too cool for crafts, centered him. Drive Gid home. Find out what happened. Get Gid to work tomorrow.

The drive took less than ten minutes, and neither of them spoke. When Noah pulled up to Gideon's apartment building, he glanced around out of reflex. The lights in the lot weren't the best. The cars in the lot, not much better. He doubted the residents were any less transient than his brother. He knew Gideon's life was in constant flux, his furniture rented, and his gear probably already packed. His brother might screw up the rest of his life, but as a firefighter, he was at the top of his game.

"Aren't you going to ask?" The voice from the other seat was subdued.

"I figure it is the booze talking. You didn't exactly go easy on the beer."

Gideon's bark of laughter held bitterness. "You missed the shots of Maker's Mark that came before the beer."

Noah sighed before he could stop himself.

"I heard that. Look, I know you don't understand, but every time I go out on the line now, I'm scared. Scared it will happen again. Scared something will happen to one of my crew. Just plain terrified."

A fresh wave of frustration broke over Noah. It had to be the alcohol talking. His brother was drunk, and he didn't know what he was saying. He was the bravest, most confident firefighter Noah had ever met. Fearless, in fact.

"I know what you're thinking. You're saying to yourself, he's drunk. He doesn't know what he's saying. I talk a good game and I put on a great show. But deep down, these days? It's all a front."

Noah pushed open the door, unwilling to hear things he couldn't comprehend. He crossed around the hood and stopped far enough away so Gideon could swing out the door, but his brother sat still. His unfocused stare out the windshield increased Noah's unease.

"Come on, Gid. Let's hydrate you with something healthy. You can get to bed, and have a decent night's sleep," to sleep it off, he continued in his mind. "By the time you reach camp tomorrow, you'll be ready to take on any spark from here to the Canadian border." Or so Noah hoped. He said, "Tell me what you need, Gid. You know I'd do anything to help you."

The relief on his brother's face seemed out of proportion with the offer. Gid said, "Everything's packed for the fire line. Furniture's gone. I was kind of hoping to get lucky tonight. You know, spend the night in some fair lady's bed." His smile was melancholy.

Frustration warred with worry, rolling around Noah's gut until acid began creeping up his throat.

"Get your gear. You're coming home with me tonight."

And God help him if he heard something he had to share, like with law enforcement, because the last thing Noah wanted to do was rat out his only sibling.

Chapter 8

Nici checked her pack one last time, though she knew everything was there. Things were simpler on the line. No room for clothes other than the basics. No space to bring things that didn't matter. No time or energy for social activities. She zipped the duffel with a rasp that sounded ominous in the comfortable bedroom.

"How long, do you think?" Her twin leaned against the doorframe, a steaming mug in her hand filled with coffee strong enough to hold a spoon upright. Nici took the cracked off-white ceramic, grinned fondly at the French saying on the side, and met her sister's eyes as she took a sip.

"Ugh, you put sugar in it. What's that about?"

Danielle smiled, a splash of straight white teeth. The expression reached her eyes, but there, the tiredness shown. Today was a rare day off, and if they both were home, they'd probably go for a run together or head to the gym for a workout, pick up some self-indulgent junk food, and watch a chick flick. Even if they had no time for romance, they liked to see other women finding it.

They were both out of balance, though Nici thought her sister might have a slightly better handle on things than she did. At least Danielle could still get close to a guy without freaking out. The best she did was ooh and ahh at them from afar. Like that nice guy helping the little girls at the office supply store. She didn't understand why he lingered on her mind.

"You, ah, going out with any of the all-male crews?"

Nici hid the frown of annoyance by turning her back on the pretext of looking inside her backpack. She knew what was in there down to the last paperclip. Danielle tended to be overprotective. Most of the time, Nici found it endearing. It pissed her off today. Someday, somehow, she had to get past it, and only she could make that happen.

Danielle asked, "Any new info on the firebug?"

Her sister was a fountain of questions, and Nici didn't want to answer any of them. Besides, Danielle had access to the same briefings she did.

"You haven't answered any of my questions. Are you pissed with me? Because I can't help it. Ever since – well, you know – I can't help but worry about you. You're the other half of my yolk."

The phrase made Nicolle grin, and her anger melted away. When they learned about the birds and the bees and how twins came into being, they used that line with each other. It never lost its charm.

"I'm not mad at you. I have no idea how long, which you know. Yes, I might be out with all-males crews, but not like before. And you know as much as I do about the situation report. Briefing concluded. I need to haul."

Nici grabbed her backpack, and by the time she had it on her shoulder, Danielle had the duffel and was out the door. She didn't stop until she deposited it in the back of Nicolle's pick-up. When she turned back, her expression was grave and Nici felt her worry. That twin thing.

"You'll be careful." It wasn't a question but a command.

"You be careful. I don't need a gun on my hip to do my job."

Danielle's frown deepened. "Maybe that wouldn't be such a bad idea."

Nici blew out a sigh. It was a discussion they had often, or rather, an issue Danielle raised often.

Ignoring the comment, she said, "Be safe," hugging her sister hard.

"Be safe," Danielle echoed, pushing her into the truck. Nici reversed out of her parking spot and gave a final wave in the rear view mirror, watching Danielle toast her with her mug while giving her the finger.

The usual send off made Nici smile.

She wasn't smiling by the time she reached the fire line's base camp. Having her personal vehicle meant she could travel wherever she was needed. Today, the forward defensive line was a scant two miles from the advancing fire. As she turned off the ignition, she noted the support crew providing food, showers and other necessities was already packing up, ready to fall back when necessary.

"Trajan, glad you finally decided to join us."

The smoke jumper razzing her promptly dismissed her with as much ease. Not everyone believed a fire behaviorist was necessary on the line. Some thought she belonged in a remote office somewhere, providing a hypothetical assessment of how the fire might react next. Others felt that, as a woman, she didn't belong on the line at all, except perhaps as a cook or server.

The best place to assess a fire was where it was happening. She could pull up weather data, terrain and population maps, and resource deployment on her laptop anywhere, linked through the mobile wifi hotspot carried by the base trailer or remotely through existing towers. Or she relied on radio waves. Cap's voice boomed through the comm. unit clipped to her shirt.

"Okay Kinkead, take a truck up and check on those two ridges. There are four cabins along the ridge, and two are occupied by full timers."

"Copy." A voice she'd become familiar with repeated the coordinates. He annoyed her to no end, in large part because he didn't want to share what he knew about the fires.

He'd merely shrugged it off, and anger flashed across his features when she pressed him.

Keying the radio, she reported in to Cap and confirmed her position.

"What the hell, Trajan? You got a handle on this bugger yet?" Bugger would normally be another word, but since the channel was monitored, he tempered his vocabulary.

Dropped into the middle of the incident, her orientation to its status would happen fast. She gripped her laptop and let her long strides carry her across the camp to the command center.

"Not yet, Cap. Just arrived. I'll report back shortly."

A fire service truck revved to her right and sprang out of a line of vehicles. Surprise had her stopping, wondering why someone would race around an area crowded with people. The truck accelerated instead of slowing, and it shifted in direction until its grill headed for her without any sign of recognition.

Instinct had her diving to the side, out of range of the big tires and steel grillwork. She anchored the laptop to her chest, using her body to cushion it as she fell. Her left shoulder took the brunt of impact as dust swirled around her.

The rumble passed her, and she sucked in a deep breath, bringing the sting of particulates into her lungs. That made her cough, and she stayed on the ground, curled around her computer, as she attempted to find clean air.

"Trajan, what the fuck are you doing standing in the middle of the road?"

That voice again, that aggravating voice. Tears washed out her eyes and she let them. Her face was probably already streaked, given the dust. It wasn't that unusual a look for a firefighter.

When she stopped coughing, she rolled to her feet in an easy movement. Natural athleticism made her recovery easier to manage, but a big hand closed on her upper arm in any case. When it shook her, Nici's anger rose further.

"What the hell are you doing racing through camp?" She spat out the words as she shook off the hand.

Kinkead barked out irate words. "Curtis and I need to clear the ridge. The houses up there." He stabbed a finger toward an area almost invisible beyond blowing smoke.

"We don't need to be mowing down crew in the process, now do we?" Anger made her want to get in his face, but that close proximity no longer made her comfortable.

"Kinkead, come on," a male voice yelled from behind them.

He stared at her as if he was about to yell at her, and she noted the ruddy complexion and bloodshot eyes. The contrast to his usual easygoing disposition made her nerves prickle.

"Watch where you're going, Trajan," he said. The menace in his voice sent her survival instincts on high alert.

Before she could respond, he spun away and leaped into the truck. It was in gear and hurtling away in a handful of seconds, a new cloud of dust rising in its wake. She couldn't stop the involuntary shaking of her limbs as her anger drained way.

Her radio crackled again, breaking into her swirling emotions. "Trajan, where the hell are you?"

>>>>>

She poured over the maps, attempting to find patterns hidden in the fire's progress. Wind, vegetation and terrain affected its direction, speed and intensity. Dozer lines dug across where possible, and hand breaks had been cut in terrain too steep for equipment. Still, a random gust of wind or a shower of embers carried from pine to treetop, even at a distance, could disrupt the best containment plans.

Her fingers ran again to the ridge Curtis and Kinkead were on. Four major structures sat high on the mountain's shoulder. They must enjoy a great view, one she herself might appreciate on a clear day. But fire moved uphill in canyons like this, and any home in its path was at risk. Even a crew of hotshots couldn't prevent a flashover.

"This is a motherfucker of a motherfucker," said Cap over her shoulder. "Got a source point yet?"

She shook her head, though she knew where she'd look first. It was easy to approximate where the fire began in its pattern, and as soon as that area cooled, she'd investigate. She didn't need to share what Cap already suspected. This fire was suspicious in origin.

There had been no dry lightning to spark this. No burn permits were issued, and open fires of any kind were strictly prohibited. That left other manmade causes. It could be as simple as a downed electrical line. She didn't want to consider other, more deliberate reasons, not when they were in the midst of a firebug's busy season.

"Kinkead, what'd you find?" Cap's voice bellowed into the radio, and the words echoed in her ears. She tried to tune him out, tracing again the one lane road passing up to the ridge top. If the fire continued on its present trajectory, it would be on the ridge in half an hour. Less than that, if it jumped a line.

"Where the hell is he?" Cap let loose with a string of curses. "Curtis, Kinkead, where the hell are you?"

Trajan gave up on the pretext of examining the map and turned to wait for a response. Cap's lined face was set in deep crevasses of worried wrinkles as his eyes stared unfocused at the mic in his hand. Despite her animosity toward Kinkead, she'd never wish a fellow firefighter harm, and she willed a voice to come through and report they were okay.

No response sounded through the airwaves. As if the crew was holding its collective breath, the radio stayed silent for other calls as well, and she turned down the other channel she monitored to concentrate.

When a new crackle sounded, she began to exhale, until she realized it was a different voice. "Cap, four-eight. It's jumping up the canyon. Some kind of big flare up. Flames fifty feet high. They get off the ridge yet? It's heading right for them."

"Shit. Fuck, shit, fuck." Cap paced to the trailer window facing the mountainside. Smoke billowed and occasional spears of flame broke through to color the haze. The shift in wind hadn't helped their efforts. Outside the other window, support vehicles were on the move, falling back to a new, more defensible location.

Cap keyed the mic and said, "Four-eight, check on them. Watch the road."

Silence, then "We're about half an hour out. You got anyone closer?"

Nici glanced at the deployment board, though she knew it by heart. No one was closer at this point. No one, except those left in the base camp.

She reached for her gear automatically. No one left a comrade behind. They could be deploying their fire shelters, waiting for the flames fire to race past them before hiking out. They could be fighting by hand and too busy to make contact. They could be in trouble of a different sort. Something was happening up on the ridge, and it wasn't good.

"I'll go, Cap."

Cap didn't question her decision. "Kick Ambling and Justice to life and take them with you."

She took off at a run. Finding Ambling and Justice wasn't hard. Both were throwing packs into the crew's truck in preparation to move. They'd only come back in this morning, and soot and sweat blackened their unwashed faces. But they didn't hesitate when she yelled for them as she jogged for the remaining tank truck. Her urgency said it all.

Staring at the map had helped her memorize the roads, but in the dense smoke, it remained a challenge to find the turnoff for the ridge. Justice sat in back, working GPS to find their coordinates. Ambling leaned as far forward as his turnout allowed, his eyes searching the gray as keenly as hers. When he suddenly pointed to the left, she spun the wheel. The road sign was long gone, its letters as scorched as the surrounding ground.

"This might be a mistake," Justice said.

"Curtis and Kinkead are out here somewhere," she replied.

The level of destruction around them didn't add up. The fire should have headed west. East of the line, this ridge should have been safe. No branch of the fire yet extended in this direction.

Unless this was a new fire. Four-eight's report of a sudden burst of flames also didn't add up. Unless it hit a propane tank or combustibles in storage, nothing would cause an explosion. Unless this was a new case of arson.

And Kinkead was in the middle of it.

Deep burn marks were the first clue they were close. The smoldering skeleton of a shed-sized metal frame hulked to their left. The fire had burned hot and fast here, fast enough to leave the treetops intact while it destroyed the underbrush and whatever sat on the ground. Asphalt had melted and reformed, leaving the road uneven. Gravel marked a driveway, but there was no sign of a fire truck or its remains in that direction.

"Up there," Ambling barked out, pointing out the windshield straight ahead. Through a break in the smoke, she had a quick peek of a grill she recognized before dense gray swirled shut once more.

They could be in the truck. They could be on the ground. They could be hiking out. They could be burned and on the ground.

She pulled to a stop about ten feet from the truck, and from this distance, she could see signs of obvious damage. One side of the engine lay exposed, its guts a black mess. Paint on that side peeled in places, more indications of intense heat.

"Shit, this looks bad," said Justice. He shoved open the back door and dropped to smoldering ground. Ambling did the same as Nici reported in. The men checked the truck's interior and turned to her, shaking their heads.

"No sign of them, Cap. We'll sweep the area." She slammed her helmet tighter and pushed open the door.

As soon as she drew her first outside breath, she knew it didn't smell right. A hot fire that burned quickly would smell bitter but clean. The toxic odor of chemicals ate at her lungs. Accelerant or the source? It wasn't propane or gas. She'd have to find the reason it hung in the air. But their first priority was locating the men.

She joined Ambling and Justice as they scanned the area. Beyond the rough burn line, the road again looked normal except for the smoke. Stepping past the cinders, she could make out roofs of the remaining three homes. Justice was already jogging towards them. Perhaps Kinkead and Curtis had taken shelter there.

Unless Kinkead was the cause. What did that mean for Curtis? He was as by the book as they came. No one would dare go against the rules with him around. Unless Kinkead took care of him too.

She examined the ground in a rough grid pattern, distracted by the signs of causes for the blast. It was clearly an explosion of some magnitude, and she'd need to question the crew on four-eight to determine what they'd seen. When her feet hit a more solid surface, she knelt to examine it. A ridge of blocks marked what must have been a foundation. On the top of the concrete, ash still smoldered.

She took another step forward, cautious about disturbing what could be a crime scene. Creeping across the space, she noted the circular outflow pattern of debris. The source, whatever it had been, was near here.

In her ear, Ambling said he'd help Justice check the other structures, and she confirmed she'd heard while continuing her inspection. Ahead of her, shards of glass and twisted pieces of metal littered the ground. This was the safer side of the blast, the side away from direct detonation. A couple of walls might have once stood between the source and the exterior, but those were gone in the fire. How far did the debris field extend? That would tell her about the strength of the accelerant and its possible type of ignition.

A puff of breeze raised by heat currents blew another hole in the smoke, and she scanned a greater distance. A large reflection sparkled on the ground.

Silver. Two silver mounds. Deployed fire shelters.

"Found them," she shouted in her mic, as she took off at a racing pace.

Chapter 9

"Two fire victims coming in, Doctor."

His head nurse already shot out orders like a gruff sergeant. She'd been that in the army medical corps. Her voice carried better than the PA system.

Noah's pulse picked up as it always did before it settled. The routine, the pace, the need. That's what centered him.

Fire victims were always harder. Burns required special services, though they were staffed for them. Too many years of drought and wildfires assured they were prepared. He tried not to think of Gideon. They hadn't parted on the best of terms. He accepted the sterile gown from an aide and reached for his gloves, his thoughts wandering back to their argument.

"You remember last year, the cabin where the child was burned?" Gideon had said.

Last night, Noah heard more of the story. It was not the child alone, but a grandfather and his granddaughter. The old man would not leave, despite the smattering of flames licking the cabin's roof. Gideon said the little girl's wide blue eyes staring at him as she clung to her grandfather's hand haunted his memory. Both died because of that fire.

"I'm sure you did all you could," Noah assured him.

His brother's sudden snarl as he jumped to his feet surprised him. "You got any booze in this place?"

"Don't you think you've had enough?" He hated his patronizing tone, but it needed to be said.

"What do you know about it, huh?" Belligerence made Gideon's words sound like he spit them out.

"I think you drink to escape your memories. Gid, it wasn't your fault." Noah reached out a hand to calm the agitation.

Gideon shook it off. His face was stormy, and he began opening and shutting kitchen cabinets with jerky movements. Noah sat still, refusing to help or hinder his search. He wouldn't find anything.

Gid spun suddenly and headed for the front hallway. "I'm heading out," he said.

"Where to?"

"Anywhere!"

"I'll drive you," Noah replied, reaching for his keys.

"I'd rather walk."

They stared at each other. Gideon hefted his backpack and duffel as he broke the gaze. He opened the door and marched over the threshold without looking back.

Noah knew better than to insist. His brother did things his own way. Noah could follow him at walking speed in his car as Gideon paced into town, and the man would never agree to the ride.

"Stay safe," Noah said, his words ringing out in the early morning silence.

In response, Gideon raised a single middle finger.

"One minute out." Bridget the sergeant snapped on gloves and headed for the ambulance bay. Noah followed, checking his own gloves as he emptied his mind.

Paramedics swarmed the ER entrance as he reached the doors. Two ambos stood with their back doors crashed open and gurneys already emerging. Around the vehicles, firefighters crowded to assist with the transfers. Noah focused on the two victims, both covered to the chin by stained white sheets.

One paramedic began the recitation without looking up. "Probable smoke inhalation, possible concussion, hasn't regained consciousness since we picked him up." He reviewed the patient's vitals, and Noah moved swiftly to flash a light in the man's eyes. Responsive. Hopefully not as bad as it sounded. He issued orders and moved to the second gurney.

A female paramedic shook her head and said, "This guy got it bad. Blown away from an explosion, by the look of it. Multiple fractures and contusions. Only came to long enough to moan and ask about the other guy. But he's alive and he didn't burn. This smoke jockey's one lucky dude." She shifted as Noah stepped in.

He stilled, unable to move, as he looked into his brother's battered face.

>>>>>

As Noah lingered outside the glass partition less than an hour later, the day felt as if it passed in slow motion. He wanted to be in there helping Gideon, but the line of authority was clear. Doctors didn't work on relatives except when no one else was available.

"How is Mr. Curtis?" The low voice of the hospital's medical director sounded at his shoulder.

Noah replied without taking his eyes off the activity in the room. "Stable. He woke up while we were assessing him. He has a probable concussion, and he swallowed a lot of smoke. The fire team asked us to bag his clothes for the crime lab." He paused, wondering if he should share the other news, but the doctor beside him had probably already heard. "They think this is another arson."

He saw the man's nod out of the corner of his eye. "Your brother is in good hands, and we'll take the best possible care of him. If we have to send him to the trauma center, I'll authorize the transfer immediately. Don't worry, Noah."

Those parting words didn't bring any relief. A mix of anger and worry kept his heart rate higher than it was in any other emergency. Gideon hadn't been responsive since they'd wheeled him into this room. He was bound for body scans, testing, and surgery to put broken bones back together. Luckily, his burns were minor. His turnout had protected him from the worst of the explosion, but not from the sheer force of being thrown a distance. The specialists were on their way.

All Noah could do was wait. It gave him a fresh appreciation for what families went through when they pounced on him with anxious questions in every waiting room. Impatience, worry, and demands for information – they cycled through him like a speeding merry-go-round, making him nauseous. He slumped against the metal window frame and continued to stare.

With every nerve in his body, he willed Gideon to wake up. The fact that they parted on less than stellar terms was only half of it. This was Gideon, his big brother, his champion when he hadn't been able to stand up for himself. Gid had been a strong kid ahead of his years, while Noah took longer to grow his muscles. Noah had been the convenient target of every neighborhood bully, but only until Gid found out and put an end to their menacing ways. It only took an icy blue stare and a fast right fist.

Now his brother lay unconscious, probably because of a deliberate act of violence. If this was the arsonist, Noah wanted to have first crack at him. His body shook with the need to do something, anything.

The cell phone in his pocket buzzed, the vibration signaling the call was from his ex-wife. A new layer of concern enveloped him, more choking than the smoke hanging over the town. Elena and Char. Why else would Barbara call in the middle of the day?

Activating the call with a swipe of his finger, he kept his eyes on Gideon as he said, "Hello Barbara."

No response. Over the blare of an overhead page, he thought he heard something, but it wasn't words.

"Hello? Who's there?" He pulled the phone away to see if the call was still connected.

Sudden rapid activity in the treatment room beyond the glass caught his attention. To the uninformed, it would look like chaos. He knew it for what it was. Gideon was crashing and the team leaped into controlled action to save him. Noah felt a paralysis take over his limbs. He wanted to be in there, fighting for his brother's life. But he'd only be in the way, since he couldn't seem to get his body under control.

"Daddy?" A faint voice sounded in a sudden moment of silence in the hallway. He pressed the phone to his ear with new fear. When a sob sounded on the line, it sharpened his senses into focus immediately.

"Charlotte? What's wrong, sunshine?"

Another sob, this one wet and more painful to listen to. He wished he could wrap his arms around his daughter and pull her in for a big hug. God knows he needed one too.

"Daddy, I want to come home."

He straightened his shoulders. He had expected this. Char hadn't wanted to go, didn't want to leave her friends and the place they now called home. Elena, on the other hand, couldn't wait to get out of town and back to what she called civilization.

"Baby, we talked about this. You get to spend the summer with your mother. She misses you. Don't you like going to the pool and seeing your old friends?"

Char sniffed on the other end. "I miss my real friends, my new ones. And it's not a pool. It's fancy and it's called a club and there are lots of rules. The kids are snobby and I hate them."

This statement brought on a fresh round of sobs.

"Char, is it okay if I talk to your mother?" He wanted to hop on a plane and bring his baby girl home this minute. Then he tuned in to the renewed buzz of action in the room in front of him. The specialists had arrived at Gideon's bedside, and they swarmed the place and demanded vitals and updates, the volume of their voices rising to cross each other apparent in the hall.

"Mommy's busy. She told me to call you. Daddy, I don't like it here."

Damn the timing. He needed to be in there, serving as Gid's advocate even if he couldn't treat him. His daughter needed him too.

"Baby, listen to me. I hear you, and I know you're upset. I need to think about how to fix this, okay? And I need you to talk it over with your mother and see what other fun activities she has planned. Swimming at her club isn't the only thing. I bet there's something that will really make you happy."

Noah scowled as the doctors working over Gideon shared a laugh. One of them shook his head and said something, and on cue, the specialists raised their eyes and turned to stare at him, as if suddenly aware that they were treating the relative of one of their own. Grins disappeared when they noted Noah's angry expression. This hospital prided itself on its staff being mindful of the patient's experience, because the patient was most important. Egos should be checked before you reached the front door. Some doctors were better at this than others.

Sobs turned to sniffs again. "Can I call you tonight to tell me a story?"

"Ah, sure, baby. It's just that the hospital is really busy with people I need to help today, so I might not be able to answer the phone. I'll try, though. I'll try really hard."

"That's okay. I feel better now. Go save people, Daddy. I love you."

It broke his heart to tell her he loved her more than anything and hang up. He compartmentalized the pain, because that's what he was trained to do. It was difficult to manage, even harder when it was Gideon's bedside he paced to. Doctors, nurses and techs parted the way for him and all grew silent as he took Gid's available hand in his and stared down at his brother's closed eyes.

"Where do we start, folks?" He let his tone send the message behind his words. He was going to be watching over every step of his brother's care. He would, because Gid always fought for him. Now, it was his turn to do the fighting.

His gaze stayed on his brother's face. Smoke and ash still colored it in some places. A gash at his hairline had been cleaned and no longer bled. Noah couldn't help squeezing Gideon's hand to let him know he was there, even if Gid wouldn't feel it. He sucked in a fast breath when weak fingers squeezed back. Eyelids fluttered and slits formed to show bloodshot blue.

"Don't worry, Gid. You will get the best of care. I'm not leaving you. I'm here for you."

Noah expected the intense pain in Gideon's gaze. He expected the relief he caught as his brother realized he wasn't alone. But he didn't anticipate what came next.

Fear.

>>>>>

"How is he?"

Jake signed the form attached to the side of the bag of Gideon's clothes, maintaining the chain of evidence they would need once they caught this bastard. Noah was sure they would eventually. That time couldn't come soon enough for him. He rubbed a hand over his face, scrubbing the stubble of beard from the hours he paced the hospital halls.

"He did well through the surgery to straighten his leg and pop his shoulder in place. That was the worst. The ortho says he should regain full use of both with rehab. I'm more worried about how he's going to take being on medical for so long. Gideon does not like inactivity."

Jake nodded at Noah, understanding in his expression. "Can I talk to him today? We interviewed Curtis, but he was a distance away from the actual blast and we need your brother's take on it."

Noah knew Jake was only doing his job. That didn't stop him from wanting to barricade the room where Gideon's road to recovery now began so his brother would concentrate on what was important. He also wanted to keep the monster who did this far away. Locking the door and throwing away the key came to mind.

Torn, he said, "He might be groggy. I don't know if he remembers anything. We haven't talked about it." He didn't add what he knew. Gideon closed his eyes and turned his head away with an expression of pain on his face when Noah asked what happened.

Jake waved a hand down the corridor as if asking for permission. Noah moved forward with reluctance. Things hummed at a slower pace here on the med-surg floor. Once upon a time, he'd pictured himself as a general practice physician, with visits when his patients stayed in the hospital as part of his care. It only took those first few days in his emergency department rotation, though, for him to realize it was where he was supposed to serve.

Noah stopped at the open door to room 303 and reached for the dispenser of antibacterial gel to apply to his hands.

"You might want to leave the bag out here." He gestured to the evidence held in Jake's left hand.

The deputy grimaced and set it down, staring at it for a moment longer. "Can't. Chain of custody. I'll leave it just inside so he won't see it. We haven't gotten anything consistent from the past scenes. No prints. No common signature on materials. Nothing we can use to trace this guy. Not a single damned thing in common, except your brother."

Noah tried to keep himself from bristling at the implication.

"Let's do this," Jake said, straightening his equipment belt and his shoulders as if preparing for the worst. He followed Noah's lead and slathered on gel, then nodded his readiness. Noah entered first, intent on protecting Gideon if he wasn't capable of coherent conversation. He had to push aside the privacy drape a few inches to check in the lowered light.

The bed was empty. Sheets were pulled tight, meaning the aide had just changed them. The various medications and monitors assured Noah his brother was still in the land of the living, probably out for more tests. He could avoid interrogation for now. On a wave of relief, he turned to Jake to reroute him.

But Jake's gaze focused on the empty bed. "What the hell?" He was already reaching into a pocket of his vest.

Noah swung back. A single red rose lay draped across the fluffed up pillow.

Chapter 10

Nici kicked out with her left foot, reaching her target solidly with a definite thump. A grunt, not hers, answered the noise. She spun out of reach as her opponent's leg wound up for a retaliatory hit, then bounced to the side and got in two good punches before the defender's guard came up. Another whirl brought her around once more for a knee to the side. Strike three.

The spit of the mouth guard served as a prelude to the comment. "Fuck." Danielle's eyes flashed with annoyance along with the commentary. She pulled tape from her hands and flung it to the side of the mat, already shaking her head in apparent disgust. "I can't believe you tagged me."

It wasn't the norm when they sparred. Most of the time they were so evenly matched, the trainer had to call time so others could use the ring. But not today.

"Your head isn't in it." Nici lifted two towels from the bench and tossed one to her twin. Danielle caught it with one hand as she glugged water from a plastic bottle. When she lowered the water, she buried her face in the cotton and groaned.

"No, no, it is not. I keep running through the arson case. It's not like it's the only open crime file we have now, but it's certainly the one with the most potential for combustion."

Nici barked out a harsh laugh. She supposed others would think her sister threw out that pun on purpose, but she was probably unaware of it. Her focus was one thousand percent on the bad guy and why they couldn't apprehend him.

There was nothing new, unless you counted the plastic flower left on Gideon Kinkead's bed at the hospital. One look at it, and Jake had sealed the room and begun interviewing the staff, starting with the aide who'd made up the room only minutes before.

"You know what really burns me?" Danielle rubbed her neck with the towel as if trying to get rid of a bad memory.

"Are you doing this on purpose?" Punning was not their norm.

Danielle frowned at her. "Doing what?"

Nici waved a dismissive hand, and said, "What burns you?"

This time, Danielle gave her a funny look before the light dawned in her eyes. The corners of her mouth turned up a little as a sheepish expression crept over her face. "Sorry, this case is obviously getting to me."

Nici ripped the zipper of her duffel closed a little harder than necessary, then wrapped an arm around her twin's shoulders as they marched out of the gym in rhythm. "It's getting to all of us, girl."

Danielle sighed and pulled out her keys, her eyes sweeping the parking lot in a habit Nici recognized. Ever since her sister became a cop, her demeanor and public persona had changed. The higher she rose in the ranks, the more watchful and wary she'd become. Nici wondered if Danielle ever relaxed completely.

"How do you do it?"

Nici's step faltered at the unexpected question. "Do what?" She synchronized her pace again, but Danielle broke their physical connection as they approached the truck. She gave it a visual examination without stopping. Ever careful, ever worried.

As they stowed their gear in the back seat and climbed in, Danielle shook her head. "You know. Be so upbeat. You're positive and smiling when the world is falling apart. Despite everything you've been through, you never lose that happy face."

If Danielle only knew. The one thing Nici had never confessed, not even to Danielle, was why she kept that sunny demeanor firmly in place. If she lost it, the bad guys won.

Instead, she said, "Did they get anything from Kinkead? I haven't had a chance to visit him yet."

Danielle's negative head shake and scowl told that story. "Kermarrec was going to interview him, but once they found the rose, things rolled in a different direction. I'm going over to the hospital tomorrow. I want to hear what he has to say for myself." She paused. "Want to come with?"

It was Nici's turn to shake her head and scowl. A fourth red rose, and this one even more personal to Kinkead, in his hospital bed. She said, "No, I'm going to the blast scene tomorrow. Your crime scene folks plan to come along. It's finally cooled enough to sift through the debris and hope for a miracle." She didn't add that she thought it was going to be a long shot, but then, she specialized in long shots.

Neither of them said anything more, and that was okay with Nici. Her mind was on the photos of smoldering wood and metal, ground zero of the explosion. In some ways, Kinkead's survival was a miracle. According to Curtis, Gideon had stopped the truck a distance away from the cabin, intending to make sure the place was empty. They'd seen tire tracks, but the paths were confusing. They couldn't afford to leave anyone behind, not with the fire moving up the canyon with astounding speed.

Curtis had climbed out of their truck, heading for a shed to check its status. He was about eight paces away when he heard the combustion and felt the force of the blast to his back. Something hit his head, and he was out and didn't remember anything more until the hospital.

Something blocked the worst of the blast from Gideon. Nici and the crew rescuing him hadn't bothered to stick around for an analysis. With the fuel from the structure added to the explosive material and the wind carrying sparks up from the fire's main line, they had no time to do anything other than grab their men and race for the only escape path still open. With luck, she'd find whatever saved Gideon's life. With perseverance, she'd find something to nail the bastard who did this.

"Are you sure it was deliberate?"

Danielle's question pulled her back to the present, in the driveway of their compact house, neither of them making a move to exit the vehicle. It would be nice to sugarcoat things, but that wasn't the way they rolled.

"There's no mistake about it. The patterns of the initial explosion and the debris we've identified so far aren't consistent with a propane tank or a gas bottle. This was something different. And you know what scares me the most about it, Dani?"

Her sister regarded her warily from across the darkening truck cab. She shook her head, her eyes intense and focused on Nici.

"It started out with basic bottle rockets and delayed trigger fires. Then things escalated. A more dangerous accelerant. A trigger that didn't rely on a simple timer but on-demand instead. New materials each time."

"Maybe we're not looking for a single arsonist. Maybe it's coincidence that we've had so many suspicious cases."

Yeah, as if Danielle really believed that. Nici inhaled deeply, smelling the tinge of smoke in the air. Fire was in her blood and smoke part of her everyday diet. She blew out that breath and turned to meet her sister's eyes. "How do you explain the red roses?"

Danielle breathed deep in turn, and her frown cut sharp lines in her face. She didn't say anything.

Nici continued, sharing her worst fear. "I'm afraid our arsonist is getting smarter and more sophisticated, and I'm not sure how we're going to stay ahead of him."

Chapter 11

"Not taking it." A mixture of pain and refusal contorted Gideon's face.

Noah sighed, wondering if it would be inappropriate to get a syringe and inject a muscle relaxant into his stubborn-as-an-ass brother's ass. He had to pick up more quarters for that jar on the kitchen counter. The girls would be astounded how full it had become while they were gone.

"This will ease the cramps and make it easier for you to rest. I heard you refused the sleep aid last night too."

Gid looked even more determined as he shook his head, but he didn't say anything.

Noah knew he had to be in a lot of pain. The broken bones weren't as much of a concern as the torn muscles and tendons, some from the blast, and some because of the surgery. His brother healed remarkably fast, and his sutures hadn't taken on the angry red sported by many patients. That wasn't an excuse to refuse something to help him heal even faster.

He tried that tactic. "You'll be able to come home more quickly if we have your pain under control."

Gid's gaze grew mutinous. With one leg in a cast and his shoulder braced and immobile, he needed assistance. Not that there weren't many willing volunteers to nurse him back to full recovery among the ladies in town, but he said he didn't want to talk with any of them. He'd even been unwilling to spend much time with the firefighters who visited. He stayed mum on why he sent them all away.

"I am not, repeat, not, moving in with you. Bro, that is too many kinds of weird."

Noah noted the attempt at a cajoling smile, but a sharp lance of pain cut through it. Gideon winced and turned his head away. "I need to sleep."

He stared at his brother's back for a time before slipping out the door.

"Dr. Kinkead, I'm sorry. We keep trying to get him to take his meds, but you can guess how he is."

Noah nodded at the young nurse and tried to add a tired smile. He felt more exhausted than he did after a crazy busy night under a full moon. Gideon's recuperation remained a high priority. But then there was Char, upset and homesick in LA. His ex-wife hadn't been sympathetic either.

"I don't know what's wrong with her. She has the best of everything here. She has the club and there are plenty of children from good families to play with. She just has to put herself out a little more. I took her shopping, because the clothes in her suitcase weren't appropriate, but she didn't like anything. All she wants to do is read. I mean, who spends a summer reading?" Barbara's complaining ended on a sputter of disgust.

Noah had spent his summers like that. Reading was still his number one downtime guilty pleasure, not that he had much time to indulge in it. That was one of the things he'd promised himself he'd do more of over the summer, to pass the time faster when the girls were gone. Now it looked like his spare time would be filled in other ways.

A voice rose louder than the general conversation caught his attention. "I need to interview him. It can't be delayed any longer."

His attention sharpened as he viewed the nurses' station at the intersection of corridors. In profile, he noted the sharp nose with a slight upturn at the end. Red hair tied up in a knot fastened tight to the back of the woman's head, and her sheriff's deputy uniform pleats were crisp and straight. Everything about her was precise, put together and exacting. She didn't even slump in her posture as she bent down over the nurse's desk. There was no mistaking that face, that hair.

"I'm sorry, but only family are allowed. Doctor's orders." The nurse shot Noah a glance as she said it.

The deputy turned then, and if he needed further confirmation, Noah had it. It was her, the woman from the office supply store and the meat counter. The one who danced with him one time and treated him like he was a predator the next. He stepped closer, because he wanted to see the color of her eyes.

She stared back at him, not in curiosity but suspicion. The shift in her stance was almost negligible, but he saw the second she recognized him too. Her lips pursed and she frowned.

"I'm sorry, Dr. Kinkead. I've told the deputy Mr. Kinkead can't have visitors, but she's insisting."

He waved in understanding, and only avoided putting a hand on the deputy's arm to guide her out of the flow of traffic because she stepped aside first. Not back, but toward him.

"You're Gideon Kinkead's brother?" While she posed it as a question, he suspected she wasn't treating it as one.

Noah nodded. He wanted to ask her name. He wanted to ask why she wasn't smiling at him as she had months ago. Despite her forbidding expression, he wanted to ask her out.

"Lieutenant Trajan, Doctor. I'm sorry your brother was injured. I understand he's doing better. I'd like to speak with him." Her hand came out to shake his in a firm and unforgiving grip. Her movements were as clipped as her speech. Whatever had happened over the past few months, she was no longer, as Char had put it, a woman who looked like fun.

He attempted to let go of his disappointment. Not that he'd planned to act out on the sudden need to get to know her better, but over the last few months, this mysterious woman with the laughing expression had come to signify what he wanted to find in his new life. Up close, she was nothing like what he imagined.

The lieutenant shifted to allow a wheelchair to pass, and he took the opportunity to step down the corridor in the opposite direction of Gideon's room. Gid was in no condition to talk about the blast with anyone, least of all cops. He'd still been evasive when Noah asked him about it yesterday. Noah would honor that for now. As much as he wanted the arsonist caught, if his brother wasn't ready and willing to discuss the situation, he'd protect him for as long as he could. Based on the determination on Trajan's face, he wasn't sure how much longer that would be.

"Gideon continues to be in significant pain, and he's not completely cognizant of what he's saying due to his medications. I don't think he's able to recall the incident in full at this point, and I'd hate to have him mislead you because he isn't thinking clearly."

Trajan nodded as if she understood, and Noah thought for a moment Gid was off the hook for the time being. Then she added, "The sooner we have anything to go on, anything at all, the sooner the community will be safer from this criminal. This was a deliberate act, Dr. Kinkead. Even if your brother feels he can't contribute anything, I don't want to miss an opportunity to gather any intelligence he might have, however incomplete or minor."

A rap of knuckles on the wall saved Noah from answering immediately, and he turned to see Gid's surgeon with an expectant look on her face. "Dr. Kinkead, a word, if you have time?"

Noah nodded and gave Trajan a shrug. The surgeon glanced at her and took in the uniform as her gaze sharpened. She said, "I assume you're here to see Gideon."

Trajan nodded, and the surgeon shook her head emphatically in the negative. "I'm sorry you've wasted a trip. I can't let you interview him now. He's in considerable pain and we've had to sedate him. If you leave your card with the nurses, I'll make sure they call you when he's able to talk."

She put a hand on Noah's arm and pulled him away. The last Noah saw of Trajan's face, frustration and anger had replaced cool and calm. She reached into her pocket as they rounded a corner.

Noah focused back on what the surgeon had said. "Gideon's worse? I left him a little while ago and he seemed to be tolerating his pain. I tried to convince him to take his meds, but he's being a stubborn bastard about it."

The surgeon nodded, glancing around as if confirming they were alone. Apparently satisfied that the lieutenant hadn't followed them, she lowered her voice as she said, "The first part of what I said is true. Gideon is in considerable discomfort from his injuries and the subsequent surgeries, and it's been difficult to get him to move around as much as he should. But I haven't sedated him. No, I didn't want the deputy to hear him. He's raving about something I can't quite make out, but it appears he thinks that somehow, the explosion was his fault."

Nici poked through the ash and debris with care, even more cautiously than the crime scene technicians gathering material for evidence. The young man and woman photographed, bagged and labeled anything that could be part of the bomb or fragments of what it damaged. The debris field was large, larger than Nici would have figured it would be. She moved out in ever-increasing circles, searching for any clues to identify the explosive materials or the arsonist.

She found what she assumed had protected Kinkead from greater injury. The scorched heavy door of the cabin lay a distance from the spot where boot-trampled ground indicated his fellow firefighters had hefted him up and carried him to safety. Even the persistent flurry of ash in the explosion and later fire's aftermath hadn't buried the marks completely. Two discarded fire shields caught like tissue on each shift of the breeze. In the center of a piece of earth bare to minerals, large spots now almost black marked where his blood had dried. Kinkead had been incredibly lucky.

Yellow plastic tents with numbers marked the evidence the techs still had to gather. The blood was flagged, as were the door and the shields. Nici had already given the techs a list of the chemicals she wanted to eliminate or confirm. Maybe they'd all get lucky and find a clear set of fingerprints on the inside door handle, and those prints would be in the system.

Nah, she didn't believe in luck. She believed in training, perseverance, and hard work, and learning from the times when even that wasn't enough.

She straightened and put her hands on her hips, continuing a visual sweep over the area past where she found Gideon and Curtis. Nothing unexpected came into view.

"Ma'am? Found something you might want to see." The young woman crouched low and pointed to mangled material on the ground near the cabin's former foundation.

"What is it?" Nici moved closer, flexing her fingers in their sterile gloves. Until the tech photographed it and bagged it, the examination would be limited to her crouched appraisal.

"Looks like part of a cell phone or other small electronic device. It could be random, something left inside the cabin. But the type of circuit structure remaining looks unusual." The woman pointed and they peered down at it with their shoulders together.

"The detonation device?"

"We just bag 'em and tag 'em, ma'am. We leave the assuming to the ones in the air conditioned labs." The young man's intonation indicated more boredom than resignation, earning him a sharp glance from his coworker.

"Sorry about Harry, ma'am. He just got turned down for a promotion, so he's a little pissy." The woman shook her head. "I promise you it won't affect his thoroughness.

Otherwise, he's not getting another chance at, well, you know, me."

That brought the man's eyes up fast, surprise and incredulity on his face. It was so comical an expression that Nici almost laughed aloud. As it was, she gave the woman a nudge with an elbow and a wink.

"Possible evidence it is. I'll wait to receive that lab report. Thank you, by the way, both of you. I appreciate that this isn't the most glamorous crime scene or the most pleasant location. But two firefighters were seriously injured here. Anything we find that can help catch who did this will be greatly appreciated."

Both techs nodded and lowered their heads again. "How are they, the firefighters?" the young woman asked.

"One has already been released, a concussion the worse of his injuries. The other may get to go home from the hospital tomorrow." Nici intended to talk with him sooner rather than later, to see what light he could shed on what happened. Danielle might have learned something today to help the crime investigation, but Nici's focus would be on the fire aspects of the case.

"You're very different from your twin, you know." The woman continued to mark evidence bags and lift pieces inside.

The man snorted and said, "Different, I'll say. The lieutenant barks first and asks questions later, right, Chrissy?" He glanced up at Nici suddenly as if realizing how that sounded. With a stricken face, he stumbled over his words. "I mean no disrespect or anything. It's just that she's very demanding and she can be kind of overwhelming at times." He reddened and shifted toward a new set of markers as if he couldn't wait to, as he put it, bag 'em and tag 'em.

Nici stood and smiled. Yes, that described Danielle. The whole catch-more-flies-with-honey thing was lost on her.

"No offense taken. I know how she can be. I think that's what makes her such a good cop."

The techs nodded, intent again on their work. Restless, Nici wandered in a direction opposite to the trajectory of the blasted door and away from the mishmash of foot tracks. Thick tree trunks about forty feet away stood scarred with black. The scent of smoke and char made her throat sore and her eyes sting. Behind her, the male tech coughed, and the female responded with a comment Nicolle couldn't hear. Their camaraderie was clear in their shared laughter.

She was content to be working alone again. Serving on a squad of firefighters, often among men she didn't know, had tamed any desire she had to be part of a team. One team burned her. Whether Gideon had lied to her as well remained to be seen.

Her eyes followed blackened remnants of shrubs and bushes. Here and there, rocks stuck through barren soil. Ash coating lifted and swirled on the breeze from a wind caused by the fire still raging further to the east. She hoped they could control it soon. Left to run, it would take off into steep canyons that made fighting it all but impossible.

Another gust eddied and her eyes stopped on a pattern in the underlying debris. Heavier ash, fallout from the initial cabin fire, lay in a thick layer below lighter fluffy stuff put off by torching trees and other vegetative matter. Changing the angle of her perspective, she confirmed what she suspected.

"Hey, get a camera over here," she yelled, even as she lifted her own to her face to snap off a few shots.

"What is it?" Harry came over at a trot, his attention focused on the ground where she stared. Chrissy was a step behind, and she dropped to a crouch, pointing in the next second.

"Is that what I think it is?" The camera muffled some of Harry's words.

Nici nodded, a triumphant grimace coming to her face.

"That, kids, is a tire track. We might have found the escape route our arsonist took after he blew the place up."

Chapter 12

"Good catch up there," Cap said.

Nici nodded, not bothering to make eye contact. She typed as fast as she could, only breaking to examine the coordinates on a map.

"What else have you found?" Cap's tone held excitement as well as humor. Nicolle was hot on the trail, and he knew it. She lifted a corner of her mouth in a half-grin of acknowledgment. You caught a break only rarely. When you did, you shook out every bit of understanding you could from it until it resembled a rung-out rag.

"Here," she pointed at the screen.

The map was set to wide view, covering the greater part of the western county and the adjacent one to its north. Nici tapped the plus sign and it zoomed in. Once, twice, three times. Then she dragged her finger until the location of the cabin appeared at the bottom as a bright red dot. A dashed line away from it heading roughly northwest continued for the distance of an inch and a half in this view. Then it crossed a lighter off-white line, thicker and more pronounced.

"That his escape route?" Cap traced the markings on the screen a couple of times as if memorizing their placement.

Nici nodded, zooming out one click again. "I followed it through the trees. The ground is covered in denser dark debris as the fire ran upslope. It's the opposite direction from the explosion's debris field."

She toggled the programs on her laptop and brought up the photos she'd taken. "Here's the really sick part. See this, where there's a large rectangular shape? I think that's where the arsonist had his truck. See what's around it?"

Cap leaned closer, squinting before pulling on a pair of reading glasses. When he focused on the screen, he swore in language colorful enough to make Nici smile, despite the situation.

"He watched," Cap said. Nici nodded, transfixed by the shapes.

"My guess is that whoever detonated the device waited in the woods. When Kinkead and Curtis arrived, he triggered the explosives. He knew firefighters would be injured. In fact, the arsonist might still have been sitting there when we arrived. There wasn't time to canvas the area before we picked up Kinkead and Curtis."

Cap nodded, sighing deeply enough to cause a wind in the trailer office. "Blew them up, watched them suffer, and didn't make his own escape until the flames got too close – or he saw he was outnumbered."

She knew the moment the implication dawned on her boss by the expression on his face. She nodded as if she read his mind. "This one couldn't have been Kinkead."

Cap nodded, then shook his head. "He could have ignited this sucker, then it misfired and he got caught." He held up a hand as if anticipating her dispute. "But that doesn't explain the place where there's no debris or the fresh tire tracks after the blast."

It still didn't explain a lot of things, and Nici knew one person who might be able to provide answers.

"I'm sorry, miss, but Mr. Kinkead isn't seeing anyone except family." The nurse behind the tall counter resumed clicking the keyboard, her eyes glued on the screen in front of her. "Besides, you should know that from when you visited before."

It wasn't the first time someone mistook Nicolle for Danielle, or vice versa. They used to enjoy it when they were younger, even going so far as to test people's observational abilities by switching places on purpose. As adults, the game lost its charm.

"Ms. Capriano, the person you saw before was my sister, my twin sister, and she's a sheriff's department lieutenant. I'm a fire investigator, and I'm in charge of investigating the arson that injured Mr. Kinkead. I'm the fire side and she's the crime side. Though we both want to catch the bastard, of course." She waited for the words to sink in.

They did, though slower than she had anticipated. The woman finally looked up, and her expression softened into concern and worry. "I can't believe someone would start fires on purpose. I mean, everything's as dry as paper out there. What are they thinking?" She shook her head.

Nici mimicked the gesture in the hope of gaining entry to the castle. She thought about wandering the halls herself, peeking in rooms until she found Kinkead, but the direct approach was always better. She'd be less likely to warrant a security escort off the premises this way.

"The person who did this set off a bomb. I'm hoping Mr. Kinkead can provide insights to help us catch him. Any information, no matter how minor, is critical. I really need to speak with him."

The young woman shook her head at Nici's comment, and she glanced up and down the hall as if afraid she'd be overheard. "I know you're just doing your job, hon, but I'll get in big trouble if I let you back there." Another glance, then a more conspiratorial look and a little lean forward as her voice dropped. "But let's say you hang around here for a few minutes, you know, just passing the time. Someone just might pass by." She winked.

Nici gave her a wink and a smile in return. She could wait. It was too early to bug the crime lab about any findings and there was nothing more for her to do on the line. She could wait until day turned to night if necessary.

In the end, she didn't have to wait long. She had examined the contents of her tote bag twice and reorganized its already perfectly organized interior when she heard her name.

"Trajan, what the hell?" She turned to find Kinkead being wheeled down the corridor toward her.

He looked like hell. Bruises on his face had faded to an ugly yellow-green. His left arm was in a black sling, a stark contrast to a hospital gown and robe in the color of a robin's egg. His right leg stuck out in front, propped up and sporting a bright blue cast. He looked decidedly pissed off and miserable.

"What the hell, Kinkead? Though I have to say, you look like hell."

His grimace deepened. "Yeah, I'm getting that a lot these days. Any word on whose pretty face I can mess for this?"

She gave him an understanding grin. While Gideon wasn't going to be throwing any punches for a while, she echoed the sentiment.

"I think that by the time you're ready to rumble, we might have a name for you, but now, no."

He swore, then apologized to the older woman in pink who pushed his chair. She smiled and patted his uninjured shoulder and said it didn't bother her a bit. She added, "Would you and your young lady like to sit outside and chat for a while? It's very pleasant in the courtyard today."

"Why don't I push him along? I think we could both use the fresh air." Nici reached for the handles on the wheelchair as the woman protested before bowing out with accepting grace.

As Nici hit the automatic opener and slid the chair outside, a fresh breeze hit her square in the face. It didn't carry smoke on it, a wonderful change of pace. That didn't mean it wouldn't in a few minutes.

"I expected to see you before now," Gideon said with a complaining grumble in his voice. He grunted as the wheels bumped over a crack in the concrete, and held up his good hand as she started to apologize.

"Not necessary. Trust me, I've been bumped, prodded, poked and generally made uncomfortable. My brother says it will get better, but not before it feels bad first."

She didn't respond, maneuvering the chair next to a bench under a maple tree.

"What have you found?" Gideon pinned her with a direct blue gaze.

"Why don't you tell me what you remember?" He began to argue, but she waved a placating hand. "I don't want your recollection to be tainted. You haven't explained it to anyone yet have you?"

He shook his head. "Some deputies were here to interview me, but Noah chased them off. He's very protective."

"Noah?"

"My brother. He's a doctor here, in Emergency. He was on duty when they brought me in. He said it aged him twenty years to see me on that stretcher. I'm kind of following his instructions for the moment, since I gave him such a bad scare."

Nici smiled. "The no-visitors rule?"

Gideon nodded. "Yup, that's Noah. I think he's worried the arsonist will come by to finish the job." His face clouded and a deep frown joined the multicolored mottle.

Nici froze, running the implication of his words through her mind. "You think the explosion was aimed at you?"

Gideon's face became even glummer, and he nodded as he glanced at their surroundings. Wings of the hospital provided a barrier on all sides of the courtyard. Two doors from the interior sat at opposite corners of the rectangle. Next to one, a narrow passage to the parking lot on the exterior lay open to anyone's access. It wasn't the most secure place in the world.

A light shiver of worry ran up Nici's arms. She reached into her tote and pulled out a tape recorder, turning it on and testing it. Then she said the date, time, and hers and Gideon's names, and settled it on the bench next to his wheelchair. "Talk," she said.

A deep sigh and a shake of his head was Gideon's only initial response, and he stared at a tree a few feet away as if gathering his thoughts. Then he nodded as if deciding something and leaned forward slightly with a grimace of pain.

"I've been getting death threats."

>>>>>

Noah thought the top of his head would blow off. Settling a difficult and unwilling Gideon at home had been a piece of cake compared to hearing the story of what had been going on the past few months. He was only glad the girls weren't home so that he could concentrate his attention on one thing and one thing only. Someone was possibly trying to kill his brother.

"So you can tell me I'm crazy now. Imagining things. You know, the concussion blew a screw or two loose in my head and I'm nuts." Gid toyed with the edge of his sleeveless t-shirt. He'd been stubborn about telling the story in fits and starts, as if unsure how much Noah could take.

Just when he got used to the latest chapter of the story, his brother added a new aspect weird enough to make Noah's head spin. Anger warred with worry as the implications of the arsons and Gid's role in fighting the resulting fires loomed larger in Noah's thoughts. Why the hell hadn't Gid said something about this when it began happening?

"I didn't want to worry you," Gideon said, as if reading his mind.

Noah brushed a hand over his head, not caring that his hair probably stood up in every direction with the movement he'd repeated often over the last half an hour. Coupled with his worry, he felt a little hurt that Gideon confided this in a colleague before he shared it with his only sibling.

"Nicolle is solid, a good investigator. A good firefighter, for that matter. She knows what to do with the information." The assurance in Gid's voice did nothing to allay Noah's concern.

"First of all, I'm not sure how she got an opportunity to talk to you, since you weren't supposed to have any visitors. Then you tell her what's been going on, but not me. And to top it all off, you haven't talked to the sheriff's deputies I've been fending off, and they might want to know a little about this too, you know?"

Gideon nodded, taking a pull on the straw Noah had stuck in his juice can and making a disgusted face.

"I'm sorry, Noah, really. I thought it was a prank at first. Then I didn't know what to do with my assumptions."

"What's different now?"

Gid took another sip of juice, setting the can down on a table and managing to miss the coaster completely. Noah crossed the room and remedied the situation, earning himself a glare from his older brother.

"I got a note, something tangible. A threatening note. I kept it, in large part because I didn't want to be pulled from the fire line."

"Did you give the note to this investigator?" Noah tried to keep his voice modulated in an even tone to hide his worry.

"Nicolle, yeah. Or anyway, I told her where I had it. They are in my pack at the base camp. She's probably going to get the pack today or tomorrow, depending. She said she'll bring my shit here. Not that there's much, but anyway." Gid's voice trailed off.

"They? As in more than one?" Noah thought he might hyperventilate.

Gid nodded with a dark frown.

Noah fought hard to keep his shit together. Forget the quarter jar. He needed to open a new bank account to accommodate the debt he was racking up with the curses running through his brain. A threatening letter, and his brother didn't think to tell him anything.

He didn't have a chance to ask another question as his brother's cell phone rang across the room. That it functioned at all was a testament to the resilience of technology. It had been in Gideon's front pocket when the blast occurred, and his body landed on it after he was propelled across the clearing. Other than a crack in the screen, it worked like a charm.

"Kinkead," Gideon said, holding the phone at an awkward angle with his good hand. He nodded to whoever was speaking, and replied, "I'm not going anywhere, so yeah, tomorrow morning is fine." He raised an eyebrow at Noah as if inquiring if there was any problem with that.

Noah shrugged. He wanted to question his brother more closely, and he wanted to do it now, before any more time passed. Protection was obviously required. What kind of protection, he wasn't sure, but he would take care of whatever was needed.

His head snapped back to the one-sided conversation when Gideon said, "Okay, I won't discuss it anymore until then. I'm sure Noah's going to be pissed, because he wants all the details, as in yesterday. But he can wait until you get here." He nodded and signed off the call in the next few seconds, keying the phone and throwing it next to the juice can.

"That was Nicolle. She's coming by in the morning with my gear, and she wants to ask me more questions. And she's bringing a sheriff's deputy with her. Satisfied, bro? You can listen in on the whole thing, and then maybe we'll both get some answers."

For Noah, they couldn't come fast enough.

Chapter 13

"I'm sorry, I'm sure this seems like overkill, but it's necessary."

Jake stood in the middle of Noah's living room, surveying it as if assessing how many more people would fit into the space. According to him, the sheriff's lieutenant and the fire investigator were driving together. Jake, a court reporter, and a sketch artist arrived ahead to get situated.

Noah paced with nervous energy. He worried about Elena and Charlotte, without his protection in Los Angeles. He'd received an email from a former colleague at his old hospital who said gang members had been in for a visit, and it wasn't a friendly one. Leading that pack was someone Noah was familiar with. No one could trace his transfer up here. His daughters, on the other hand, were another story. Barbara had scoffed at his request to be extra careful.

And he worried about Gideon, because before the phone call announcing today's visit, he'd been shaken as he related the threats against him. All because he had done his job to the best of his ability.

Just like Noah.

"Noah? You okay, man?"

Noah looked up to find Gideon and Jake staring at him. Gid looked concerned. Jake looked interested, as if his serve-and-protect radar had picked up a blip.

Noah shook his head to discourage any further discussion. "This is a sick, fucked up, shitty situation." He figured twenty dollars in the jar could cover him for the day.

He moved across the room and checked the angle of Gideon's leg. The wheelchair was designed for practicality, but not necessarily ease of use in a compact space. It sat in a corner now, and Gideon draped himself across the sofa with his leg propped on the coffee table. Noah had given up trying to get him to use the coaster for what was now a large glass of ice water. He'd deal with the stains on the wood later. Hell, he'd buy a new end table when this was over.

That was if it was ever over.

>>>>>

"This sucks hindquarters six ways to Sunday."

Nici preferred this adage to the pronouncements Danielle had made earlier this morning, when the phone call came. That string of profanity made even her ears burn.

The voice was apologetic but business-like. The officer reported the missing man's particulars as if he was reading the phone book. Nici's face must have given something away, because Danielle was at her side in an instant, hitting the speaker button and identifying herself to a suddenly silent caller.

When the conversation began again, Danielle's eyes met hers and she didn't so much as blink.

"I can't believe they can't find him. I mean, his parole was a mistake. They should have recaptured him right away. How could he have slipped out of sight already?" Danielle slammed a fist on the steering wheel of her cruiser in emphasis. Worry made the lines on her face more pronounced, until she looked like the craggy cliffs higher up in the Sierras.

Nici closed her eyes. She didn't want to think about it, and Danielle didn't want to talk about anything else. Nicolle tried to convince herself that he wouldn't care about her. Even after the letter announcing his early release, she continued to tell herself it didn't matter. He'd be too busy celebrating his mistaken freedom to track her down.

Now he was out of sight, and that made her nervous. Danielle swore she'd protect her with menace dripping in her voice, but Nici knew that was impossible. Her twin wouldn't always be with her.

"Here we are." Danielle turned off the ignition and turned to look at Nici, her professional demeanor softening into worry and understanding. "You don't have to do this, you know. I'll give you the transcript, just like you let me read yours last night. No secrets between us, even professional, right?"

Nici swallowed but nodded and tried out a small smile. The pointed stare she received in return told her she wasn't successful.

"No, I need to do this. We need to catch this guy before he torches something else. The next time, anyone in the line of fire might not be so lucky."

>>>>>

"They're here," Jake announced from his post at the front window. The sketch artist had set up an easel, and a rough drawing of the cabin and surrounding area covered the first sheet. Lines shown through pages underneath, but Noah hadn't asked what was on them. All would be revealed soon enough, and then maybe he'd finally have the full story.

Jake moved to the front door and opened it, nodding to the people outside. "All set up, Lieutenant." And he stepped aside.

Noah's eyes froze on the person coming in the door. The woman's red hair was wrapped up as before, and she carried her patrol hat under her arm. The same precise creases lined her uniform, bulging and hiding her curves under what was undoubtedly the same kind of bulletproof vest Jake wore.

"This is Lieutenant Trajan."

Noah moved forward automatically to shake her hand. She nodded in recognition but didn't say anything. He wanted to look away, but up close like this, he noticed the freckles on the bridge of her nose and the lines at the corners of her eyes. She didn't look like she smiled often, certainly not like she had at the end of the binder aisle all those months ago.

Her attention turned to Jake's introduction of Gideon, and she took a step in his brother's direction. Noah turned as well and took in the comical picture of his brother's mouth hanging open like a cavern in his confused face. It took a lot to faze Gid around a woman, but this must be one of those rare times.

Yeah, when he'd tried to explain how hot that woman had been as they'd been singing their proverbial hearts out and dancing like it was two-thousand-and-two, Noah hadn't done her beauty justice. Even frowning as she was now, the sharp features unsoftened by her expression, she would be considered good-looking in anyone's book. But she didn't do it for him as she had before. The scowl probably killed it. This woman was much harder than the fun-loving woman he thought she was that day.

Jake said, "And this is Fire Investigations Specialist Trajan."

What the hell? Noah didn't miss the same last name and spun toward the door. A carbon copy of the first redhead strode in, dressed in a different uniform and without the disguise of Kevlar to hide unmistakably fit curves. He gaped at the woman inside the doorway, who happened to be staring at him too. A vague confusion chased across her features before she suddenly smiled, and he recognized her immediately.

Behind him, Gideon's voice sounded perplexed when he said, "There are two of you?"

The fire investigator's smile grew even broader. "Yes, Gideon, two of us. Two peas in a pod, mirror images, so to speak."

Noah broke free of her gaze long enough to glance over at his brother. Gid was still staring, his eyes flipping between the two gorgeous women, one of them still scowling. At least he'd closed his mouth, and Noah made a point of closing his too.

The lieutenant turned to him and narrowed her eyes. "You're the one from the fish counter."

Ah, so it hadn't been his dance partner but her twin. He turned to the investigator, stepping forward. "It was you at the office supply store." He put out his hand. "Noah Kinkead."

She smirked, one side of her mouth higher than the other. "Nicolle Trajan. You play a mean air guitar, and that lip-sync? Awesome." She closed her hand around his and squeezed.

A spark rose up his arm and sent hairs standing up straight. He realized the second she felt it too. Her eyes widened, and he felt his do the same.

He didn't turn when Gideon said, "Whoa, Nicolle. You could have told me you had a twin sister. Gideon Kinkead, ma'am, and I'm so very happy to meet you." The warmth in his tone could raise the average world temperature by ten degrees.

A cold biting wind blew in next. "Danielle Trajan, Mr. Kinkead. And frankly, I'm not sure what to make of you."

>>>>>

Gideon stared at Danielle, then flipped his gaze over to Nici. When he caught her watching him, he grinned in that self-deprecating way she supposed men thought would get them off with less than a warning. Danielle could more than take care of herself. If Gideon came on too strong, she wouldn't put it past her sister to throw him to the mat as she had in their martial arts bouts, cast and sling or not.

Nici's eyes tracked over to Noah and found him watching her with an assessing expression. He looked curious, as if he was trying to figure something out. His eyes didn't snake over to Danielle's as if he was trying to spot the differences between them. That's what most people did when they first encountered them together. He smiled and gave the slightest of head weaves and bops.

It struck her funny bone. She hadn't forgotten how unashamed he seemed to be, caught dancing to elevator-styled rock music without lyrics attached, as he helped two little girls who called him Daddy.

That stopped her cold. Children. Children had mothers. He was married, and he was coming on to her as if it didn't matter.

She dropped her stoniest expression on her face, the one other firefighters called balls-to-the-wall retardant. They swore a fire would put itself out under the chill in that stare. The good doctor blinked at her, obviously noticing the sudden change in attitude. His head cocked to one side and he looked perplexed, as if he couldn't figure out what he'd done.

"Mr. Kinkead, I sincerely doubt you are without any information that can help us. By your own admission when working with my," Danielle bit off her next word, and Nici reset her focus on her twin, "with Investigator Trajan, strange things have happened on a few fires since last fall. And then there are the trophies."

"Trophies?" The other Kinkead took a step forward, though Nici couldn't tell if it was to come between Danielle and his brother or to confront someone. She moved forward on instinct, considering she had someone to protect too.

Danielle glanced at Noah, then back at Gideon. She shook her head. "You haven't told Mr. Kinkead, the other Mr. Kinkead, about – "

"Doctor Kinkead, Lieutenant."

Danielle pursed her lips at the interruption. Nici sensed her growing frustration with the delays.

"I repeat, you haven't told Dr. Kinkead about the flowers left behind, have you, Mr. Kinkead?"

"What the hell, Gid? There was more than one?" Noah took another step forward, and Nici read the worry and anger on his face. If there weren't witnesses, she bet one massive family argument would explode.

Gideon seemed to feel enough unease with the line of questioning to look away. "Probably someone playing a prank, that's all." He directed his mumbling voice toward the wall.

"What about the phone calls?" Danielle's bullet-fired question seemed to throw him off guard, and he looked not at his questioner, but at Nici.

"You told her about those?"

The accusation in his eyes almost made Nici sorry she'd done so. Almost, but not completely. She was a fire investigator. Her sister was the head of the interagency task force after the arsonist. Gideon was at the center of these mystery blazes.

"Phone calls? What calls?" Noah turned to her too, and under his scrutiny, she straightened up to meet his gaze head on.

"Gideon's been receiving threats. Death threats, to be specific. The calls arrive before each fire. They appear to escalate in level of promised violence." Nici felt her throat close up, knowing it was a personal reaction she shouldn't have.

Noah swung back toward his brother and took a step forward. As if recognizing a situation about to turn ugly, Danielle and Jake stepped forward too. Jake went so far as to put a restraining hand on Noah's arm.

"Why didn't you tell me?" Noah didn't bother to shake off the hand as his voice dropped with the question. Nici read his emotions in the words. Worry, disappointment, pain, anger.

"You have enough on your plate with the girls, and well, everything else." Gid waved his uninjured hand as if this explained it all. What he left out in his recitation made her wonder where the wife was in all this. Was she part of the 'everything else'?

"I'm here for you. We're here because you're here. I could have easily taken them to Seattle or Chicago or another big city. We came here so the girls can get to know you better."

Gideon frowned at his brother's words, turning his face to the far wall as if he could block out the emotions by turning away from their source. "Yeah, the princess would have squawked even louder to be that far away from her precious LA."

Noah pulled in a breath that sounded like part injured gasp, part struggle for control. He closed his eyes, a pained look coming to his face. "Elena wouldn't like it, you're right. But I'm in charge of my family. She can complain all she likes, but her place is with me."

A wife whose wishes he ignored, even distained, and a control freak to boot. Nicolle liked him less and less, the more he opened his mouth. It was too bad, because he was easy on the eyes and built better than some firefighters she knew.

Jake put a hand out in each brother's direction, his palms falling in slow movements as if to placate them. "Hey, come on guys. I know this is hard to talk about but it is serious business. We need to get to the bottom of what's happening. It's not like people receive death threats every day."

Nici forced herself to stay still when she wanted to dart her eyes to Danielle to see how she'd react to that statement. She kept her eyes on Noah instead.

What she saw made her forget her personal concerns. Noah's eyes widened and his nostrils flared. Then his face went blank of any fixed expression. His eyes, though, were another story. They stayed wide and focused on Jake's face.

What was there in his gaze? Was that fear? Or guilt?

>>>>>

It was as if Jake knew his darkest fears. As if he saw through Noah's façade and figured it out. He'd never breathed a word of it to anyone, not even to Barbara when he told her he was taking the girls north. Not even to his divorce attorney when the man asked for a good reason to share with the judge so Noah wouldn't be in violation of the intent of his custody agreement. Noah had simply explained more than once that his work brought him to Flynn's Crossing.

The only one who knew was Marcus, and Noah only took his boss into his confidence because he felt he owed him. The public hospital he served in LA was difficult to staff, and Noah was a respected member of their medical team. His paycheck came from Marcus's business. The threat, though, came from the environment.

"Given the circumstances, I can understand why you'd want to move, Noah. You realize, though, that taking yourself out of this county won't necessarily take you out of harm's way." As word through the grapevine proved, out of sight wasn't out of mind. It appeared they hadn't forgotten about him, and they vowed to get even.

He forced himself to look away from Jake, his wandering gaze landing on the face of the happy twin, as he'd decided to think of her. Nicolle Trajan had laugh lines where her sister carried marks of her frowns, like the thunderous expression she wore now. But Nicolle's face was a study too, a study in frozen incapacitation.

He'd seen that look too many times to contemplate. Usually it came to a person when they faced the unbelievable. A terminal diagnosis. The death or disability of a loved one. The lack of a way out, of hope, of choices.

As quickly as he cataloged the expression, it was gone. Nicolle's eyes sought out her sister and the lieutenant's frown deepened. Some kind of communication happened between the women, and tension increased in the room.

He turned toward the sofa and found his brother watching him with a questioning expression. Gideon focused on him to the exclusion of the rest of the occupants of the room. His frown rivaled the lieutenant's.

"Noah? What's on your mind?" The question came not from Gid, as Noah expected, but from Jake.

"Dr. Kinkead, do you have any insights you can share with us about the threats to Mr. Kinkead, or the letters or trophies?" This came from the frowning twin, though now, both were frowning.

"He doesn't have anything to share, because I hadn't told him about all of it before. He's probably pissed with me. That's what you're seeing." Gid flashed Noah a warning look as he lifted his chin toward the cops.

"I get the impression there's something we need to know but no one's sharing." Jake scratched his head, keeping his eyes fixed on Noah as he resettled his uniform hat and tapped the pen against his thigh.

"Kermarrec, why don't you get pictures of the letters? I assume you kept them, Mr. Kinkead?"

Gideon nodded in a resigned fashion. "Yes, I did, and I kept them in plastic bags too, just in case they were needed for evidence someday."

The lieutenant cocked her head and nodded as if in approval. With his attention focused on his brother, Noah all but jumped out of his skin when a hand touched his arm.

"Dr. Kinkead, are you sure there isn't anything else you can tell us?"

A single glance engulfed him in smoky eyes the color of a winter dawn sky. They were anything but cold. Heat rose like freshly caught kindling, strong enough that the others must feel it too.

"Doctor?" Her voice fell softly on his ears, as softly as her strands of hair if she wore it lose. Pulled back tight into a ponytail, she was as fresh-faced as a teenager.

"I'm, ah, I'm sorry. What did you ask me?"

She stared at him, the tip of her tongue appearing and tapping at her top lip once before hiding again. He didn't miss the slight widening of her eyes or the puff of breath stirring against his face.

"Trajan? Nicolle?" Gideon's voice sounded like it came from a great distance away, and Noah wanted to kick him in his bad leg for interrupting the most entrancing moment he'd experienced in a long time.

"Coming?" The more authoritative tones of the other twin broke the spell.

Nicolle shook her head as if she too had been mesmerized and gave an all too brief apologetic smile before spinning for the door without another word.

"What the hell was that about?" Gideon's voice held more curiosity than anger, but Noah remained rooted to the spot, staring at the empty doorway after it swallowed up the woman he couldn't forget.

Chapter 14

"Someone want to fill me in?"

Danielle shook her head at Jake's question as Nici busied herself with her tablet. She was suddenly all thumbs and couldn't get it in its case if her life depended on it. The doctor unnerved her, and she hated the feeling.

"Dani, if there's something I should know that would help with the case – " Jake let the words trail off as if unwilling to push harder.

"Thanks Jake. No, this in no way affects or impedes the investigation into the arsons. I was curious about Noah Kinkead's reaction, though. What do you think he's hiding?"

Nici finally got the tablet's sleeve shut and pushed it back into her briefcase. Up close and personal, the doctor looked even better than he had in her dreams. Blond good looks with firmly movements under control in contrast to his brother's wildness. Blue eyes the color of a bright spring sky. Grooves in his face said he laughed easily, worried a lot, and lived life. She forced herself to look at Jake with mild interest, though she doubted her nonchalance fooled Danielle.

"I know both Kinkeads, though Gideon better than Noah. Gideon's lived around here for a few years, ever since he was assigned to one of the wildfire hotshot crews. He's had a couple of drunken episodes at local bars. If I were to guess based on the timeline we're working with, something happened last summer, and Gideon's train comes off the track every once in a while as a result of it."

Nici slid a look to Danielle, but her sister was intent on Jake's words.

"What about the doctor?" Danielle moved and turned as if to keep an eye on the house. If Nici did the same, they'd be too obvious.

Jake shrugged. "He moved up here to work at Armstrong in the ER. A good doc, from what I can tell. He took care of me when I was hit in the winter. He has two little girls and rarely hangs out with us because he's a single parent. I think there was a messy divorce involved."

Nicolle barely avoided spinning to him in surprise, but nothing stopped the unbidden bubble of delight forming in her belly.

>>>>>

"You heard me, bro. I saw that look on your face. Tell me what the fuck is wrong, and tell me now."

Noah stacked Gideon's discharge papers and snapped them straight on the dining table to buy time. He had nothing he could tell. If he did, Gid would worry. Gid would worry anyway, but at least he wouldn't have a clue about how dark the situation in LA had been. Of course, he'd also be in the dark about the current potential for risks. Noah had to believe they were safe, if only to cope.

His thoughts slipped to his girls, and he examined the wisdom or folly of not telling Barbara the true reason why he'd moved them north. His only reassurance was in believing the punks who'd come into the hospital that night had no way of knowing he had children.

"Noah, I'm asking for the last time. You need to tell me. What is it you're keeping from me?"

Noah spun and stared at his brother. Gid was barely in a place where he could take himself to the bathroom, much less be a hero on Noah's behalf. It was Noah's turn now.

"Hey, relax, okay? I am worried about you. Why didn't you tell me about the phone calls?" He walked toward Gid as he spoke, dropping to the edge of the coffee table and sitting at eye level. Using his best compassionate stare, he mustered sympathy and worry and let his brother see it all.

Gid shook his head. "Okay. I know what you're doing. You're trying to turn this around on me, and I deserve some of that. But don't give me that shit. You're still keeping something from me, and you're going to tell me if I have to beat it out of you."

Noah let his eyes slip in slow motion from his brother's face to the sling, then over to the cast propped beside him on the table. When he shot his brother a bland look accompanied by a single raised eyebrow, Gid wore a wry smile.

"I'll pay someone to beat it out of you then. Trust me, Noah, I am going to find out what's going on."

>>>>>

"We should have told them."

Across the cab of the truck, Danielle's impatient tapping of fingers against steering wheel plastic was loud enough to be audible over the hiss of tires on asphalt.

Nici watched trees flash by, many already turning brown on leaf tips from drought stress. The summer would be long and hot, even without help from a firebug.

"What should I have told whom?" She didn't need the clarification, but she didn't want the past to come between her and the nice buzz she had going. Noah Kinkead was a single dad. Not that it changed things, but it was nice to know. She hated to think he'd been flirting with her and flaunting a relationship at the same time.

"You know who and you know what. Listen to me. This is serious business. Who knows where this jerk is coming from or why he's starting these blazes? In the interest of full disclosure, we should have told them, but it's your story to tell."

Swinging back, Nici took stock of the tension drawing deeper grooves than usual around her sister's eyes. While they stayed on the road, she sensed her darting occasional glances as if Danielle gauged her level of attention.

"My situation has nothing to do with these arsons. They began last fall. He didn't get out until April."

Neither of them needed to specify who 'he' was.

Danielle fidgeted behind the wheel in an uncharacteristic exhibition of nerves. Curious now, Nici said, "Why are you so worried about this? What do you know that I don't?"

Danielle opened her mouth, shut it with an audible snap, and deepened her frown. She looked like she would speak again, only to shake her head in a movement hard enough to dislodge part of her tight bun. "I would feel better if we had back-up," she said.

Nici grinned, though she doubted Danielle saw it. "Um, you're a sheriff's lieutenant, I'm a firefighter, and we both kick ass in three different forms of self defense. I think we can handle anything that comes our way."

That brought a rueful half-smile to her sister's face, though the worry lines around her eyes hadn't dissipated.

"All I'm saying is that it wouldn't hurt to have a few more pairs of eyes open around town, you know, just in case."

"We live in Flynn's Crossing. People know what we're buying at the grocery store practically as soon as we approach the cash register."

"Trained eyes, Nici, trained eyes." But she let the subject drop.

It didn't disappear from Nici's mind, though. It was impossible to let it go. Until her attacker was caught, she wouldn't rest easy. And there was the arsonist to consider too.

Chapter 15

Noah was only a little surprised when a scant week passed before Gideon suffered a total loss of patience and demanded to be driven to the fire team's headquarters.

"Yes, I'm sure I'm up to it, and no, I don't need to rest in that neat as a granny's house of yours and keep my leg up and my arm down. I'm tired of feeling useless. My leg was broken and my shoulder was dislocated. My brain still works fine."

Noah sighed and made one more attempt to argue with him, which he knew would be useless. It might be good for Gid to be contributing to the search for the arsonist. Firebugs, from what Gideon had told him, start fires for the thrill of watching them burn, and secondarily, for the mayhem they produced. Hidden somewhere in the data were clues to the identity of that individual, and Gid was good at ferreting out clues.

Noah had nearly spilled out a few of his own. His worry over the girls hadn't abated when no new messages came from the LA hospital. He noted Gid's careful consideration of him more than once over the past few days.

"I know you, bro. Something's bugging you. If it's me going to work, don't spend any time thinking about it. It's the best place. At least then I'll feel useful."

"I understand, I swear I do." Noah hesitated before adding, "But that's not it."

Gid stopped rummaging through a tote bag he was packing for his day and glanced up, concern marring his features. "So what is bothering you?"

Noah walked to the fireplace and stared at the pictures placed strategically across the mantle. Family photos from happy times. The girls at Disneyland. Char with a tooth gap in front, riding her first bike. Elena with a grin as she showed off her model wannabe walk. Both of them with him, taken at the beach, probably Santa Monica. One shot with their mother, so he couldn't be accused of turning them against Barbara.

Then there were the older shots. He and Gideon on their matching bikes. Gid all surfer-dude tan and bleached blond hair, sporting lifeguard wear at the beach, with Noah looking pale and skinny in comparison. He had been eighteen in that shot to Gideon's almost twenty-one. Just accepted in an intense pre-med program and so damned proud of it. He'd urged Gid to join him in college, but his brother had other plans. The day he turned twenty-one, he joined the fire academy and never looked back.

And here he was, wrapped in plastic casting and Velcro straps. If a bad guy walked in the door right now, what could he do? Swing a crutch at him?

"Noah?" Gideon's tone mimicked the voice of the big guy before the flood.

"Gideon?" Noah copied the tone, a game they'd played since they were boys. If he expected a smile in response, it looked like he was going to be disappointed. Gideon waited, his face serious with a troubled set to his raised eyebrows.

Flicking a glance at his watch, Noah sat in the chair at an angle to the wheelchair, where he didn't need to look his brother in the eye unless he wanted to.

"You remember when you asked me why I thought moving to Flynn's Crossing was such a great idea?"

Gid nodded. Noah fidgeted with the crease in his slacks, though it was perfect.

"There were more reasons than the ones I shared with you."

Gid nodded once but said nothing.

"I mean, getting the girls out of the craziness of that city was the primary factor, and being near you, so they could get to know their uncle, made the selection of a location easy."

This time, Gid didn't bother acknowledging the statement.

Noah straightened his neatly aligned tie, the pattern a collage of comic book heroes Char had found for him at a local shop. His younger decided he needed a different tie for each day of the month, and she was determined that each one would be a fun one. He didn't argue with her. His patients seemed to appreciate the humor.

The whine of tires on the road outside caught his attention. The street was quiet but well traveled. Its curve meant an approaching vehicle wasn't visible until it was a few doors down. How hard would it be for someone who meant harm to sneak up on them?

Noah rose, feeling a wave of agitation course through him. It would be a bad idea to involve his brother in this. It was probably nothing. The warning from his old colleagues was an overreaction. No one would trace him here.

"You're stalling."

"Listen, we better get going. You don't want to be late." He moved forward to grab the handles of Gideon's wheelchair.

His brother snagged his good hand on the brake, engaging it so the wheel moved nowhere. Then he put the hand on the wheel itself to hold it as if for good measure. While he couldn't turn around, Noah guessed the expression on his face. Pissed off.

"I have all the time in the world, since they don't know I'm coming in. And you don't have to be in for another," he made a show of consulting his watch, "two hours. We have beaucoup time, and I am not going anywhere until you tell me the whole story."

Noah let go of the chair and shut his eyes, rubbing the bridge of his nose in frustration. He'd opened this discussion, and Gideon wouldn't drop it until he was satisfied with an explanation.

He crossed the room and opened the fridge, grabbing water bottles for the two of them. Without being asked, he cracked the top on one and handed it over. Then he sat down with his, broke the seal, and took a long drink. When he lowered the bottle, Gid was still staring at him, the bottle's condensation already building up on his hand. Noah dropped his eyes from that intense assessment and picked at the bottle's paper label.

"You were in the throes of last year's fire season. I didn't want to bother you." The label came off, glue sticking to his thumbnail. A drip of water fell off the side and landed on his polished loafers.

An irked snort sounded next to him. "For fuck's sake, get on with it." The grumble in his brother's voice more than his words told Noah his patience had almost evaporated.

"There was an incident at the hospital. A teenager came in with multiple gunshot wounds, most of them to his midsection. Bleeding everywhere, but still wild on a high the likes of which I never want to see again. It took three police officers and two orderlies to hold him down, and treating him was difficult."

The tick and wheeze of the icemaker echoed from the kitchen. Another set of tires passed on the street, slower this time. Was it someone casing the house? Noah fought the urge to sneak to the window and peer around its frame.

"He'd been shot in a gang-related drive-by, according to the cops. He wasn't much older than Elena. He should have been in school, playing sports, chasing his first crush." Noah fell silent.

A woman's voice called out down the street. He'd never noticed how quiet things got when no one spoke here. With the girls around, the noise level hummed along at a constant low roar. Gideon had filled it with sports and movies for the last week. Now, all was silent.

"Let me guess. You lost the kid, and you were tired of the painful grind of lost causes and bad cases. Plus, you were worried the girls would get caught up in that same hell, and one day, one of them would be on that gurney."

Noah inclined his head at his brother's partial guess. An uneasy edginess made him shoot to his feet and pace to the window. He contemplated lowering the blinds against the peaceful setting. What if that peace was all a charade?

"The kid died a painful and gruesome death by any stretch of the imagination. I found out later that the cocktail of drugs in his system would have killed him soon, even if he wasn't bleeding out. The drugs made that part worse too. I did everything I could. In the end, he died."

A woman walked a small dog down the street, pausing as the dog peed and sniffed around. She had a headset on and appeared to be having a conversation. Didn't she realize she should be vigilant? Someone could walk up behind her and –

"Noah, you did everything you could. Sometimes, kids die before their time because the world is a hellhole. He was in a gang, he took drugs, and he was shot. You tried to save him from himself, but by the time he got to you, it was already over. His fate might have been sealed long before that night." The soft words trailed off, as if his brother couldn't think of how else to comfort him.

He watched the retreating back of the woman and the butt of the dog as they disappeared around the curve up the street. A small car, old and noisy, raced by. High schoolers, probably, just like that young man.

Noah ran a hand over his hair. Old habits were hard to break, and when he was stressed, he still found himself fussing with the same old things. Only in the ER did he feel completely in control. He'd lost patients before that night. He'd lost patients since. But none had affected him in the same way.

"I know you're right. I know he was probably a lost cause before they ever rolled him in the doors. If not that night, then another. I know all that, but that's not the part that worries me." Noah stopped again, unable to form the words.

"So what's bothering you?" The delivery of the question came with a sharp snap, and with that tone, Noah felt his uncertainty snap too. If he was going to face this thing head-on, he needed to come clean with his brother. Together, they could be vigilant, even if they couldn't fix it.

He sat back in the chair, looked his brother in the eye, and told him.

>>>>>

Nici walked her fingers through the stack of files, looking for the one she'd tabbed and cross-referenced. The maps inside provided little in terms of new information, but she'd examined everything else multiple times and no fresh ideas sprang out.

A cheer and shouts of good-natured cursing sounded from the other side of the squad room, and she turned to see the Kinkead brothers making an entrance. The doctor stood behind Gideon with his arms partially raised, as if ready to catch him as he tottered on his crutches. With his good hand, Gid slapped palms with men and women along a path to the desk where she worked. Their progress halted a few times as people rose for a word with the man trussed up like a half-done holiday turkey.

Her eyes rose to the doctor, to find him watching her. His face was pale, which she expected on someone who worked inside. A flashy tie with Superman in his traditional fist raised pose made her crack a smile. The man had a sense of humor. She should know this. Their pseudo-duet in the binder aisle wasn't a single fling in letting his hair down.

His gaze was intense, hotter than a flash-bang when it hit the ground and ignited. At this distance, his eyes appeared a darker blue than his brother's, his hair a darker blond. He looked tame, but some unidentified emotion in his expression eyes made her heart pound.

"Trajan, move over. I need to get back to work." The pair stumped into the room, and Gideon indicated the pile of folders with a lift of his chin. "Anything new?"

Nici would have answered, but she was momentarily speechless. Dr. Noah Kinkead had taken her hand in his, the shake perfunctory. But he held on to it, and she wasn't willing to yank away, not yet. The firm grip did weird things to her insides, nerve endings sizzling so hot, she swore others would hear them.

"Trajan? You with me?"

She shook her head and closed her eyes against the mesmerizing blue gaze of the good doctor. "Nothing new, Kinkead. What are you doing here?"

The doctor answered. "He insisted on coming to work. He insists his brain is fine, even if his body is not. In my medical opinion, I'm not sure his brain is ever right, but there you go."

The words got him a middle finger from his brother. He didn't crack a smile at the gesture, but his eyes twinkled with mischief. She liked him more and more by the minute, and that might not be wise.

Noah lifted a hand and waved at Gideon as if he was an exhibit in the room. "I'm the younger one, so I have no say in the matter. Ignore the fact that I'm a doctor and he's not. He says he's good enough to come back."

"He's older?" She inclined her head in Gideon's direction.

"Oh yeah," said Noah, and the tone said it all. How many times had she rolled her eyes at her twin over the years? That older sibling stuff burned, sisters or brothers.

"Right here, guys, right here. I'll thank you, little brother, to avoid casting aspersions on my intelligence."

Noah raised a conspiratorial hand and stage-whispered from behind it. "He's been watching those deep, intellectual programs. You know, the ones with the big words. I'm hoping more rubbed off on him."

The middle finger popped up before returning to trace a line on a map on the table. Gideon didn't bother to turn around to see if they noticed.

"Trajan? What the fuck? I heard Kinkead's here and he thinks he's going to work. What are we going to do, carry him to the fire line? Oh, there you are, you lucky bastard. How you feeling?"

Nici saw the slight widening of Noah's eyes that accompanied Cap's appearance in the doorway. His gaze flashed from head to toe on the man, settling on his missing fingers for a moment before the startled expression softened.

"Cap, this is Gideon's brother, Dr. Noah Kinkead."

Cap extended a hand and squeezed, and she sincerely hoped he toned down the grip for a change. The doctor must be strong, because Noah didn't flinch.

Cap said, "Kinkead, Kinkead. ER doc, right? Heard about you. You do good work." He slapped Noah on the shoulder before turning back to Gideon.

"Kinkead, in my office. We're going to discuss the advisability of this return to work. You're going to have to convince me that blast didn't loosen more screws in your head than were clanging around already."

Gideon started to protest, but he didn't stand a chance. Cap put big hands on the back of the wheeled office chair and nearly launched it through the door. They were gone before three seconds had passed.

"Well, he's a force of nature, isn't he?" Noah watched the retreating back as if calculating the force of a firestorm.

Then he smiled, and the air crackled with a sudden static charge when he turned the grin on her.

She pulled her tongue off the roof of her mouth and said, "Yeah, Cap is that. I adore the man. Working for him, I learn more every day. He's more like a mentor to me than a boss."

She clamped her mouth shut with sudden force. She didn't mean to sound like a one-woman cheering section. It wasn't like Noah would care.

"I have a mentor like that too. The man walks on water when it comes to understanding people and where they'll thrive. What he doesn't know about emergency medicine, well, I'm not sure it's worth knowing."

That intense gaze turned thoughtful and serious once more. "Actually, I'm glad Gideon's been hauled out for a few moments. I have something to tell you that I think might be germane to the arson cases. G d doesn't agree with me, but he's not the only one with a nose for trouble."

She motioned a hand to the chair next to her, kicking it out with her foot by way of invitation. He glanced at the chair, then his watch. He frowned.

When his gaze locked with hers once more, his head took a slight tilt right as if trying to figure her out. She found his youthful genuineness and warm eyes comforting. What was his bedside manner like? It took her two heartbeats to realize she wasn't thinking about a hospital bedside.

Snapping her eyes away, she shuffled papers and shoved them into a random folder with more force than required. She'd have to dig them out later. She wandered in the smoke without a clue, and she couldn't see a thing except those dark blue eyes and that smile.

"I can't stay now. I'm due at the hospital." His words stopped, forcing her to look up at him when they didn't continue.

Noah regarded her with a pensive gaze, his eyes flicking over her features as if memorizing her face. She felt the lash of each movement like a caress of his fingers. What a hell of a time to have a reaction to a man.

"Can you meet me later, after my shift? I'll hope for a quiet day so I leave on time. Say, seven o'clock at Mallory's? I do think it's important in solving these arsons, or I wouldn't mention it."

What else could she say?

"Sure. Do you want me to bring anyone else?"

He shook his head, and if she was correct, the movement was more vehement than called for. He searched around the overflowing table and found a stack of sticky notes. A shiny pen appeared from his pocket and he wrote something down.

"Here's my number, in case he gets to be too much for you."

Her tongue was stuck again as he handed over the orange slip. Their fingers grazed and she swore she felt a spark ignite. He stood in front of her, his hand extended, when she yanked hers back.

He stared as if waiting for a response. She discovered her voice from wherever it was hiding. "Okay, good. Though one of us can run him home if he gets too tired."

Noah smiled again, the grin so boyish and full of fun that she forgot why he was there. "I'm more worried that he'll drive you all crazy. Can't have our crack fire squad racing for freedom. Where would the town be?"

She couldn't help the bubble of laughter rising, and she giggled in response. It felt good to laugh with him, even if she sounded like a simpering idiot. If his eyebrows rose in surprise, she probably imagined it.

He still hesitated, and she swore he shuffled one foot in a gesture of shyness.

"It would probably be a good idea for me to have your number too, in case we have a train wreck or something that keeps me late at the hospital."

She blinked. Of course. That made sense. But when had she last given her phone number to a guy? It had been, quite literally, years. She pulled the same sticky note pad forward and hesitated for a second, debating giving him Danielle's instead. Her sister could let her know if he called.

She heard the lecture for her older-by-minutes sister in her head. It's a phone number. She could block him if things got weird. He was a doctor, not that this guaranteed he was a good guy. It was time to stop letting the past rule her future. She wrote down her number, tore off the page in a sharp motion and handed it to him before she could change her mind.

He smiled as he looked at it, tucking it into a trouser pocket. The movement drew attention to his fit body, and her eyes popped back to his face before they wandered where they shouldn't be. He nodded once and turned for the door. With a hand on the jamb, he paused and looked back at her. "Nicolle? I'd appreciate it if you didn't tell my brother we're meeting. Okay?"

She nodded in agreement because her body was absorbing the smooth inflection he used with her name. It wasn't until he'd closed the outer door that she frowned when she realized what he said.

Chapter 16

So what if she texted her twin that she was meeting a colleague to discuss potential information about the case? The truth was close to that. Danielle said she was working late too.

And so what if, after a grueling run that did nothing to distract her nervous thoughts, she found something feminine to wear and put on a touch of make-up? She nearly poked herself in the eye with the mascara wand.

Nici had all day to think about his words. So what if she'd turned each one over carefully in her mind, looking for a hidden meaning? He had information he thought was relevant to her case. It might be something as simple as Gideon talking in his sleep and Noah wanting to share what he said.

Sure, right. Nothing was simple about this case, only deepening the mystery. Whatever he had to say might solve some portion of it.

That's why she was driving her truck at a sedate pace along the county road to Mallory's at five minutes to seven. She didn't want to be early, and she didn't like being late. Reminding herself it was all about the case wasn't working either.

Drawing close with three minutes to spare, she spotted him immediately. He stood on the broad porch to the side of the front door, and she slipped into a distant parking spot as he glanced at his watch with an impatient gesture. Maybe he wanted to get this over with. The idea didn't settle her nerves.

She should be the one impatient for this to be done. She was the one who should be itching to return to her laptop and reports and maps. She was the one tasked with solving this.

The engine died with her abrupt turn of the key. From where she sat, she could observe Noah at a distance without being noticed. Minutes ticked by. She was now officially late. Some perverse sense of wanting him to be disappointed she wasn't yet there, then elated when he saw her, made her wait.

And he did look disappointed. He watched each car approaching from either direction, then seemed to sag a little when it continued past, or when its passengers disgorged and none of them was her. She wasn't sure where this game playing came from, but she wanted to see how long he'd wait for her.

This wasn't a date, and she chided herself for toying with his good intentions. He might have legitimate facts, and here she was, acting like they were in high school. Watching him gave her time to notice that he too had changed clothes. Jeans with a decent amount of wear and a polo shirt in faded blue suited him. These clothes showed off a body that was toned and fit without being a bruiser. That suited him too, she decided.

He frowned at his watch again, then fingered his phone as if searching for a message. He slapped it a couple of times against a thigh with no give to it, and she imagined the resounding thud of its flat screen against hard muscles. He was clearly a man who took care of himself as well as he took care of his patients and reportedly, his children.

She was wasting his time. He probably had to pay a babysitter to be here and she was keeping him longer than necessary. Games again. When had she started playing games like this?

Easy to answer. Four years ago. The bite of smoke in the air, the hard ground under her back, the jeering laughter.

She pushed open the truck's door as hard as she tried to push away the memory. She kept her eyes on him as she grabbed for her monstrous bag and slammed the door on the past. When he looked up and saw her, a rewarding surge of relief flooded his expression, right before he gave her a dazzling smile and came down the steps two at a time.

"Hey, you're here. I was beginning to worry and thought I might have missed a call or text from you."

"Hi, sorry I'm late. I got stuck on something about the case." Only true in a minor way.

His smile dimmed a bit when she said that, as if suddenly reminded this wasn't a social meeting. A business-like buzz-kill dropped in place, replacing his intense smile.

"Did you learn anything new today?"

She shook her head, not wanting to lead him on.

He glanced at the door as it opened emitting noise and patrons. Then he glanced at his watch once more.

She tried to cover her disappointment with a nonchalance she wasn't feeling when she said, "Look, I know I'm probably keeping you from spending the evening with your children. Why don't you summarize what you have to tell me and you can get back to them?"

He looked up at her with sharp focus, and she fought the urge to smooth her hair, feeling overdressed and overdone. Damn, why had she worn make-up? She rarely used it anymore. It made her want to rub her eyes.

"My girls are with their mother in LA for the summer. Gideon is out, I assume with a couple of buddies. I am a free man for the evening and at your disposal." He gave a brief bow and seemed to examine her more closely. "Did I tell you how great you look?"

She was thankful for the shadows she could turn toward, so he wouldn't see the blush she felt on her cheeks. This was strictly business. If she repeated that enough times, would her body get the message?

"The timekeeping is an occupational hazard. You learn to time everything, how long it's been since the patient received a medication, how long an episode has lasted, how long ago you called the specialists. Or in this case, when the soccer game ends, meaning when the crowd thins and we stand a chance of getting a decent table." He smiled at her again, and damn her traitor body for feeling as warm and gooey as melted chocolate.

She made a show of looking at her cell phone and frowning, because she didn't want to feel this receptive to the man. He wasn't the first to look hard in her direction in the past four years. Even his brother had tried to ask her out. But he was the first to make her want to be soft and feminine and willing once more.

Damn him.

"How long do you think this will take?" Anger at herself made the bite of her words more pronounced. With them, his high wattage smile dimmed.

"It depends." He pulled the door open and motioned her ahead.

The noise from the interior hit her in a shock wave. Multiple games blaring on flat screens ringing the bar. Laughter and words mixed from raised voices, mostly male. The yell of a bartender at a server confirmed an order. From another part of the room, a baby cried.

That sound always got to her. She turned toward it without thinking. The sound ceased, but still, she sought the child in the crowd.

Next to her now, Noah followed her seeking eyes as if trying to determine what she was looking at. The baby started again, but she still couldn't find it.

"Sorry," he said. "I forgot the restaurant side is usually filled with little kids at this hour, and noisy. I've never brought the girls, but I've hung out with friends here a time or three. We usually sit at the back, by the dartboards. It's not much better in terms of the decibel level, but at least there are no kids crying."

A crying child was something she doubted she'd ever get tired of hearing. What a precious gift.

Turning resolutely toward the restaurant side, she moved forward without waiting to see if he followed. Four steps took her to the hostess stand, where a young girl probably not yet of drinking age grinned at them.

"Hi, welcome to Mallory's. You can pick anywhere in the bar, or I can seat you at a table in the restaurant. The bar's kind of crowded, but the food options are the same."

"A table, please," Nici said, not waiting for Noah. She wanted to be out in the open, not buried in the forced intimacy of bodies crammed close.

A shout went up from the bar side as they walked to their table, and she glanced back at Noah. "I'm sorry, did you want to watch the end of the game?" She wasn't sorry in the least. Why did she feel compelled to test the man?

That's easy, her devil side said. Keep pushing the man away to see how determined he is to come back. Proof that he wants to be here with you. Trust.

Oh yeah, she was ready for tonight like she was ready for a flashover in dense forest.

>>>>>

Noah didn't get it. Outside, she'd smiled at him like she was happy to see him. Now she was all business as she flicked two paper napkins like they were fine linen and tucked them on her lap. She opened the menu for only seconds before she snapped it closed again and folded her hands on top of the plastic cover. Her unblinking gaze rested on him as if she planned to interrogate him as her sister might.

Emotions could run high and uneven for first responders. Noah had done the psychological training, but that didn't make it any easier to diagnose. He watched Gideon as discreetly as possible for signs of extreme stress, signs that he was about to blow. He stared at Nicolle the same way now, but he couldn't help himself.

He cared, not just as a professional kindred soul, but because this was Nicolle Trajan, a woman he quickly found himself wanting to know better and for much, much longer. He needed to slow things down.

"Made up your mind already?" He pushed a teasing note into his words as he casually examined the main courses, then the appetizers. He knew exactly what he wanted too, but her brisk completion of a selection made him draw things out.

"This shouldn't take long. Don't feel compelled to find something on the menu. I can eat when I get home."

She froze as if she realized how dismissive her words sounded. Noah watched her for a moment, waiting for a retraction, but none came. Instead, her face shifted into that mask of indifference once more. The fascinating transition made him want to push her buttons even more.

"How about splitting an appetizer? I love the calamari here. The batter is the best – light and not greasy. I was going to follow with a burger. What do you want?"

She frowned, though this time, it was more in puzzlement. She clearly didn't know what to make of him. Blinking smoke-colored eyes narrowed and hands slowly unfolded, opening the menu once more in slow motion as her gaze lingered on his face. He missed the connection when her head dropped to peruse the pages. His heart tripped as her eyes met his once more, and a smile lifted her lips.

The smile was still there an hour later, after they devoured the squid like they hadn't eaten for weeks and their burgers as if days passed instead of minutes since the appetizer. A scent wafted across the food aromas, and Noah fought the urge to lean closer and sniff deeply. The woodsy feminine wildflowers had to be coming from her.

Noah was grateful to see Nicolle relax, mopping her plate with as much enthusiasm as Char did. The only purpose for fries in both their books was as a vehicle to consume ketchup. She took particular care to dig through the remaining potatoes for the plump ones she liked, and when she popped the last one in her mouth with a grin, he hoped he wasn't drooling. It had nothing to do with the food.

Her bell notes of laughter covered the sounds surging around them at his latest story. Noah said, "But don't tell Gideon I mentioned this. It will embarrass him."

Nicolle's laughter died down and she cocked her head to one side, as if seeing him from a new perspective. "You two aren't all that alike."

Noah shook his head to disagree. "Oh but we are. We're both single minded. We go after what we want with dedication and commitment. We believe in right and wrong but recognize the gray area in between. We believe in saving lives."

Except in some cases, things didn't work out that way. A hospital that turns into a shooting range. A cabin someone refuses to evacuate. The result is the same. Some lives can't be saved.

"Noah? What's wrong?"

Her words snapped him back from the ugly dark place. "This has been fun." He put a hand out and covered hers where it rested on the scarred wooden tabletop. Her eyes dropped to their joined hands for a moment before she pulled hers out in a slow drag. He couldn't stop the sigh of disappointment.

"I agree that this has been a nice break from reality, but we're here to deal with it, not hide. What did you want to see me about?" She was all business once more, and if her face looked somewhat pained as she dug through that big bag at her side, he knew his probably looked worse.

"I have an incident to explain to you. I think it could have something to do with this arsonist."

He let his story unwind slowly at first, and to her credit, she didn't break in with questions. She sucked in a couple of deep breaths when he described the young man's agitation and multiple hands required to keep him down. He glossed over the medical procedures. She wouldn't care how many times Noah tried to intubate the boy, or the multiple needle sticks of meds to combat the drugs and booze. The shotgun of tests in an attempt to determine what the kid was on would mean nothing to her. In the end, life's blood flowed on the slick treatment room floor and all over Noah, and there wasn't anything anyone could do about it.

"I called him about two hours after they brought him in. Pronounced him dead, I mean. He'd bled out a considerable amount before he got to us and he continued to in his struggles. At that point, he had probably suffered permanent brain damage. We tried our best to save him until there wasn't enough left to pump his heart and make his lungs work." He fell quiet, the picture in his mind of the young man's face finally at peace reminding him of the countless children lost to gangs and violence.

"You did everything you could, I'm sure." The quiet confidence in her voice made him nod, though he had a harder time convincing himself of that. She slid her hand over the table, close to his.

"We tried everything, but ultimately, it was on me. It was a public hospital, the emergency room of last resort for many patients. Our motto, though it was never formal, was treat and street." He twitched his fingers and rolled his palm up, gripping her hand. She squeezed, and he raised his eyes.

"We treat their medical crisis and release them. I can't tell you how many times someone raced up to our doors with music blaring, dumped a half-dead person on the sidewalk, and roared off. That was the case here. But it was what came later that was perhaps the worst."

He looked toward the bar where the crowd had dwindled after the soccer victory, because he didn't want to fixate on how tightly she held his hand. If it was only comfort she offered, he'd take it.

"Later that night, maybe near dawn, another car screeched to a halt outside, but this time, the motor died and a group came inside. We had two security guards assigned to the entrance, but they were no match for these big brawny types. A nurse called for police back up, but that was slow to arrive."

"I – Noah, if you don't want to tell me, I – "

"No, it's not that." He turned to gaze fully into her face, and noted the compassion and empathy filling her expression. She really was a beauty, and while she didn't need the make-up she'd added tonight, it certainly enhanced her aura. He pulled his hand away. Contact while he told this part would only make it harder. It was like he was pulling her into something dirty and ugly, and she didn't deserve it.

"Here's where I think it might have a bearing on your arsonist. The gang rolling in asked about the body still located in my treatment room. Aides had cleaned him up and mopped the area around him, but they were trying to determine an identity and find next of kin before moving him. A slightly shorter thin man who ruled the rest with authority stepped from the center of their protective circle. He identified himself as Rage, which was a street name."

'You got my brother here, doc-man, and you better take me to him. You better patch him up real good, doc-man, because if you don't, my boys gonna make life painful for you.'

"I tried to get an accurate name for the boy with holes in his dead body, but I wasn't having any luck. I could hear sirens outside, and since the wagons didn't come in lit up, I knew it had to be the cavalry. At least, that's what I tell myself now was going through my mind then. Who the hell knows what I was really thinking? The man in front of me was brandishing a gun, as were all of his cronies. All I could imagine was trying to patch up a room full of my coworkers and unsuspecting patients and families before having to start on the cops answering our distress call."

He folded his hands on the table in a duplicate of the gesture she'd used earlier. This time, she reached across the table and closed both of hers on top. They sat in silence for a few minutes while he examined a smattering of scars that looked like burns on the back of her right hand. Finally, she squeezed tighter and spoke.

"Tell me why you think this is connected. You don't have to explain anything else."

He shook his head in a slow side-to-side motion before looking up. "No, I'll finish. The gang members fanned out in the lobby and through the treatment rooms, and I heard screams and shrieks, but no gunshots. Finally, a sharper noise, a cross between a yell and a curse, sounded from the direction of the boy's room, and I ran down the hall. I'm not sure what I expected to do, other than protect a body that had already suffered too much indignity. What I found, though, chilled me."

Noah's abrupt halt inside the room's door didn't matter to the thin man, Rage. He bent across the body of the boy, shaking him and urging him to wake up. The other men turned their heads away and one seemed fixated on bloody gauze protruding from the burn barrel. Their eyes flashed up to Noah, then to the man now shrieking over the dead body. Rage spun and took two rapid steps before freezing, his wild eyes now on Noah.

'You, doc-man, you killed my brother. He only thirteen, you know that? Thirteen. He had a great future ahead of him, and you let him die.' He advanced, but Noah didn't back down. It wasn't the first time he'd been the target of a loved one's grief-stricken anger. He knew how to talk to them to help them deal with their loss. Hell, it was his loss too. He never wanted to lose a patient, particularly one so young.

'We did everything we could for your brother. What was his name? Do you know who shot him?'

Rage snarled and got in Noah's face, a finger poking and waving with a ferocity that raised the question of whether or not he too was high. 'None of your damn business who shot him. We deal with them. His name none of your business neither. But what is your business is doing something for him. I seen it on TV. Bring him back to life.'

This was a first. Noah didn't crack an expression other than sympathy. 'We tried to resuscitate him for over forty-five minutes. He'd lost too much blood. He'd lost a lot before he got here, and his drug-induced struggles against us as we tried to help him – '

That was as far as he'd gotten. The older brother went ballistic, screaming and cursing and pointing the gun that looked bigger with the barrel aimed at his nose from a foot away. 'He no druggie, doc-man. He no druggie. You done this to him, doc-man, and you gonna pay.'

Noah shook his head again, a part of him still feeling the situation had been surreal. "While it was happening, I felt like I experienced it in slow motion. Things got fast and furious after that. A male voice, loud and assertive, called for me from down the hallway, asking me to show myself so they could ascertain where the gunmen were. By now, the gang was melting out of the room on silent feet and I had no idea which way they were going. The last to go was Rage. I felt his pain when he took a final look at his brother. He then walked up to me, grabbed the hospital identification off my scrubs, and was gone."

Nicolle hadn't removed her hands, and her face held as much sympathy as Noah had felt that troubled evening.

"Noah, that happened hundreds of miles from here. I think you're safe."

Using Marcus's words, Noah said, "Trouble can come from anywhere."

A fleeting expression of worry might have crossed her face, but it was gone before he could be certain. He squeezed her hands and released them, feeling a new sense of chill in his heart. She lounged back, though her posture wasn't casual. "Tell me why you think this is connected to the arsons."

Noah mirrored her pose, feeling anything but relaxed himself. "After that, there were random problems. My tires were slashed in the hospital parking lot, so they moved me to an interior garage with no outside access. My badge was deactivated and reissued. But he had my name, my photo, and because of my public position, easy access. Strange people would hang out in the waiting room. I took to exiting and entering the hospital from different side doors, never taking the same path."

Their server came by and asked if they wanted dessert, and Noah gave her a forced smile and declined, asking for the check. When he looked back at Nicolle, her eyes were on him but far away, and wherever that was, it didn't look like a place she wanted to be.

"So, let me wrap this up for you. These gangs aren't just thugs. They're sophisticated, often with cyber hackers on their payroll and who knows what other skills. Soon there were strange cars cruising by the house at all hours, and threats appearing in the form of things thrown at the house. I feared for the girls, so I sent them to their mother's, but we were all unhappy with that arrangement. I went to my boss and asked for a change of assignment, anywhere that wasn't LA. Gideon lived here, so I requested something in this area. It so happened that my company staffs the doctors for Armstrong's emergency department. I packed up the girls and we moved here over the Christmas holiday."

"Ergo, the dancing in the office supplies aisle," she said, flashing a sudden smile that lit up her face and made her eyes glow.

"Ergo, the dancing." His own smile flashed and faded. "But then, I received a message from a former colleague in LA. It seems the gang is trying to track down where I am now. Their reach is long and their lack of forgiveness even longer. It didn't matter that I did everything I could to save that boy. To Rage, I was at fault. And now I'm wondering how strong their urge for revenge is, and if it would extend to arson aimed at a firefighter related to me."

Nicolle shifted and looked away, her face turned to a big screen TV but her eyes unfocused. When they finally came, her words were slow and delivered in a flat tone. "I guess any threat is a possibility. You're right, danger can come from any direction. I'll have the task force look into it."

There wasn't much conviction in her voice. Had he made a mistake in sharing this with her? Some date he was. The evening had started out with that joy of new discovery, a friendship building with little steps. Then he'd unloaded this on her and the fun was gone. He pulled out cash and left it in the server's tray over the check.

She shook her head as if denying something she was thinking and turned back to him. Glancing down at the bills, she reached into her big bag. "Let me split that with you."

He shook his head and attempted to bring back some of the levity from earlier. "Don't you know doctors are loaded? Our date was at my invitation, and therefore my treat. No arguments."

Did she get a shade paler?

"Um, this was a date? I'm sorry. I don't exactly date."

Noah chuckled as he pushed back and rose. She sat, uncertainty on her face as she looked up at him. He assumed she wasn't waiting for him to pull out her chair, but he did it anyway. She seemed to come back from wherever her mind had wandered, though she still looked confused as they made their way to the door.

The press of night air felt good, cooler than the day and with only a hint of smoke on the evening breeze. He knew this would change by morning. In hours, the smoke from adjacent fires would drift back to cover the area in a hazy orange glow and people would line his lobby complaining of coughs and headaches. But for the moment, he could almost imagine things were normal.

He wanted to put a hand under her elbow, not because he thought she needed help but because he wanted to touch her. Their linked hands before had felt nice, nicer than any encounter he could remember. That moment's hesitation cost him, when she stepped a few feet into the parking lot and turned to him. "I will look into the issue you brought up, Noah."

He nodded, mesmerized by how the limited glow outside the bar made her hair glossy and radiant. She stared back at him as if she too examined him in this different light, and he hoped she found something she liked.

She broke the spell with a drop of her mesmerizing eyes and put out her hand. "Thanks for dinner."

This was not going to end like this, he decided. He took her hand in both of his, and her gaze snapped up in surprise. He stepped in closer and leaned down before she could react. A single kiss, light and too brief, made him realize her lips were even more tempting up close than they were from a distance. He pulled back to find her eyes closed, and he figured, what the hell.

He moved across the small gap between them and lowered his head again. This time he put more pressure into the kiss. The sensation of keeping his lips locked on hers made his body respond in a way it hadn't in years, a surge of emotion and a rush of blood. He wasn't sure how long their connection lasted. This time, he pulled back more slowly and forced his eyes wide.

Nicolle's gray eyes fluttered open, as if she woke up under protest, and her lids were at half-mast as she looked at him. Then she took a step back, and night air rushed in where warmth had been moments before. Another step, and their hands fell apart.

But she kept watching him as she took slow steps backward. One hand raised and she pressed two fingers to her lips. Then she smiled.

His heart did an abrupt flop as he grinned in response.

Chapter 17

Nothing was going to kill her good mood. Not Danielle, who'd gone bonkers when she found out how Nici had spent her evening. A date? Not really, no matter what her twin said to the contrary.

Cap grousing about budgets and shortfalls and requisitions didn't dim her lights either. If he looked at her with suspicion when she gave him a bright, cheery good morning and an affectionate pat on the cheek, it only made her smile bigger. She whistled as she crossed the squad room, making more than one head lift and stare at her in shock. Nope, nothing was going to blow a hole in her day.

Okay, so she didn't get to sleep easily last night, and she would probably be running on fumes in a few hours, but what the hell? It appeared she had a man interested in her, a good decent man, someone who made caring his life's calling and did it well. He was easy on her eyes too, which didn't hurt things in the least.

Noah had flirted with her early in their dinner. When it came time to share his information, he'd allowed her to comfort him. Then he'd kissed her good night. A blazing flame of a kiss. Two, actually. If things got hotter between them last night, she'd be on a new fire line this morning and the conflagration would be their fault.

The good doctor had texted her this morning, just a few words about how he enjoyed last night and hoped they could do it again soon. His sense of humor popped through when he added, "Minus the heart-wrenching life story stuff, of course." Then he added a smiley face.

A clatter and cursing announced the arrival of her officemate, and she looked up in time to take in Gideon's struggle with crutches between narrowly set desks and boxes of supplies. His backpack looked like it weighed a ton and a sheen of sweat marked his forehead. She rushed forward to grab his arm as he upended a trashcan.

"Are you supposed to be up so much already?"

Gideon huffed and blew out another curse. "I can't stay cooped up. I don't care what the doctors say. I can't stand feeling helpless." He shrugged out of her grasp and continued into their cubbyhole, falling into a chair with little grace and nearly ending up on the floor when its wheels propelled it backwards.

"Fuck. I hate this. I need a walking cast but the doctor won't give me one for another two weeks. Two weeks. Can you believe that? I even asked Noah to put in a good word for me, but my brother is in cahoots with the ortho." He wiped his sleeve across his forehead and met her gaze, followed by an exaggerated double take. "Well, someone sure looks happy this morning. Are you enjoying my show? Tickets cost three kisses, Trajan."

She barked out a laugh at that and settled into her own chair to examine him more closely. There was a definite resemblance between them, Gid and Noah. She hadn't equated Gideon's unruly looks with Noah's textured blond hair and blue eyes, but the younger brother was a more refined version of the older one. More to the point, where she originally thought Noah would be a soft, unmuscled type, the kind you'd expect to find working in a hospital, she'd been surprised. When he pulled her in close for that second kiss last night, the outline of toned body was unmistakable. As was the hard outline of something else. She wasn't yet sure how she'd handle that, so she chose not to think about it. Not yet. It was too soon.

"Ah, Trajan? Nici?"

Her eyes popped open. She hadn't even realized she'd closed them. She was lost in the memory of those kisses. Gideon regarded her with a bemused expression, as if he too was lost in thought. His question, however, was the last thing she expected. "Tell me the truth, Nici. Does your twin ever relax and let her guard down?"

Gideon and Dani? Not in a million years could she see it. In fact, the more she thought about it, the harder it was to imagine. She giggled, and he looked startled by the sound. That made her laugh harder, and by the time she got herself under control, he was shaking his head and staring at her like she'd lost her mind.

She pulled a folder forward and woke her laptop from its binary slumber, pushing both toward Gideon. "No time for twenty questions, I'm afraid. Tell me, what do you know about incendiary ignition devices?"

He sent a final strange glance in her direction before rolling his chair forward and pulling the laptop closer. He frowned at the screen, then flipped open the folder and ran a finger down the list inside. His fingers were broad, like someone who worked hard in physical labor. Noah's fingers were different, tapered and fine but with that same sense of strength. A doctor probably had to be strong. Of course, his hands when he pulled her closer were gentle and –

Not going there. She'd combust and the only thing left of her would be a charred spot in the chair.

Gideon hummed and toggled her screen, then flipped the pages as if seeking something in the file. She knew the second he found it, the same anomaly she'd discovered. She had hoped, and his small smile of shared triumph confirmed it. "You found a signature. The bug's using a nonstandard trigger device to start these fuckers, and now we have something to trace." His fingers began typing on her keyboard before he'd even broken eye contact.

"Yeah, well, don't get your hopes up. I searched for that configuration and there are about two hundred videos online about how to make a trigger like it. And the number of sources we would have to run down is ridiculous. Still, it ties the fires together in a way other than – " She broke off.

Gideon's face tightened into granite and he typed faster. "You can say it. Other than that damned piece of plastic he leaves behind every time." His eyes rose to meet hers. "Other than me."

She nodded, because denying it wouldn't make it go away. Now would be as good a time as any to bring up Noah's theory.

"Your brother thinks the fires might be related to what happened at the hospital where he worked in LA. You know, the incident with the kid and his gang-banger brother." For Noah's sake, she wanted him to be wrong.

Gideon's gaze rose so quickly, she wondered if his head would pop off. His sharp stare and pinched face communicated his anger over the idea.

"Did I tell you Noah didn't bother to share that little bit of news with me until a few nights ago? I didn't? Well, he didn't. You would think he would have told me last year when it happened. You would think he would have mentioned it when he moved here. No, he waits until now, and despite the fact that LA is a world away from here, he thinks these things are connected."

He went back to banging keys, and if her laptop survived the brutal assault, it would be a miracle of modern engineering. His fingers rammed hard enough to make the table shake. With a sudden exclamation, he pushed the machine away and dropped his face into his hands. It muffled his voice when he finally spoke.

"I cannot believe Noah didn't tell me sooner. I'm his only brother. Did he tell you about the threats the other hospital reported? These goons could be in the neighborhood right now, and we wouldn't know it." Gideon's head shot up and he pinned her with a puzzled gaze. "When did Noah tell you this?"

"I didn't know before you, if that's what you're asking." She knew damn well that was not what he was asking her.

"You're evading my question. When exactly did Noah tell you this?"

Why was she suddenly feeling shy, like a high school bookworm caught going out with the favored college-aged jock? She busied herself reordering the files in front of her and reached for her laptop when Gideon leaned back. His gaze, speculative and narrowed, stayed on her without blinking.

When he continued to stare, she said, "He told me about it yesterday."

Gideon jumped on that. "He was at the hospital all day yesterday." He snapped his fingers. "The working late excuse. You two were on a date."

Too surprised to catch herself, her eyes jerked up in time to see Gideon's sudden sly smile. Feeling color heat her face, Nici said, "It wasn't a date."

"Who paid?" He flashed the words out like lightning.

"He did, but – " She didn't get a chance to finish.

"Date," he said, waving away her objections.

She pushed her chair back to pace, stopping at the small window overlooking the beehive of activity in the fire camp. It didn't hold her attention. She selected her words carefully. "Your brother is a nice man, and I admire his devotion to his family and his profession." She turned around and sat on the table, meeting Gideon's eyes.

His face had turned serious. Gideon's words were quiet when he finally spoke. "Yes, Noah is a good man. He deserves better than he's gotten, more often than not. I worry about him, Nicolle. I worry about him a lot."

She realized as her heart did a sudden quick uptick that she was worried about Noah now too.

She grabbed her laptop and returned to studying the arsonist signatures. Gideon eyed her with musing intensity a couple of times but confined his comments to their investigation. By lunchtime, the sky had again turned orange and brittle, and the smell of smoke overwhelmed everything else. They hadn't progressed past the single common signature.

A ripple of greetings rolled to them from the outer room, followed by a perfunctory knock on the doorjamb. The space filled with a tall, boney man wearing a creased uniform and a hardhat that read 'Safety' across the front in bold lettering.

"Trajan, Cap said I'd find you here." The man moved forward and eyed Gideon. "Kinkead, sorry to hear about your injuries. It's a bitch."

Nici said, "What can I do for you, Clyde? I know you have jurisdiction here, so my findings are all yours." She updated him with their results from the morning. "If you'd like to step in with your big resources, feel free," she said.

"Well, thanks, but I'm not here to shovel your embers. I came because I received a report on the materials located at the points of ignition for the cases where we're suspecting arson. We got lucky." Clyde frowned and pulled a sheaf of papers from his back pocket, referring to them over his glasses. "In one of the last arson fires, we found a common trigger mechanism, a cell phone. It's the disposable kind, so untraceable."

Nici nodded. This wasn't news.

"But a corner of the case remained intact, protected enough during the blast to let us lift a print. We got a hit on it. A con with priors."

He looked like a kid given his birthday presents early.

Gideon said, "Did someone pull him in?"

Clyde's grin died. "No can do. He was released right before the fire in April. Mean bastard, by the sound of him.

One Clovis Mitchell left the Idaho pen on a mistaken early release."

Nici's good mood vaporized in a gasp. Her heart skipped and thudded before picking up speed, and she wondered if the past could ever be left behind.

Chapter 18

It was a hell of a day, and he wasn't even going to put a quarter in the jar for thinking it. A layer of dust had formed on the coins at the top, because despite the increased pressures and associated cursing Gideon brought into the house, Noah didn't have the heart to enforce his system. What kind of message would it send his girls when they returned and found the jar overflowing?

The ER had been hammered from early morning on, with the first serious cases arriving before eight and maintaining a steady flow ever since. Added to the flood of people with legitimate issues, the frequent flyers came in droves seeking social support. They were parking gurneys in the hallways and begging for help from the hospital's main floors. He'd changed clothes three times already, his back-up slacks and shirt long gone and replaced by scrubs.

The young boy in front of him now had decided to test the theory that anything could and would fit in his nose. Age four, his nose was small, and the marble lodged there was not. He cried until Noah let him hear his own heart beat. Then he became fascinated with whatever instrument Noah produced, and the marble removal was accomplished with minimal tears. He declared, over a residual stuffy nasal whine, that he was going to be a doctor when he grew up.

"I think that's admirable. But you know," Noah winked at the boy while he gave the mother a reassuring smile over his head, "doctors have to know what belongs in a hole in your head and what doesn't. Do you think you could learn that?"

The boy nodded vigorously, almost dislodging the gauze used to stem a small trickle of blood.

"Thank you, doctor. I can't thank you enough. You're so wonderful with kids. Do you have children of your own?"

This was not his first ride on the turnip truck. The woman's hopeful smile and flicker of attention to his ring finger told him she was flirting with him, even as she batted her eyelashes and pushed a slow hand through her hair. He merely smiled in response, signaling the aide to show mother and son out to the discharge desk.

He glanced at his watch, wondering how many seconds he'd have before the next summons, the next page, or the next person needed him. He'd meant to call Nicolle long before this. He didn't want her to think she was far from his mind. Whatever brainpower he had that was not dedicated to his patients returned to last evening, again and again.

Her gentle understanding. The feel of her hands on his. Her laugh, that musical rise of sunshine on a cloudy day. Yes, he thought about her, and when he wasn't thinking, he could still feel her hands grasping his and taste her warm lips.

Slipping down the crowded hall, he murmured to the desk clerk that he needed a short break, indicating the door to the staff quarters. She nodded with sympathy. It wasn't until the door to the men's room closed after him and he flicked the lock shut that he let go of the breath he'd been holding. Escape was bliss.

Taking care of business was quick, a skill most doctors developed as residents. You never had enough time, not with your patients, not for your research, not for yourself. He checked his watch once more. Two minutes had elapsed since he'd checked out. He was owed a few more.

Scrolling down his phone contacts, he took a seat on the sink counter, swinging his legs as the phone dialed her number.

"Hello," she answered. He heard the cautious warning tone in her voice. She was probably not alone. Gideon could be leering at her at this very moment. Lucky guy.

"Hi Nicolle, it's Noah. How's your day going?"

He heard the phone being covered, a mumble of sound followed by a longer pause and the increase of background noise.

"Hi again." She didn't say anything more past those wary words.

Noah felt a sudden need to treat lightly. Had he misread her possible interest last night? Did she have second thoughts? Or worst of all, did she compare him to Gideon and find him lacking? His spurt of jealousy at his brother startled him.

"So, how's your day going?" The delivery of her question made him pause before answering. Tension laced her voice. If Gideon had been making things difficult for her, Noah would make his recovery a little more uncomfortable than necessary.

He said, "We're getting hammered. Is it a full moon? Even the cockroaches have come out."

"Cockroaches?" He heard the distraction his words caused.

"Sorry, that's a bad term. Frequent flyers. You know, the people who come to an ER rather than go to a clinic or individual practice. Some even have insurance. I think they want to engage in witty repartee with yours truly."

Silence made his mood sink.

"Look, if this is a bad time," he said.

She rushed in with quick words. "No, it's not, and thank you for the break. It's been kind of a mess here. We got a hit on the possible arsonist, at least someone who might be involved with one fire. And we learned the chemicals used are also common to meth labs and other drug processing. It's been kind of crazy."

"Isn't this good news? You sound worried." He'd become very good at reading people's voice tones over his professional years. Sometimes they hesitated to explain why they really sought treatment, either because of the problem or its cause. Coaxing reality out of them had become one of his specialties.

He imagined her face, the pinch of worry at the outer edges of her eyes, the tense line of her lips. Very kissable lips. It would be good to hold her again. For her comfort, of course.

Who was he kidding?

"Listen, I can't stay out here for much longer," Nicolle said. A hand hammered on Noah's locked bathroom door at the same moment. A nurse delivered the particulars of a case in rapid-fire words.

"I have to go too. Can I call you tonight?"

She seemed to hesitate before saying, "I don't know how long I'll be – "

"Me neither," to more knocking.

"Okay." And for the first time, it sounded like she was pleased.

That kept him going through the long day. It was later, much later than he wanted, when he devoted his thoughts on his short drive home to what he planned to say to Nicolle. Convincing words about another date, less business and more personal this time, ran through his head as he made the final turn into his street. The reveal of his home around the curve was normally a welcome sight after a very long day, and with no worries about the girls stuck with a sitter, he could feel his stress draining away as he slowed down the road.

Except his house was overrun with cars. His driveway stood full, two cars across and two deep. Unfamiliar cars and a white van with a logo he couldn't read in the dark lined the street. He stopped at the curb a couple of doors down. Every light on the inside was on. Gideon hadn't mentioned inviting company over. He thought about going in the back door. He might be able to creep in unnoticed, because he wasn't in the mood for people.

As he tried to make a decision, a sheriff's SUV pulled in behind him. He watched in his mirror as it parked on his rear bumper and Jake got out and walked to his door. So much for stealth.

He rolled down the window. "Hey, Jake. Just trying to figure out where to park. It looks like Gideon decided to have a party. Glad you could make it."

Jake glanced toward the house, then back at Noah. "He didn't call you? It's no party. Your house is the new command post for this arson case."

That explained the vehicles and the lights. Noah gave up the pretense of sneaking in and turned off his engine. As he and Jake strode up the walkway, Noah thought back to his cryptic conversation with Nicolle. He said, "Was there another fire?"

Jake put out a hand to hold the front door open. "No, but there's been a break in the case."

Noah froze inside the door, his eyes scanning the living room and dining room. Gideon, propped on the sofa with an ashen face and twisted mouth, flipped through pages in his lap. The way he absently rubbed his thigh above the cast told Noah his brother was hours past his endurance point in terms of pain. Yet he knew if he said as much, Gid wouldn't listen.

The woman standing over him made him do a double take. Nicolle? The redhead was dressed in civilian clothes, but as he looked closer, he noted the more deeply grooved lines in her face. A bulge at the back of her waistband proved to be a gun. Danielle turned to look in their direction, narrowing her eyes, and Noah tried to hide his disappointment.

The old fire captain stood at the dining table with another older man, tall enough to challenge the chandelier when he leaned over. They stabbed at a computer screen, one of three open laptops. Voices, subdued and intense, came from the kitchen, and a man stood with his back in that doorway. He turned and spotted Noah as a blonde woman strode out.

"Okay, you're all set. You have hot food and cold, dinner and breakfast, just in case. When you need a resupply, let me know. Now that they've been here, the interns will be fine making the next delivery."

He recognized the woman. None other than chef Roxy LaFollette stood at the entry to his kitchen, backed up by her movie star partner Mac Smythe. He didn't know Roxy made personal takeout deliveries. He didn't know Mac helped her out. Despite having spent a couple of evenings in the man's company, Noah was still a little star struck.

Mac saw him first. "Hey, Noah, food's fresh and hot, so I hope you didn't eat at the hospital. Hell of a day, isn't it? I can't believe it." He shook his head.

Roxy let Mac loop an arm over her shoulders as she surveyed the room. Her stillness only lasted a moment before she began to move through the space, picking up used mugs and glasses and shoving them at Mac with a silent nod toward the kitchen. With a sigh and a shrug at Noah and Jake, Mac began shuttling things back and forth.

"Roxy, you don't need to do that. I'll clean up later. I hope Noah understands – "

Nicolle burst out of the kitchen and stopped, her eyes zooming in on him fast with an electric pull that must be mutual. Her mouth closed and her chest rose on what might have been a sigh. He certainly hoped it was, because it answered the sudden speed of his heart.

"Hi," she said. It appeared she didn't know what else to say.

He lifted his chin in acknowledgement, but before he could say anything, his brother's voice rose from the sofa.

"Sorry, bro. The squad HQ needed to move with the fire line. No room at the sheriff's office. We need to be here. There wasn't anywhere else to meet."

Taking in the worried, exhausted and generally pissed off expressions of everyone in the room, Noah shook his head to let them know he didn't mind. He thanked Roxy and Mac on their way out. By the time he turned to her again, Nicolle sat in a chair at the dining table, her eyes down on the laptop in front of her. He didn't miss the subtle moves of her twin as she placed herself between them.

He tossed his briefcase on the entry table. "Catch me up."

A few minutes later, he wished he'd stayed at the hospital, elbows deep in blood and bones. Catching him up didn't take long. A match to a former prisoner in Idaho, now paroled and missing, was not an answer for the first few fires. The next part made Noah feel sick.

"The chemicals found at the source of the latest fires are all consistent with those used to process various street drugs." This assertion came from Nicolle, who moved to his side but didn't touch him.

Her twin added, "Based on what you told Nicolle, I made a couple of calls to resources in Southern California, and they tell me the gang you faced in that incident last year, Dr. Kinkead, is a major player in the manufacturing and distribution of these same types of drugs. We've sent our chemical analyses to them for review, to see if they match anything they've confiscated. We won't hear back until tomorrow."

His greatest fear that the past would catch up to him was being realized. And Gideon had been hurt because of him.

"I know that look. No, this didn't happen because of you. Noah, are you listening to me?" Gideon's voice rose and popped Noah out of his reverie.

"Yeah, well, the drug angle only gives us part of an answer. There's the guy from Idaho. And what about the anomalies from the cases last year? I'm glad this is your turf and not mine, Cap." The tall man, unidentified and leaving, slapped Cap on the shoulder once and disappeared out the front door like a puff of smoke.

"Noah, can I talk to you for a minute?" Nicolle's voice, pitched low, went unheard by the others as they began jockeying for position through the kitchen door. Gideon remained on the sofa, his head back and eyes closed.

"Don't mind me. I'll take a powernap and be ready for the next round."

Noah moved forward automatically and checked the circulation around his brother's cast. Then he eyed the dislocated shoulder. The sling lay partially hidden under Gideon's butt, and while his brother didn't appear to be using the arm much, it still should be immobilized.

"I don't need a lecture. I know, I know." Gideon cracked his eyes open and looked up at Noah. "I'm trying to watch it. I couldn't manage the papers with only one hand."

From the kitchen, a female voice said, "I bet you can manage a damn lot with one hand, Kinkead. Now is not the time to boast about your prowess."

Beside him, Nicolle shot a puzzled glance in that direction. The only other woman here was Danielle. When she stared back at Noah, she looked perplexed.

Gideon's eyes were closed once more, but Noah noticed his triumphant smile. Another conquest, though he had less concern about Danielle Trajan being able to handle herself. Gid might have met his match.

He gave up trying to figure out what had happened with his brother and took Nicolle's arm in a gentle grip. The house wasn't large, and the only rooms not visible were bedrooms. Char's room was Gideon's for the time being. Elena's had become the storage area for Gideon's few boxes and bags. That left his bedroom. The implied intimacy would have to be something they overlooked. Still, after guiding her up the stairs and closing the door, he felt their isolation.

Nicolle looked at the bed once before turning toward the opposite side of the room, the entrance to the attached bathroom. There wasn't much room to pace, but pace she did. Back and forth, her eyes studiously ignored the largest piece of furniture. She finally sat on the only other appropriate surface, the chair in front of his desk, and Noah sank to the edge of the bed.

She looked nervous, her ill ease making his more acute. Her hands, curled together in her lap, were never still. He wanted to grab them and hold on, though for his own comfort or hers, he wasn't sure.

"I'm sorry your home has been invaded like this. Gideon wasn't in any shape to travel with the convoy to the new fire line, but we need him on this case. He suggested we move our headquarters here for the time being."

"That's fine. I understand. Without the girls, the house is too empty anyway."

His attempt at easing their tension fell flat, slipping and falling like unaware residents on wet exam room floors.

"Anyway, there's something you need to know." She glanced toward the closed door and bit her lower lip.

That single act made him tense in a different way. He'd forgotten how tempting those lips were. Not forgotten. Lost in the terror of knowing his problems were now his brother's, and found again in her single movement.

When he spoke, he couldn't control the spasm in his voice, and it came out rougher than he intended. "I figured it out. Rage and his gang found me. They're behind this. What do you need me to do?"

She was shaking her head even before he finished. "No, that's not it. I need to tell you about – "

"Nici? Eat something. Then we need to go over Mitchell's potential threat. I know you don't want to, but we can't avoid it any longer. Nici? Where the hell are you?"

Nicolle turned to the door at the sound of her sister's voice, and Noah noticed the paling of her usually healthy complexion and the faster ringing of her hands. A knock sounded as she rose, brushing past him as he too stood and made a grab for her arm. He missed, she yanked open the door, and her sister stood on the threshold with an assessing expression in her narrowed eyes.

Chapter 19

She wasn't sure if she felt disappointment or relief. Nici brushed by Danielle the same way she brushed by Noah, so neither of them would notice her over-bright eyes and unshed tears. Her past was catching up with her, with all of them. Clovis Mitchell would exact his revenge.

"Nicolle, wait," Noah called after her, and she heard her sister's murmur to distract him. She hoped he could at least look at her with something other than pity and disgust when the truth came out. Because come out it would.

The living room was silent and empty without the crowd from before. Gideon still lay on the sofa, taking bites of a sandwich at a rate guaranteed to empty the plate within minutes. Everyone else was gone.

"Where's Cap?"

"Following the convoy," he mumbled around chewing.

"And Jake?"

He swallowed this time and took a long drink from a can of soda. "Danielle sent him out with a list of tasks. Things to look up, people to contact, arrangements to be made. Sheriff stuff." He eyed her with more alertness than the late hour and his condition should allow.

He said, "Did you tell Noah?"

"Tell me what?"

Crisp delivery of the words swung her to the hallway's entrance. Noah stood just inside, his eyes on her. She noted the lift on to the balls of his feet, and the balancing shift as if he centered himself. She'd seem that move more than once, and usually in the sparring ring. He was preparing for an attack.

As well he should. Not willing to explain, she countered with, "We should eat."

"I'm. Not. Hungry. You said this isn't about Rage. Tell me what?" He hadn't moved, but she sensed his bristling energy, his anger and worry and god only knows what else.

Danielle darted around Noah and took Nicolle's arm, pulled her forward, and grabbed Noah's. He didn't put up a fight, and she couldn't. Danielle said, "Why don't you two go in the kitchen, eat something, and then we'll all talk." She all but propelled them through the room with a force Nicolle knew she usually reserved for throw downs.

"Are you sure?" Gideon's tense question wasn't muffled by distance.

"Yes, I'm damned sure," she heard her twin hiss back. Their siblings fell silent. The door to the kitchen swung shut on quiet hinges pushed by an unseen hand.

"Tell me what?" She should have known Noah wouldn't give up.

Nici turned toward the trays of food loaded to feed a small army. It was too bad her appetite fled with their retreat. "We should eat before this gets cold," she said, picking up a plate she didn't need and spooning on food she didn't want.

Noah grabbed a plate, ladling food with an appearance of the same disinterest she exhibited. He pulled out two chairs at the round table tucked into a corner. Nici imagined this is where the girls did their homework and discussed the important matters of their lives while he prepared their meals. The surge of domesticity swamped her and her throat closed. Everything she was missing, as if she needed more reminders.

"What's wrong, Nicolle?" His question's quiet tone seemed more suited to his doctor guise. That too was probably deeply ingrained in him, as deeply as the spurts of adrenalin followed by crashes of tedium were for her.

She forced herself to fork in food as an excuse not to speak. Delicious flavors burst on her tongue and under other circumstances, she would have moaned from the pleasure. Her emotions, though, were elsewhere.

A warm hand covered hers on the table. She stared at his ring finger, its shape unmarred by a band or any sign he'd ever worn one. What kind of marriage had he shared with his wife? There must have been some passion. His children were living proof.

Darkened blond hairs sprang from the back of his hand offering sparse coverage. Would he have a trail of those same hairs on his chest? She'd never been attracted to hairy men, and after, well, after, definitely not. The mere thought brought a shiver to her body, one she didn't try to quell.

"You can tell me anything, you know. I've heard it all. I'm a doctor."

His statement almost made her smile. "Is that like a bartender?"

He squeezed but didn't let go. "Kind of. You'd be surprised what people tell me. It must be because of something they see in my face. I'm told it's not the norm."

She lifted her gaze to meet his darkened blue eyes, serious and intense. The smile marking his lips didn't reach the rest of his expression. Hesitancy drew deeper lines, as if he sensed whatever she was going to say would change things.

"You do have a kind face, Noah. Kind eyes. I get the feeling I could tell you anything, and ask you to keep it a secret, and you would. I – I trust you."

She trusted few people.

He seemed to pause as if considering what he wanted to say. The tilt of his head accompanied eyes flicking over her features. It had been a long time since she'd been this close to an interested man who had good intentions. She hoped he'd still want to be as close again, once he knew.

"I'm sure you hear this all the time, but your eyes match your profession well. Smoky, with swirling emotions and tiny flecks of bright light that could be sparks and fire."

"Ah, no, I've never heard that before." His words pleased her in an extraordinary way. Her smile grew wider, the feeling more sincere, and his grew to match it.

"What's going on in there? If the two of you are getting it on, could you at least send out more of that lasagna before things get any crazier?"

Gideon's voice, loud and teasing, rang through the closed door. It should have broken the spell, but she was still staring, and so was Noah.

Nici felt the sigh rise from him as if his breath caressed her face. What would he make of her news, of the pivotal point in her life that now marked everything with a before and after? Would he still look at her with the same longing that marked his intensity now?

>>>>>

He wanted to break Gideon's other leg, and maybe his jaw as well. His mouth wired shut seemed like a great idea.

He gave Nicolle's soft hand a final squeeze. Soft, but marked by scars and calluses. He suspected her heart was the same. It was there on her face, in her eyes, in the aura of sadness she carried with her.

"Guess our time is up. Do you want to finish that?" He nodded toward her plate, where she'd moved food from side to side but left most uneaten.

She shook her head, standing and putting her back between them on her way to the sink. She stopped there, settling her dish against the stainless steel with a clatter but not moving away.

"You're going to hear some things, things about me. You won't like them. Please don't judge me, okay?"

He thought perhaps he'd misheard her. He didn't let any time pass before saying, "Believe me when I say I'm the last person to judge anyone else. Not with my track record."

That made her turn. "I hardly think defending your patients and your staff against the brutality of gang members is a failing mark on your report card."

He froze at the admiration evident on her face and her trace of an admiring smile. Her trim body turned toward him, and he imagined he could see the deeper inhales against the outline of her shirt. Whatever other emotions it hid weren't obvious, but he hoped more than he thought possible that she felt safe enough to share them. It moved him to think someone would believe in him and hold him up as a hero, even when he knew differently. If he'd handled that night better –

"Noah, haul ass out here. We need to get things organized and decide what we do next."

Gideon's no-nonsense tone broke the mood and forced Noah to shake his head at his betraying thoughts. He had no right complicating this situation by drawing Nicolle into a relationship. Why would she want one with him? She was single, in a high-powered job and probably looking for the same in a man. He was a single dad, and while he had no doubts about the esteem assigned to his job and how hard he worked, he wasn't in the sexiest of medical professions.

"We should go," she said. Was that regret in her words, on her face? He didn't have time to look more closely before she walked to the door and placed a hand on its old wooden frame.

"I am sorry you're getting pulled into this." Then she was gone, leaving a slow swing to the door as it closed behind her.

He wasn't ready to confront their problems, not yet. If there was a way for him to stop this craziness before it went further, he would, but he had no idea how. On autopilot, he covered food containers and dug in a cabinet for plastic bowls and lids. He'd talked with security experts. Other than cautioning vigilance and suggesting he keep the police informed about any supposed incidents, there was little he could do shy of wrapping his family in a ring of protection well beyond his salary to provide.

The door swung open, and he turned toward it, hoping Nicolle had come back. But Danielle's raised eyebrows and regretful gaze met his.

"I'm coming." He wiped his hands on a towel and looked around the kitchen. Nothing that couldn't wait remained on the counters.

"She wants to tell the story herself." Danielle's statement hurried his steps. Her eyes, identical to Nicolle's in coloring, hardened. "If I had my way, she'd never have to talk about this again."

Noah followed her into the living room, his gaze finding Nicolle. Her perch on the edge of a stiff chair didn't look comfortable, but then neither did her expression. She stared at her hands as if she didn't recognize them. Her clasp was tight enough to paint her knuckles white, a pale comparison to the tan of her hands. Noah glanced at her twin to see if the other woman planned to comfort her, but she stood at the wall, leaning against it with her arms crossed and staring into the distance.

He crossed the room and knelt next to the chair, covering Nicolle's hands with his own and squeezing as she had for him. Her startled eyes rose to meet his and she frowned as if she didn't understand the gesture.

"Please don't make this more difficult for me." Her whispered words carried so much anguish that he retreated without asking what was wrong.

"Nici, let's get this over with," Danielle said, the gentleness of her voice in sharp contrast to the warrior appearance of her face. Noah found himself staring at her now, wondering how she could be so cruel and unfeeling to her sister.

"Give her time, Danielle. She deserves that, don't you think?"

Noah rotated to gawk at Gideon. His brother's anger communicated itself clearly in his words. His dark look was aimed at the lieutenant as if he already knew what was coming.

Noah had had enough. "Leave her alone, Gid. Whatever Nicolle has to say, she can say in her own time. Hell, where are your manners?"

If his sudden outburst surprised his brother, he didn't show it. He merely threw a significant glance at Danielle and gave her a tight smile, one she didn't return.

"It began four years ago." Nicolle's quiet words drew him back to what was important. He moved toward her again, only to have her shake her head to stop him. He sank into Char's favorite beanbag chair, his knees rising almost to his chin as he wrapped his arms around his legs.

"I was responsible for an inmate firefighter crew. Do you know about those programs?"

Noah shook his head, though a quick sideways glance told him he was the only one in the room in the dark. "Give me a case summary."

She nodded at his request. "These are inmates who have earned job training as firefighters. My crew had worked the previous season. Most were due for parole soon. Some had already secured jobs on fire crews for the following year. It was considered a safe group."

Her use of the past tense captured his immediate attention. Nicolle waved a hand when he opened his mouth to comment. The fact that she wouldn't meet his eyes closed it again.

"We were fighting a particularly nasty blaze up in the northeast corner of the state, and the fire proved to be unpredictable. It would die down, only to flare up somewhere else. The terrain was rough and mountainous, making accessibility an issue. The smoke was dense and we couldn't count on air support." She paused, back to wringing her hands. "Because we chased the fire, my crew became separated from the main body. And because conditions blew up, my men were separated into small groups as well."

"They aren't supposed to do that," Gideon said.

Noah couldn't take his eyes off Nicolle. He felt her profound distress, wishing he could take it over for her. Part of him wished she didn't say anything more because he guessed he'd hate what came next.

"No, no, we weren't, and believe me, I heard all about that. But it happened. One minute we were facing an inferno, and then the fire died back and shifted directions. By then, we were off course behind a ridge. The radios wouldn't work. I couldn't find most of my crew." She fell silent.

"It wasn't your fault." The protest bit out of Danielle as if she couldn't help it.

Nicolle shook her head again. "We've been over that, Dani, and in the end, it doesn't matter. What happened, happened. I didn't follow procedure and put myself at risk."

He crawled forward and covered her hands once more, and when she tried to shake him off, he tightened his hold instead. "You don't have to say anything more."

She wouldn't look at him, examining their joined hands instead as if they carried important messages. "Yes, I need to finish this. I'll cut to the end. Some of the inmates held a grudge against me, feeling they were somehow getting less respect because they reported to a woman. One of those inmates was in the small group around me when the fire calmed. He decided to take advantage of the situation."

Nicolle lifted her face and he saw the unshed tears filling her eyes. They made the depths appear endless, like bottomless pools reflecting his face back to him. It was then he realized he showed no obvious emotion. A trick doctors developed, a mechanism to keep the bad news or doubts to themselves, was handy at times of crisis. It was something his ex-wife hated, what she called his emotionless soul stare.

Nicolle flinched and tried again to withdraw her hands. Noah could kick himself for causing her additional grief. He forced his face to soften and his words to lose their bitter pitch when he said, "What did he do?"

A sniff, a shrug, a quick intake of breath. Then she said, "He attacked me."

"Son of a bitch, the fucker." This from Gideon.

Noah remained kneeling, his thoughts in unfocused turmoil. How could any man hurt a woman? It was beyond his comprehension.

His eyes met Nicolle's, and he read her unsaid request. Ask no questions. It was enough that she shared this. He nodded to let her know he understood.

"Some of the others on the crew found Nicolle and the man and broke things up. They took control of the situation, to their credit. They got the assailant back to camp where he was turned over to authorities. Nicolle went to the hospital and – "

"That's enough, Dani." Nicolle's sharp words sliced through the conversation. That silence hung in the room for so long, Noah swore they were smothering. He stared at Nicolle, wanting to pull her into his arms and comfort her for the tragedy. Obviously, she wasn't over it yet.

"I don't understand how this impacts our arsonist," Gideon said.

Danielle pushed off the wall and paused by the side of Nicolle's chair. Her hand dropped to her twin's shoulder and Noah could see her fingers tighten before she moved off to pace the room. Nicolle's face turned into a stony mask of cold indifference.

As if she knew it would be impossible for her sister to continue, Danielle answered. "That man, Clovis Mitchell, received an extended prison term and is banned from firefighting. He screwed up his chance of changing his life when he gets out, at least as far as firefighting is concerned. He blames Nicolle."

Noah couldn't keep the words from bursting out of his chest. "How the hell can he blame her? He caused his problem. He hurt Nicolle." The idea bit stabbed into his gut until he was sure he must be bleeding inside.

Nicolle's voice was tiny when she responded. "He doesn't see it that way. And the worst part is that Mitchell was released from prison in April. His parole officer and local authorities can't find him, but his fingerprint has been identified on one of the arson trigger devices."

Her face reflected the feelings roiling inside him. Sudden fear brought its icy grip to his heart as Nicolle's lifted her devastated gaze to his with a single tear falling down her cheek.

>>>>>

Nici kept her face averted, though she didn't notice the streets as Danielle drove them home. All she could see was Noah's stricken face, the anger he didn't bother hiding, and the pity in his eyes. She didn't want his pity. She wanted ignorance. If he never knew, they might have stood a chance.

"You were right to tell him. Besides, I think Noah took things well, given the circumstances."

"Whose side are you on, anyway?" Nici couldn't help letting bitterness filter into her tone.

Danielle seemed to hesitate a few seconds before saying, "Hey, yours of course. But this isn't about sides. Gideon blames himself, Noah blames himself, and you blame yourself. The only person to blame is the criminal who hurt you and your firebug." Danielle's reasonable tone held nothing but logic, but that didn't make it any easier to hear. Nici sensed her fidgeting nerves, chalking them up to her twin's frustration with their lack of progress.

They drove in silence as Nicolle relived the telling twice more in her mind before she could find words again. "Sorry. I didn't want Noah to know. You're right, they deserved to know. But that doesn't help how I feel."

A hand grabbed her shoulder and squeezed. Damn, her sister had a firm grip. And she didn't let go.

Nicolle turned and said, "So what do we do now? We have three potential sources of risk we can't locate, we're no closer to linking igniters or accelerants to an individual, and fire season rages on."

Danielle's mouth pulled into a grim line, and her hand dropped to the steering wheel so her other could comb through her hair. She had it down tonight, a rarity when she left their house. With the few brainwaves left after the emotional night, Nici wondered why her sister suddenly decided to do something so girlish.

"We keep looking. We hope someone makes a mistake and we find a clue. Or, worst case, we catch them in the act next time."

"There can't be a next time. Too much of the state is already burning, and the crews are stretched past thin. We have to stop him, and we have to do it before he torches anything else."

The tires whined against worn asphalt in the sudden silence. The air between them hung with tension as thick as new smoke.

"I'll catch Mitchell, Nici. I promise you."

Determination rang out in her sister's tone, but her soft words didn't bring reassurance. She blinked back tears as she thought of that pity on Noah's face and mourned what could have been.

Chapter 20

Gideon's drawn face told Noah more than words how much their struggles overnight had worn on him. The fact that he didn't even argue with Noah's directive to stay home and rest spoke even louder. His shouts asking where Noah was going when the front door slammed were something to ignore. Gid was a bright guy. He'd figure it out.

Noah had been chasing ghosts, though. A drive by Nicolle's house revealed an empty driveway. He needed to see her, to assure her everything was all right between them. Or maybe he was the one needing that security.

She might have gone to work this morning. He was due at the hospital in less than an hour. Driving around with a random hope of locating her wasn't possible for much longer, and calling would only produce protective stonewalling by all parties. He understood everyone's desire to keep Nicolle safe. That's what he wanted to do too. The urgency he felt to comfort them both would have to wait.

Even as busy as his day was, she was never far from his thoughts. Smoke invaded the town with a shift in the winds, and the resulting flare-ups of respiratory distress kept the ER staff busy without breaks. In between cases, his mind always strayed to her stricken face and the devastation in her eyes last night after she'd shared her story. There was more to it, he was sure of that. He guessed it wouldn't be pretty.

They all had secrets. He, Nicolle, Gideon. What hid inside Danielle's psyche, waiting to spring?

He sat in the hospital parking lot after his shift, drumming his fingers on the steering wheel with newfound energy as he debated his next move. Nicolle hadn't reached out to him during the long day. His texts and voicemails went unanswered. What could he say to make things comfortable and safe between them? When his cell phone rang, he nearly tore his pocket in an attempt to get at it. Disappointment coursed through him on faster heartbeats as he realized the screen revealed his ex-wife's number. He hesitated a moment to collect himself before answering.

"Hello."

"Hi Daddy. Are you working?"

Despite his mood, Charlotte's voice calmed him without effort. "No, sunshine, I just got done. How was your day?"

He let the chirp of words sooth him. It was best the girls weren't here now. Too much was happening. He only hoped they would remain safe in LA.

Starting the ignition and driving on autopilot, he made appropriate noises when Char paused long enough to draw breath. Busy Main Street gave way to the quieter lane he'd found himself on this morning. This time, though, a dusty truck he recognized stood in the driveway. He parked behind it and shut down the engine.

"I got to go, Daddy. Mommy's husband is taking us out for ice cream tonight. You know what, Daddy? I miss you."

His little girl's words tugged at his heart, but at least she wasn't crying to return. Perhaps she'd come to terms with the summer visit. Or maybe ice cream was enough to cure all ills.

"I miss you and love you too, sunshine. Can I talk to Elena?"

Learning his older daughter was off with friends for the evening brought a momentary frown, but he shook it off. He had to trust Barbara to keep an eye her. He had to, or he'd drive himself nuts worrying.

The world was oddly silent after he hung up, like all sound had been sucked clean. A hole opened up in his heart.

He had to learn to get used to this. Over the coming years, there would be other separations. Soon, too soon, the girls would grow up.

The phone rang again as he sat staring at the little bungalow. There must have been a second in her day Char had neglected to tell him about. He answered without looking. "What you'd forget, sunshine?"

Silence.

"Hello?" He pulled the phone away to glance down at the display, noting the restricted number. Alert and focused once more, he said, "I'm sorry, I was expecting my daughter. Who is this?"

He stared at the house as the silence continued. He was tempted to hang up when the front door opened. Nicolle stood framed against its dark interior with a cordless phone to her ear.

"Are you going to come in or sit there like a stalker?"

"Um, would you like me to come in?" A sudden flash of nerves ripped through him.

"Honestly, I'm not sure. But I think we should have this out so we can both get on with our lives." She disappeared inside as the call disconnected. The door stayed wide.

He whipped the car door open so hard, it bounced on its hinges and swung back on him, banging him in the shin. Pain made him pause long enough to consider whether this was a good idea. If he forced her to reveal what she wasn't ready to share, there was no guarantee they'd return to their easy camaraderie. There might be no chance of returning to that, no matter what.

He reached the house before he had a conscious answer. He put a cautious hand on the door to swing it inward. The interior sat darker than expected in the early evening light, and his eyes had to adjust before he found her. Nicolle sat on a couch in that same posture she'd held last night, linked hands resting on her knees. He thought she jumped when he pushed the door closed, but he wasn't sure when it shut out the brighter exterior.

"Are you all right?" He promptly gave himself a mental kick for asking such an inane question. People who were all right didn't sit in the darkness, looking like they expected to be blindsided by an attack.

"It was a tough day," she replied, but by her flat tone of voice, she could have been reciting the phone book.

"May I sit down?" He gestured to the couch next to her. In the dim light, he saw her shrug as if it didn't matter.

He sat as close as he could without touching her. He wanted to press next to her, near enough to take her hands in his and unweave her tightened fingers. He wanted to wrap his arms around her and tell her it would all be okay, just as he did with his girls on a rough day. He didn't think Nicolle would take that well.

"Listen, Noah, we should cool things off. We don't have much in common, and I, well, I don't have much to offer. In a relationship, I mean."

He opened his mouth to protest when chimes sounded across the room. Nicolle frowned in that direction but rose before he could place his outstretched hand on her arm. It was probably just as well. How would she react if she knew what he was thinking?

She picked up a cell phone from the table by the door and her frown deepened as she stared at the display. She raised it to her ear and greeted the caller.

Whoever it was did a lot of talking, with Nicolle issuing occasional sounds of agreement or comments like, "I see" and "I understand." Noah gathered it wasn't good news. Her face fell into deep lines of stress. The hand clutching the phone tightened. Her breathing accelerated and her eyes grew large, larger than last night during her explanation.

She was almost hyperventilating by the time she said, "Do what you think is best. Yes, I understand." The phone clattered to the table when her fingers gave up their grip. Her huge eyes stared at a wall, unseeing, and her breathing came in tiny gasps.

Noah couldn't stand to see her so upset. He wanted to kill whoever had called her. He wanted to make everything that worried her disappear in a puff of smoke. When he crossed the room and pulled her into his arms, she didn't resist him.

"Nicolle, let me help you." He tucked her head until his shoulder. As he'd suspected months ago, her height matched his, but in this position, he felt like he sheltered her from whatever storm was headed in their direction.

Nicolle's arms crept around his waist, and she nuzzled closer to him. She didn't say anything, and he felt torn. He wanted to demand to know who called her, but he enjoyed the feel of her in his arms too much to protest any reason for her actions.

"Hold me, Noah. Just hold me." The plea in her voice did him in and he forgot why he should be worried as he tightened his arms.

Her hair tickled his cheek where her face burrowed deeper into his neck. Her body trembled, and he wanted it to be because of their embrace. He didn't think that was the case. A part of him that hadn't seen any action in so long sprang to sudden attention at having her soft womanly body pressed against him from thigh to chest. Even if the reason for them being in this clutch was the wrong one, the result was the same.

He wanted her. Knowing there were things needing to be said between them didn't change it. Those casual kisses days ago hadn't been enough. If anything, they'd only fed his appetite for her.

"That was Mitchell's parole officer, in case you're wondering." Her voice was small and strained. "An update, not that there was anything to report."

Against her back, his hands clenched and he forced his fingers to relax. If he ever had a chance at pounding the man with his bare fists, he'd take it.

"I am sorry for using you like this." Her muffled words, issued in a voice as soft as the hair caressing his face, hinted at her dismay.

"There's nothing to be sorry about. I understand you're upset. I'm glad I'm here to comfort you."

She pulled back fast, and surprise made him loosen his grip. Her piercing examination of his features was as extensive as any intake he performed on a new patient. If she looked too closely, she'd find evidence of his need for her, and he didn't want to scare her away. He shifted on his feet, attempting to ease the pressure in his slacks. All she had to do was look down.

But Nicolle broke free and crossed the room into even deeper shadows. She stared at the pristine dining room table as if studying it for flaws, her fingers trailing along the carved edge. The jerk behind his fly as he thought about those fingers on him made him clear his throat and consider bolting for the door.

"You know this won't go anywhere."

Her words snagged him in. "I'm not inclined to share other people's private business with anyone. I am a doctor. I hear things people would rather not tell anyone else all the time. Whatever you say to me will stay with me, and me alone."

She shook her head, making the cascade of red hair dance across her shoulders. "No, you're misunderstanding me. Deliberately, I think, and probably to spare my feelings. I said it before. You're a kind man." She glanced up at him, over her shoulder and sharing a small smile. The faded light hid her eyes and her expression.

She turned to him fully and walked in a slow pace back towards him. Blood drummed in his ears. He felt like prey being stalked by a lioness, and damn if it didn't make him feel even hotter.

Nicolle stopped in front of him and raised a hand, letting her fingers trace his cheek and linger on his chin. "No, I'm talking about you and me, Noah. I don't have much left to give a man, and I can't be sure I won't react badly even if I want to try. It's best if we agree to be friends and leave it there."

Her words drew him forward, suddenly uncaring about what she might see. Even in the dimly lit room, he discerned her rapid breathing in the quick rise and fall of her chest. Fright would be a logical diagnosis.

"Are you afraid of me? Right now, this instant, are you afraid of me?" He kept his words gentle.

She shook her head, a puzzled expression wiping away the smile. Then he was correct. He could only interpret her heightened respiration and sudden stillness one way. She was as affected by him as he was by her.

He stepped closer so their toes almost touched. She didn't back away. At this distance, they were eye to eye, and he recognized the caution she used like a shield.

He put a hand to her cheek as she had to his before, stroking back and allowing his fingers to linger in her hair and tease her earlobe. She stilled but didn't back down. "I promise to always be careful with you, Nicolle. I don't agree that you have nothing left to give. You're funny, wise, and understanding, and you know the lyrics to kick-ass rock songs, always a plus in my book."

This time she chuckled, even as her eyes sparkled with what he suspected were tears. Her body melted a little into a more relaxed stance. She said, "What do you get out of the deal?"

It was his turn to laugh, and he didn't bother to hide the wry tone. "I get to hold a beautiful woman in my arms, all night if she lets me. That's hardly hazardous duty."

She was the one to step closer this time, but not before letting her eyes flick down his body and rest for a moment on the obvious tent in his dress slacks. "I can't do anything about that, you know." She nodded down, then let her eyes linger there again. He felt the gaze through the fabric as intimately as if her hand caressed him.

"I don't expect you to. Just, ah, stop staring at it, okay? I don't want anything to, ah, come between us."

She laughed this time, and he sighed in relief at the sound. She stepped to his side and linked her arm through his, leaning her head on his shoulder.

"You are a good man, Doctor Noah Kinkead. If it's okay with you, I'd like to snuggle up against you and fall asleep with your arms around me. I feel safe with you."

He didn't know how to reply and wasn't sure he could get his throat to work even if he did. She pulled him down the hallway, and he let her. He thought fleetingly of calling his brother to let him know he wouldn't be coming home tonight. He reached into his pocket and pulled out his cell phone.

"Let me text Gideon, so he doesn't worry."

She released his arm and crossed her own in front of her. "Does he have to know you're here?" The sunny light faded from her eyes once more.

"No, I'll say I'm working."

Looking at her, his breath caught. She was so amazing, both outside and in. Danielle had a harder edge to her, but Nicolle retained a gentle softness. Even now, the resignation he saw on her face did nothing to harden her. He rapidly changed his mind.

"You know what? He probably won't even notice I'm not there. Let's forget about him."

The flush of relief on Nicolle's face made him feel like he'd just made a perfect decision. Then another thought occurred to him.

"Will you sister be upset to find me here?"

Nicolle giggled with a sudden mischievous glint in her eyes. "You are right to fear my twin, Dr. Kinkead. She is quite formidable, and she looks incredibly kick-ass with a gun in her hand. For your future reference, you don't want to challenge her to hand-to-hand combat either. But you don't need to worry tonight. Danielle called to say she's working late. I doubt we'll see her until morning."

>>>>>

She couldn't remember when she'd last slept so deeply or so long without strange dreams or nightmares. It had been quite literally years. As an added bonus, she could stare into the boyish face of a truly amazing, caring man.

Noah hadn't stirred since she untangled her limbs from his. Even as she pulled away, his arms tightened as if trying to keep her close. Safe. He made her feel safe. How many men would be satisfied with holding her as they promised and asking nothing in return?

It wasn't as if he didn't want more, Nici knew. She'd felt the press of his erection during the night, but he remained the perfect gentleman. It wasn't until she initiated a few brief kisses that he gave in and returned the embraces with a heat leaving no doubt in her mind. He wanted her.

If she was going to get over her past, she couldn't find a more gentle but willing partner. If only she could. She wasn't sure she could go through with it.

His eyelids fluttered at the same moment she heard the big engine turn into the driveway. A glance at the clock told her she better rouse him anyway. He probably had to work today, and he couldn't go back to the hospital in the wrinkled slacks he'd slept in without being asked. She kept on the t-shirt and gym pants she'd greeted him in last night, but there were a few times during the night when she wished they were skin to skin. Her eyes traveled down to the light tuff of blond hair peaking out over the top of his t-shirt, leaving her aching to follow the trail down to the promised land.

"You are a beautiful sight first thing in the morning, Investigator Trajan."

Nici lifted her gaze to find Noah's half-mast eyelids and suggestive smile directed at her. He was heart stopping handsome, and coupled with the kind demeanor and commitment to his profession, she was sure he was going to prove irresistible. On impulse, she leaned forward to give his lips a quick kiss and felt gratified when he wrapped a hand around the back of her neck and pulled her back in for a second, deeper one.

"Good morning," he whispered, as his day-old beard tickled her jaw.

She couldn't keep the shy tone from her voice. "Good morning yourself. I could say the same thing about you, Dr. Kinkead."

He grinned as if the comment pleased him, and after another quick kiss, he rolled to his back and stretched. She heard things pop, tendons and joints getting back into place. It couldn't have been comfortable for him to wrap himself around her all night long, constrained by his work clothes, but that's what he did without complaint.

"See anything you like?" His teasing made her realize she was staring again.

She leaned back and ran her eyes up and down his body with more boldness than she'd used before. "I'd have to consider the question but only after an extended examination."

He laughed, a full throaty sound that did melting things to her insides and brought quivering questions to her nerve endings. With a wicked grin on his face, he said, "Want to play doctor? I'm more than happy to give you the stethoscope."

She giggled in return, feeling more lighthearted than she had in a long time.

A hand rapped on the bedroom door in a quick staccato. "Nicolle, is that the doctor's car outside? Are you all right?"

Danielle's worried tone also demanded an answer, and with a last regret-filled look at Noah, Nici rose.

"I'm fine. We'll be right out. Can you start the coffee?"

No response. She knew it wasn't because Danielle wasn't full of questions. A man's car parked in front of the house would raise curiosity enough. Nici wouldn't be surprised if Danielle had put a hand on the hood to check the engine temperature to gauge how long he'd been here. She'd deal with her twin later.

She turned to find Noah standing and pulling on his dress shirt. His sober eyes were on her, though, and he froze in a motion to reach for his socks and shoes.

"Are we okay?" He didn't move, as if the world rode on her answer.

She gave him her biggest smile and nodded. "Oh yeah, we're better than okay."

He grinned as he turned toward the bathroom, whistling a rock and roll tune from twenty years ago. If she remembered correctly, the words were something like, 'It was a hot, hot, hot, hot night.'

That made her smile even wider. Yes, it had been, and it might be even hotter the next time. She bopped out of the room to find Danielle in the kitchen, staring at the coffeemaker with a tired sag to her body.

"Tough night at the office?" Nici tapped her twin on the shoulder in passing and expected to hear a response. When none came, she put mugs on the counter and turned Danielle toward her.

Her twin worked harder than most, as if she still needed to prove to the force and herself that she had earned her leadership position. Too many nights passed with no sleep when cases were complicated or staffing was short. Dedicated was too small a word to describe her.

But Nici didn't see the worn frown she expected. It looked like Danielle hadn't showered, and she wore yesterday's workout clothes, the same type of outfit she wore to and from the station each day. An embarrassed red stained her cheeks. When Nici had last seen that, she couldn't remember.

"What happened last night?" Nici asked the question with a hand on her sister's arm in rising alarm.

Danielle pushed her loose hair behind her ear as if impatient with it. Straightening, she examined Nici's face with sharp glances. "I could ask the same thing. What is Kinkead's car doing in the driveway? Are you okay?"

Nici wasn't ready to explain, not when the feelings were tender and new and needing more analysis. She turned the question back on Danielle. "Are you okay? Your face is red, and you look strange. Maybe Noah needs to check you out."

A deeper voice broke into their staring contest. "Check what out? Danielle, do you need a doctor?" Noah stood in the hallway entrance, as subtly commanding as if he was in the emergency room. His face was gentle, wearing a genuine concern she considered professional but kind. The authoritative calm was a sharp contrast to the man who'd teased her moments before, and this time, Nici felt her cheeks heat with what was undoubtedly a blush. On cue, his gaze cut back to her, and she saw the slight widening of his eyes even as his smile stayed polite. The temperature was rising and she was clueless about how she would cool things down.

Danielle's sharp gaze probably looked him up and down, no doubt taking in the shirt as perfect as if he'd pulled it from a hangar and the slacks crisscrossed with creases where none should be. Nici didn't want to come up with explanations. To cover her turmoil, Nici said, "I, ah, need to use the room. I'll be right back. Help yourself to coffee, Noah." She gave her twin a hard stare and whispered, "Be nice to him."

Ah yes, Noah Kinkead did all sorts of crazy things to her insides and made her almost believe she could leave the past in the past and find a new kind of future. Then her eyes snagged on her flat belly in the bathroom mirror, and her heart squeezed like a fist held it in its unyielding grip. Damaged goods. She was damaged goods. She wanted to hide and have a good cry, reality pressing in with the light of day. But there was no time.

Voices rose and fell from the kitchen. Danielle's was louder, and Noah's sounded patient and even. Nici cracked open the door as she brushed her hair and dragged it into a quick ponytail. Their conversation made her pause.

"So help me, Gideon's brother or not, if you do anything, anything at all, to hurt my little sister, you'll have to answer to me, Noah."

He didn't respond immediately, as if he weighed his answer first. Then Nici heard, "I would never do anything to hurt your sister, Lieutenant. I know it might be hard to understand, given that we haven't spent much time together, but I care about Nicolle, care about her a lot as a matter of fact. I am a patient man. We're taking things slow. Maybe someday she'll trust me, and then we can see where the future takes us."

Trust. Nicolle stared at her face in the mirror, wondering if it was a feeling she could ever use again. Her trust was in short supply and she wasn't sure she'd ever be able to find it. For Noah's sake as well as her own, she certainly hoped she could.

Chapter 21

That might have been the most peculiar send-off in history. First Danielle's threat, and it could only be called that. Then Nicolle's quick dismissal, as if she couldn't wait to see the back of him. Her eyes, though, told a different story. Dismay, despair, denial. When Noah leaned forward to kiss her lips, she'd turned her face and offered her cheek instead.

He diagnosed it as self-consciousness in front of her twin. She might not want to explain what they'd shared, a night more intimate in some ways than if they'd made love.

Making love with Nicolle would be a phenomenal experience, of that Noah was certain. The mere thought of it made focusing on driving an instant challenge. He also had to school his expression so Gideon wouldn't see. His brother could be sharp as a scalpel when he wanted, and he'd pick up on the change in Noah in an instant.

Because he was changed. Whatever wrongs had befallen Nicolle in the past, they would face the future together. He didn't want her to stand against those demons alone. He'd be by her side, and together, they'd overcome them, however long it took. He would devote himself to making it work, and he had all the time in the world.

A block later, reality struck. Who was he fooling? The girls would be gone for another few weeks. Once they returned, it would be hard to grab time for coffee, much less a relationship. His daughters were his highest priority. The clock was ticking. He needed to convince Nicolle they had a shared future and soon.

He pulled into his driveway, relieved to see the window blinds open and no cars blocking his entrance. At least he and

Gid could talk. If Gid was even here, that is, because no sign of him appeared.

It was strange Gideon hadn't at least texted him last night to find out where he was. Noah glanced at his phone to see if he'd missed a message. It was tuned off, which he didn't remember doing. Gideon was probably sleeping, and probably pissed to be left out of the action for so long. He might have been chasing a woman.

He remembered Danielle's flushed face and strange comment. "Gideon's brother or not." He didn't see the abrasive lieutenant swayed by his brother's easy charm. And use of Gid's first name? When had that started?

Noah put his hand on the front door handle, surprised to find it unlocked. Caution emptied his thoughts as he stepped inside the entry on light feet. He pulled up abruptly, watching Gideon glare at him with anger in his expression.

"You didn't call me last night."

The bite in Gideon's words carried censure more than concern. Noah felt an instant wave of anger in response.

"I'm sorry, I didn't know that at my age, I still had a curfew. Or that I needed to report my whereabouts to my brother, who often doesn't let me know for days where he is and what he's doing. I'm sorry I left you alone and worrying last night." But he didn't feel guilty in the least.

Gideon raised his hands as if in surrender, but his expression didn't change. Pensiveness hid his usual good nature. He held up the phone, the cordless unit from the landline, and shook it at Noah.

"This is a phone. Until we get this thing with the arsonist cleared up, you call me. Where were you anyway? Your cell went to voicemail. Things go crazy at the hospital?"

Noah walked through the living room and began undressing, one eye on the clock as he realized he needed to haul his butt into the shower fast to make it in to work on time.

But the night had been worth it. He grinned as he thought about Nicolle's teasing smile.

"Oh man. If you had a flare-up at the hospital, you wouldn't be smiling this morning." Gideon's words stopped abruptly.

The silence was complete enough to make Noah turn in curiosity. It wasn't like Gid to leave an opportunity for good-natured grief to go wanting. Gideon hadn't moved, though. He sat in the chair facing the front window, and he stared at the couch with a guilty expression. His eyes rose and he pinned Noah with a serious stare.

"Bro, if you're doing what I think you are, you have to be careful," Gideon said.

Noah circled his head and heard his neck pop, then did the same with his wrists. It bought him time to decide how much he should tell Gideon. Then he remembered Danielle's guilty look. The idea dawned and rose to full brightness as he chuckled.

"Seems I'm not the only one," Noah said. Gideon shook his head and stared at the couch once more. Noah couldn't bring himself to consider why he was now looking at it with such tenderness. The contrast when his face darkened with worry forced Noah closer. "What happened here last night, Gid?"

Without turning, Gid said, "Noah, we found another red rose this morning, on the doormat here at the house."

He processed the statement, thinking first that he wanted to know who the other part of 'we' was. The second implication of the sentence hit him with enough force to knock him back on his heels. He couldn't process the threat fast enough to decide what to ask next.

They both jumped when the phone rang in Gideon's hand, the noise drilling through their stillness. He held it out without raising his eyes, and by the time it rang again, Noah flopped back on to the opposite chair and connected the call.

What he heard next made him stop breathing as he clutched the plastic harder.

>>>>>

"Damn it. Damn it. Damn it." The words, delivered in an even tone with almost pleasant sincerity, should strike him as funny. The woman uttering them loomed over the others in the room as if about to interrogate them.

His house never felt this stifling and undersized to Noah, not even when filled with his daughters' friends. Gideon sat in the same chair. Noah paced the length of the room in growing agitation. Nicolle arrived with Danielle, both already in uniform. Nicolle met his eyes with a worried glance but Noah had no chance to console her. A quick call to Marcus had settled staffing for the day. Noah wasn't going in.

In fact, Noah wasn't going anywhere for a while, not with this hanging over his head. The call had been brief, but not brief enough to be forgettable based on its contents. Gid's subsequent anger was as drenching as Noah's fear.

A knock sounded on the door, and Danielle frowned at it, holding out a hand to stop Noah when he would have answered. He jumped at the metallic click when she unsnapped her holster. Her tension relaxed when she looked through the peephole, and she unlocked the door with swift fingers and opened it to Jake on the threshold.

"Good, I'm glad you're here. Noah, go over it again for Jake."

It wasn't like he hadn't gone over it multiple times already. Luckily, he'd had the presence to hit the speaker button on the phone when he recognized the voice, and Gideon had heard the second half of the explosion of words too.

Jake had yet to say anything as he pulled a small notebook from the pocket of his safety vest and clicked the pen. He stared at Noah expectantly, then glanced at Danielle when Noah didn't say anything.

He couldn't go over it again.

"Noah, it's important."

Nicolle's quiet words made him inhale to steady himself. When a hand settled on his back, he wasn't surprised to find her standing behind him, understanding filling her sad eyes. Keeping his gaze locked with hers gave him courage.

"It was Rage."

Jake said, "Did he identify himself?"

Noah shook his head, then turned fully when the deputy raised a skeptical eyebrow. "Have you ever had something burn itself into your memory? A gesture? A face? For me, it's his voice. I will never forget it. I can't." A shudder ran up his spine and made his scalp prickle.

Danielle responded first. "Go on, Noah. No one here questions your identification."

He grabbed Nicolle's hand in his and lifted it to his lips. The quick kiss didn't go unnoticed by the others in the room, and he saw Danielle and Gideon in particular exchange a longer glance. The tension between them added more electricity to the already overcharged air. He gave Nicolle's hands a final squeeze, letting go with reluctance.

Noah resumed pacing. "He said I have a nice little thing going on here. He knew the girls weren't here, which means he must be close by and watching me. He wanted to know who the crip was, as he put it." He stopped to glance at Gid, who, with a sharp nod, urged him to say the rest. "He said by the time he was done with me, he'd cut up every person I cared about, just to watch me suffer."

He swung around and stared at Nicolle. "This isn't going to work. You need to stay away from me. I need to keep you safe."

Sudden anger blossomed on her face, making her look as fierce as her sister. She stalked across the room and slammed a fist on his sternum, not hard but with enough force to grab his undivided attention.

"If you think some punk is going to keep me away from you, you don't know me very well, now do you? I will not be chased off." She grabbed his cheeks, pulled him forward, and kissed him hard enough to make his ears ring. When she let go, he felt dazed by the determined light in her eyes.

"He's skimmed over things, but that's the gist of it," Danielle said. "It is clearly a threat to Noah and his family. I might take exception to the assumption that he's watching, because the town's pretty good at identifying outsiders."

Noah rubbed his hand over his head, wishing he could brush away his darker thoughts as easily. "I already called Barbara and warned her. She isn't taking it as seriously as I want her to, but all things considered, I think the girls are safe in LA."

Jake finally spoke. "I'll notify the locals. It doesn't hurt to have them watching out for credible threats." He hesitated, then said, "Do we think this guy has anything to do with the fires?"

Gideon nodded along with Noah. "He knew about the wildfires. He mentioned being able to burn the town down if he wanted. Much as I didn't believe it would be anything related to Noah when this started, I have to think this Rage guy could pay someone to start them."

Jake frowned and shook his head as if he disagreed. Danielle said, "What, Jake? He would be capable of hiring a torch, and it would be a nice way for Rage to keep his hands clean."

"That's not what I mean." He hurried through the words as if expecting to be interrupted again. "That's not why I'm here." Now he turned and looked directly at Nicolle, and Noah felt the hairs on the back of his neck stand at attention.

Jake said, "Remember what we said about the town picking out people who don't belong? We had three calls today, and all of them identified a stranger matching the picture and description we circulated last week. I'm sorry, Nicolle. The witnesses are credible. Mitchell is in town."

Noah heard Nicolle's gasp and saw the flash of pain before she threw herself into his arms. He buried his face in her neck. He wasn't sure which of them shook harder. Bitter words delivered in rapid fire burned across the room behind his back, but Noah wasn't letting go. Much as he wanted to keep Nicolle away from him, away from his mess, it didn't appear she was in any less danger.

"Every agency, every level, every jurisdiction. I want his poster up in every public place, and I want a front page story in the paper tomorrow."

Seeing the terror she was trying to hide, he felt Nicolle's pain course through him. Danielle's wrath made Rage's sound like a child's laughter, Noah thought. He would feel sorry for the inmate Mitchell, except he didn't deserve anyone's pity for what he did. And if he ever got his hands on the guy, Noah would forget he was a healer for a while.

Chapter 22

"This is a hell of a mess."

Gideon punctuated his pronouncement by throwing a crutch across the living room. Noah didn't flinch when a vase crashed to the floor. He stared down at the shattered pieces, thinking how much they resembled the current state of his life.

"This is a fucking mess, and I'm a cripple and can't take care of things for you, damn it."

Noah turned, feeling more weariness than he did after a nonstop thirty-six hour shift. "It isn't your fault, Gid."

That seemed to do little to quiet his brother's anger. "No, but we could have been following up sooner if we hadn't been so distracted by the red herring of those stupid roses. Who knows what they symbolize, but they didn't have anything to do with these threats." He stopped and eyed Noah carefully. "Sorry about the mess for Nicolle too. I've never seen Danielle so upset."

Welcoming any distraction, Noah jumped on it. "How often have you seen the good lieutenant upset?"

He almost smiled when Gideon's eyes suddenly widened as he realized he gave himself away. His brother's expression turned self-conscious, then contemplative, and his eyes darted to the couch. "Often enough," he said, his voice subdued.

An intriguing statement, and one Noah felt compelled to pursue. "I didn't know you and the lieutenant were that well-acquainted. Did this arise through professional," he paused until Gideon looked up at him, "or personal connections?"

Gid grabbed the remaining crutch and struggled to his feet. "It doesn't matter. What are you going to do about Nicolle?"

"What do you mean, what am I going to do about her? I plan to clean up this mess," he waved a hand at the vase to symbolize everything in his life, "and then I hope we have a chance at a relationship."

Gid shuffled over to the broken vase and bent as if he planned to clean it up. Balanced on a crutch and a cast, he was in danger of toppling into the fireplace. Noah reached out and caught him in the second before his forehead made impact with brick.

"I'll take care of this. I am competent at cleaning up messes too, you know." When Gideon didn't move, Noah added in an even tone, "They teach us that in medical school."

That prompted a smile out of his brother. Gideon met his eyes and scrutinized him, finally nodding as if liking what he saw. "It's about damn time," he said, and retrieved the missing crutch before hobbling back to his chair. "I thought Barbara had scarred you for life."

"She didn't scar me. The truth is, we drifted apart long before her eyes wandered. She was smarter about our relationship than me. I didn't have my priorities straight." Noah picked up the largest ceramic pieces and headed for the kitchen trash.

"How did you have your priorities screwed up? You always put Elena and Char first." Anger made Gideon's raised voice even louder.

Noah returned with a dustpan and whiskbroom, going to work on shards of pottery and finding stray dust devils in the process. He wasn't a stickler about keeping the house operating room clean, but with the distractions of his brother and everything else going on, he'd let this deteriorate too.

In time to the rhythm of his sweeping, he said, "I did put the girls first, but only them. Barb and I were more like roommates than a couple, both tasked with whatever the girls needed but not listening to each other about our own needs. Work absorbed me. I thought it did for her too." He straightened and searched the area for more debris, more to avoid his brother's steady gaze burning into his back than a need for cleanliness.

"Can I say I'm glad you're no longer with her? Has enough time passed?"

Noah smiled, though he didn't feel happy at the words.

"You can say that. I think even when we split, I was more hurt for the girls than I was for me. I felt – relieved." He was sure the pause wouldn't be lost on Gideon.

"So what are you waiting for?"

Noah turned to look at his brother. Gideon's lazy smile had returned, and with it, a gleam in his eye said more than the words.

"I can't very well drag Nicolle into this problem, now can I?" A new surge of emotion, anger paired with crushing disappointment, made his tone harsh.

"I agree. Let's take care of the problem, so you can go after the girl." Gid struggled to his feet once more, as Noah made another trip to the trash. When he returned, Gideon was almost to the front door.

"Where do you think you're going?"

"We need to get you some protection so you aren't completely unarmed if and when this dude comes for you. If I'm not there, you need help. I'm not an advocate of guns, but you need one." Gid put his hand on the front knob and turned. If he was surprised by the anger in Noah's eyes when the door slammed shut before it swung more than a few inches, he didn't show it.

"You have no clue what I can do, or what kind of protection I need. I will not, repeat, will not bring a gun into the house, not with the girls."

Gideon nodded, his face cautious and unreadable.

Noah was tired of it. Tired of being threatened. Tired of being thought of as a patsy. Damned tired of reacting to the world rather than taking action. And he was donating the quarters in the curse jar to the kids fund at the hospital. Elena could swear all she wanted. He no longer wanted to be considered an example of constant control.

He grabbed his keys and yanked the door open, barely missing Gideon's good set of toes in the process. "Come on," he hissed, barreling out the door and uncaring if Gid followed him or not.

He stayed silent on the drive to Sacramento, even brushing off his brother's tentative questions about their destination. If Gideon was surprised when they arrived at the tilt-up building in a rundown industrial area, he hid it well. Noah pulled a gym bag from the back of the minivan and barreled for the metal door, and he didn't think about waiting to see how well his brother could maneuver the uneven asphalt and parking bumpers. His anger hadn't cooled a single degree during the drive.

He was Noah, the well-behaved brother. The doctor with clean, soft hands. The pacifist who would rather turn the other cheek. The weak link in the chain. The smiling, quiet, good-natured man no one saw as a threat.

That had changed, and no one knew how much in the last year. He'd never had to use his hands for anything but good before. Since that night in the ER, his definition of good experienced an earthshaking shift.

Punching his card into the electronic slot, he grabbed the door handle a second after its ping of acknowledgement, throwing it wide enough for Gideon to catch it before it closed. He headed for the swinging doors to the left, with no anticipation about his brother's path behind him. He had to give Gid points for keeping his mouth shut while his curiosity must be glowing with intensity.

"Hey Doc. You looking for a workout or a match today?" The large man stacking folded towels on shelves outside the lockers smiled in greeting.

"Anyone around, Devin?" Noah changed his clothes quickly in a habit born in med school and perfected with years of practice.

"Just me for the time being. You feeling feisty today, Doc?" Devin stood to his full height, almost a foot taller than Noah, and flexed ample muscles on his refrigerator-sized build.

"Yeah, you could say that. I want to kick some ass, and I don't care whose it is. I might just level you today, my friend."

Devin laughed, flexed again as if anticipating some fun, and pulled the sweatshirt over his head. "Game on."

Noah was out the door in less than a minute, stretching a few seconds later. It helped to concentrate on this. He could take out his anger and frustration on the movements. A few well-placed kicks, a rapid-fire series of punches, and the grunt and sweat of hard work would level his memory of the fear on Nicolle's face when she heard her attacker was asking about her. He wasn't only fighting against his own threat any longer. He had Nicolle to protect too.

Men's voices sounded, with greetings exchanged in pleasant voices. The scrape of chair legs on the concrete floor. The whispering zip of wrap unwound and applied to knuckles and hands. Finally, the metal on metal clink that marked the opening of the cage.

"What is this place?" Noah hadn't heard Gideon's approach, despite the thumping crutches and cast.

"It's a gym."

"I see that."

Silence. Noah executed a few turns in quick succession, spinning him away from where Gid stood.

"You should wear gloves. You don't want to get hurt."

Noah swung back around and stepped nose-to-nose with his brother who, under normal conditions, used to be able to throw him. Even now, Gideon's shoulders seemed to swell with muscle and skill.

"When they come to find me, I won't have time to wrap my hands. I won't have time to put on gloves. When they come for me, I want to be prepared no matter what I'm doing at that time."

Gideon's somber face didn't shift. He didn't say anything. After examining Noah's face for a moment, he nodded. "Be careful in there," he said.

Noah saw blood then. Being careful wouldn't protect Nicolle, his family or his friends. If Rage and his posse decided to burst through the door of his home or the hospital, careful wouldn't cut it. He spun away before he decked his brother, injured or not. When he came to the steps up to the ring, he took them three at a time and slammed the cage gate hard enough for the sound to echo like gunfire in the old building.

>>>>>

"It's a good time for a refresher. Devin said he didn't have any appointments today. He can watch us spar and tell us what we should work on next."

With her twin's words, Nici's hands tightened on the steering wheel in anticipation. Danielle rode shotgun, only because she sent text messages with both thumbs blazing when she wasn't talking on her cell. Occupied as she was, she had little time for idle chitchat, which left Nici to her own ugly thoughts.

Like the picture of Noah's face when he heard she was being stalked. He was a gentle soul, a healer instead of a fighter. No man would want to get involved with a woman who was the target of an out of control maniac. And that whole issue of involvement. Did she even want to get involved? Was she ready? Noah's charm and agreeable nature made him nearly irresistible. But when it came time to take things further, would she recoil?

There was no doubting at least some of these fires were tied to her. A firefighter knew how to set a fire. Training and experience honed those skills. Even an inmate firefighter had knowledge of those basics.

"Are you coming in, or are we guarding the parking lot?"

Danielle's sarcastic question shook her out of her head. On rote, she'd backed into a slot a few feet from the door, nose pointed toward an escape route. What fire experience hadn't taught her, she'd learned over the past few years from trainers and coaches and law enforcement. And Danielle. Her sister could be a real bitch about protection and logistics.

Nici grabbed the bag from the backseat. She didn't need the fresh clothes in the other case, her go-bag for the times she was called into the field from somewhere other than home. It never hurt to be prepared. She watched Danielle reach for her wallet to access her keycard, and when she moved aside the big shirt she wore, the grip of her weapon gleamed in the late afternoon sun. The sight of it did nothing to steady Nici.

The door swung wide to blackness after the sun outside, and while her eyes adjusted, she took in the sounds of shuffling feet, grunts, and slams shaking metal. Light glowed down on the cage where two men, one significantly shorter than the other, took no prisoners.

"Looks like Devin's having some fun," Danielle said, stopping outside the flood of illumination.

"Or getting his ass handed to him. Look at that guy's moves. He's small, but he's quick and accurate. Have we seen him before?" Nici took a step further to get a closer look.

"Yes, yes you have."

Nici felt Danielle's lunge of protection at the same time they both swung toward the voice. Gideon Kinkead sat on a metal folding chair at the edge of the circle of light, his expression a mixture of pissed off and wonder.

"Kinkead? What the fuck are you doing here?" Danielle's pace forward defined anger, and Nici felt her twin's pulse pick up. The other feeling she picked up made no sense at all. Excitement?

Gideon turned back to the cage. "I'm still a little unclear about this, but I think Noah's showing me he doesn't need me to protect him."

A jolt of recognition made Nici spin as a swift undercut of legs collapsed Devin to the mat with a tree-worthy thud. The other man shifted and flexed his shoulders, raising his face to the light overhead. Doctor Noah Kinkead.

Gideon said, "Who is this Devin guy?"

Danielle seemed to have regained some of her composure. "You haven't heard of him? Mixed martial arts champion. He doesn't compete anymore, but he offers training. He's very particular about who he takes on, preferring people who want to learn for legitimate self-defense purposes than those who want to follow in his footsteps in the competitive ring."

Nici watched Noah dodge, cut and land a good lock to Devin's upper arm, effectively pinning him to the side of the cage with a clang that shook the structure. Sweat dripped from his hair, but his face was a picture of feral concentration. She doubted he was aware of anything outside the ring, even when Devin gave a self-deprecating laugh and called uncle.

Even then, it seemed to take a minute for him to shake out of his intensity. A deep breath only eased his stance slightly, and when Devin delivered a few quiet words, he nodded his head once and moved to the far side of the cage facing away from them. The clang of the gate closing with Devin's exit left him unmoved.

Nici didn't realize she stood at the base of the cage, staring up at Noah's heaving back, transfixed. The well-worn tank top sported a couple of holes, and baggie trunks reached halfway down his thighs. His bare skin gleamed, highlighting the cut of muscles and tendons. Nici found herself breathing in time to Noah's urgent rise and fall, even though she hadn't exerted a muscle.

"Go on, if you want." Danielle's voice came as if she stood a great distance away.

"Go on what?" Nici's voice sounded husky to her own ears, and she cleared a suddenly parched throat. Noah apparently didn't hear her, because he still stood, arms raised and fingers clenched in the cage's intricate webbing.

"You want to spar? I warmed him up for you." Devin stood at her shoulder.

"What? No. I, ah, I thought Danielle and I were going to work out, then maybe you could watch us."

When the big man didn't respond, Nici forced her eyes off Noah and back to the trainer. He smiled at her, a knowing gleam in his eye. "He's good, about good as you. But he's riled up. Not sure what made him so crazy today. I'd watch his left foot. Got a mean old sneaky shuffle and sweep." Devin backed away, shouting up to the cage, "Noah, next up."

Danielle wasn't stopping her as she dropped her bag where she stood, along with her light sweatshirt. Her hair was already in a knot and she grabbed for the wrap for her hands as she noticed Noah didn't have anything covering his fingers. What the hell was he thinking? He needed his hands to work.

Nici turned, intending to yell at Devin for allowing Noah to work out without a guard on his hands. Her eyes fell on her sister instead.

Danielle stood next to Gideon where shadows pressed against the ring's halo. Her head bent to his raised face, and their conversation had every indication of an argument. Every indication, except for the hand Danielle rested on Gideon's shoulder and the fact that her heart pounded. Nici could feel it from here. By the look on Gideon's face, he was excited as well. Danielle's hand didn't restrain him. It appeared to caress his injured shoulder through his t-shirt.

"What the hell?" Nici stalked over to them, and Danielle glanced her way with a face that screamed guilt. She pulled her hand back as if suddenly burned, putting it behind her back. Very much not the actions of her badass sheriff's lieutenant twin.

"Gideon says Noah's itching for a fight. I say go give him one." Danielle put her other hand behind her back and stood at parade rest as if that was her intention all along. Too bad they had that twin thing going, because Nici could read her emotions. She was hiding something, and it wasn't a little something.

"What's going on here?"

Gideon responded to her abrupt question instead of Danielle. "She's been telling me about Devin, and about how you two have been training with him. I think it's a great thing, learning to defend yourself. It gives you an element of surprise if you ever get overtaken again, and it could delay your attacker until help can arrive."

Delay her attacker? She didn't train this hard to delay him. She planned to take him down.

Nicolle felt that spurt of rage, at her life not being her own and choice being taken away from her, at others thinking they knew what was best and willing to pat her on the head and say what a brave girl she was. Brave her ass. She could kick them from here to Japan.

She spun toward the cage, kicking off her shoes and only pausing long enough to yank her socks inside out before throwing them into the darkness.

>>>>>

Noah heard the clang of the gate and footsteps on the mat. His next opponent stood a few feet from the center and waited, breath coming fast. Noah's breathing had settled, but his mind was still in turmoil. He thought he smelled wildflowers, a fragrance he'd come to associate with Nicolle. That would have to be wishful thinking. The guys frequented this place smelled like high school locker rooms.

Devin hadn't gone easy on him, and he'd feel every stroke, chop and jab tomorrow. It was a clean feeling, though, like he had something under control in the otherwise chaos. He closed his eyes to center himself. He turned and took a step forward, keeping his head down in the stance and positioning that were a precursor to every match. He might not have been doing this for long, but every hour he could afford away from his daughters or the hospital, he'd spent training and honing skills he hoped he never had to use. Except he now probably would have to use them.

The finality of that thought brought his eyes open with the mat in view, along with the feet of his opponent. A wide-stance set, but not too so wide as to indicate a tall person. Narrow feet, almost delicate, settled lightly on the mat in a ready position. Slender feet with pink-painted toenails.

His head snapped up at the same moment as an arm grabbed and twisted his body. In the blur of action, he caught the determined expression on the woman's face. With that came recognition, and with recognition, he let his body go limp.

"What the hell are you doing in here?"

His voice sounded low and raspy, like he couldn't catch his breath. And he couldn't. Nicolle made sure of that, with enough pressure on his windpipe to limit his air supply without seriously hurting him.

"I could ask you the exact damn same thing." She sounded ferocious, like her anger could almost match his.

"We aren't doing this." He tried to shift her off-center and break the hold, but she wasn't giving up.

"We fucking well are. And while we're at it, either wrap your hands or deal with the consequences."

For the first time in hours, Noah felt like smiling.

Chapter 23

"Here's your bag."

Danielle shoved the go-bag into her hand before Nici could process the action. Her mind and her body were still in the cage, still fighting with Noah in a match that should have exhausted them both.

"I'll shower when we get home." She tried to push the bag back, but her twin glanced over Nicolle's shoulder.

"I'm taking the truck, and Gideon's coming with me. You're going with Noah." She lowered a shoulder to move past, but Nici gripped a hand on her arm.

"What are you talking about?" The idea of being in close quarters with the man wasn't a problem. She could hold her own against him, as she had proven in the ring. The fact that they were evenly matched wasn't an issue either. But the wave of elemental heat she felt when she was around him was a definite factor.

Danielle's gaze fixed on something behind Nicolle's back, and she turned to see what her sister was watching with such attention. Gideon and Noah were having a heated discussion, and Nici guessed she knew the reason. At that moment, both men looked up, and there was no doubt where Gideon's eyes landed.

"What is up with you?" Nici swung back around in time to see a blush rise on Danielle's cheeks. Her face held an uncharacteristic softness before she let the expression drop, pulling on her non-emotional mask once more. But the touch of color lingered.

"Oh, so that's how it is." Nici didn't bother hiding her smirk.

"That is not how it is." Danielle took a step forward until they were nose to nose. "I am trying to gain his trust so I can determine if he's had anything to do with the fires. Come on, you're the one who pointed out his proximity and opportunity in these cases. I'm going to learn more."

"Yeah, sure. Tell yourself whatever you need to, sis. Just," she paused, knowing the words wouldn't be welcomed, "just be careful."

Danielle snorted, her attention again wandering to the men. Sounds from that direction indicated they were moving. The thump of Gideon's crutches echoed on the concrete. Noah's steps fell silently. Nici fought the urge to turn and watch them approach.

"I'm a cop, Nici, and I can take care of myself."

Nici kept her eyes on her sister and said, "It's not your body I'm worried about."

Danielle frowned but dropped it quickly and didn't reply. Her face became impassive and bored, as if she was waiting in line to buy a box of cereal. The rhythm of rubber tips stopped behind her, and Nicolle felt the elevated heat of Noah's body as he brushed by them and put a hand on the outside door.

"We're all set," Gideon said, in a cheerful voice that seemed too loud in the empty gym.

"Are you sure?" Noah hadn't turned from his position at the door, and Nici watched his back rise and fall with his heavier breathing. Their bout could no longer be the reason for his agitation. He might not be happy with the arrangements. If he didn't like it, he could speak up.

"Noah," Gideon said with a warning in his voice, his eyes on Danielle.

Noah turned, but his gaze didn't fall on his brother. His scrutiny fell on Nicolle instead, and her body jarred with recognition of hunger and edginess mirroring her own. Their duel in the ring had done nothing to appease those feelings, and it appeared they hadn't helped Noah either.

He pushed open the door with one hand, the gym bag slung over his shoulder ramming into the side frame in the process. With his free hand, he waved her through the opening and out into sunlight. "After you," he said, and he didn't sound happy about it. The bold challenge in his tone kicked her heart rate up further than it should have been.

He beeped open the minivan and held the passenger door open for her. Sweaty, not meeting her eyes, and clutching the straps of his gym bag with white-knuckled fingers, he seemed anything but pleased with their situation. And yet he remained a gentleman, a trait she found endearing. When he started the engine, his face held irritation as he watched the other two making slower progress to the pick-up. If he didn't want her here, why had he agreed?

Without conversation or the radio, Nici had nothing to distract her from the feelings of growing dismay. Never had she been so at a loss for words. She stopped herself more than once from apologizing for whatever Danielle cooked up, until she realized the idea could just as well have been Gideon's. Neither one of them seemed to mind disappearing in each other's company.

In a desperate attempt to make small talk, she glanced around the interior of the minivan and said the first obvious thing that popped into her head. "Wow, your daughters are neatniks, aren't they?" Not so much as a gum wrapper littered the back seat or floor.

Noah didn't say anything. His hands tightened on the steering wheel. Nici somehow doubted he usually drove with his fists clenched in that perfect ten and two positioning.

She returned to staring out the windshield. On the horizon, columns of smoke rose into the sky indicating each of the main fires, discoloring the otherwise pale summer blue. At least the smoke was more white than dark, a sign they were gaining a handle on perimeters.

Nicolle cast around for a safe topic of conversation. "How are they enjoying their summer?"

Noah gave her a quick glance, and she read the disbelief and anger on his face. This was very different from the easygoing man she'd come to expect. "Elena is delighted to be with her friends, because she believes she is above anyone and everyone here in Flynn's Crossing. Char is miserable and lonely because the children she considers her friends are all here. Char can't wait to come home and Elena is already complaining about it. It sucks no matter what." He bit out the words as if the effort cost him.

That was the most honesty she'd heard from him regarding his kids. It didn't sound like he felt anything against the girls, but the situation. She respected his openness and took a breath to tell him so.

"Before you tell me it's going to be okay, don't. I'm worried about them being anywhere near that monster who threatened to hurt them. At the same time, if he's sent someone here to go after me, I'd rather they weren't around. Barbara isn't a bad mother. Her husband isn't a bad guy. But the whole situation sucks."

He fell silent, one hand moving to a more natural position at the bottom of the steering wheel with his fingers loose. The other combed through his hair as if trying to use the movement to settle turbulent thoughts.

She understood how he felt. Every time she thought about her monster, she felt like puking.

"We'll get to the bottom of it, Noah. Every resource we can spare is working to find the firebug, and I know Danielle was notified all local departments to be on alert for anyone who could be associated with your gangster. Things might take time, but we'll get them resolved and keep everyone safe." At least, she'd like to believe that.

He glanced over at her before returning his eyes to the road. He seemed to be relaxing, his body no longer thrumming with angry energy. The tension in his face dissipated and he looked more like the Noah she'd come to know. A few more minutes passed in silence until the sign for the town turnoff noted three more miles.

"I got it detailed," he said suddenly. It took her a moment to realize what he was talking about.

"I take it after the girls left?"

He nodded. "And I had a service do a deep cleaning on the house, not that this mattered much once Gideon moved in. I pay someone to take care of the lawn and garden. When things are really crazy, I even have groceries delivered." He fell silent, and the look on his face seemed to say he wasn't proud of his coping mechanisms.

Nici put a hand on his arm and felt the muscles under her fingers stiffen immediately. She pulled her hand back, savoring the residual heat from skin on skin contact. The click of the turn signal sounded overly loud in the car. "You do what you have to do so you have time for your daughters."

He gave a terse nod, signaling again for the turn up to the main residential area. "The hospital and the girls, and Gideon, and working out, that's the sum total of my life. I sometimes feel it's more about survival than living." His voice dropped on the last sentence as he pulled into a driveway around the curve of the road.

He shut the engine off but didn't move, and Nici tore her eyes away from his profile to look at the house. The two-story bungalow had once been a single level, the addition something typical in the town as t grew. The yard held bushes and shrubs, but no flowers. Noah probably didn't have time for that.

"You've seen the inside. It's not very much. I bought it in a rush last December, since I needed to settle the girls before school started. There hasn't been time since then to make it our own." He sounded mournful about that reality. She didn't know how to respond.

He turned toward her then, and she had a hard time reading his expression. Confusion and doubt seemed to swirl together, along with a lack of confidence, foreign to what she'd come to expect of him.

"Are you sure about this?" His words whispered across the front seat, his eyes intent on her.

"About what, exactly?" Her nerves rippled, though whether she was feeling excitement or apprehension, she wasn't sure.

One side of his mouth quirked up, though it wasn't quite a smile. Humor returned to his eyes as he continued to stare at her. He shook his head. "Danielle didn't tell you?"

Nicolle shook her head, and Noah gave a quick snort and shook his head as if he found the situation mildly unbelievable. He pushed open his door and paused, eyes on her once more.

"How do you feel about a sleepover?"

>>>>>

Gideon was unbelievable. Leg in a cast, shoulder still on the mend, wrongly under suspicion in these fires, and intending to sleep with the cop heading the investigation. Noah didn't want to think about it because it brought fresh suggestions to his mind, and he didn't need that encouragement.

He pointed Nicolle toward the bathroom on the first floor while apologizing for its condition. Gideon's things were spread across the counter, but Noah swept them into a drawer and pushed the basket of miscellaneous toiletries into Nicolle's hands, along with fresh towels. He didn't want to think about what she would do in that shower, but his libido ignored his efforts.

His shower was faster, and his clothing choices deliberate. He didn't want her to see him as a potential threat, but no matter what he chose, she would undoubtedly notice. His body wasn't listening to his mind when it came to silencing the need she awoke in him.

Who knew how stimulating a friendly competition in the ring could be? All it took was the right competitor, and boom, his body wanted nothing better than to fold her in and take them both on a ride they'd never forget. He didn't think Nicolle was ready for that.

He busied himself in the fridge, pulling out salad ingredients and two small beefsteaks, hoping it would be enough. He didn't have much to offer in the way of an elaborate dinner. Mostly, he shopped for quick and nutritious on the way home, and with Gideon around, that often included something precooked from the deli, easy to reheat. His brother ate like a fireman, so leftovers were sparse.

The sound of the door to the kitchen opening, a slight squeak he kept meaning to get to, alerted him to her entrance. He kept his head in the fridge as he inhaled the wildflower fragrance he didn't remember from his daughters' many choices. It would have been easier if she smelled like his girls. Then he might convince his body she was off limits.

"What can I do to help?"

Her voice was soft and a little rough, as if she wasn't sure how to use it. If she was uncertain about this strange arrangement, he could understand. It wasn't as if she wanted this. He wondered what kinds of arguments this would raise between Nicolle and her twin. His own disagreement with Gideon was just beginning.

He stayed hidden, willing his body to calm and his face to settle into casual friendliness. "I've got this. What would you prefer to drink? I don't keep soda in the house, so there's sparkling water, milk, and an abbreviated juice collection picked over by my brother."

He didn't hear her moving around, and the silence lasted for so long that he finally forced himself to stand and look around. Nicolle now stood at the sink gazing out over the empty yard. Her hands rested on the counter and she lifted on her toes as if stretching. Shorts and a t-shirt did nothing to hide her body in profile, and that view alone brought Noah a fresh wave of desire with stat urgency. Inside boxers intended to hide his interest, a growing erection twitched and stretched with the movements of her body.

As if she felt his eyes on her, she turned her head and regarded him solemnly. Her feet drifted to the floor and her fingers dug into the hard surface before releasing. Her eyes drifted down his body. And stopped.

And she burst out laughing.

A man could only take so much abuse.

"What?" He stepped fully into view and raised his arms wide.

Nicolle wrapped her arms at her waist and bent over, laughing harder. She pointed, then convulsed with fresh giggles.

Noah felt his face redden. At least her reaction took care of his overzealous body. Things had deflated and gone into hiding, and might not be seen again for months at this rate. She wiped her eyes on the backs of her hands, pulling a piece of paper towel off a stand and mopping further while still occasionally giving a hiccup of a chuckle.

He pushed the fridge door closed with more force than was probably necessary, given the rattle of bottles inside. Mission accomplished. She wouldn't be looking at him with anything other than amusement.

"Those are the cutest pajamas I have ever seen, bar none." She stared at his legs, shaking her head. He glanced down, beginning to appreciate the humor too.

"Yeah, I know, pretty adorable. I bought them for the nights the girls have sleepovers, so I look like an unassuming dad. I hadn't realized the giggle factor until I wore them the first time Elena had a friend over. She was appalled, needless to say. Do you think Goofy's nightcap is too over the top?"

Nicolle began laughing one more, pointing and doubling over with tears pouring down her face. Goofy wore a nightshirt matching the long stocking cap on his head, his ears flopping out and nearly landing in the candle in the character's hand. Daffy's sleeping costume didn't cover his waddling tail, and Mickey's defied explanation. Repetition of the characters in material covering waist to feet only emphasized the unmanliness of the get-up. Noah felt his own laughter bubble up and overflow, until he and Nicolle held on to each other and roared like they'd both been hitting the pharmacy.

It felt good to laugh like th s, and Noah felt freer than he had in ages. Their laughter slowed to chuckles. When they were down to only a sporadic giggle, Noah stared at a woman who looked as fun and carefree as the one he'd seen months ago in the store. His heart rate accelerated once more.

His hands were on her arms. One of hers rested on his shoulder and the other on his waist, and the heat of her palms penetrated the fabric to burn into his skin. He could do nothing to keep his pulse under control. If she felt it, at least she didn't give any sign that it frightened her.

His eyes dropped to her parted lips, and he heard her gasp. He focused fully on her face. He didn't want to frighten her.

But fright wasn't what he saw. Arousal and hunger found an answering beat in his body, because she didn't look in the least bit put off by his intense interest. As much as he regretted it, he needed to slow things down. One of them needed to stay sane.

He stepped back, but not before giving her arms a quick caress, fingers trailing on her bare skin. Regret washed through him even as his feet made the journey across the room, until his back pressed up against the fridge door. Nicolle looked disappointed.

"I don't want you to be afraid of me." He kept his eyes on hers, even when he wanted to roam down creamy flesh that looked too soft to hold the powerful muscles he'd felt in the ring that afternoon.

"I'm not afraid. But I don't want to lead you on." A waving gesture of her hands looked to Noah like birds ready to take flight. Yes, she might still cut and run.

Her sudden restlessness communicated itself loud and clear as she began to prowl the small confines of the kitchen, all the while keeping as much distance as possible between the two of them. "I might not be able to act on what I want, what you want," she said.

He cleared his throat, having a hard time verbalizing what was going through his mind. "I want you to feel safe with me and with whatever pace of things you want. I'll control my expectations."

She glanced over at him as if understanding what that cost him. But she smiled and nodded. "Can you just hold me through the night?"

He exhaled and nodded, wondering how big a liar his body was going to make of him.

Chapter 24

Noah was true to his word. After she'd asked, he'd gone about making their dinner as if they did this all the time. He'd even changed the conversation to innocuous subjects. Where they went to college. Why she picked firefighting. Why he selected medicine. General get-to-know-you kinds of things. Safe.

He was wonderful, a perfect gentleman, until Nici wondered why she'd asked for this. She wanted to jump him and find out what hid under those cartoon characters. She'd had a sense for the shape of things when they sparred, and everything she felt left her craving more.

But she didn't trust her body not to betray her. When conversation winded down and night fell, there was nothing more they could say to avoid the inevitable.

"You can sleep in my room." His face remained amiable but the tension in the lines of his body gave him away. He expected her to change her mind. "I'll take one of the girls' beds."

"I thought a sleepover meant we slept together," she said. She didn't bother to hide the husky tone of her voice or the obvious desire laced in her words.

She watched Noah's throat work in a swallow ending in an audible gulp. "I can hold you through the night, Nicolle, but I can't guarantee you won't feel things my body can't hide. Are you okay with that?"

Oh hell yes she was. She wanted to know his desire for her was real. Maybe, with time, she could move on to something more.

Hours later, she lay encased in strong arms with tough muscles pressed against her back, staring at a clock that said the hour approached one in the morning. She couldn't sleep, and she didn't think Noah did either, based on the uneven cadence of his breaths. They'd matched each other without conscious effort, even when one or the other took a sudden deeper gulp as if to steady themselves.

Darkness was often her enemy, but tonight, it offered her bravado.

"I want to tell you how it happened."

She felt his arms tighten imperceptibly. "You don't have to," he said.

"No, I want to. It's better this way, in the dark. I'm being a coward. I don't want to see your face."

"Nicolle, there isn't anything you – "

"Sshhh. This is my story and I want you to hear it. It isn't pretty. It isn't easy for me to share. But you've become important to me, so you deserve to know."

He pulled her in closer, nestling his nose behind her ear, and for a moment, she forgot about the ugly past and the mess it made of her future. The present was too delightful.

He whispered his response in her ear. "I like who you are now, the woman you've become. We're each a sum of our pasts, living in our presents and hoping for better futures. If we wish things were different in the past, we'd be different people. I'll repeat myself and say I like who you are now."

She sighed, resignation settling in her gut and churning the salad and steak.

"You know the basics already. In the remote terrain, the fire shifted on a minute-by-minute basis, creating its own weather systems. While the inmate crew had skills and experienced, anyone would have struggled under these conditions. We were supposed to be mopping up hotspots, but winds blew the fire back across our escape route. We had to fight it where we stood."

A muscle in his arm functioning as her pillow twitched as if he was there fighting the fire with her. His fingers flexed against her belly, flattening until his palm began a tender circling motion. That gentle calming motion helped her go on.

"The crew split when a tree crashed. The fire had topped it, so when it fell, it exploded into new blazes. Most of the crew was on the other side, and I yelled for them to head down the hill, away from these new fires. That left me with three men and very few options available to us."

She smelled the smoke from that day, acrid and sharp. Heat made more intense by the new flames choked her. She pointed out a clearing to the others, joining them in a fast trot as they ran for its safety. Surprisingly, it led down a canyon that had burned before and now stood quiet after the chaos up the hillside.

"One of the men fell, crying out. He said he tripped on a log in the ash. He tried to walk on it, but he said it was too painful. The others planned to carry him out, but it would slow all of us down. The fire road and resupply lines were at the bottom of the ravine, and I sent the other two down for help. By this time, the man was weep ng and saying he thought his ankle might be broken. I tried my best to make him comfortable."

She thought she'd done the right thing. His face tracked with tears, but then hers did too, a symptom of the smoke. She'd had a split second to recognize the danger she was in when his face changed to a leering smile and he punched her hard enough to make stars float in front of her eyes.

Behind her, she felt Noah's body stiffen and still. This would be it. He would ease away from her, knowing what would come next. He'd offer words of condolence, even though he didn't have a clue about the scope of what she had lost. They would lapse into an uneasy friendship, until that too faded to nothing.

She soldiered on. "By the time I could think again, I was on my back, and he was on top of me. How he got through my turnouts in that amount of time, I'm still not sure. He had my pants down below my knees, and his were open." She stopped, aware that Noah had now ceased to breathe. "Do you want me to continue?"

When Noah's arms pulled from around her, she set her face in an understanding mask of indifference, even though it killed her inside. The end was coming.

He surprised her by rolling her in his bed until they lay face to face. A gentle hand caressed her hair back and a finger lifted her chin until they were staring at each other. The room held enough ambient light for her to read his expression.

Anger, understanding, hurt, calm. They were all there, along with others she didn't quite comprehend. Of course he would understand. He was a doctor, and he probably saw more than one woman come in the emergency room door after rape. She didn't need to spell it out for him.

"Go on if you need to," he said, his voice a hush in the stillness. "I'm listening, and I'm here for you." He tucked a hand behind the nape of her neck, his fingers moving in a comforting circle that almost made her believe the ache would someday recede.

Taking him at his word, she continued, knowing that her voice took on a cold, empty quality when she said the words. The violence of the rape. The strength with which Mitchell pinned her to the ground. Her assailant's laughter as he pounded away. Her feelings of helplessness that lived to this day.

Running out of steam, she stopped talking, but she couldn't stop the shaking in her bones. His rhythmic strokes hadn't slowed, and his eyes held only concern as he watched her.

"I am sorry you had to go through that," Noah said, patience and calm radiating from his tone.

She couldn't see his face, but she bet he'd be closing himself off and withdrawing any second now. Nicolle shook her head, effectively dislodging herself from Noah's embrace. He would move away soon enough. It was always best to be the first one to decide things.

"Hey, don't leave." His hands gently stroked her arms as she leaned back, intending to stand.

"Oh come on. I'm damaged goods. You can't wait for me to go."

She turned her back, not wanting to see the relief for her first move written on his face. When her feet hit the floor, she shivered despite the warmth of the room. Alone. She too often felt completely alone.

Light flooded the room with a click of a bedside lamp. "What makes you think I want you to go?"

She heard him rise on the other side of the bed, and she shifted to stand and turn with as much nonchalance as she could manage. Meeting his eyes was hard, but not the most difficult thing she'd ever done. She'd done that when she faced her attacker in court.

While his voice held frustration by the truckload, disappointment colored his expression. Hair standing on end would have been comical, if not for the color darkening his cheekbones and the fingers flexing at his sides. In his pj's, the remnants of the curve of a bump behind Mickey marked his former ardor.

It was pointless to think about it now. She had deflated his interest, and while he was upset now, at any moment he'd realize he was getting away easy. Nicolle would walk first before he needed to make up any excuses.

She reached for her clothes, neatly stacked on a chair by the bureau courtesy of Noah. Shoes. Where were her shoes? In the living room under the coffee table?

"What are you doing?" His question was softer than his previous exclamation.

"What does it look like I'm doing? I'm getting dressed. I'm going home. I don't care what Danielle and Gideon have heating up. I don't belong here." She yanked on her shirt and bit off a curse when her hair snagged on a button in front.

That was why her eyes filled with tears, she assured herself. Pulling harder jarred her scalp and made her wince. Damn it, why couldn't she even make a clean exit?

Hands stopped her impatient fingers with the barest amount of pressure. "For the record, you do belong here. I want you here. And hold still before you end up bald. I have two young daughters with long locks and short fuses. I've got this."

The tender untangling of her hair echoed in her heart, and she felt the barrier she worked so hard to defend begin to crumble. When her head popped out and Noah stroked the shirt into place, she could only stare at him.

"In case you didn't hear me, let me repeat. You belong here. Is that so hard to believe?"

The backs of his fingers soothed her cheeks in feathery strokes as she felt tears track down. She couldn't stop them. Few people knew her secret, and even fewer treated her with this compassionate care once they learned it. Her parents, doctors, and counselors all seemed to think if she bucked up, she could survive this and thrive on the other side. Only Danielle took her pain and fear to heart.

She nodded to answer his question, unable to speak.

"All right then. Come back to bed. I'll hold you quietly or tell you a story, whatever you want." He stepped back, pulling her with him, and she gulped in air. He knelt on the bed and kept his touch gentle, as if he gave her every opportunity to make the choice of staying by herself. He looked silly dressed in cartoons, and yet she had ever confidence he would keep his word. If she demanded to leave, he would let her go.

But he wanted her to stay.

Nici sniffed and rubbed her cheeks, realizing her tears had abated. Tissues appeared in front of her face, blocking her view of the man offering them. How many men kept a box of tissues by the bedside? One who knew how to listen without judgment and dry tears when needed. A good man.

She sniffed again, feeling the release of emotions as a catharsis. Noah lounged on his back on the bed, patting the mattress next to him as he opened an arm for her to nestle in. Her knees hit the sheets before her mind consciously decided she wanted to stay.

"Any story?"

Noah nodded.

"What if you don't know the story I want you to tell?"

He smiled then. Was that relief in his eyes? "Oh baby, I can make up any kind of story you like. Princesses, dragon slayers, animals that talk, spaceship travel. You name it, I've probably made it up. Two daughters, remember?"

He chuckled as he gave a rueful shake to his head. Nici couldn't help the answering chuckle bubbling up in her. Without pausing to analyze it, she plopped herself down and snuggled in close, laying her cheek against his chest and hearing the reassuring, constant hard beat of a good heart.

"Tell me the story about why you became an ER doctor," she said.

>>>>>

Nicolle Trajan was a tough one. Noah had no doubt she'd made herself that way as protection from the harsh reality of what she'd experienced. No one should ever suffer like that.

He'd treated too many women who came into the ER post-trauma from a sexual assault. Their situation called to something in him, a burning need to help them cope with their attack while he tended their wounds with gentle care. The female nurses took primary responsibility, but when a doctor was needed and no woman was available, he was it. In these cases, his shorter stature and usual calm nature helped, but he still saw residual terror in their eyes.

That same kind of feeling had sparked in Nicolle's face moments ago. She pushed it down with what he had no doubt was superhuman effort. He wanted her to feel safe with him, without a need to hide anything. But he had to earn that trust. She felt safe enough to cuddle in his bed with clothes on, but true trust would take time.

He had all the time it took.

Keeping his movements comforting and steady, he used his best singsong grammar school paper voice to say, "Why I Became An ER Doctor, by Dr. Noah Kinkead, Emergency Medicine."

She giggled. He liked the sound.

"It's not exactly exciting."

She shoved him, not hard enough to move him but enough of a tease to warm his heart. "I want to know. Tell me the story."

He propped them both up higher on the pillows and returned to tracing his fingertips down her bare arm. He liked the goose bumps that rose in his path. It made other parts of him warm. He couldn't act on it, didn't even want to think about it. Nicolle needed to trust him. This would all be about her.

"I was nine and Gideon and I were goofing off, climbing trees and doing typical boy things. Gid fell out of the tree, and he cried. I mean, he never cried, but his arm hurt a lot and he cried. I wanted to help him feel better, but I was a kid. I went with him to the emergency room. The x-rays looked scary, but this nice doctor did things to help the pain go away. He listened to Gideon's worries about being able to play ball after the bones healed like he understood his concerns, and even made him laugh. I think it was the laugh that did it."

He fell silent, thinking back to the sounds and smells of that ER long ago. Those things hadn't changed over the years. Noises of machines and people and rushing energy. Antiseptic, bodily fluids, people drenched in panic sweats. It didn't gross him out back then, not like it had Gid or their mother. To him, the scents belonged to the place where caring people made things better.

Coming back to the present slowly, he realized Nicolle rubbed a hand on his arm in a mirror of his strokes. It was comforting, a nice familiar feeling when they were only beginning to know each other. A little grin lit up her face, and her gaze stayed on his.

"That's not too bad a story," she said.

He shrugged, knowing it wasn't his best. But it was the truth. "Yes, I learned people have the power to heal, and I wanted to be one of those good guys. Besides, I have it on sound authority that healing is sexy."

She giggled again, and he wished he could make her do that all the time.

She said, "Whose authority is that?"

Noah shifted in sudden discomfort, wishing he'd kept the remark to himself. "Gideon, but then, he does have a reputation."

Her smile disappeared as she glanced out the window with a frown.

He pulled her closer when she began to rise, resisting the urge to squeeze her. He spoke quickly. "Danielle is fine, Nicolle. Things have changed for Gideon. He's experienced fear and he's wiser now. He thinks before he acts."

Or at least he hoped his brother did. Noah thought he might be praying with those words. He pushed a strand of hair behind her ear, letting his fingers linger at the delicate shell. "Danielle is strong, like you. You've overcome an ultimate violation, and you haven't let it stop you from dancing."

She coughed out a sound he took for disbelief. "What are you talking about?"

"Dancing, you know, like you did in the store. Do you want to know how many times I thought about you, about that day, since then? I kept hoping I'd run into you so I could introduce myself formally and show you my better moves."

Her open laughter rewarded him. In fact, she kept laughing. He could choose to take offense, but he didn't. He did have some moves. She just hadn't seen them yet.

When her laughter died down to hiccups, he pulled her close. His nose pressed against hers, rubbing back and forth in a playful way. Her gulps quieted and her eyes grew wide, and finally she nudged her nose back at him. She didn't move away when he came closer and gave her a light kiss on the lips. In that brief contact, he felt her tremble.

He wanted to pull her in tight and keep kissing her, deep kisses to see where passion could take them. But he kept his expression calm and his touch light when he drew away. "Good night, Nicolle."

Wide eyes stayed linked to his. She stared at him unspeaking. Then she wrapped his face in her trembling fingers and placed a longer, deeper kiss on his mouth.

It was the sweetest of feelings, her lips pressed to his. He didn't want to frighten her away, so he kept still. When she retreated, her intense examination of his face would have rivaled a specialist with a particularly puzzling patient. When she smiled, it lit up the room like sunlight. She shifted to cuddle in close again and he exhaled the breath he didn't realize he'd been holding. Her relaxed tone more than her quiet words calmed the accelerated beating of his heart.

"Good night, Noah."

He tightened his arms around her, only satisfied when he finally heard her even breathing. It was a long time before he slept.

Chapter 25

Sunlight tickled the windows, overwhelming the small lamp still burning next to the bed and forcing her eyelids to half-mast. Even she still left the light on some nights when residual panic turned the shadows dangerous. Nici wondered which of the girls felt the presence of monsters under the bed. Clearly, the daddy behind her didn't mandate darkness to get over fear.

Noah had her wrapped in a protective cocoon of his arms and legs. Her back pressed to his front, and an impressive bulge dug into her buttocks. Curiosity warred with common sense. She should leave the peace he brought to her last night in the safety of the first light. Get dressed. Make coffee. Thank him for his comfort, but recognize it wouldn't stand up to the reality of the new day.

But yearning built a rough demand inside her. She pulled away, and Noah shifted with a quiet moan of protest before resettling. Mickey was a darned sight bigger this morning, and Nici felt her cheeks heat up with the idea of what thin flannel hid from her view.

Those thoughts made her restless, itching with need and forced to the solitude of the bathroom. She stared at herself in the mirror over the sink. She had shared some of her darkest secrets, and the man who was as good and kind as his brother said hadn't flinched away. Could she be brave enough to do the same with him if they took things further?

When she returned to the bedroom, Noah had rolled to his back, an arm thrown over his eyes and the other reaching to the side of the bed she'd occupied, palm up, as if waiting to pull her back when she returned. Her eyes drifted downward. Mickey did a hula twitch as if he knew she watched.

She knelt on the bed and ran her fingers up Noah's palm, rewarded by his grasping for her. She put a palm on his chest, enjoying his warmth and the beat of his heart. Steady. That was Noah. She suspected he would always be steady.

And steady was what she needed. Perhaps someday, she'd be able to let go and feel free once more. She could be that woman he'd seen dancing in a rare unguarded moment of invincibility. For now, she could give him all she had.

Nici ran her palm lower, following the dips of his body down his centerline. Noah stirred. He drew in a slow breath as if waking from a dream. Her gaze slipped from his face, from ridiculously long lashes resting on cheeks smooth except for an early morning fuzz of beard. His chest rose and fell, a pace that seemed to quicken as she watched. Then her hand and her eyes drifted lower, and she let one finger trace the line of him, Mickey's knowing smile egging her on.

Noah's breathing changed, a sudden gulp followed by no sound or movement. He released it in a hard sigh.

"Good morning," she said. She heard the purr in her voice, the tone husky and deep. She couldn't help it.

He didn't pull away, and when she glanced at his face, his expression didn't give her a clue about what he was thinking.

"Good morning yourself," he said. She let two fingers drift along the outline this time, feeling the surge of heat. If anything, Noah grew larger under her hand.

"What are we doing?" His question came from a gruffer place, but his tone remained conversational.

"You are not doing anything. I am looking for my dancing shoes."

She caught his quick grin before he hid it, but his eyes told tales.

"So, these dancing shoes. Are they spiky heels, or cowboy boots, or what?"

She added another finger, gave herself permission, and wrapped a hand around him. Noah sucked in a gasp that she thoroughly enjoyed.

"Boots, the rock and roll kind. Big heels, chunky. Black leather up to the knee. A low cut t-shirt, and a very, very short skirt."

She could feel his pulse rise with her description, and the idea she could rev him up like this made her absurdly happy. That, and the steel-hard length of him throbbing in her palm.

"It's a good thing you weren't wearing that kind of get-up when you were shopping for office supplies," he said, the sound of his words clipped as if it cost him to speak.

She tightened her grip, loving the control and the fact that he was secure enough to let her keep it.

"And why is that?" The feel of him in her hand made her wet in places that hadn't enjoyed good sex in so long, she might now officially re-qualify as a virgin.

"I don't want the girls to see this before they're at least thirty," he said. He bolted upright and grabbed her face between his hands, his eyes wide and staying open as his mouth closed over hers.

Her mind wiped clean of everything other than sensation. She knew Noah could kiss. He'd proven that fact already. She knew he could be gentle and kind, comforting and funny. He'd proven that last night.

But this Noah was different. Intense. Purposeful. Driven as if making her crazy with need was his only reason for being on the planet. And boy oh boy, was he succeeding.

Nici had a split second of indecision, holding back in case this was all a dream, or in case memories flooded in and pushed them apart. But the past stayed where it should be and the heat they shared brought her closer.

She'd experienced Noah's lightning fast reflexes in the ring. He used those now to lift his t-shirt out of the way, so fast that it didn't feel like he broke their lip lock. Another snap of magic fingers, and her shirt flew off into a corner. She wasn't sure if she pulled him in or he did the honors, but they were now pressed skin to skin. Her nipples hardened to painful points from the friction of fine chest hair.

It was as if an incendiary device exploded in the middle of the bedroom, and they were both torches in the aftermath. She should be afraid. Flashbacks should be smothering her like retardant. Why wasn't she scared of this with him?

Noah broke the string of kisses, pulling back only far enough to settle his forehead against hers. Their pants matched in ferocity. His eyelids lifted and his eyes met hers, and his hands clutched in restless movements on her waist. As if he could read her mind, he said, "You may be over-thinking this."

Was she? She attempted to find words to explain. "I should be feeling hesitation, or fear, or something, don't you think?"

He blew out a huff of air. "I can't say that's within my realm of expertise to answer." He inhaled deeply, leaning away from her and examining her face closely enough to make her wish they were in darkness. "Are you feeling hesitation, or fear, or anything other than, ah, heat?"

She felt the grin on her face at his careful wording. Heat worked.

She shifted closer. "I feel enough heat to torch the western United States."

He chuckled, leaning back and pulling her with him. When she lay cushioned by his body, he said, "What do you say we do something about that?"

>>>>>

When a predatory smile broke across Nicolle's face, Noah kept the groan of delight to himself. Originally, he thought he would take things slow, but the picture Nicolle painted of heavy metal rocker chick ignited something inside him. He could see her like that, in control and taking no prisoners. He imagined her expression would be like the one she wore now, as her eyes raked him from the top of his head to the place where her body rested on his.

And god help him, Mickey, Donald and Goofy weren't an appropriate audience for the heat pouring from her, where her fiery core met an erection that didn't want to hesitate either. If he gave in to the intense desire making his pulse pound at a dangerously high level, he would scare her off. She deserved his best behavior, and she deserved to be in charge.

She shifted, lifting her hair and letting it cascade like a rich waterfall over her arms. He forgot what he was thinking when her hips settled into a rhythm sure to make him go off like a rocket in no time at all.

He dug fingers into her hips, intended to lessen the friction and her pace, but instructions weren't getting through from his brain to his hands. Instead of slowing her, he sped up the motion as fever built inside him. When she groaned, he bit his lip in a vain attempt at control.

"I think we're still wearing too many clothes," Nicolle said in a husky voice he'd dream about for nights on end.

"I agree. We need to get rid of this audience."

She glanced down at the characters and laughed, and the sound did crazy things to his nerve endings. He might be short-circuiting important neurons and synapses, but if he needed them in the future, he didn't care. All he could focus on was the strong beauty above him and the passion glowing in her eyes.

She slipped off him and he immediately missed her heat. Without it, he felt empty and jittery. He wanted to be close to her, closer than they had been and maybe closer than she would allow. But she stripped off her shorts without hesitation, glancing down at him with a pointed expression.

"Do you need help with anything?" There was no mistaking the yearning in her voice or on her face when she met his eyes again. He shucked off the bottoms and the briefs he'd donned underneath in deference to her.

She tilted her head and stared down at him, eyes widening slightly. Yeah, she should be surprised. She did that to him. He doubted he had ever been harder, and the ache settling into his balls made movement a challenge.

Nicolle cleared her throat and glanced around the room. "Do you, um, have any protection? I didn't think of that." A nervous laugh punctuated her statement.

Noah exhaled with a wheeze, reaching for the nightstand. As his agitated fingers closed around the drawer pull, a nipple swung enticingly close, and he couldn't resist a quick kiss.

Nicolle hissed a shocked sound.

"Sorry. It was too tempting." He settled back, crossing his ankles to assume a position of nonchalance as he handed her the box of condoms. He laced his fingers behind his head to keep them from wrapping around her waist and pulling her down on top of him.

"These haven't been opened." She examined both ends.

Noah wondered why discussing this was such a turn-on. The sight of her kneeling on his bed, the discreet packaging cradled in her hand and the puzzled tilt to her head, did insane things to his central nervous system. He didn't think his anatomy professor had this in mind when he described the interconnectedness of neurophysiology. Everything twitched.

He tried to speak, cleared his throat, and tried again. "I had the talk with Elena, and since she's twelve going on thirty, she asked me what kind of protection I use. Why she assumes I have an opportunity for a relationship, I'm not sure. She wanted proof. I only hope she's as demanding with boys in her own age group."

Nicolle laughed then, a full burst of high spirits that made his erection dance. He felt the burning need to bury himself inside her and experience her laughter from the inside out. He couldn't allow himself to move in fear that he'd rip control away from her.

Her mirth subsided and her face took on an expression of wonder. She traced fingers across his eyebrows, down his cheeks, and across his lips. He chanced a couple of kisses as she passed. He felt her deep inhalation as if it sucked all oxygen from the room.

"You said relationship," she whispered.

Not trusting words, he nodded.

"Not sex."

He nodded again. "Sex is a bodily function. Relationships are emotions."

She tilted her head as if considering his words. He enjoyed her total focus, as if a philosophical intellectual discussion was normal when their bodies should be rubbing in frictional urgency. No matter what she thought, for him, both his body and his mind were full in on this moment.

His hand lifted in slow motion to push hair behind her ear. The path it took after that, down her ribs and into the tangle of hair at her apex, was inevitable. He was rewarded by her sharp intake and quick grasp of him at the root. It was his turn to hiss now.

"This is sex, you know," she said, stroking with a purposeful force.

His eyes might be crossed, but he could still see her clearly.

"It's also a relationship, Nicolle." He wasn't sure how much longer he was going to hang on.

"I haven't had a relationship in a very long time." Her coarse whisper made every hair on his body stand up on end.

"Neither have I."

As if the words flipped a switch inside her, Nicolle tore open the box, scattering foil envelopes in every direction. Grabbing one, she ripped it open with a triumphant moan. Her touch was delicate and inflaming as she positioned it on him, and Noah gave up the fight. Covering her hand with his, he stroked the condom in place just as she climbed over him. Her eyes linked to his gaze and her fingers wound through his as she dropped on him.

"Oh god."

He wasn't sure who said it, or maybe it was both of them. Nothing ever felt this good, he was sure of that. It was everything else he wasn't sure of.

"Help me, Noah."

Hell yes. He freed a hand and traveled down her body, willing his own needs to wait, but she moved with a feverish urgency that wasn't making it easy.

"I am not going to last long if you keep that up."

She gave a knowing grin full of strain. "That's my point."

He found her core, letting his fingers trace her in exploration. She sucked in another groan and shoved hard against his hand.

"Now."

He couldn't help the choke of laughter, even as he felt his own explosion starting in his spine.

"Are you always this demanding?"

As he knew he would, he felt her ripple of laughter inside her body, where he was buried deeper than he thought possible.

"Oh baby, you ain't seen nothing yet."

This time they both laughed, until the fire flashed over and consumed them.

Chapter 26

She drifted in and out of a doze, her mind hazy with random thoughts. Noah's arms were still around her, his fingers laced together in the middle of her back. The sanctuary his body offered was the best kind of mooring. He hadn't let her go since she collapsed in a heap on top of his heaving chest.

Nici wanted to say something, but she couldn't seem to string words together in any way that made sense. That was, ah – no, inadequate. Thank you for making this – no, too formal. I've never – too soon, too personal.

But this was personal, at least for her. She would never have dreamed of coming on to any man who knew her troubled past. But with Noah, she felt safe. She should tell him that.

He wasn't asleep. She could hear the occasional hitch in his breathing, the flex of muscles where their cooling skin met. His hands never left her, though. Steady Noah Kinkead. Steady and a firestorm in the sack. Who would have guessed?

His fingers shifted then, stroking her spine in a way that fanned her embers all over again. When he spoke, his voice sounded well used and raspy.

"That was amazing, beyond amazing. Thank you for making my life complete. I've never had an experience like it."

Not only did he know what to do, he knew what to say.

She tried to lift off so she could see his face. His hands came to her shoulders and held her at a distance, a short distance. She found comfort in that.

"Me too," she said, the need to reply making her feel shy all of a sudden.

Noah's gaze narrowed, his eyes flicking across her features as if checking to make sure she was being honest with him. The shyness grew more acute.

"What?" She tried to pull away, embarrassed by the frank assessment in his face.

"You are the most beautiful woman, Nicolle Trajan. Outside and in. Your face is a picture of happy perfection, and thoughts about your body will feed my dreams for months if not years. But it's your strength, heart and determination that blow me away."

A blush made her cheeks beyond warm.

She ran a finger down a pectoral better chiseled than many of the firefighters she knew. His shiver and sudden peak of his nipple rewarded her, as did his slow mischievous smile. Where her belly met his groin, his erection twitched and demanded new attention.

"Really, Doctor?" She wiggled, producing the desired effect of another more substantial arch from him.

"Really." He paused, serious once more. "Unless it's too much for you."

She finger-walked her way down until her lips pressed his. "You're sweet to worry about me. But I'd rather play doctor again. And this time, I want to be on the bottom."

Noah groaned, and she giggled into his mouth.

He kissed back her laughter, beginning to turn them, and then froze. She felt his body tense. Then she heard it too.

Chimes. Music. In tandem.

He broke off the kiss, though he gave her a heated look she could easily read. Reluctance. She doubted she regarded him any differently.

"That's my phone," he said, offering one harder kiss before sliding off the bed and grabbing it in one smooth move.

"And that's Dani's ring," she replied, watching his firm backside as it disappeared toward the bathroom. She only bit off her sigh when her sister's chirp sounded again.

She heard him answer with a gruff hello, and she forced herself to head to the pile of clothes on the chair. Her phone stuck out of a jeans pocket, and she pressed the button without looking at the display. Her vision filled with the set of Noah's back, tension in every muscle.

"Hey," she said, distracted by a mole on his right buttock. It flexed as he shifted his weight. Definitely something to explore further.

"There is a fucking shit storm in progress, and I need you to get to the station, now," Danielle said. The bark of her furious words focused Nici faster than an explosion. She moved toward her clothes on autopilot.

"What's happening?" Her reply was muffled by the bra she attempted to handle with one hand, getting caught in the cell in the process.

"I'll tell you when you get here. Bring Kinkead with you. You both need to be here."

"Dani, tell me what is going on." Nici's surge of adrenaline made her words cut off sharper than she intended.

"Just get here. And Nici?"

"Yeah."

The pause was longer this time. "Be very careful."

>>>>>

Noah checked his rearview mirror so many times, his eyes ached from the constant readjustment. Every dark vehicle was a sudden potential threat. Anyone who followed for more than a block, suspect. Gideon's words bounced around in his brain until he thought he might have an aneurism.

"Rage made an appearance at the hospital. Here, at Armstrong. Asking for you."

His heart pounded as he glanced at Nicolle in the passenger seat. He didn't want to bring her into this.

"What did Gideon tell you?"

She'd asked that question twice already, and he'd told her the same thing each time. But her expression remained puzzled with a frown marring her features.

"I don't understand why Danielle wants me there so urgently then. I mean, this guy is after you. He doesn't know we have a – " Her words petered out.

"A relationship?"

She nodded.

He slipped a hand across the wide front seat and covered her fingers. They were cold, but then his own weren't much better.

"I'm sorry I got you involved in this. I should have kept my distance. You don't deserve to be sucked into my mess." He regretted it more than he could explain.

She turned her palm over and linked fingers with him, giving a tight squeeze. "You didn't get me involved in a mess. We're involved in a wonderful beginning of what I hope will be a fascinating relationship. For as long as it lasts, Noah."

He opened his mouth to respond in kind, then stopped. For as long as it lasts? Was she already thinking there was an end to what they had? Because he wasn't, not by a long shot. He was thinking about introducing her to the girls, and all the fun they would have with a great female role model like Nicolle. Strong, intelligent, wise, professional, humorous, kind. All the things he wanted his daughters to grow up to be.

He pulled into a visitor stall at the sheriff's station and turned to respond. He didn't have a chance before both of the van's front doors were yanked open.

"About damned time," yelled Gideon.

"Off the streets, now," barked Danielle.

Noah barely had time to beep the vehicle locked as his brother dragged him along. The crutch didn't slow Gideon down or make his grip less demanding. In front of them, Danielle had an arm around Nicolle's shoulders, ushering her inside without pausing.

Noah stopped, needing to gather his thoughts and emotions for what would undoubtedly be a hellish situation. Gid took one more step and pulled, but once momentum was gone, his leg slowed him down.

"Come on, Noah. Now." He glowered as if to add weight to his words. Then he stared more closely.

"What happened to you?" Gideon dropped his hand and stepped to the side as if trying to find better light.

"Nothing. Listen, we need to keep Nicolle away from this. It isn't her fault, and she's not involved."

Gideon's sudden stillness made Noah shut up. A shift of expression, Gid's eyes sliding to the side and examining the asphalt with sudden interest, made Noah's pulse rise.

"Gid, what is it?"

"Dani didn't want to tell her, not on the phone. That guy, the one who attacked her, was spotted outside their house."

Noah headed for the station door at a run.

Nici gulped from the water bottle, willing her face to remain calm as she attempted to steady her insides. Across the room, Noah looked like he was going to explode.

"What do you mean he's waltzing around town? Isn't he in violation of something? Can't you pick him up?" He paced to a far wall, stretched his shoulders and cracked his knuckles, and paced back with no more composure on his face. His eyes said it all. He was pissed, and on her behalf. She wasn't sure why that made her feel better, but it did.

From her seat behind the desk, Danielle said, "To pick him up, one of my deputies or the local police need to see him. He's done a good job hiding himself, though how he's doing that, I don't know. An unfamiliar dog gets reported in this town faster than I can find this asshole."

Nici cleared her throat, wishing she could center her thoughts as easily. "And Rage? You said there are multiple warrants out on him. Including murder, now, wasn't it?"

Danielle nodded, her expression thunderous. Gideon stood propped on the credenza behind her, and he put a restraining hand on her shoulder. Danielle stilled and seemed to tilt her head toward that hand. Under other circumstances, Nici would have questioned her twin on the motion, but they needed to deal with other issues.

Gideon nodded to Noah and said, "I called Dawson and told him you had been called out of town."

Noah's face lost all color and became as frosty as the middle of winter.

"You called Marcus? Why?"

Gideon only stared, his lips a thin line.

"Cap knows you're not going to be at work until we catch this bastard," Danielle said, pulling paperwork from a stack on her desk and writing something without looking up.

"Hell no," Nici bit out, unable to keep her fury in check as well as Noah did. "I am not going to be scared off my job because this jerk is on the loose. I can protect myself."

"And I can protect her," Noah said, coming to stand next to her and sliding his hand into hers. She tightened their grip, grateful for the support.

"As I can protect Noah. We will take care of each other. So you see, there's nothing to worry about." Except Nici felt the worry banging like a drum in her temples.

Danielle didn't even look up. She tore a piece of paper from the pad and waved it toward her twin. Nici didn't move. Danielle's eyes drifted down to the linked hands and her face softened.

She said, "Shit, Nici. Take the paper. It's directions to an address in Tahoe. You and Noah hang out for a few days and stay out of sight. Gid and I will clean this up. Then you can come back and resume whatever it is you're doing." She waved the page at their joined hands.

Nici felt her stubborn streak flash up like a flare. Danielle was always like this, appointing herself in charge like eight minutes between them made that much difference. She owned her problems or they owned her, and she was tired of backing away.

"No," she said, and had the satisfaction of seeing Danielle's eyes flash surprise at the vehemence in her voice. Beside her, she felt Noah's body shift closer as if he agreed.

"Damn it, Noah, Dani's right. Do it. You two can have a little vacation, nothing fancy, but I hear the cabin has a hot tub and a killer view of the lake." Gideon's voice took on a pleading note.

Out of the corner of her eye, she saw Noah bounce as if readying for a fight, but his unruffled words hit her with blindsiding shock. "Let's do it, Nicolle."

She turned to him, ready to argue, and clipped off whatever words she meant to say. His face was impassive, but his eyes flashed with fury and hard resolution. He wasn't planning on following orders, and she was right there with him.

"Okay," she said, trying to make her voice as sound agreeable as she could. Noah rewarded her with a quick wink the others couldn't see and a fast squeeze of her fingers. He reached for the paper from Danielle's outstretched hand, examining the address.

"This is a good idea. Nicolle and I will leave the two of you to handle this. We'll check in daily and see how things are going. Do we have time to pack some clothes?"

Dani nodded, her face puzzled as she looked between the two of them. Over her shoulder, Gideon frowned as if mystified by their sudden capitulation.

Nici backed toward the door and Noah followed. They were almost outside when she heard a quick, "What the fuck?" Gideon sounded like he didn't believe them.

Her twin's voice faded as they put distance between them, saying, "That was too easy."

Chapter 27

An hour later, the hum of tires on the highway was the only sound in Nicolle's truck. Noah forced his hands to relax on the wheel. Inside, his thoughts churned to match his gut.

"This handles well," he said.

Her eyes remained on the road in front of them. Twenty minutes out of town, she had yet to say anything substantial. He glanced in the mirror again, finally convinced no one followed them toward Tahoe.

"We're not going to the cabin," Nicolle said. "I mean, I'm not going. You can go, but I'm not." Her voice rang with a firmness he appreciated. Rock steady and unwilling to back down.

"We are going to the cabin."

She started to sputter another protest, as she had a number of times when they gathered essentials. She didn't agree with him, and Noah checked the mirror before yanking the wheel to the side and settling them on a turnout overlooking the river. She continued to protest until he grabbed for her and pulled her across the center console, kissing her with every emotion that had built inside him since this morning.

Despite her anger, she didn't resist, threading her fingers into his hair and holding on hard. At least it confirmed the heat between them wasn't something he imagined. Noah released her, unwilling to stop but knowing making out on the side of a busy road would be a huge risk. With regret, he pushed her back into her seat and stared at her. Her lips were wet and her eyes huge, but she didn't seem inclined to argue with him anymore.

"We are going to the cabin," he repeated, keeping his voice soft. Her face fell in shards of disappointment, an expression he never wanted to put there. He continued, "But we aren't going to stay there, and we aren't going to wait like the obedient younger siblings while big brother and big sister fix things."

A sudden triumph sparked in Nicolle's eyes, and it took everything he had not to pull her back into his arms and pick things up again. But they had to plan. They had bad guys to take down. It was time this madness ended for both of them.

Nicolle smiled at him and tapped impatient fingers on the dashboard. "Well what are we waiting for, Dr. Kinkead? Let's get this show on the road."

Grinning, he put the truck in gear and pulled back on to the highway. Their shared silence was amiable now. The only difficult moment was when a fire service helicopter passed low overhead, moving rapidly toward town. Nicolle scowled up at it, but said nothing. The scowl remained in place for a few miles, until Noah squeezed their joined hands. Her expression shifted to regret and she sighed.

"I should be there," she said.

"And I should be at the hospital, but let's face it. Until we get this straightened out, we're more of a hazard than anything else. Are you sure this is the right road?"

Ornate mountain homes rose on either side as the road climbed to heights overlooking the south shore of Lake Tahoe. Through the pines, Noah caught glimpses of crystal blue water and sun shimmering on its surface. Little snow marked the peaks this summer, but the Sierras were still magnificent.

"Oh yes, this is the right road. The cabin belongs to friends of our parents." Nicolle didn't gawk out the windows as they cruised through the wealthy neighborhood.

"We've involved more people? This keeps getting better and better."

"Relax. Dad does their taxes, and has been for years. They're always urging my parents to take advantage of the place. They issued the same open invitation to Dani and me years ago. Looks like we'll finally get a chance to use it."

The disembodied voice of the GPS system alerted them they'd reached their destination on the left and Noah pulled into the driveway of a house four times larger than the one he lived in now.

"Why aren't your parents' friends here?"

Nicolle flashed him an indulgent smile filled with humor. "It's their vacation home, one of three they own. I think they're currently someplace in South America."

"Huh," he said, staring at the portico entryway framed in warm wood and stonework. Nicolle was already at the front door, punching a code into a wall pad and disappearing inside. Seconds later, the garage door lifted, and she waved him in.

The garage was larger than the house he first lived in with Barbara. He could probably operate on the space's pristine floor. He already had a hard time calling this a cabin, and he hadn't even seen the inside yet.

Nicolle leaned against the interior door with her thumbs linked in her jeans pockets, looking like she enjoyed the surprise in his wide eyes. He couldn't help it. Despite being a doctor, he didn't know many people with this kind of wealth. He was still paying off his student loans, and he'd probably finish about the time he'd need to start paying for Elena's college years. When he trailed after Nicolle into the kitchen and adjacent living room, he barely avoided gasping in amazement.

"I wish we were here under better circumstances," Nicolle said softly, coming up behind him. She joined him in staring at the all-encompassing view with the lake like a jewel gleaming at the foot of the surrounding mountains.

Noah wrapped an arm around her and pulled her close. "We'll make the best of it. I have to say, it's going to take me a few minutes to remember why we're here in the first place. Give me time."

She chuckled. "I'm going to check the fridge and see what we have on tap for dinner."

He frowned, realizing they hadn't thought to bring groceries. "I can go out for something."

This time, she laughed. "If I know the Bennigans, the pantry is full, the fridge is stocked, and nothing is past its expiration date. Oh, and the wine cellar will have anything you have a taste for too."

This time, some of Noah's tension drained away as he shook his head in amazement. Nicolle took this in stride, and her authority and comfort calmed him. They would make the best of this. They would persevere, get rid of Mitchell and Rage, and continue to explore what was growing between them. Despite the astounding vistas framed by two-story windows, his gaze locked on Nicolle. She was prettier than any outdoor view. As if she knew what he was thinking, she grinned at him with a pronounced wink before sauntering off in an exaggerated sway for the open kitchen. He had to remind himself they were in danger, because he wanted them to cause some trouble all by themselves.

With her head in the freezer, she said, "Do you want to consult on our selection, or should I make an executive decision?"

"Go ahead, whatever you want. I'm going to call the girls."

He heard her acknowledgment as he moved to a couch that could easily hold eight people with room to spare and sank into its welcoming cushions. What would his girls think of a place like this? It might even silence the worldly Elena. Char would have a field day exploring the many rooms.

God, he missed them. At the same time, he knew it was best they weren't around right now. Two less people he loved to worry about. As it was, his concerns about Nicolle, Gid and Danielle dominated his thoughts.

Nicolle. Love. In the same thought. His heart pounded again. He swore he'd keep her safe.

Needing the distraction, he pulled out his phone and dialed Elena's cell number. The picture on the screen was one of both girls taken last summer. Elena hated it, saying it made her look like a kid. Char loved their laughing poses. Perhaps he needed to think about a phone for Char.

"Hello?"

"Char? What are you doing with Elena's phone?" His eldest would never share it, not by choice.

"Hi Daddy. She's in the shower, and the phone was ringing, and I could see it was you, so I answered it. How are you, Daddy? I miss you." She finally ran out of breath and stopped the rush of words.

"I miss you too, sunshine. What did you do today?"

Char chattered about a visit to a theme park and how cranky Elena got, and how their mother was kind of mad at her husband and how their mother said he was now in the doghouse. "But they don't have a dog," she finished.

Noah smiled. "It's an expression grown-ups use. It means he's in trouble."

He could picture Char processing this, twirling a strand of blonde hair around and around until the already curly piece tightened. She said, "What are you doing today?"

"Well, I'm on a little vacation."

"You went on a vacation without us?" He could tell this idea produced great consternation in his youngest.

"It's more like a date," he clarified.

"You're on a date?" Char sounded fascinated by the idea. "El, Daddy's on a date," she yelled, not bothering to move the phone away from her mouth as she delivered the message.

Noah winced, realizing this might not be acceptable news. He hadn't dated since the divorce. He hadn't prepared them for this eventuality, not when it seemed like a vague and distant possibility. They might not approve.

He heard squabbling in the background and Char's continuing excited chatter. Then a rustle sounded from the phone and another voice came on the line.

"Father? You're on a date?" Disbelief made Elena's voice sound squeaky.

"Hi Elena. How are you, honey? I heard you had a nice day today."

An exasperated whine sounded through the connection. "You will not change the subject. A date. Honestly. When we're home, all you do is work. Who is she? What do you know about her?"

He grinned at the third degree. In the background, he heard Char demanding to know more too.

"Her name is Nicolle, and Uncle Gideon introduced us."

Elena snorted. "If Gideon introduced you, she's not going to be appropriate."

"What do you mean? She's a firefighter, and she saves people. That's cool, right?"

Behind him, he heard a chuckle, and he turned to find Nicolle watching from across the room, two frosty glasses of clear liquid in her hands. She raised one to him and he nodded.

"Father, everyone knows Gideon is a player. Yeesh." Elena paused to shush Char.

"How do you know what a player is?" Where did his daughter learn this stuff, and how did she know about Gid's less than stellar example of dating life?

"Father, come on. It's time to introduce you to the twenty-first century. Oh, I have a call coming in," she said in a sudden breathless rush. "It's Richard. I need to take it."

Noah bolted up straight in alarm. "Who's Richard?"

"A guy I'm seeing. He's older. People my age are much more mature and sophisticated here, Father. Say goodbye, Char."

"Wait. Does your mother know this boy? How much older?"

But he didn't get a response. Char yelled 'I love you' in the distance, Elena echoed 'yeah, me too', and the line went dead.

He dropped his head into one hand and thumped his phone against his skull with the other. He'd have to call Barbara, never a fun event, and ask if she was paying attention to what their daughter was doing. That would crowd him in that doghouse with the current husband.

"That sounded interesting," Nicolle said, dropping on to the couch next to him.

He continued to beat the phone, hoping for wisdom. He asked, "Tell me, at the age of twelve, what were you doing?"

He glanced over to find her face screwed up in concentration as she tapped a finger to her cheek.

"Twelve, twelve, let me think. Girl Scouts? Softball? Oh yeah, and sewing classes." She snapped her fingers and grinned at him. "The sewing didn't take."

"You were a Girl Scout? You play softball?" There was so much he still didn't know about her, and he wanted to learn it all.

"Oh yeah, and drama club, and the student newspaper in high school. And in college, I worked as a waitress. I was lousy at that too."

Her comical expression made him laugh.

"My girls do none of those things. I suppose I should be concerned about it. But right now, I'm worried about Elena dating a boy she labels as older. She's only twelve. Both the dating part and the older part are torture."

He leaned back, pulling her with him until his chin could rest on the top of her head. The sensation of her arms encircling his waist brought him peace. "They're growing up so fast, and I worry I'll miss things, important things. My life is pretty much work and the girls. Or at least, it was until you came into it."

He felt her still in his arms. He didn't want to drive a distance between them, so he hurried on. "Do you want kids?" Why that popped out of his mouth now, he wasn't sure. He could picture Nicolle laughing and sharing things with his girls, but she might not be on board with that.

A ripple of tension ran through her body and communicated to his. When she spoke, her tone was reserved. "Kids are wonderful. I've been working on my career, so I haven't had time to think much about it. Why do you ask?"

He blew out a sigh and wished he'd filtered his thoughts before speaking.

"Your career is important. You have plenty of time. You're young."

Did he imagine the sudden uptick in her pulse? He wanted to check her reaction. But she pushed away and stood, pacing away on thumping feet with her back to him. From the kitchen, she said, "I pulled out the makings for burgers for dinner, and I thought we'd have baked potatoes and asparagus with them. Then we should start planning, Noah."

He stared openly, trying to read her emotions with her face hidden from view. As a change of subject went, that was an extreme shift. Curiosity warred with concern.

Finally, she looked up at him, and no feelings showed on her face. With an objective distance in her tone, she said, "How are we going to draw the bad guys out, and how are we going to keep Dani and Gid off our trail as we do it?"

>>>>>

Oh god, oh god, oh god. Nici had repeated that litany in her brain numerous times since this afternoon. Any time Noah strayed into personal territory, she veered them away once more. He must know she was evading something.

Not that their plans to bring down the bad guys were developing well either. Neither one of them were trained in this sort of thing. Short of making themselves into targets, they hadn't come up with any workable ideas. That didn't wash, since targets on their backs put unsuspecting innocent people at risk as well.

"I think we should call it a night. Maybe if we sleep on it, we'll come up with better ideas in the morning." Noah took their wine glasses into the kitchen and loaded the dishwasher. He stayed silent as he hunted under a cabinet and emerged with cleaning spray. With dedicated precision, he wiped down the counters and sink until everything sparkled. Nici felt the distance growing between them.

"Planning on performing surgery on that counter later on?" She injected humor into her words so he would stop being so on edge with her. She wanted them to slip back into the easy camaraderie they shared before she'd sidestepped the kids issue.

"Never hurts to be prepared," he said, washing his hands and drying them on a paper towel. He pitched it into the trash and paused briefly, watching her. Then he came toward her in slow steps. Damn if he wasn't giving her a seductive grin too.

She grinned back, matching it and raising the heat up a notch. His pace sped up.

When she rose into his waiting arms, his grin widened further and he began to hum. The beat wasn't exactly a slow dance number. Then she recognized the tune. The music from the office supply store, the first time they'd danced together.

"Smooth move, Dr. Kinkead."

"Ah yes, Ms. Trajan, and I have a list of them. Care to try out that king bed and experience some of my favorites?" He dipped her low and kissed her in a quick hit.

"How about trying out the hot tub first?"

He hummed some more, whirling them in a circle that ended at the entrance to the bedroom hallway. "I'm not sure those condoms are rated for water use. In fact, I'm not sure any brands are."

She stopped, watching his face. In the space of a few short days, he'd become so important to her. She didn't trust the rising wave of her emotions. She could easily fall in love with this man, too easily in fact. He deserved more than she could offer him.

She couldn't keep the husky note out of her voice when she said, "Noah, I'm protected. I've had a clean health check since, well, then. I have them every three months, to be sure." She stopped, wondering what he would think of her bumbling explanation.

His grin faded and his eyes darkened to a blue closer to midnight than the ocean. "What are you saying?"

She shrugged, suddenly unsure she should have rocked the boat. "Just that if you want, we don't need the condoms, and we could try the hot tub. I'm sure you're fine. After all, you're a doctor, and I trust you."

Relief crossed his face first, right before he frowned. "I don't want you to do anything you're not ready for, Nicolle. We have all the time in the world."

Her heart surged with the sincerity ringing in his words. Protective, gentle Noah. Despite their circumstances, her spirit felt lighter than it had in years.

She took his hands and walked backwards toward the bedroom, gratified by the joy blooming on his face. When he halted, she did too and leaned into the light caress of his fingers on her cheek.

"I am honored you trust me with your secrets and with the gift that is you. And I promise never to let anything happen to you."

The sharp pang his words caused made her happiness to dim for a moment. She didn't expect him to control the future, but that was for tomorrow. Tonight, they had all night.

"Make love to me, Noah." She let her eyes drift shut as his mouth closed over hers.

>>>>>

He hadn't been completely truthful with his daughter when he said the woman in his arms was cool. Nicolle was scorching hot, and she was heating Noah up faster than a wildfire as seconds ticked by.

The lips under his inspired him. Poetry in motion, as she was in the sparring ring, as she was in firefighting gear, and as she was when she delivered an impassioned declaration that she could take care of herself. But he wouldn't let her stand alone.

He allowed his mouth to move away from the enticement hers offered to drift along her cheek. Settling a string of kisses on her neck, he enjoyed the sensation of her shiver and the moan that followed. Her shell of an ear tempted him, and he gave it a quick bite, happy to hear her gasp in reply.

"Come to bed with me, Nicolle." He guided her steps in an exotic dance down the darkened hallway.

Her reply, delivered in the vicinity of his shoulder as her hands reached out to lift off his shirt, held a teasing tone. "I thought you wanted to try out that hot tub."

He stifled an exclamation when her teeth closed on a bundle of nerves in his neck with a gentle bite. She soothed it with warm kisses, making him inhale sharply. "Later. Now, bed," he said, barely getting the words out.

Who removed clothing faster, he couldn't say for sure. This wasn't a race, but eagerness. He wanted to explore her naked body in ways he hadn't had time for before. She seemed equally eager to chart new territory as her hands stayed restless in their movements and her eyes glowed in the moon's light through the window.

In that glow, her skin took on an incandescent sheen, and the dark red of her hair blazed golden. She looked like some sort of fire goddess, bright and immortal, a siren calling men to their everlasting home. And he didn't mind burning, not one cinder.

"You are so beautiful," he said, letting his hands follow the paths his eyes traveled over her porcelain skin. He didn't hide the reverence in his tone or the admiration in his touch as he explored muscle and strength as well as softness and femininity.

She didn't respond, her eyes glazed and following his movements as if mesmerized. He cupped her breasts, the perfect size for his hands, and let his thumbs brush her nipples in slow strokes until she groaned.

"Good, gentle Noah," she said in a murmur so soft, he had to lean closer to hear her. "What does it take to make you lose that careful control?"

He would never violate Nicolle like that. Never. She deserved to be worshiped and cherished. Those words left his lips without thinking.

Her immediate frown stopped his roaming hands. "I trust you, Noah."

He nodded, uncertain where she was going with that statement.

"I'm not made of china, or did you forget the times I threw you in the ring?"

She flipped him on his back and jumped on top before he had time to react. She was breathing hard, but he didn't think it had anything to do with exertion.

She leaned back, pressing her palms to his chest as she did so, and her fingers raked across his abdomen, making his muscles quake. A surge of blood hardened him and made every thought race out of his brain. When she lifted her hair and let it fall back in an elegant slide, he forgot about being kind and gentle and reached for her hips.

He whirled her, his chest coming to rest pressed against her back. Her quick gasp of shock made him wonder if he'd moved too quickly, but her body pushed tighter against him. His blood boiled so fast, it was a miracle he didn't suffer an immediate and life-ending stroke. If she wanted to see him lose control, she was doing a damned effective job of driving him over the edge.

"Feel what you do to me," he demanded, his teeth sinking into her shoulder. Her moan was full of desire and she rubbed her body against his. When she spun beneath him and opened her legs, he followed her down on the bed with a chant in his head of mine, mine, mine.

She wrapped her legs around him and her fingers closed on his arms. He kept his gaze fixed on hers, unwilling to let a second go by without every possible connection between them.

"You are mine, Nicolle, mine to cherish and mine to protect." He pumped into her in one hard stroke, and she cried out. Then a wicked smile curved her mouth and she twisted her hips, taking him impossibly deeper. A curse burst out before he could stop it.

"That would make you mine too," she said, shifting once more in a way that made him throb harder. Every muscle in his body wanted to move, to pound into her at a pace that could stop hearts. She was true to her word, driving him past control.

He wrapped a hand around the back of her neck, lifting her for an open-mouthed kiss, tongues tangled and breaths hard. The pistoning of his body was answered by the frantic thrusts of hers. Releasing her neck, he positioned a hand between them and rubbed her core, setting up a cadence that matched the force of their pumping.

His balls pulled up tight and it felt like thousands of scalpels tore down his spine. Beneath him, he heard Nicolle's cries and the tightened sheath of her body grasping him. Then his vision blurred and stars danced in front of his eyes as he cried out her name and poured into her.

Chapter 28

Nici hummed, allowing the bubbles to tickle her in places Noah had visited throughout the night. Oh so many places. She was pleasantly sore, incredibly stretched, happily sated and content to stay still.

Then the man of the night walked out on the deck wearing nothing but a smile and she thought maybe she could go a few more rounds. A girl needed a regular workout, right?

"What's that grin for?" He punctuated the question with a kiss as he handed her a steaming mug of coffee.

"I was appreciating my sparring partner. He has an excellent physique, or maybe you doctors call it anatomy. Yes, a truly inspiring anatomy." She reached out and playfully ran a finger down one of her new favorite parts. That part surged and began an upward transit with her movements.

"You are going to kill me, woman. Give me a few minutes, and we'll see if I die a happy man." He slipped into the hot water next to her with a hiss.

She took a sip of the coffee, trying to force her gaze to the view and away from Noah's face in contented repose. He looked younger with his eyes closed and his head back, the only emotion on his face one of bliss. She figured her own face probably matched it. Never had she imagined so much passion could burn all night and be nowhere near containment.

When she woke from a dreamless deep sleep to find Noah making love to her, his tongue dancing at the hot spot between her legs, she nearly cried out from the intensity of acceleration alone. The fact that he moaned and writhed later when she returned the favor, loving every inch of his impressive length, made her smile even now.

"I guess it isn't true what they say."

Noah said, "Hhmmm?"

Realizing she'd said the words out loud, she felt the blush rise on her cheeks. "Oh, um, nothing."

He opened one eye to regard her quizzically. The other eye popped wide to join in the stare at what she knew was heat on her cheeks. "Come on, you can't lead with a sentence like that and then say it's nothing."

She shifted, which only put a jet in a spot that Noah had given particular attention to a number of times. Her eyes unfocused as she tried to form words.

"Nicolle Trajan, are you having impure thoughts?" He took her coffee cup and put it on the ledge of the hot tub. His arms came around her and lifted her, turning her on to his lap. When she settled, she realized another myth was debunked.

"Ok, fine, you got me. Two urban legends, torched."

He laughed, his face filled with curiosity. "And those would be?"

She traced his collarbone, noting with some satisfaction that red marks still showed from her more exuberant kisses during the night. "Well, if you must know, there's the legend that the size of a man's equipment is in proportion to his height. I'd say you are particularly well-endowed, Doctor."

She shifted in his lap to emphasize her point and was rewarded when he further disproved the second myth.

"I can tell you with medical certainty this myth is just that, a myth. In fact, height has nothing to do with length, or girth for that matter. Nor does anything correspond to the size of a man's thumb. That story about creases in the earlobe and sexual prowess, on the other hand, has not been adequately researched."

Enjoying this playful side of him, Nici reached for his head, turning his face away. "I didn't get a clear view of your earlobes last night. Maybe I should check to see if they live up to your, ah, capabilities."

His chuckle made her heat up in ways that had nothing to do with the foaming water swirling around them. She nibbled his earlobe, loving the sound of his moan and tightening of muscles under her fingers.

"Was there anything else you need debunked, madam?"

"Oh, I think you've settled that one already." She gave him a cheeky grin with a kiss.

His face grew pseudo-serious. "And that is?"

"Certain things don't grow in hot water."

His laughter rang out as he lifted and proved how big things could grow, given the right conditions. They'd never made it to the hot tub phase of their explorations last night. Now might be that perfect time.

She leaned into Noah just as a chime sounded from the opposite edge of the tub. A second chime followed. Her cell phone vibrated from its damp perch to accentuate the sounds.

Her forehead landed on his, even as he began to straighten. She didn't want this time to end, wrapped in a blanket of loving and caring and forgetting about the harsh reality existing outside their little world. He ran a towel over his hand and reached for her phone. When he passed it to her display side up, his expression mirrored the disappointment she felt.

Texts from Danielle, two of them.

'Talk?'

'Unless ur busy?'

The sly insinuation wasn't lost on Nicolle.

Noah moved her to the side, reaching for a towel and standing. She gave his butt one final lingering glance and said, "It's Dani. She wants to talk."

He nodded, his eyes on the lake below them. He hid under the towel and rubbed his hair with fierce movements, and when his face emerged, regret filled his gaze.

"I should call Gid and see what's happening."

She nodded, feeling a chill despite the cheerful burble of water.

"I'll call Dani."

He wrapped the towel around his waist, leaned over to give her a hard kiss, and disappeared inside before she blinked an eye. With an empty sigh, she hit speed dial.

"Are you behaving yourself?" Danielle's question sounded distracted instead of playful, raising hairs on Nici's neck immediately.

"Well hello to you too. How are the investigations coming? Any progress?"

Nici heard the long sigh and a clatter than could have been a pen thrown against a solid object.

"No, I'm sorry to say we are not making much progress. We are getting a lot of reported sightings, but none of them pan out." Her twin sighed again, inhaled deeply, and added the next words in a softer tone. "How are you and Noah doing?"

Despite the tension of the call, Nici smiled. "We're doing good, better than good, great."

Another sigh. "That's terrific, sis. I'm happy for you." Danielle hesitated again, long enough this time for Nici to worry.

"Dani? What's wrong?"

An uncharacteristic doubtful tone filled her twin's voice when she replied. "Listen, when things quiet down some, I have something I need to tell you."

"Tell me now, Dani. It's obviously bothering you, so get it off your chest."

Nici could almost feel the determined shake of her sister's head. "No, later. Like I said, when things quiet down. I'll get that bastard, Nici, I promise you. And while I'm at it, I'll catch Noah's bad guy too."

>>>>>

"It is fucking frustrating, and that's all I can tell you."

Noah nodded, knowing no response would be required. Gid would rant for a while, and until he calmed down, there wasn't much point in trying to direct the conversation.

"I mean, how hard can it be to locate a guy covered with gold bling and probably driving a car that stands out just as much?"

"Gid, that's profiling."

A string of curses shot through the phone. "I'm not being prejudiced. Would you like to hear what I think of the guy who attacked your girlfriend?"

Noah didn't say anything.

"Did you hear me?"

"Yes, I heard you, and since I share your sentiment, I don't need to respond."

Gideon stayed quiet long enough for Noah to pull a shirt over his head against the morning chill.

"So, she is your girlfriend now, am I right?"

What was Nicolle? The term girlfriend sounded like high school. His woman made him sound like a caveman. She deserved more respect than that.

"She's the woman I care about deeply, and I plan to continue caring about her even more as time goes on. Satisfied?" He wasn't sure why he sounded angry about it.

Noah stopped where he stood to examine his emotions. It wasn't anger. Now that he listened to it, allowed himself to feel it, he recognized it for what it was.

Fear.

Fear that she wouldn't reciprocate his caring. Fear of the unknown, when so much of his life felt uncertain. Fear she could be taken away before they had a chance.

This had to end, and end soon.

"Where do we go from here?" He forced his voice into a level modulation, even as he wanted to bite out the words.

His brother gave a disgusted mutter, saying, "You and Nicolle don't go anywhere. Dani and I have this."

"And how is the lieutenant?" Considering this was the longest Gideon had ever been with the same woman, Noah thought it was a fair question.

Silence bare of background noise crackled through the phone.

"Gid?"

"She's pissed. Fine, but pissed. Listen, I have to go. Dani's waving me over."

Out of extreme curiosity, Noah said, "Where are you?"

"Doesn't matter. I'll check in with you later. Until then, lay low, okay?" Gideon paused, then added, "Take care of yourself, bro." It was the closest they ever got to any stronger word for their feelings.

"You too," Noah said, emotions swamping him. They never said they loved each other. It wasn't a phrase common in their vocabulary. Noah realized he didn't use it much either, except when it came to the girls. He tried to tell them all the time.

Now he had someone else to tell too.

Nicolle appeared in the doorway as if he summoned her with his thought, tapping her phone to her lips with her gaze on the floor as if deep in thought. She stopped and looked up, worry filling her features. He saw the force in her eyes, the same force he knew filled his own.

Realization. Fear. And something more.

She said, "We have to finish this."

He nodded, crossing the space between them. When he reached her, he wrapped his arms around her. Nicolle's came around him, tightening more with each moment they stood there. A knot formed in his throat, big enough to make it hard for him to breathe. He wouldn't, couldn't lose her.

Chapter 29

Nicolle didn't want Noah at the hospital. Noah didn't want her at the fire camp. They shouldn't be seen in public. But these were the best ways to draw out both of their bad guys. They were out of other options.

With consensus formed, they stared at each other. Nici drank in the sight of him, standing straight with his shoulders back, balancing on the balls of his feet as he did before charging in the ring. Electric forces seemed to spark from him. Noah was itching for a fight, and the fact that he would probably get one, one that might injure him or worse, left her empty inside.

She did the only thing that made sense, the thing her mind, body and spirit needed, and she climbed him like a crazy woman. Pushing him against the nearest wall, her hands couldn't rid him of clothes fast enough. When his need rose in an instant to meet hers, his hands were everywhere, and seams ripped in their eagerness. Her legs anchored him to her and he slammed into her hard enough to make pictures rattle. Passion made the moments a blur, but that was how she wanted it.

Fast, hard, mind emptying. It blocked the one emotion she didn't want to feel. Fear.

The clench of her orgasm made even yelling his name impossible and his answering groan as he pulsed inside her was more gratifying than anything she'd ever accomplished. They slid to the floor, his arms locked around her and his face hidden in her neck. His exhalations bellowed in her ear. She felt tears falling like light rain and knew nothing could ever be the same between them.

"Promise me something," he said in muffled words.

"Yes."

She felt his smile on her neck. "You don't even know what I'm asking yet."

She chuckled, the need for tears disappearing. They would weather this. What the world looked like on the other side remained to be seen.

"Yes," she said again.

He pulled back, his hands coming to her face and cradling it. He inspected her features one by one in thorough examination. It was probably too soon to use the words, but that didn't mean they didn't live in her heart. If they were in her heart, they were probably in her gaze too.

His face fell, as if what he saw pained him, and she vowed to keep things light. If she never said it, he could never be certain. She attempted a smile, and he answered in a moan. He closed his eyes, shook his head, and blinked open. When he repeated the blinks, his eyes shined with suspicious moisture.

His voice was guttural when he said, "Promise me you'll be very careful, Nicolle Trajan. Promise me."

She nodded, finding words hard to come by. "You too, Noah Kinkead."

He nodded with vigor as he tightened his hold on her face and gave her a kiss, not of passion, but deeper. Commitment. She returned it with everything inside of her.

When he pulled back, his eyes searched hers once more. "I can't believe I'm saying this, because we've only known each other a short time, and I don't act on a spur of the moment." He cleared his throat before continuing. "Nicolle, I love you, and I can't stand the idea of anyone hurting you."

She gulped in surprise, a surge of giddy happiness filling her chest. He loved her. In the craziness of their situation, something good had taken root and begun to grow.

She stared at him in amazement, unable to speak. And she watched his face fall, his expression growing sadder and more distant with each passing second.

Nici hadn't said the words, not out loud. When he started to shift her away, his face averted, her fingers tunneled into his hair to stop him.

"Noah, look at me."

His head turned with obvious reluctance. His shuttered expression, a calm empty mask, told her more than words what he felt. He didn't want her to say anything out of pity or empty emotion.

She drew him close, so close that they shared the same breaths. When she felt the tension between them reaching a breaking point, she whispered, "I love you, Noah."

He crushed her to him with a triumphant cry, and she marveled at the magic of three simple words.

>>>>>

Two hours later, they drove down the mountain, their free hands linked over the center console. They hadn't said much after those magic words, letting their bodies do the communicating. Despite what they faced ahead of them, Noah didn't think he'd ever been so at peace.

Based on appearances when he glanced over, he suspected Nicolle felt the same. There was a glow to her skin, a shining light in her eyes, and the safe, constant pulse of her blood where he could feel it in the tight grip of their fingers. Lives coming together, a life to share. He was damned tempted to turn around and hope their siblings could make the terrors go away.

That wasn't how he wanted to live. As a child, having his brother defending him had comforted him and kept him safe, but they were adults now. This was his battle, his and Nicolle's.

His phone buzzed in the console, and Nicolle reached for it and read the display aloud.

'Sighting at hospital.'

"Type back, 'Rage'?"

The short click of keys filled the truck cab.

The phone dinged again.

'Y'

Noah blew out a breath. "So I guess our plan is solid."

"Why didn't they arrest him?" Nicolle's question hung in the air.

"Maybe he disappeared by the time the cops arrived. Maybe they couldn't verify it was him. Who knows?" He let his words drift off, reassured when Nicolle gripped his open palm once more.

"They'll get him, Noah. Give Dani time. She has everyone in local law enforcement on their toes."

He didn't want to bring up the other looming danger.

"And the firebug?"

Out of the corner of his eye, he saw her shake her head. "I don't know. I have a hard time believing it's Mitchell. I mean, the fires began before he was released. I'll know more once I examine the most recent source to see if it could have been the same arsonist."

Their one source of disagreement. In the hospital, he was surrounded by a crowd of others, including armed security and hospital staff with sedatives in syringes. In the field, even with a crew in the area, she was exposed and most often alone.

"I'm going with you, so that will be tomorrow."

She shook her head to disagree and he heard her accompanying deep inhalation. "Noah, I can do this. It will be safe. Besides, after working the night shift, you'll need to sleep tomorrow."

"I'll sleep when they're both caught and behind bars." He squeezed her hand for emphasis and released it, returning both to the steering wheel as they entered the outskirts of town.

She didn't reply, and another peek at her face revealed a stubborn frown. Bottom line, if she decided to take matters into her own hands, there was little he could do to stop her.

"I love you," he said, as the sudden need to remind her how important she was in his life overwhelmed him.

She turned in the seat, facing him with a radiant smile. "Oh Noah, I love you too. We'll get though this and then we'll decide what comes next." A shadow crossed her features, an expression so quickly gone, he might have imagined it.

"Where we go next is we continue to spend all of our free time together. When the girls come back, we do things as a family. I guess we better read Gideon and Danielle in on this." He suspected both had some explaining of their own to do.

Nicolle didn't respond, and he couldn't concentrate on the flush of traffic and watch her reaction too. The dinner hour made Main Street more crowded than usual, and he noted a more visible police presence with mixed feelings.

"Are you sure about this?" Her voice sounded strong, so he made a point to answer in kind.

"Without any hesitation." He pulled into the hospital parking lot. The lingering kiss they shared held too much worry, fear and poignancy to make it feel romantic. He wiped a single tear from her cheek, allowing himself the luxury of examining every feature of her face. She smiled, and he realized he did too despite the pain of their separation. He didn't look back as he marched toward the hospital's door, afraid his resolve to carry through with this would waver. The screech of tires leaving the parking lot was unmistakably hers.

Nicolle's kisses lingered on his lips, and he fought the urge to cover them with his fingers to preserve the sensation. That would make him look silly when he walked in the staff entrance, and above all, he needed to appear unwavering in his resolve.

It was his choice to be here. Drawing out Rage was Noah's primary intention, but in all truth, he needed to be here too. His identity was wrapped up in being a doctor, in helping others, in saving people. The fierce competitor in the ring was only due to the requirement to protect his family. He wasn't a fighter by nature.

But he would fight. He would fight for Nicolle, his girls, and his brother. They were his family. They were his priority. The nuance of Nicolle being at the head of the list wasn't lost on him.

He entered the small back office behind the ER reserved for doctors' use. A satchel rested on the floor behind the desk, and a briefcase leaned against the wall. He recognized the satchel as belonging to the woman who usually covered the day shift, but the briefcase was unfamiliar. Bare of any monogram, he had no clue who might be filling in for him.

Night shifts were often the worst. People came in with complicated needs, sometimes drunk or high, or with complicated conditions that couldn't wait until morning. When the girls were home, he limited his nights to one week a month. This summer, he'd worked whenever he was needed to give his colleagues a break. He doubted they'd be upset he returned early from this unplanned absence.

He dropped his worn case in its usual corner and opened his locker to retrieve his white coat. Freshly laundered and pressed, he pulled it on, feeling like he donned armor for battle. The war was coming and he would be ready for it. Just in case, he flexed his hands and feet, tightened and loosened his core muscles, and thought about the best ways to disarm a lunatic in case Rage made an appearance. His perverse sense of being prepared left him with scant satisfaction. This wasn't over yet, even if he felt confident it would be soon.

The door swung inward and the tall willowy woman entering stopped short in surprise. "Noah, what are you doing here?"

"Hi Monica. Night shift. It's my week, remember? Or did they call you in instead?"

She shook her head, moving toward the satchel as she shed her coat. It bore stains and marks from the day, and she gave it a one-handed toss into the corner laundry bin. Hefting her personal bag, she gave him a tired smile.

"No, I've been on today. You wouldn't think I'd have a problem with that, but it's been busy and I'm pooped. Your replacement's read in on our cases, and he has it handled." She disappeared out the door before he had a chance to ask who was already on the floor.

Putting things off wouldn't catch a bad guy. He pushed through the door and strode to the nurses' station with determination, intent on getting up to speed on waiting patients and dismissing his substitute.

"Noah?"

The deep voice brought him up short. He turned mid-step.

"Good evening, Marcus."

His boss stared at him with open curiosity. The white coat wrapping his large frame made him seem bigger than street clothes would. Even decades off the football field, he looked like he could take down a lineman without breaking a sweat.

"What are you doing here?"

Noah shrugged as if nothing was unusual. "Night shift." He eyed Marcus more closely. "What are you doing here?"

Marcus shifted a shoulder and pushed his glasses further up his nose. He broke into a smile that made his pearly whites stand out in sharp contrast to his black skin.

"I still practice. Got to keep my hand in so I know what you guys face. Besides, who better to find a puny black guy than a big black guy?" He let out a laugh, and voices around them dropped to listen.

Noah couldn't stop the responding smile. His boss was more friend than supervisor. In the early years, he served as a confidante when Noah mourned the loss of patients. They celebrated the birth of the girls. When his marriage when sideways, Marcus provided sound advice. When all hell broke loose last year, Marcus urged Noah to get back to work and stop feeling sorry for himself. Putting his friend in the line of fire was not something Noah would tolerate.

"I've got this, Marcus."

A big hand clutched his shoulder. "You don't fight alone, Noah. Let Rage show his ferret face and toy gun here. We've got this together."

Noah thought the big man sounded like he relished the idea.

>>>>>

The camp was never quiet, not with active incidents underway. It probably shouldn't have surprised her when Cap's signature hand appeared on the corner of her desk.

"What the fuck, Trajan?"

"What the fuck, Cap." She booted up her laptop and moved folders to the side to give her notepad room.

"You are off-duty until we catch this fucker."

She kept her eyes on the scrolling programs on her screen. "Which fucker are we referring to, Cap?"

He huffed out an exasperated string of expletives, some of which made Nicolle smile because they were so imaginative. "You know damn well who I'm talking about. Mitchell is still on the loose, in case you haven't been kept in the loop, wherever you were that brought such a bloom of color to your cheeks." Cap leaned closer and stared at her face. "What the hell have you been up to?"

Her face heated in a probable blush as she thought about Noah, about the cabin, about being in love. A shiver of apprehension followed, shaking through her at the thought of how much danger he put himself in.

The outer door burst open and bounced on its hinges, hitting something hard again before bouncing shut. Nici couldn't see who'd come in because Cap put his body between her and the intruder. That was the last thing she wanted on her conscience. Her intention was to draw Mitchell out by being accessible, not putting the lives of those around her at risk.

"I've got this, Cap," she said, rising to make eye contact.

"No, I've got this, and you're going back to the cabin," said her sister.

Voice tone alone communicated Danielle's rejection of any argument, which pissed Nici off to no end. Eight minutes was a spark of time. It didn't give her twin any special rights. Cap's glaze flicked between them and he wisely stepped out of the way.

Danielle marched up and came nose to nose with Nici, her breathing hard and her eyes snapping with barely suppressed anger. Doing the twin connection thing, Nici read her emotions. Yeah, she was angry. She was also afraid and worried.

"We had a deal. You out of sight, and me doing my job." Danielle hadn't bothered to lower her voice. Around them, Nici heard scurrying feet as people exited the building.

"You gave a directive. It doesn't work for me. So I'm here, doing my job." Nicolle took a step back and returned to her seat with as much nonchalance as possible.

Danielle's next comments were almost as imaginative as Cap's had been. The comparison made Nici smile. When her twin ran out of steam, she pulled a chair out from a nearby desk and dropped into it.

"Why didn't Noah have the good sense to stay in place?"

They knew their secrets wouldn't last long. If someone called her sister, someone also probably called Gideon. Nici shook her head, and Danielle groaned.

"Gid is going ballistic. I swear, cast or not, he is ready to kick some ass. It might be his brother's."

Nici typed meaningless words on to her laptop as if continuing to work. "Yeah, tell me about that. How would you know how Gideon's feeling? You two seem to have gotten very cozy over the past few days."

Her sister didn't respond. Nici shifted to watch a flush of pink start at Danielle's neckline and work its way to the roots of her hair, and a red abrasion under her ear turned darker with the blush. It looked remarkably like stubble burn, another reason to grin. Danielle caught the expression.

"It's nothing, and you're trying to deflect." Her twin leaned closer with narrowed eyes. "What's different about you?"

Despite the mixture of fear and worry swirling inside her, Nici couldn't help it. Her broad grin made her face ache and her sister's answering groan turned that into a delighted laugh.

Chapter 30

His Friday night waiting room was getting damned crowded, packed enough for staff to grow jumpy and make Noah wish he had an outlet for the tension inside him. These people weren't even patients.

The current deputy on duty happened to be Jake. In civilian clothes, he blended in and was better at looking inconspicuous than the constant scowl Gid provided. Noah had watched his brother's silent glare as he took up residence in the corner of the room, his back to two walls as if he expected to make a stand. More than one person walked in the door, caught his brother's eye, and backed out again.

The hospital administrator hadn't raised too much of a fuss at the added security. In fact, the dude at the top, a hippy type who seemed to relish the idea they could catch a real criminal on his watch, stopped by every couple of hours when he was on campus, just to check in. He looked like he'd be ready for a rumble too.

Add these folks, the occasional local cop, and additional sheriff's deputies to the myriad staff who wanted to see what was going on, and Noah considered perhaps they should close down and direct people who were seeking services to an urgent care center. It was getting harder to tell the patients from the gawkers.

At the sound of a clumping gait, Noah turned to find Gideon standing at his shoulder, a dense frown tightening his features. Marcus loomed behind him, and Jake approached and completed their tight circle.

"I can't believe he hasn't made a move," Gid said, a frustrated note in his voice. Noah could understand. It had been a long week, made worse by Nicolle's absence. Two off-duty deputies volunteered to cover her trip to the site of the last fire's start. Danielle insisted they hunker down at home when Nicolle wasn't working. If Danielle wasn't with her, another cop was. That made Noah feel marginally better, but it also meant he and Nicolle weren't together. Not a single moment of private time, unless you counted late night phone calls often interrupted by a page for his services in the ER.

"Relax, he'll show eventually. We've made it known Noah's here. The newspaper was very accommodating in running a story on him. If this character is in town, he'll show." Jake checked the display on his cell phone and stepped out of the group.

Marcus nodded at Jake's retreating back. "He's right, you know. Though I swear, every African-American man who comes in those doors is making people nervous. I even caught someone eyeing me funny." He gave a chuckle as if the idea amused him to no end.

"Look, Marcus, I'm sorry. These people aren't prejudice but they also don't always think. You really don't have to be here."

Marcus stared at Noah as if absorbing his words, then shook his head to disagree. "Noah, I do need to be here. As I told you, you aren't in this alone. Besides, I'm looking forward to crushing the little bastard as much as any of you, for what he does as a representative of my race if nothing else." He stalked away, calling out to a nurse for a patient update.

Noah appreciated the sentiment and the support, but the idea of anyone providing enough protection for all of these family and friends didn't make sense. If he stood alone, he only had to worry about himself.

"He's a force of nature," Gideon said, and Noah swung his attention away from his boss to his brother's curious comment.

"Yes, he is that."

"After all of the times you told me what a mentor and role model he is for you, I get it. He is a man to be admired. But then, so are you. I've watched you with patients, people who are scared or hurting or just plain nuts. You give them all dignity and respect as you care for them, and you are the best example of the good, kind doctor he represents."

Noah did a double take to stare more closely at Gideon. Never before had his brother complimented his choice of profession, much less commented specifically on how he performed his duties. As if knowing he'd caught Noah unaware, Gid shrugged and gave a lopsided grin.

"Hey, I know quality when I see it."

"Dr. Kinkead? Did you want to talk with the young woman in six again? Other than that clean break, she isn't complaining about anything else. I've already called ortho. She's still jumpy but she's not talking. The social worker is tied up and will be here as soon as she can."

A young woman of college age had come in crying with her wrist at an odd angle. She refused to say how it happened, though the bruises on her forearm would seem to indicate she'd been mistreated. Her clothes were clean but more suggestive than was common in the area. Her identification said she was nineteen, old enough to be treated without a parent or guardian present. The address listed a central valley town as her home, and it wasn't clear what she was doing in Flynn's Crossing. There wasn't any law stating she had to tell them how it happened. Noah had called for a social worker to talk with her, because something told him she was in trouble.

Now he wanted to delay her discharge a bit, to give the social worker time to come down. If the girl had been attacked, she deserved a chance to discuss it with someone who could help. The guilty party deserved to be caught. Once she had a cast on her wrist, there was no reason for her to stick around.

Gid waved him on his way as the outside doors opened and both their gazes shifted to see who entered. When Noah's eyes fell on Nicolle, he couldn't help the delighted grin that followed.

They had precious minimal time this week to talk, very little privacy when they did, and limited ways to celebrate their new feelings. And yet, with each passing moment, Noah felt they'd grown closer, as if their shared risk made them appreciate their love even more.

When Nicolle's eyes swept the room and landed on him, she smiled too, a softening to her tired face and a glow brightening her eyes. He loved her, the depth of emotion still rocking him like a low punch. No doubt about it, he'd fallen fast and hard, and he didn't plan on fighting it.

He crossed the room and pulled her in for a quick kiss, uncaring about the spectators around them. It seemed a hush fell over the room, or it could be the peace descending on his heart. Things always felt better aligned when she was around.

"Hi," she said, giving him a shy grin.

"Hi yourself." He rested his forehead against hers and wrapped caressing fingers under her braid to massage her neck. It was stiff with tension. Her days were as long as his nights, with no more success than he was having. Both his bad guy and hers stayed hidden.

She pushed back, lifting a hand to trace the lines between his eyebrows. His worry lines, she'd teased, and he admitted he thought they were getting deeper. "If this keeps up, I'll look like a wizen little old man next to your youthful beauty," he'd teased back. She pressed her thumb there now as if to erase them.

"How was your day?" He took her arm and led her down the corridor, away from the waiting room and its multiple sets of curious eyes.

"Long, hot, smoky. The blaze that began two days ago looks like arson, and it should be cool enough tomorrow for an initial assessment. No other new fires, so that's a relief. The summer isn't over yet, though. There are bound to be more started by nature, if not by human intervention." She sighed and put her hand to her back, rubbing low.

He placed his knuckles over the spot and worked at the knots. Maybe when this was over, before the girls returned, they'd take a little vacation, a real one, and he'd treat them to a couples massage. They both needed it.

"That feels incredible." Her eyes fell shut and a blissed-out look came to her face.

"Happy to be of service to a particularly fine firefighter defending our town," he said, dropping his face into the curve of her neck. He felt calm descending on his soul as he held her.

"Excuse me, Doctor." The receptionist stood at the end of the corridor, a sheaf of papers in her hands and an apologetic look on her face. Noah released Nicolle with heavy regrets.

"Yes, Cammy?"

"I'm sorry, Doctor, but the social worker still isn't here. Ortho wants to move Ms. Presley to get her taped up, but I wanted to check with you first to make sure it was okay."

Only one social worker was on call during the night. He hated the idea that someone hurt the girl and she had no one to talk with about it. Ortho would be getting impatient with the delay.

Noah turned to Nicolle, wondering if it was out of bounds to ask it of her. Nicolle returned his steady gaze with growing curiosity, as if she knew something was up. He told her about the girl and his suspicions.

"If she's been attacked, she needs to have the opportunity to talk about it. File charges. Ask for a rape kit to be done if she was violated. She has rights." Nicolle's words became more vehement as they continued.

Noah nodded in agreement. "But the social worker isn't down yet, and the girl needs to have her arm set." He hesitated, trying to read the situation from Nicolle's perspective. The look in her eye was determined. If she didn't want to, Noah had no doubts she'd tell him so.

"Can you come in while I examine her and explain what's going to happen? You might be able to read between the lines on her case. If you think it's appropriate, signal me and I'll leave the room. Maybe she'll feel more comfortable talking with you, woman to woman." He didn't want to add that since she'd been in similar circumstances, she had a better chance than he did of best knowing what to say.

Nicolle threaded her fingers through his and faced him. "Which room?"

He gave her a quick kiss of appreciation, wishing they had more time. When things were resolved, he swore he'd make it up to her, but for now, he turned them down the corridor with Nicolle's pace matching his. They stopped in front of room six.

Its door was closed, which made Noah frown. Perhaps the nurses thought it would make the woman feel more comfortable to have this kind of privacy, but it wasn't protocol. Next to him, Nicolle took a deep breath, and he watched her calm her expression into friendly sympathy. She nodded her readiness. He knocked, and after the space of a few seconds when no answer sounded, pushed the door open.

The curtain strung across the room to block the view of the empty second bed narrowed the space. Ms. Presley sat on the edge of her bed, a warming blanket wrapped around her shoulders and another across her legs. Her eyes darted from Noah to Nicolle and back again, then down at the cold pack wrapping her injured wrist. Her nervousness seemed to have increased since he'd examined her before, but he suspected her pain level had also grown with the passing time.

"Ms. Presley, I'm betting that arm of yours is feeling pretty awful by now. We're going to get you into the orthopedics department where they'll set your wrist and put a cast on it. Then we'll get you some painkillers and send you on your way. Were you able to contact anyone to drive you home?"

The woman's cell phone sat on the bed next to her. She glanced at it before her eyes darted around the room in a wild random pattern. Her agitation was obvious in the jittery beat of her feet against the bed frame and sharp twitches from her body. Noah suspected she was coming down off something, but test results on the blood they'd drawn were also slow to return. He couldn't prescribe anything until he knew what was in her system.

Nicolle stood to the side, her stance casual and unhurried. When the patient glanced at her again, Noah paused in his slow deliberate examination of her arm and said, "This is Nicolle. I know male doctors can sometimes be overwhelming to talk to, so I thought you might like a woman around to discuss how this happened. If you like, I can leave the room and you can talk with her alone."

Ms. Presley yanked her arm back in a move that had to hurt, her eyes widening unnaturally and flashing around the small room. She didn't seem to want to talk with Nicolle, nor did she want Noah to touch her when he reached out to stabilize her arm. At the rate she was thrashing, she'd injure herself even more.

He backed away slowly with his hands raised to make his movements reassuring and stepped to the panel on the wall. Pressing the green button, he leaned against the wall as if ready for a casual conversation. The button would light at the nursing station, and someone would come to assist in case the high this girl was one turned out to be dangerous.

Mirroring his movements, Nicolle also stepped back until she was against the curtain. Noah smiled inside at the thought of how well they worked together as a team. But even with their retreat and attempts at ease, the girl's turmoil escalated further.

Noah concentrated on her, trying to figure out how to encourage her to communicate. They couldn't force her to talk. If she didn't want to reveal the cause of her injury, he'd have to release her from the hospital's care.

A metallic grating sound made by the privacy curtain's hangars moving on their ceiling rail clanged through the room. With it came Nicolle's gasp, probably surprised that she backed into it. The patient's eyes became even larger, her good hand flying to her mouth to cover a parody of a scream. The curtain rattled again, and Noah turned to reassure Nicolle he had this handled.

And realized he didn't.

"Well, lookie here. Doc-man, look what I got here. I got the great equalizer."

Rage stood inside the shadow of the curtain, his arm around Nicolle's windpipe and a black and silver gun pointed sideways at her temple. Noah shot Nicolle a quick glance to find her looking more pissed off than scared.

Shifting on to the balls of his feet, Noah straightened his body but stayed near the wall console. He tried to assess the situation objectively, but despite the many times he'd trained himself to think about a situation like this, he wasn't prepared for the onslaught of feelings brought on by seeing the gun pointed at Nicolle. If his apologies showed on his face, he doubted Nicolle would notice. She appeared to be absorbed by the metal making a dent in her temple.

"So, doc-man, long time no see, eh? Oh, that's right, you haven't seen me. But I've seen you, lots of times. As a matter of fact, I seen those little girls of yours last week too. Little one all pretty in a pink bathing suit, and the big one trying to act all adult-like up in a blue bikini. Going to grow up to be beauties, if you cooperate. Eye for an eye, doc-man. You know how it goes."

Noah's blood froze in his veins, and he saw Nicolle jerk in concern as well. Char's favorite swimsuit was a bright princess pink. The blue two-piece was modest and Noah's only concession to Elena's desire to grow up too quickly. Oh yeah, this guy had seen them all right.

Denial wouldn't work, and neither would blustering his way through apologies and explanations again. Rage hadn't listened at the hospital the night his brother died, and he hadn't listened to reason on the times he'd threatened Noah since. Tonight wouldn't be any different in that regard.

"You realize there are sheriff's deputies covering every entrance and exit, and any disturbance in here will be heard by them. No matter what you choose to do, it won't bring your brother back."

Rage began to laugh, and the sound wasn't pretty. Out of the corner of his eye, Noah noted Ms. Presley wept openly, shaking her head from side to side as if anticipating the worst. She slipped off the bed and huddled on the floor, pulling the blanket up over her head. Only her injured arm was visible as it extended through an opening.

"You know what, doc-man? All that security didn't make a difference when I brought in my girl here. Everyone was so damned busy watching her sashay her tight little ass across that waiting room, all weepy and sexy and shit, that they didn't see me slide in behind her and walk right down this here hallway. Didn't even have to work hard to hide. So much for your big fucking security, doc-man."

Rage yanked his arm around Nicolle's neck. She was now up on her toes as if attempting to ease the pressure to her throat. Too much pressure, and she'd pass out. Noah met her eyes, and her anger seemed to have abated into calculation. She stared back at him as if waiting for him to communicate what they could do to get themselves out of this hellish situation.

"Eyes on me, doc-man, not your pretty little girlfriend here. Oh yeah, I know all about you two. Got to admit, there is something to that whole girl in uniform thing. Tell me, do you play doctor or fireman when you get together, eh?" He said the last words close to Nicolle's ear, and she grimaced in apparent disgust.

Noah kept his eyes steady on Rage, blinking only when necessary. He forced calm he was far from feeling into his voice. "What do you want?"

Rage laughed again, the sound becoming more maniacal. "That gimpy brother of yours, call him in here. Say goodbye to him, we take care of business, then I leave you alone. Eye for an eye."

He noted Nicolle's sudden frantic blinking as if to get his attention. She might have tried to shake her head, but the grip on her was too tight. Rage cackled again as he jerked her hard. "None of that, bitch. Otherwise you end up worse than that bitch on the floor."

Noah shook his head to dissuade Nicolle from doing anything that could make her situation more deadly. He had no doubt the gun was loaded and Rage would have no trouble pulling the trigger. The man had killed before.

Everyone froze when a knock sounded on the door. "Yes, Doctor?"

As if in warning, Rage shoved the gun barrel harder against Nicolle's head above her ear. Noah didn't want to think about the potential for damage. Not a hair on Nicolle's head would be harmed, not while he was in the room. He worked to steady his pulse and his tone.

Raising his voice to be heard by the nurse outside, he said, "Could you please page Doctors Armstrong and Silver for me, please? I'd like to get Ms. Presley casted and discharged as soon as possible. Thank you."

To her credit, the nurse's voice didn't waver as she said, "Of course, Doctor, right away."

Nicolle looked at him as if he'd lost his marbles. Maybe he had. If he waited for help to arrive, there was every possibility one or more of them would suffer multiple GSWs, and blood would coat the tan lincleum floor.

Rage's weird laugh rang through the room once more. "Discharge? Discharge? You wanna see a discharge, doc-man? How about I discharge into one of these bitches here? Or maybe into you?"

He shoved Nicolle to the floor to land next to Ms. Presley. A grunt as her knees hit the hard surface mixed with a sob from the patient. Noah kept his eyes on the gun now aimed at his chest, prepared to throw his body between the bullets and the women if necessary.

Time seemed to have slowed. Seconds took minutes to pass, until it felt like the maniac's laugh came in single prolonged notes. In a brief glance to Nicolle, he read the concern in her eyes, the tight lines of her face making her look older than her years. He wanted to see her grow old in real time, and he wanted to be next to her to enjoy it. The six feet separating them could have been an ocean.

His skin felt too tight and his hands clenched in empty frustration. He had no weapon in the room, unless he attempted to swing an empty IV pole or a monitor stand. Neither would be subtle, not like a scalpel or syringe would have been. Even if he kicked the gun from Rage's grip, he would risk the weapon firing when the man jerked in reaction. In a small space like this, a deadly ricochet wouldn't be out of the realm of possibility.

Calculation of speed and trajectory wasn't conscious. Noah had spent hours kicking a bag, hitting a specific tiny spot repeatedly until he could do it without thinking. He knew how hard, how far, and how lethal his delivery could be, but that was on a bag in a gym, an inanimate object. He was dealing with a gun-toting lunatic bent on misplaced revenge.

A firm knock on the door froze all of them.

"Yes?" Noah maintained a professional tone, as if this was business as usual. Nothing about this was normal. Hopefully, Rage had no clue about what would unfold.

On the floor, Nicolle attempted to wiggle into a better position. From his angle, Noah could see no way for her to get her feet under her without alerting the man with the gun. His woman's eyes flashed at him in frustration as if she too realized her predicament. He hoped his look reassured her. He would find a way to get her out of this unscathed.

He had lesser hopes for himself.

"Doctor Kinkead? I wanted to confirm that you were requesting Doctor Silver. Is that correct, sir?"

Jake's voice held a hint of boredom, as if this was an everyday occurrence. Noah knew how much urgency would now be evident in the emergency department. Security would be clearing the waiting room. Patients were being hustled away. Those who were too unstable to transfer would be locked down in treatment rooms with staff surrounding them. Sheriff's deputies would be planning how they would proceed to neutralize the threat.

All because Noah had sent his SOS. Doctor Armstrong – a threat that required security. Doctor Silver – a threat with a gun.

Understanding had dawned on Nicolle's face when his gaze next swept the room in a continuous circle. Jake's presence and his casual question alerted her. As if in response to his silent wishes, she curled to make herself smaller and tucked part of her body in with the patient, her braid dangling over her shoulder and brushing the floor as she crouched low.

At least she was marginally safer. The women were out of a direct line of fire between the doorway and Rage. Noah, on the other hand, wasn't so lucky. Exposed by the door's opening swing, if anyone came in firing, he'd be the first one hit. Rage could wreak havoc behind the relative protection of the barrier. Despite his ranting, the man's gun didn't waver from its aim at Noah's chest.

"You know what, doc-man? I was gonna do your bro like you did mine. Make you suffer like me, watching him die. Eye for an eye. Now I'm gonna shoot this bitch of yours instead. Gonna like watching all that blood flow, doc-man. How about you?"

Anger surged through Noah with cold precision. He shoved off the wall with one foot and propelled himself into Rage's chest with an extended elbow, grabbing the arm holding the gun and aiming it upward. The guy was probably high and unnaturally strong as a result, but Noah's fury drove him harder. The gun discharged into the ceiling, bringing a round of curses from outside the door. He noted the door's rapid inward swing out of the corner of his eye, but he couldn't pause to determine who entered.

Rage stayed on his feet, the gun still in his hand in a grip Noah wrenched to break. This time, the bullet pinged against metal and glass, and lights flickered out. Rage knocked Noah to the side in the darkness, and the buzz of emergency lights flickering on came with the blast of another bullet.

"Noah?" Nicolle's worried voice came from the floor and it sounded like she'd moved to the end of the bed. Rage's crazy laugh came next. As new illumination glowed from the warming emergency light, Noah saw the man aim at the dark shadow he took to be her body.

He acted on fury and instinct, kicking out with more force than he had ever used. The contact of his foot on ribs jarred his leg, but he welcomed the extra adrenalin that came with the surge of pain. Harnessing that power, he launched his shoulder toward the hand holding the gun, and crashed both of them into the empty bed on the other side of the curtain. Trapped in the fabric, he kept punching and kicking until he heard nothing more from the man under his fists.

"Noah, I've got this."

"Shit, Noah, you're bleeding."

"Stop, Noah. Stop."

The voices in sequence, Jake, Marcus, and Nicolle, finally penetrated the flood of fight hormones coursing through his system. His fists stopped pumping, and in detached observation, he noted blood staining the white curtain. Hands lifted him to legs made shaky in sudden reaction. He fell back and landed on bodies struggling to support his weight.

"Where are you hit?" Marcus's face appeared in his view, rapidly moving hands over Noah's frame.

The sound of groans came to him next, and he turned toward the noises. Jake had Rage laid out on his bloodied face, pinning his arms behind him as he fastened handcuffs on his wrists. To the side, Gideon held Rage's gun dangling from two fingers extended far from his body as if he didn't want to come closer to it than necessary.

But it was Nicolle Noah wanted to see. He needed to know she was okay. Had she been injured in the chaos? Bullets could do damage even after two or three rebounds.

Her face appeared in front of his, and her hands landed on his cheeks a second later. Tears ran down her face and she bit her lip. He thought the tremulous smile she gave him was brighter than the sun, and the most beautiful thing he'd ever seen.

He struggled to lift hands that would not cooperate to cover hers, and said, "Are you okay?"

She nodded vigorously. Her lips opened as if she wanted to say something, but she sobbed instead and yanked him in. The urgency in her kiss provided more reassurance than her words alone would have.

Against his mouth, she said, "My hero. You were amazing. I love you."

Two deputies dragged Rage to his feet, one reading him his rights as they pulled him out of the room. Jake followed, reporting into the mic on his shoulder that they'd apprehended him. At the door, he stopped and looked back, giving him a jaunty salute. Noah's elation bounced around as those bullets had, and he fought the urge to giggle.

A poke in his shoulder began to bring things back into perspective. He turned in time to see Marcus cut the sleeve off his shirt and raise a swab of disinfectant to torn skin. The big man's pearly grin glowed in his dark face.

"Now, this is going to sting a bit."

Damn, it did, and more than a bit. He'd never use that line again. Noah felt Nicolle's head on his other shoulder, her arms wrapped around him as if holding him up.

All of them turned when a fierce voice sounded from under the bed.

"Did you kill the bastard? I hope you did. He broke my arm." And Ms. Presley began to cry in earnest.

Chapter 31

Hustling into a clean exam room, Marcus insisted on attending to the injury himself, and Noah gave him credit. Perfect, neat stitches from the bullet that grazed him would barely leave a scar on his arm. Those big hands could work little miracles.

Statements took time too, as sheriff's deputies flooded the emergency department. Danielle barreled into the exam room with shouts sending her deputies scattering. When the door closed on them, her bluster deflated and she grabbed Nicolle and hung on to her for a long time.

And finally, when Noah had been given another shot of antibiotics, a sling to immobilize his arm, and aftercare orders, he'd argued with Marcus about taking the following week off.

"You need to heal, and you might want to talk to someone. This was a trauma, you know."

Noah shook his head to disagree, then flashed back to the fear he felt when the gun pressed against Nicolle's temple. Instead of arguing further, he wrapped his good arm around his woman and nodded. Marcus gave a satisfied smile and waved them out the emergency department's double doors. Even with this threat eliminated, Noah doubted things inside the department or his heart would return to any semblance of normal for quite some time.

"You should be resting."

"It's a scratch." They'd had this conversation repeatedly in the past hours.

Resting easy had been the last thing on his mind when he finally got Nicolle home and alone midday after the attack. Her insistence on a shower had been an excellent idea with the waterproof bandage wrapping his arm. She was damned inventive when they made it to bed, and afterwards, they fell into an exhausted sleep that lasted until the early hours of morning. With a satisfied grin, he remembered how they started all over again.

Their escape from reality lasted until almost noon, when his cell phone chimed with Elena's designated ring. After everything that happened, he needed to hear his child's voice no matter what the message. He dropped his fork into the half-eaten plate of eggs and nearly tripped over Nicolle's feet in an effort to pick up immediately.

"Hi Elena. How are you?"

Silence first greeted his words. Then he heard a quick intake of breath.

"Daddy?"

His heart stuttered. The word alone sent a message about the depth of her anguish.

"Sweetheart, what's wrong?" He tried to listen for background noises as an indication of where she was.

"I hate LA, Daddy."

That was a first.

"What happening? What's wrong? Where's your mother?"

A sob and a sniffle sounded through the line. "She's off buying Char some stuff. I didn't want to go. I don't want anything here." Another wet sniffle.

Elena always wanted to go shopping. It had appeared to be her all-time favorite sport, closely followed by fixating on the latest boy band.

Noah looked at Nicolle, who motioned she would leave the room. He waved her back into her chair and moved to the table to settle next to her.

"Wow, the shopping malls might have to close down," he said, putting a teasing note into his voice. A watery chuckle from the other end rewarded him.

"Father, don't be silly." But she chuckled again, and this time, the sniff was more of disapproval than tears.

"What are you doing?" When was the last time his older daughter asked anything about him? His eyes settled on Nicolle, who shook her head with a frenzy that sent her long hair dancing around her shoulders.

"Ah, nothing new. Tell me what's going on there."

Silence. He sometimes forgot she was soon turning thirteen and her hormones were already raging. The rapid shifts in mood were not yet something he was used to. He hoped Nicolle could weather them better than he would over the coming months. How would he explain this latest turn of events to his daughters?

But that worry fled when Elena burst into tears once more.

>>>>>

Nici leaned away from the table, trying to give Noah and his daughter some privacy for what was clearly an emotional moment. She could hear the girl's sobs even as Noah pressed the phone tight to his ear, as if to reduce their distance. The child's voice rang out loudly enough for her to hear the conversation too.

He was a wonderful father. Nicolle could tell that by his devotion to his daughters at the expense of personal time and his concentration on whatever crisis the girl suffered. His pain at their separation made his face solemn and tight. He raked a hand through his hair in apparent frustration, wincing when the stitches in his arm pulled against the movement.

"I'll stay on the phone with you as long as you want, sweetie. No, don't worry. I love you, and nothing in the world is more important to me than your happiness, yours and Char's."

A gut-jarring tension gripped her with his words. Her brain understood. This was his daughter, and she deserved his unfettered love and commitment.

But her heart wasn't used to this, not yet, if it ever would be. Nici didn't want to have expectations of this fledgling relationship, even as she recognized she already did. Noah didn't know everything about her. He deserved to have a woman who was whole, and she could never be that woman.

"Elena, are you sure you're okay now? Because I can stay on. We can wait for your mother, and we'll all talk together."

His patience, the calm tone, and the love shining on his face made Nicolle sigh in regret. She shouldn't be here for this intimate moment. His daughter deserved his undivided attention.

But when she tried to stand, his hand clamped on to her thigh and held her in place with a strength that belied the injury to his arm. He frowned at her, even as his soothing words continued. Shaking his head, he squeezed her thigh again, and she dropped back into her seat. His brief smile as he removed his hand telegraphed his relief.

"Call me later when we can all talk about it, okay? Or I can call your mother tonight. It's your choice."

He nodded at whatever the girl said. More reassurances.

He said, "I love you, Elena. We'll talk later. We'll work this out, I promise." He disconnected the call.

Not even a second passed by before he swung to her and frowned. "What's happening? What's wrong?" The demand and worry in his voice spoke louder than his strained low volume.

No transition. No desire to discuss what was happening with his daughter. Right for the heart of things, and with the same words he'd used moments before. Nici wondered if he ever got tired of dealing with excitable females.

His hand returned to her thigh and he turned her chair to face him nose to nose. The anger in his eyes made her reconsider blowing this off with a teasing comment.

Her eyes fell to her hands, her fingers twisting in her lap. Her tell. She knew it. Noah probably recognized it. His fingers closed over hers in a quick movement, but his grip was gentle.

"Nicolle? Why didn't you want me to tell Elena about you? I want my girls to enjoy knowing you as much as I do."

One hand moved to her chin, tilting her head up until the only way she could avoid his eyes would be to close hers. She couldn't delay this conversation any longer.

"You love your children very much."

He nodded, puzzled confusion on his features. "I love you too, Nicolle. Where did you think you were going?"

"I wanted to give you some privacy, so you and Elena could talk without me listening in."

He shook his head, the confusion more evident. "Thank you, but I didn't feel like you were intruding. I would have moved myself if I thought it wasn't appropriate." He leaned forward to give her a lingering kiss, the kind that made her lips feel like flames. When he moved away, she swore she heard a pop and sizzle.

"What is this about?" His voice was tender and worried, and as she tried to back up, he drew her in closer.

Nicolle tried to meet his gaze with honest openness, but her heart wanted to protect itself. Every strong breath he took as she continued to hesitate wafted across her cheeks. Her lids dropped enough to filter his face through her lashes, giving her somewhere to hide.

"You have your girls, Noah. When they get back, they'll need all of your time and energy, and that's what they should have." He started to speak, and she shushed him. "They are your children, and they deserve to have a full time father."

If he was confused before, now he looked completely perplexed. "And?"

She pulled her hands out of his and waved them in the air. "And, they need you."

Concern retreated in his expression and a grin turned up one side of his mouth. "Oh, I'm not letting you get away, not easily and not at all."

She frowned at the sudden good humor in his voice. "Noah, you're not listening to reason."

He gave her a kiss that surprised her in its quickness. The man could strike like a rattler when he wanted to. When he sat back in his chair, his grin widened to a full smile, making the lines at the corners of his eyes crinkle.

"I am being all kinds of reasonable." He leaned in close, his nose inches from hers and the depths of his blue eyes darkening. "I love you, Nicolle Trajan. I hope my girls love you too. Char's easy, since she already thinks you look like fun. Elena doesn't like anyone right now, but she'll come around in her own time."

She frowned this time. "Why would Char think I'm fun? And what if Elena doesn't come around?"

He laughed this time, a deep chord that made parts of her zing with renewed energy. She would miss his laugh. She would miss his caring nature. She would miss everything about him. The depth of her impending misery exhausted her.

"You don't need to worry about the girls. Allow me to repeat myself. I love you, and I'd like us to keep exploring where this takes us. Though I have to admit, I'm sure I'm further down the road of commitment than you are. Open book, Nicolle. That's what I always want to be with you. And that includes sharing my girls and my future."

The thud in her ears from her racing pulse made it hard to hear his words. The rapid beating of her heart should be something he could see, because it hurt in her chest like it wanted to break out and reach for him. There was only one thing she could do.

"Open book? Everything?"

He grinned and nodded vigorously.

She wouldn't allow herself to hesitate. "I can't have children."

>>>>>

The flat tone of her voice warred with the crushed expression on her face. Noah heard the words, his brain processing each letter and trying to make sense of them. The longer he delayed speaking, the more destroyed she looked, until he forced himself to say something, anything, to filled his stunned silence.

"Why?"

He kicked himself almost immediately for the stupid question. He tried to reach for her hands to pull her nearer, but she slipped out of the chair and wrapped her arms around her middle. When she paced away from him, he felt like he was losing her.

"I'm sorry. That was inappropriate. What I meant to say was – "

She fluttered a dismissive wave, keeping her back to him. "I know. It's not what guys want to hear. That's why I didn't want us to have any expectations or get too attached. But you and I zoomed along and I never had the courage to tell you. I'm sorry. That's why I think it's best if we go our separate ways. You deserve a big family, Noah. You're a great dad." She headed for the living room at a trot.

No. Hell no. He sprang out of the chair, uncaring when it bounced off the fridge and hit a cabinet. He caught up with her as she snagged her purse off the floor by the front door, his hand closing over hers on the knob she had already turned. "We need to talk."

She shook her head, and when her waterfall of hair swung away from her face, he saw she was crying. It broke him. He executed a clench that would have made his martial arts instructor cheer and hauled Nicolle over his shoulder. If there was pain in his arm from the process, the fear and ache in his heart masked it.

"What the hell?" She burst out the exclamation, hanging like a stunned doll as he climbed the stairs and dumped her on his bed. Without pausing, he had her pinned, her purse scattered to one side and her hair in a wild mess around her face. When she spit out a strand, she stared up at him in disbelief.

He felt the sting of arousal run through him, but he forced it down. She deserved a chance to tell him what happened before he showed her it didn't matter. He could be honest and tell her he'd already fantasized about a little girl or boy that looked like the best of her and some of him. A younger sibling for his daughters. Evidence of the love he had for Nicolle and the kind he suspected she had for him, if she just let herself act on it. But he loved her without a shared child too.

"I love you," he said, happy to hear his voice sounded more level than he felt.

She pleaded with him. "I love you too, but don't you see, that's why – "

He cut her off, because he didn't want to hear her faulty reasoning. They loved each other, and that took a backseat to his fantasies. "Tell me what happened."

She looked away. "Did anyone ever tell you that you move faster than a snake when you want to?"

He laughed at the change of subject, and his body relaxed. Somehow, this would be okay. He released her hands and moved off her body, coming to rest next to her with a hand on her heart. Its beat was fast and strong, like the woman. Reaching over, he placed the gentlest of kisses and felt her quiet sob like a breeze on his lips.

"You aren't going to like hearing this."

He examined her dejected expression. "I know that because I can see how much grief it causes you. But it's part of you, and I want to know everything about you. Open and honest, Nicolle. No secrets. We can do this."

She shook her head as if she was going to disagree with him again, but instead, she gave a deep sigh and turned on her side to face him. Her fingers intertwined with his.

"It was Mitchell. The rape. We'd been in the field for days, under less than sanitary conditions. Topping that, Mitchell had a sexually transmitted infection. I didn't have any symptoms to begin with, but then, I started to have problems."

Noah knew where he wanted to vent his rage. Beating the man's face to pulp after kicking his privates up into his intestines would be a good start.

"What kind of infection?"

She hesitated, told him in stuttering words, and followed with, "That's why I get checked so frequently, because I'm always worried it will come back. The doctors assure me it won't, but I still worry. I'm sorry, I should have insisted we always use protection."

"How long have the test results been negative?"

"Over two years. But now you understand. I can't keep seeing you because someday, you'll find a woman who can give you more kids. The infection spread far enough in me to ensure I never can. And what if the infection comes back and I hurt you?"

He wasn't sure whether he should laugh or cry. Her earnest concern for his future sex life was endearing, even though he could already tell her there wouldn't be anyone in his future but her. It was also clear she mourned the fact she couldn't have children of her own. That complex side effect of sexually transmitted diseases was more common than most people wanted to believe.

He leaned forward, resting his forehead against hers while maintaining eye contact. He wanted her to hear him without any doubts about his sincerity.

"Now I understand, Nicolle. I understand this hurt is something you bottle up inside and probably few people know about, because that's the kind of person you are. You don't want sympathy or pity, or a break, or anything other than a level playing field. I appreciate that. And I can't see you without having sex, because god knows, you are one hell of a sexy woman and I can't help making love to you. Now understand this."

He reached out and brought their bodies flush, and the warmth flooding through him at her closeness was better than any rush from the ER or the ring. Other than the birth of his daughters and the constant surprises they brought to his life, he didn't have anything to compare it to. He put his lips over hers in a gentle kiss.

"I love you, and you aren't going to scare me away. I have two beautiful daughters to share with you, and they're going to come to mean everything to you and you to them. As long as I have you beside me, I have everything I want or need."

He kissed her, smiling as he did so to swallow her protest in one fast bite. She shoved at him, pushing herself away. Her panting gasps made him smile wider.

"But what? Why? Noah, you could do so much better than me."

He gave an exaggerated sigh of exasperation. "No one is better medicine for me than you, Nicolle. I know this without any doubts. I'm a doctor, so you have to trust me. Now quit talking and kiss me."

Uncertainty still raced across her features, even as she leaned in closer. "Are you sure?"

He tweaked a lock of her hair. "Madame, I took an oath. You have to believe me."

Her eyes narrowed with a slight frown. "Which oath is that?"

He closed the distance between them. "The one where I say I love you."

This time, her smile challenged his in brilliance as she reached for him.

Chapter 32

Despite his best attempts to distract her, Nicolle remained adamant about returning to work. Since Noah had nowhere he had to be until his arm healed, he appointed himself her personal protection detail. She protested, but he saw the secret delighted smile fill her face as she turned away from his stern assertion. The next day, her mood shifted to melancholy as they drove through burnt forest.

From the driver's seat, Nicolle said, "I don't believe it's Mitchell."

Noah's eyes drifted from the smoky road to her averted face. "We know it wasn't Rage. His actions were all about revenge. Danielle said his reaction to our assumption that he would hire an arsonist didn't even register a blip on her radar. He didn't start any fires."

Nicolle's face fell into a more troubled frown as she stayed silent. Noah paused as the next option occurred to him and swung around in his seat, the bite of stitches nothing compared to the pain of the idea. "You can't still think it could be Gideon."

Nicolle shook her head, but he didn't think she appeared certain. He barreled out the words as disappointment surged. "How could he have started the last fires? He can't drive."

She braked the truck with a jerk that had him propping a hand on the dash. When she turned to him, she put out a placating palm.

"Look, not even Dani really believes he's guilty anymore." She stammered to a stop.

His voice dropped with cold tension gripping his gut. "Not even? Anymore? What aren't you telling me?"

Her eyes pleaded as both palms extended to him. "You have to understand Dani's point of view. She's a cop, and she's trained to gather the evidence and draw conclusions from it. The only fingerprints on the notes are Gideon's. Granted, that's circumstantial and there's a good reason for them, but there's no tangible sign of another guy except for these written threats. Anyone could have written them."

The unspoken words hung in the truck cab. Gideon could have written them himself.

"So how does the lieutenant think Gid got to the fires?" He heard the rasp of pained disbelief in his voice but could do nothing to calm it. His brother couldn't be the source of these fires. But then again, things had changed for him last year, and Noah wasn't sure he knew the man he was today as well as he should. Gideon harbored secrets.

Nicolle withdrew her hands and examined her fingers before twisting them together. "An accomplice, or driving with his left foot. Noah, she doesn't want to think he could do it, but she's a cop."

He turned to stare at the damaged forest around them. Damaged, as Gid could be. No, that could not be an option.

"What about the last fire? There is no way Gid could have started it. He and Danielle were together."

Nicolle faced forward and put the truck in drive. Her fingers showed stark white against the black plastic steering wheel. "It was ruled natural causes, a probable lightning strike." Her expression in profile remained troubled.

Noah felt ripped in two. The woman he loved or his brother? He didn't want to be forced into a choice, because either option was a higher price than he was willing to pay.

Softening his voice, he said, "Let's hope this one was manmade. Gid had no opportunity to go anywhere, not while he babysat me twenty-four-seven."

She nodded, but misery made her features tense. He reached across the cab and squeezed her shoulder. "Don't worry. We're okay, you and me. We'll all get through this."

Her frown deepened, which only increased the tension he felt. She said, "Noah, what if it comes down to believing your brother or my sister? It might a choice you have to make. Things are so complicated, and you deserve more."

He laughed, though it wasn't humor he felt. "Stop the truck."

"What?" Her foot came off the accelerator.

"Pull over, and I'll show you just how much more I have for you. Hell, Nicolle, I'm a doctor. I thrive on complicated. You and I love each other. Our meddling siblings will have to figure things out on their own."

Their speed increased again as she chuckled, and a lightness Noah hadn't experienced over the last few tense days made him join in. Things might be crazy around them, but he and Nicolle would be better than good.

Her chuckles faded along with her grin as they passed into an area where smoldering remains of trees stood close to the road on either side. She said, "You don't need to come with me. I doubt Mitchell is lurking at the scene of his latest inferno, if it was even him."

He didn't say anything, enjoying her profile despite the slight frown on her face. Her expressions chased across her features with an ease Noah had come to appreciate. She didn't hold back like her sister did. When she was upset, he knew it. A happy Nicolle challenged the radiance of the sun.

She glanced over and did a double take. "What are you smiling at?"

He continued to stare, noting the blush rising from the neck of her regulation uniform shirt as if she guessed.

"Oh, nothing. Enjoying the beautiful scenery."

She grumbled in response and waved a hand out the windshield. "What scenery?" She slowed the truck at the entrance to the restricted area around the fire camp and glanced at him. Her grim expression lightened, and she reached a hand out to squeeze his arm.

Just that touch was enough to make his body heat up like the brush must have before it torched to the skies. Like he did, whenever they were alone. He'd have to put a lock on the bedroom door once the girls were used to Nicolle being around all the time. He planned to have her around forever, if she'd only agree.

"You should be getting ready for the girls to come home on Wednesday," she said as she pulled back.

"I'm already prepared, because I never put anything away. I never had a chance. I cleaned up Gideon's stuff, dropped it off with him, and made a list of what we need to stock the fridge. Are you always going to argue with me?"

She chuckled. "I'm not arguing. I'm merely pointing out that you have other more pressing things to do today than babysitting me. I'm be fine, Noah. Picky Peter will be with me."

The nickname did not inspire confidence, and Noah wanted to make sure someone had her back. The incident meteorologist scheduled to accompany her into the field wanted to examine the area for signs of weather forces that fanned the fire faster than it should have spread. He didn't trust him to watch out for his woman, not when the unknown man had another agenda.

His woman. He was used to that phrase already. If he could only convince her it was true.

"Are you worried about the girls coming home?" He asked the question with offhand neutrality, suspecting he already knew the answer.

"Not worried so much as missing you already. Once they get home, they deserve to have you all to themselves. You know, to reconnect and adjust."

He sighed. "It will be fine. Yes, there will be a period of adjustment for all four of us. Gideon and Danielle too. But I'm not letting you slip any distance away."

The quick flash of her happy grin gave him a surge of energy. He'd do anything he could to keep a smile on his girls' faces, all three of them. One major thing hung over his lovely fire investigator's happiness.

"I wish he'd show himself so we could catch him," Nicolle said.

"Amen to that."

Twenty minutes later, Noah road shotgun in a fire service truck. In the back seat, Picky Peter, clearly not a Pete kind of guy, tapped away on his tablet computer and mumbled to himself. A couple of times, Noah thought the man made an attempt at conversation, and he said, "I'm sorry, I didn't get that, Peter." No response.

Nicolle reached across the larger space between them and patted his hand. "He mutters to himself all the time. It drove us crazy at the beginning, until we realized that's the way he is. He doesn't hear himself, and he won't hear you when he's like this. He'll pop up with a comment soon and you'll know he's back among the land of the living."

They drove up a narrow road made bumpier by scorched asphalt and downed branches. All bore signs of charring, with melt marks on the edges of what was once a single lane street. The higher they climbed, the harder it became for Noah to look at the signs of destruction. Trees sixty feet or taller with scars up their trunks. Little left along the ground smaller around than his arm. No sign of anything green. No signs of animals or birds.

"It is eerie," Nicolle said, reading his thoughts as she swerved to avoid a larger fallen trunk. The road became gravel, exaggerating the lurching movements of the truck. Noah braced himself on the dash, feeling the sweat roll down under his shirt. Turnout coats and hard hats were something

Cap mandated. Noah had accepted the pants as well, given that he didn't know what he was getting himself into. He was grateful Nicolle warned him about bringing heavy-soled boots. Peter grumbled about the coat with a sniff of dissatisfaction and said his jeans and loafers would be adequate. She'd whispered into his ear, "Now you see why we call him Picky Peter."

All the more reason to be by her side. Anywhere else, he'd worry.

A particularly uneven section of the road made the truck shimmy, and Nicolle cursed softly. Her attention focused on the drive, and Noah didn't want to distract her. But she looked damned hot in her gear, and he grinned to himself when he thought about ways he could show her that later. The idea of playing doctor and firefighter was growing on him.

"Well all right then. Where are we?"

The voice from the back made Noah jump. He was so focused on his thoughts about Nicolle, he'd forgotten Peter was with them.

"About two more minutes. GPS says the cabin should be coming into view."

Noah peered through the hazy air, trying to make out structures. If there had been a cabin, it was long gone. When they were almost on top of it, Noah could make out blocks in the form of two rectangles wedged together.

Putting the truck in park and turning off the ignition, Nicolle said, "There it is." She reached for a camera and clicked off a few pictures before opening her door. Noah did the same, careful to step where she did as he followed her toward the old foundation.

Behind them, the creak of Peter pushing open his door drew Noah's attention. The man pulled out a handkerchief to cover his face. Its pristine white folds below his glasses made him look like a bandit wannabe. He shed the turnout coat next. When he tossed the hardhat back into the truck, Noah shook his head in disbelief and turned his attention back to Nicolle.

How she could step so lightly in her thick boots, he wasn't sure. Her moves when they sparred had been studied, but here in her element, they were like a dance. With a long metal stick in her hand, she turned over pieces of debris and snapped more shots. She bent low to examine something on the ground, clicking off pictures in quick succession with the addition of the flash.

He must have stayed still for too long, because she glanced in his direction as she stood. Whatever expression had been coming to her face froze in place as her body went rigid.

Picky Peter was about to get his, Noah mused. Nicolle would feel responsible for him in the field, and he ignored orders and common sense by shedding his protective gear. Turning to see what the meteorologist was now up to, Noah identified the real reason for Nicolle's sudden stillness.

A large form in worn turnouts stood behind Peter, the face obscured by the shield dropped down on the helmet. An arm wrapped around the small man's neck and lifted him, knocking his glasses askew as the handkerchief rose with the pressure. Peter kicked back ineffectually, while his attacker laughed in a deep rumbling voice. The sound echoed in the empty forest, evil in every note. On instinct, Noah moved to put himself between this intruder and Nicolle.

"Put him down, Mitchell." Nicolle's voice also echoed, sounding disembodied but steady. Noah wasn't sure where he should look, behind him to assure himself of her safe whereabouts, or at Mitchell and Peter. One of the meteorologist's kicks hit his tablet, lying face down in ash. Its blue case mocked them with its bright color in the otherwise barren landscape.

The big man lifted the shield to reveal eyes wide in madness and an insane grin. "Why Trajan, you look hot as ever. I knew you'd be glad to see me. Bet no one ever gave you a good time like I did." Mitchell laughed and gave Peter another tug off to lift his feet off the forest floor.

Noah felt the tension climb his spine and settle with a heavy beat at the back of his neck. He pushed down the rage the man's words caused. Nicolle didn't need him blurry with anger. She needed him focused and calm and ready to attack.

A rustle he missed in trying to manage his emotions grabbed his attention, and Nicolle appeared in his peripheral vision. Her camera lay cradled in her hand pointed at the two men across the clearing. An occasional click might have sounded from it, but Noah couldn't be sure. His eyes swung back to Mitchell. If the man strayed so much as an inch toward Nicolle, Noah would be on his throat in a second.

But the parolee made no attempt to move, only jerking Peter periodically and laughing in that maniacal way of his when feet swung in frantic arcs in response. The glasses were gone now, probably crushed under boots that looked like they belonged on King Kong. Noah no longer wondered how the man got the drop on Nicolle. He was the size of a tree, and being blindsided by him would be comparable to having one of the giants around them fall on their heads.

"Let him go. Peter didn't do anything to you." Nicolle issued the words in a soft but commanding tone, one Noah could appreciate. He often used the same to talk with a difficult patient.

"Ah, come on Nici baby, where's the fun in that? You think the last time was a cluster fuck of blame? Wait until you see how this is going to play out."

"Get in the truck. Lock the doors. Get on the radio." Nicolle's instructions came to Noah in rapid fire under her breath.

"Not a chance in hell," Noah replied with as much cheer as he could manage. He heard Nicolle inhale to argue with him, but she never had the chance.

Not that great a distance divided them. Nicolle was an arm's length off his left side. He could push her behind him, given the need. Peter was a different story. Besides being held captive by a lunatic, he was a good forty feet away. Based on his expression, a panic attack held him in its grip as well. Noah could read the signs but it was more important what he heard.

He and Nicolle stopped breathing at the same moment, when the lighter in Mitchell's hands flicked to life with a click loud enough to echo by itself. A stick hung from a loop in his pants' side, and he set the lighter to the rags bound around its end. This time, his cackle rose to a higher pitch, as if feeding the flames also fed his insanity.

Noah had one thought. There was nothing left to burn. Scorched ground would yield no fuel. Treetops above them were too tall. Then he realized Mitchell had none of those things in mind.

With a single arm swing, Mitchell spun the meteorologist's body in front of him and dropped the torch to strike against unprotected denim. He threw the man away as soon as the fabric caught and tossed the torch after him as if he was playing with paper matches.

Nicolle yelled something indistinguishable and furious, already running to where Peter had landed. Fire climbed his jeans, and screams that Noah knew he'd hear in nightmares sounded new echoes. Mitchell stepped back and cackled, his arms crossed in a posture of relaxed enjoyment. Noah had a moment of indecision. Help the burned man, or take down the evil one?

Nicolle thought faster than he did. She had her coat off and slapped it on Peter, yelling at the man to hold still. Noah slipped his arms out of his and followed, realizing in a split second that they both would have their backs to the devil incarnate. Throwing the coat at Nicolle, he turned to face their attacker.

Mitchell drew closer, absorbed in the fire and staring at Nicolle with rabid hunger. His eyes ran up and down her body as if remembering everything and planning to do it all again. The sick enjoyment on the crazy man's face made Noah's logical thinking short-circuit.

With a silent spring, Noah jumped across the distance between them feet first, landing with his full force on Mitchell's chest. The big man woofed out a grunt of surprise as he went down, with Noah sprawling past him in a pile of debris. Something punctured his palm and he yanked it out without looking to see what it was. He palmed the sharp item and shoved it into his pocket, in case he needed an advantage. Unfair or not, he'd take what he could find.

As if her voice came from a great distance, he heard Nicolle saying, "No, Noah, don't. He'll hurt you." Then Peter gave a weak cry and Noah heard Nicolle murmur something. He didn't dare look, keeping his eyes on Mitchell as he rose from the ashes.

For his size, he moved fast, and he was on his feet and leaping at Noah within seconds. He let out a roar like a predator deprived of its prey, and his hands aimed for Noah's throat.

Training turned decisions into microseconds. Noah judged the distance to his opponent and calculated the placement he needed for maximum effect. Hitting the bag in the gym was nothing like hitting a moving mountain of a man. But he was never this inspired or angry in the gym's sterile environment.

His first kick landed inside the right arm near the elbow, with the edge of his boot striking as close to where he wanted it as he could have hoped. Mitchell grunted and paused, his arm falling to his side. He looked down at it as if he didn't understand what had happened. When he raised his eyes again, all hint of crazed humor was gone.

"You broke my arm, you fucker."

Noah stayed where he was, stilling his body and lifting on the balls of his feet once more. He doubted this injury would be enough to stop the man. He said, "It's not broken, though it will be a while before you can use it. I'm a doctor. Why don't you sit down and we'll discuss how best to avoid a long term problem?"

The seconds of confusion were fun to watch, before anger and probable pain took over. Mitchell charged again, one arm out this time, and Noah lifted his foot and struck again. This time, he had the pleasure of hearing a distinct pop as his heel collided with the side of Mitchell's left knee, crumbling him to the ground. He jumped back to put himself out of reach.

Over Mitchell's head, Nicolle watched with her mouth open. Peter writhed on the ground next to her and reached out a blackened hand to grab at her arm, dragging her attention his way. She rose and headed for the truck, and Noah remembered they needed to contact the base. Others could take care of Mitchell now. He wasn't going anywhere. But Peter needed his assessment and any immediate aid he could provide.

He took careful steps around the big man on the ground, his concentration focused on Peter as the man let out a new shriek louder than the last, followed by wrenching sobs. Noah moved faster, his mind already on initial burn protocols using what they had to work with in the vehicle.

He didn't see the hand flash out to grab his ankle, taking him down as his body continued forward off balance. He didn't have time to center himself, because his momentum shot him toward Mitchell. The big man's injured leg was at an odd angle and the opposite arm still hung useless at his side, but that only seemed to inflame his remaining limbs into action.

Before Noah could fight him off, Mitchell pinned him in the chest with his good knee, tightened his remaining hand around Noah's throat, and squeezed. The pain reached a nine on a ten-point scale, making Noah wish he'd trained a little harder on evasive maneuvers. He heard Nicolle yell something, but he was concentrating on keeping his airway open and blood flowing to his brain. Noah reached his hands up in preparation.

The lunatic crouched closer, and at this distance, the lack of human emotion made his eyes a dense black. "Yeah, you try to peel me off you, fucker. You're a scrawny little thing, aren't you? I wonder what she sees in you when she could have me "

Not in a thousand lifetimes. Stars began to flash across his narrowing vision, and he knew he didn't have much time. Noah felt along the big hand until he reached the wrist, counting tendons and ligaments until he found the spot he wanted. He pressed one thumb into the nerve, readying his other palm to slam up into Mitchell's nose. With any luck, he'd knock it back into his brain and take a burden off the prison system.

Mitchell's fingers suddenly released, and the man stared in confusion at his limp hand. Noah readied his facial blow, pulling back with the limited space he had and concentrating his energy.

A shrill cry filled the forest, and Mitchell's body suddenly disappeared, airborne and gone over Noah's head. Nicolle sprang past and yelled again, and he heard the sound of boot against cartilage and a new shriek. Mitchell's keening wail peaked and grew silent, as if he passed out.

"Noah. Oh god, can you breathe?"

He nodded as Nicolle's face appeared, unable to speak until he inhaled deeply a few more times. Around them, ash swirled and settled like dirty snow. Some of it stuck to her face, and he lifted a hand to brush it away. That only made things worse. He realized she was crying and laughing at the same time, and rivers of black marked the lines of her tears.

"I love you, you idiot."

He coughed and tried twice before the raspy words came out. "I love you too. You're my hero. Help me up."

She gaped at him, closed her mouth, and then opened it again as if she was again going to argue with him.

"Forget about saying no. Get me up. Let's see what we can do to help Peter until others arrive."

She put an arm around Noah's back and her hands under his shoulders, and between them, they got him to his feet. He winced but kept his pain to himself. He figured there were enough injured bodies around that needed more tending than he did.

"I wasn't going to argue with you. I was going to say that I'm not a hero, but you are. I have never seen moves like that, Noah. You have to show me how you took him down."

They both glanced over at Mitchell, who lay on his side breathing heavily but apparently unconscious.

"We should tie him up," Noah said, already hobbling to the truck with more energy.

"He's not going to move for a while," Nicolle said, releasing her support but not her hold on him. Noah heard a purr of satisfaction in her voice.

He stopped and looked at her. "How can you be so sure?"

She grinned, white teeth in a face the color of ash. "I kicked his nuts into his kidneys."

Noah chuckled, despite the news stabs of pain the action produced. Nicolle soon joined in. Then she stopped, and an impish grin that held absolutely no remorse filled her face. She leaned closer and whispered, "Three times."

He couldn't stop laughing, bent at the waist until his legs cramped from the fight and the effort of staying upright. "You are incredible."

Nicolle nodded at his compliment, but her face fell into a thoughtful expression. Her words were quiet when she said, "We've slayed our dragons, Noah. Neither one of them is going to get out of prison to harm us or the people we care about. Now we can see what comes next for us." The inflections in her declaration said more than her words how she wasn't sure what that might be.

"I have a prescription for that, Ms. Trajan," he said in his best reassuring doctor tone.

Her eyes narrowed with sharp suspicion. "And that is?"

He grinned and yanked her close enough to see the sparks of surprise dancing in her smoky-colored eyes. "You and me, together forever."

He swallowed her answering laugh as their lips confirmed that diagnosis.

Epilogue

"What the fu-, I mean, fudge, guys, eh?"

Cap stood in the doorway of Noah's house, his grin of greeting switching between Noah and Nicolle.

"What the fudge, Cap," Nici replied. A small palm tucked into hers and she looked down at Char. The girl's wide eyes were on Cap's missing fingers as she pulled Nicolle's hand for attention.

"Why did you guys say fudge, and why doesn't he have all his fingers?"

Noah stepped across and reached for his daughter, throwing an apologetic look in Cap's direction. The captain moved faster and bent down until he was eyeball to eyeball with the girl.

"My name is Cap, and I'm Nicolle's boss." He dropped his voice as if sharing a secret. "Though I have to tell you, she bosses me around most of the time."

Char grinned, doing a quick curtsey she copied from the myriad princess movies she liked to watch. "I'm Char. And I guess it's okay if Nici bosses you around. She bosses Daddy around all the time too."

Nici enjoyed the disconcerted expression on Noah's face, and she gave Cap's cheek a quick kiss of greeting. An out-of-place ruddiness rose as he placed his radio belt on the entry table. "I think you know almost everyone," she said, waving him inside. "This is Marcus Dawson, Noah's boss."

Marcus moved forward and extended a hand with a smile. "More friend than boss, I'd say. Glad we finally have a chance to meet."

And with Cap's arrival, everyone was there, an impromptu party to celebrate that the bad guys were taken down and it was over. Less than a week had gone by since Mitchell was sent to a prison hospital bed in Sacramento. Danielle groused about not being able to keep him in her jail, but the medical care he needed for his injuries required more advanced services than the local cells would provide. She said as much again now.

"Come on, Dani, he's behind bars and according to his parole officer and the district attorneys in two counties, he's not going to see the light of day for a very long time. There are so many charges against him, they're pooling resources to figure out who gets him first." Nici tried to wrap an arm around Danielle's shoulders, but her twin shrugged it off and turned away.

Nici eyed her with concern. Danielle had been like this since the day of Mitchell's apprehension. Noah's brother had also been distant. Gideon sat on the couch and watched with a neutral expression as Danielle stalked over to Jake and his wife and began an animated conversation with her back turned to him. Whatever was up, Danielle didn't want to discuss it. Gid wasn't talking about things either.

A soda in hand, Cap settled on the couch and beckoned Char forward. She settled next to him and leaned in as if she'd done it a thousand times.

"She trusts so easily," Noah said, pulling Nicolle in closer.

"I hope she never has a reason to change," Nici said, putting her head on his shoulder. He lowered his face for a quick kiss, one she held on to longer than necessary. They both grinned as they moved apart in slow motion.

Behind them, a sudden tortured groan made them both turn. Elena watched them with a disgusted expression. She rolled her eyes and whipped on her heels, disappearing around the corner before either of them could say anything.

"I should reassure her," Noah said, already disengaging.

Nici knew his heart was in the right place, but the more important he made accepting Nicolle in their lives, the less the girl seemed to want to do it. They had tried talking to her as an adult, as a teenager, and when Noah got frustrated, as a child.

Marcus stepped beside them and said, "Let her be. She'll come around in her own time. When my daughters were her age, they did everything on their schedule. When you're almost thirteen, the world revolves around you."

Noah grinned but looked unconvinced. He took a step as if he planned to follow Elena, but Char's high voice called to her father. With furrows of concentration marking her smooth young forehead, Char examined Cap's missing fingers as if she saw this kind of thing all the time. Being a doctor was on the girl's future career list, along with ballerina, teacher and the latest addition, firefighter. The girl raised serious eyes and asked, "Daddy, can you fix his hand?"

Nici watched Noah's face fill with emotion as he opened his mouth to speak. He wanted to be the hero in his daughters' eyes, and after four days, Nici had seen enough evidence to be convinced he was. Elena might not be showing it, but she was confident this would change again with time.

Cap answered Char's question. "Nope, he can't fix me anymore, little one. You see, I lost those fingers a long time ago, and someday, I'll tell you the story about it. But for now, I want to hear about how your dad and Nici stopped the bad guy, okay?"

Char nodded hard enough to make her curls dance, and Nici glanced at Noah. He wouldn't want a child to hear this.

A new voice said, "Hey Char, why don't we head for the kitchen and round up more food? I have a feeling this story is going to make everyone hungry."

Nici met the eyes of Jake's wife and mouthed her thanks. She hadn't met the woman before today, but she was proving to be kind and quick. Jake had mentioned a daughter who would be in school together with Elena in the fall.

"How's Peter?" Cap asked the quiet question as he watched the little girl skipping out of the room with a fond smile on his face. This softer side of him was new, but Nici thought she could get used to it.

"He'll recover, though there will be scarring after multiple surgeries. Luckily, Nicolle acted fast and the fire didn't get a chance to do as much damage as it could have," Marcus said.

"Yeah, about that. What were you thinking, throwing yourself over a flaming man like that?" Danielle's eyes snapped as she asked the question, but Nici read the underlying fear in her sister. She raised her arm with its single slight burn as evidence.

"I acted on training, Dani. This isn't much worse than the burn from a stove. Besides, Noah is the real hero."

Cap and Danielle both turned to Noah, who shrunk away at the sudden attention. She knew he hated to recount the tale again.

Cap leaned forward over steepled fingers and said, "Tell me about the thing you hit him with. Was that some form of karate or something?"

Noah sat up and she sensed the embarrassment. He told her the more he thought about it, the more he was concerned he could have gotten them both killed. Or worse, Noah would have been incapacitated and Mitchell would have carted off an injured Nicolle. That gave him a nightmare last night, one she wasn't there to calm because they'd agreed to stay in different houses until Elena came around.

"It was a form of Chinese martial arts, using pressure points to disable an opponent. I practice the targeted kicks on a regular basis. I have to tell you, though, that kicking an inanimate bag in the gym and kicking a man flying at you and bent on hurting you are two completely different things."

They all laughed at this, Jake drawing closer in the process. He too had heard parts of the story. "Tell me where you were aiming that first kick," he said.

"The median nerve, kind of like a super hard hitting your elbow sort of thing."

Jake nodded, patting his non-existent shirt pocket as if he planned to take notes. Nici heard a chuckle from the end of the couch where Danielle perched, and she watched her sister give an indulgent grin.

"And the next one?" This from Danielle.

"The outside behind his knee. Same principle."

Cap shook his head, wonder on his face. "I might have you drill our female firefighters. The men, pah, they're on their own then."

Everyone laughed. Gideon plopped his walking cast on the table with a thud. "I want that last move, bro. That was like something in movies."

Danielle rolled her eyes, inching away from Gideon at the opposite end of the couch like he was contagious. Nici frowned at her. At some point soon, she needed to ask what had happened and not take a denial for an answer.

Noah pointed to his wrist and said, "This spot, same thing again. You lose the feeling in your hand and you can't grip anything for a while. Ladies, in case your man ever puts his hand someplace where it isn't welcomed." He pointed at the spot.

This time the laughter was sheepish or impish, depending on gender. Only Danielle and Gideon remained unmoved. Nici wondered if they'd had a falling out, or if their natures had taken over. They had each moved on. It saddened her to think Dani wasn't finding love, not like she had. It made her appreciate Noah even more.

Cap said, "So, there's that other set of injuries, the ones that knocked him out. What's the explanation for those?" He flashed an expectant look between the two of them.

Noah shook his head but didn't look at Nicolle. He leaned forward with an earnest expression and said, "I think those happened when Nicolle tried to aim for his other knee, right?" He gave her a stern glance.

She smiled back. He had insisted from the first moments after the attack that he take full responsibility for Mitchell's condition. The man hadn't said peep to the contrary, and according to his court-appointed attorney, had been reluctant to explain how he'd come by those final injuries. Nici argued with him at the beginning, but when Noah insisted, saying he didn't want her to be blame-stormed again, she relented. It was much more rewarding than arguing. And afterwards, he agreed she could claim one kick.

Cap looked between the two of them as he shook his head. "Can't say this wasn't a fun thing to write up, but what the fu-, I mean fudge, Trajan. Don't ever let me get on your bad side."

Nici rose with the escalating laughter and good-natured teasing. Noah stood as well and gave her a quick kiss on the cheek. "I have a surprise for everyone."

She nodded, curious about what he had been planning. He'd been secretive and excited about it, as he now scooted out of the room like a kid expecting Christmas.

She headed up the stairs to the bathroom, her head still in the clouds with the wonderful life she now enjoyed. It was remarkable how different things were today than they had been at the beginning of summer. Only Danielle's turbulent non-relationship with Gideon still hung over their heads. She'd help her sister get over it, whatever it was. The looks those two shot each other when they thought they were unobserved were steamy enough to douse a campfire.

The sound of a sob stopped her, and she glanced around trying to find the source. A moment later, she heard another sob. She pushed open the door to Noah's bedroom to find Elena curled into a ball in the far corner behind the bed.

The girl looked up, but didn't say anything. Nici said, "Hey." Elena stared at her a moment before dropping her face into her arms again and sobbing once more.

"I'll get your dad, sweetie."

"No." The earnest wet entreaty stopped Nici. More whimpers sounded from the corner. It hurt her heart to hear them. Whatever bothered Elena, more moody and irritable than normal according to Noah, it was something she couldn't or wouldn't discuss with her father.

Nici took a deep breath and made the short walk around the bed, dropping into a crouch a couple of feet away against the wall. After a few minutes, Elena's sobbing slowed. Nici said, "Do you want to talk about it?"

Elena's head popped up and her eyes snapped with annoyance. "Why are you asking?"

Nici remembered almost thirteen well. Boys. Hormones. Disappointments that felt like the end of the world. That was the year she realized she'd never be able to sing well enough to be a rock and roll star, and it crushed her confidence for a time.

"Because whatever is bothering you isn't something you feel you can discuss with your dad. Because your father and I love each other, and I get the added benefit of having two amazing girls who are part of his world. Because I care about you. I'd like to get to know you better, and part of that is giving you whatever support I can." Nicolle thought it was too early to say the word love.

Elena sniffed, wiping the tears on her face with the backs of her hands. Her suspicious regard lasted so long, Nicolle thought she was going to yell again.

"You kicked that guy in the nuts," Elena said.

Nici couldn't help jumping in surprise. They hadn't discussed this in front of the girls.

Elena smiled in obvious triumph. "I heard you talking about it. About how you gave it to him three times, and hard. I hope you broke something and it never works again."

Yes, she had definitely heard too much. Nicolle remembered the conversation, late the night the girls got home when she and Noah thought they were already asleep.

"Did Char hear that particular conversation too?"

Elena shook her head.

"Good, then let's keep that between us, okay? I don't think she's old enough yet to be exposed to this particular tactic."

Elena's rapid nod of agreement came after only a second. She looked down at her fingernails, peeling at the black polish as she had steadily since returning home. She didn't seem to be in any hurry to replace it, a fact Noah had remarked on that morning.

"I wish I'd kicked him in the nuts."

Nici stilled, unsure where this was going. "Mitchell? Thank you, but he was my bad guy, not yours."

Elena snorted and gave her a sideways glance. "Not your bad guy. Mine. Richard."

Noah needed to be the one hearing this. Nicolle didn't want to supplant him in this kind of discussion. If someone had forced Elena into something she didn't want to do, he should be the one listening.

But Elena didn't seem to notice her hesitancy. She said, "Richard is a dickhead. First, he acted like he was into me, and then, like, no. Then he was all over me. I pushed him away, I hit him, and he laughed at me. He said I was a prick-tease, that I led him on, but obviously I was just a baby, and a hick baby at that."

Nici absorbed the words, relying on a memory of how her rape counselor had handled their initial conversation. Her heart beat quickened, and she wished Noah would come looking for them. "Then what happened?"

Elena shrugged, adding a new black flake to the growing pile on the floor. "His friends showed up, and he, like, told them I was a baby and a PT and all that. But I didn't want to go with him, not after the way he acted with me." The girl sniffed dismissively. "Anyway, then he and his friends walked away laughing. Every time they saw me after that, they laughed at me." Another sniff. "Like it matters. I hate LA. I never want to go back there again."

Nici exhaled a breath she wasn't even aware she'd been holding in anticipation of the worst. She nudged her body closer to the girl, who didn't give any indication she noticed.

"I'm proud of you for standing up for your principles, Elena. Women need to do that to bullies. If he didn't respect what you wanted, he wasn't worth another second of your time."

Elena gave a quick nod, but Nici saw the quiver of her chin.

"Promise you won't tell Daddy, okay?"

Nici nodded into Elena's tear-filled eyes. "Of course. This is just woman stuff between you and me. But you know he'd be proud of you if you tell him. You did what you needed to protect yourself."

Elena's face pulled into a picture of frustration. She snorted, a very unladylike sound, but it made Nici want to laugh in relief. This would not scar her for life.

"Yeah, but you need to give me lessons. Next time, I'm kicking the guy in the nuts. And when I can do that, I'll tell Daddy."

>>>>>

Noah was reassured by Nicolle's smile, as she gave him a discreet thumbs-up with a point toward Elena. Whatever had happened, they must be fine, because Elena flashed a quick smile in Nicolle's direction too.

Char bounced in from the kitchen with a plate of cookies, putting them on the table with a clatter and dancing over to the cases. "Daddy, what's this?"

He opened the first case and removed the contents, hooking up the power supply with quick movements. "It's my surprise."

"But what is it?"

"Oh man, you have not done what I think you've done, have you, bro?" Gid's tone sounded like mock horror, but Noah noted the grin on his brother's face. With quick moves, Gideon removed everything from the coffee table, taking a cookie to munch on as he was suddenly on his feet. "Be right back."

Noah felt every set of eyes in the silent room on him as he opened the other case and bent to hook up the final piece. He heard an amused Marcus say, "Oh my, oh my." Gid reappeared with a couple of wooden spoons and a stack of pots. When he seated himself with a flurry of movement and placed the pieces in front of him, he grinned and nodded to Noah.

"Ladies and gentleman, for your musical pleasure tonight, let me present," Gid did the drum roll of introduction with two spoon handles on the table, and Noah finished with a chord, "the Bad Asses."

"Daddy, quarter in the jar," Char said.

"What the fuck," popped out of Cap's mouth, and Char looked at him aghast.

"Daddy, I think Cap needs to put two quarters in the jar."

Noah grinned at his family, at Elena attempting to look bored but intrigued, at Char already on her feet ready to dance, at Gid getting his groove on. Then he looked at Nicolle, and she already had a spoon up to her mouth for a mic. Marcus stood to the side, his hands at the ready for an air guitar, and lifted his chin with a grin.

He hit the first series of chords, his fingers flying like he was still a teen and his voice a bit screechy on the first words. Gideon slammed on the pots until one of the lids flew off the table, and Danielle opened her mouth as if getting ready to comment as his brother grinned up at her. She promptly shut it again and looked away from Gid with a deliberate turn of her head. Noah didn't miss the disappointment on his brother's face.

Yeah, something wasn't right, but whatever it was, Noah would help him fix it. His family was going to be all right. He met Nicolle's eyes as she watched them. She winked at him as she opened her mouth to hit the first notes.

Okay, she might call it singing, but it was awful. He flubbed a sequence.

"I know I'm bad. That's why I lip sync. Someone else needs to sing."

The sound of a harmonica caught him off guard, until Cap picked up the melody as if he had been doing it for years. "Big fan of theirs, big fan," and he went back to blowing. Marcus added his voice as a bass line. Jake and his wife danced an acceptable boogie, and Nicolle had Danielle up on the floor, the two of them joining Char in a shimmy that had Noah going hard.

Then he hit the riff, the one he loved, and a single voice screeched the lyrics along with him. He almost lost the beat in surprise as all eyes in the room turned to Elena. At the end of the stanza, which she delivered in a nearly perfect rocker imitation, she glanced around the room.

"What? I like them too. They're old and stuff, but they're cool."

Noah started laughing as he jammed with his band, complete with back-up singers and dancers. Noise filled the room, and he thought his face might ache for a week from his broad grin. Nici looked at him, and everything tilted into balance in his world.

They were on the final verse when the drums went missing. He looked at Gid to see why he'd lost the beat, and realized his brother stared at the front door. Noah's fingers slowed on the strings. Someone beat an urgent fist on the wood and called out to them in a demanding voice.

Everything fell silent as Noah slipped off the guitar. A feeling of tense doom rose in him as he made his way across the living room and checked the peephole. The uniformed person on the other side wasn't anyone he recognized. When he pulled open the door on the man's raised fist, Nicolle called out a greeting, as did Gid and Cap.

"Brody, what's going on?" Cap crossed the room and picked up his radio, swearing as he stared at its face. He turned a knob and a sudden rush of disembodied voices filled the room.

"Sorry, Cap, but I knew you'd want to know about this." He nodded as if in apology to everyone in the room, but his eyes hesitated when they rested on Gideon.

"What, Brody?" Nicolle slipped her hand into Noah's with her question.

The firefighter shifted in obvious discomfort, his gaze flashing to Gideon once more. "Another fire, arson again based on the flashpoint and velocity of the burn." He hesitated.

"Spit it out, Brody," Cap said, already pulling his communications belt across his body. Gideon rose from the couch and threw the wooden spoons on the table with dull bounces.

"We found this, Cap." He lifted a plastic bag, the clear kind commonly used to line office wastebaskets, and he glanced at Gideon.

Noah heard the steel in his brother's tone when he asked, "Where did you find it?"

Brody held the bag out in front of him as if it might ignite at any moment. "On your desk, Kinkead."

Noah exchanged a worried glance with Nicolle. It couldn't be. His brother had to be innocent. They turned as one to the room.

Gideon and Danielle stared at each other, neither face readable. Gid's nostrils flared, with anger or pain, Noah wasn't sure. Beside him, he heard Nicolle's gasp.

His pained eyes still on Danielle, Gideon said, "It's not over."

The End – And To Be Continued...

Excerpt from *LOVE'S FIERY RESOLUTION*

Check out Book 10 in the Flynn's Crossing series, **LOVE'S FIERY RESOLUTION**, *to experience the love and suspense from Gideon and Danielle's perspective – and learn the identity of the arsonist! Here's a taste of what's to come!*

Prologue – Last Autumn

Blisters formed where heat baked bare skin. Dense smoke made vision of more than a few feet impossible. Gid's tongue had long gone dry from scorching air penetrating his breather. Twin sensations of power and fear rippled through him. Conditions were beyond the realm of reason, and he loved it.

He brought the Pulaski down with a surge, intent on digging a scratch line in partially burnt ground. The understory had disappeared on the first flash and they thought they had this front contained. Madame Fire had other ideas. A gust of wind built into a flame devil, tearing a new hole in their line and racing away, even as it left behind torches skipping from treetop to treetop. There was no way down, and no way up. They were left to fight the monster, cut off from help.

Still, he felt powerful. Perhaps there was something wrong with him. Part of him fought the fire with the last surge of energy he had. The other part, the part he'd like to think was wise and objective, jittered in knowing they were five men alone in hell, and despite their best efforts, they might die on this ridge.

"Hey, hey, over here."

The disembodied voice sounded urgent but controlled. Training surpassed fear in circumstances like this. Over the roar of combustion, he heard a keening scream, and his eyes swung to the dim shape of a small building. Sparks lapped its roofline and the shingle siding smoldered.

Instructions poured over his comm unit faster than slippery retardant falling from planes above them. A fresh rain of red spattered around the team, but it made only marginal difference. Their yellow turnouts had long since turned a mixture of gray and red, making locating his men harder by the moment. Pines engulfed to their tops outraced their efforts.

"Clear a path. One evacuee, a little girl. Anyone got a spare hand?"

Gid stepped toward two waving figures. Two more flanked them with their backs turned, their faces to the advancing fire.

"Honey, we're here to help you. Please stop struggling. We'll get you out."

He heard the words of the rookie. He and the other firefighter carried a child between them. A fire shelter protected her head and shoulders, making her unrecognizable. Her feet would soon suffer from the heat in those sneakers. He wondered if she could run.

The rookie said, "She was behind the cabin. I didn't get a chance to check inside. You take her and I'll go back."

Gid shook his head. "Nah, keep moving. Might be safe in the streambed between the bounders. Head down. I'll check the cabin."

He rushed forward over their protests. Who left a child alone in a tinder dry forest? Behind him, he heard the child's startled cries. "Binky. You have to get my Binky."

Figures. Binky was probably a dog or a cat. But if it was a living thing and he could catch it, he'd bring it to her. The girl would have precious little else left.

He rammed the head of his Pulaski into the door and heard splinters of wood where the hinges left the old frame. The interior was darker than the forest, and he struggled to see through his visor. Smoke twirled in the light from the blaze outside. The space was meager but crammed with belongings. He heard his name called over the comm and acknowledged the directive to move out. It would only take another minute. There weren't many places to search.

Lifting his visor, he peered into the corners. "Here, Binky." He felt stupid, but he did it again anyway. "Binky, come on. You don't want to be a roast, do you?"

The impact came from nowhere, settling with a hard thump between his shoulders blades. Pain radiated down his arms. He tightened his grip on his equipment automatically. Whatever Binky was, it was huge. He wouldn't put it past the kid to keep a pet bear. People in these backwoods locations where never predictable.

He prepared to face his attacker when he heard shouts. The voices magnified in his earbud grew urgent.

"Kid, stop struggling. You can't go back. He'll find it. Honey –"

"Shit, she's running toward the cabin. Kid, are you crazy or –"

"Gid, get outta there. Roof's gonna go."

The cacophony of noises, the men's voices mixed with the pitched howls of the child, accompanied the raging voice of wildfire. He dropped his visor and turned toward the open doorway.

A large form filled his view of freedom. Raised like claws on the ends of arms extending from a big body, something loomed over him. Outside over the shrieks of the inferno, he heard the child's plea.

"Binky. I need Binky."

Something slammed into his face, cracking the visor's surface in a snowflake of fissures. What the hell? Another crash and he recovered his protective instincts and raised his tool to shield him from the next impact. This time, the swipe of a strike closed on the handle with a determined yank.

"Get out of my house," said a deep raspy voice, with enough rage to convince him he was hearing things. Everyone knew bears didn't talk.

The large hands closed on either side of his and pulled the handle away as if he'd been holding on with a single finger.

"Binky. Binky." The girl's sobs registered in his comm and echoed from the doorway, and he realized she was inside.

"Kinkead, outta there now. Gid, get out."

Frantic shouts in his ear went unheard when a flash from the woods lit the interior with an unearthly glow. In the light, he saw his attacker. A man taller than him by a good foot and more and with shoulders so broad, he probably needed to turn sideways to enter the door. But what scared him the most were the man's eyes. Even in the dimness, he could see their whites and the crazed expression in them. The bear of a man raised the Pulaski in the air with the fine point aimed for Gid's head. It bore down and he heard his own voice scream with the impending collision.

"Wake up, man. Kinkead, wake up. Gid?"

Rough shakes tumbled him over until his face bit into dirt. Something heavy pressed against his back, holding him in place. He struggled to free his arms, but they were pinned at his sides.

"It's okay, man. Gid, it was a dream. You're safe."

The voice penetrated. He wasn't fighting for his life. The weight on his back wasn't the bear-man. He drew deep breaths, feeling the douse of unhealthy sweat soak his sleeping bag. He stopped fighting, letting his body go limp as he turned his head.

"I'm okay." His voice came out weak without conviction and he tried again. "I'm awake."

The pressure eased, and the face of another firefighter swam into view as the man knelt next to him. Shaking his arms to stop their trembles, Gid drew a deep breath and pushed himself up to his knees. Feet shuffled in the small group surrounding him. He lifted his gaze to meet sympathetic eyes, but something else lurked behind those expressions.

Pity.

Fear.

Embarrassment.

This would never be over.

About the Author

I love to hear from readers, so feel free to contact me through my website, www.yvonnekohano.com, or directly on Facebook as Yvonne Kohano, on Twitter @yvonnekohano, and at yvonne@yvonnekohano.com. Please leave an honest review of this novel at Amazon, Goodreads, or your favorite book discovery site of choice.

A HOLT Medallion Award of Merit recipient in Romantic Suspense, Yvonne enjoys channeling her characters' voices and passions as they overcome real world problems and discover love. Her Flynn's Crossing contemporary romantic suspense series is set in a fictional northern California foothills town not unlike the one where she used to live. Of course, the beauty and wonders of the Sierra Nevada Mountains and the surrounding counties play costarring roles in her work.

The first six books in the Flynn's Crossing series follow the developing love interests of the girl tribe, a group of successful women who work through real world conflicts and challenges to find acceptance and love - with some suspenseful happenings thrown in! In the next six books, single guys in the wolf pack find their true loves, but not without their own issues to conquer. Periodically, Yvonne will be adding seasonal novellas to the series, featuring the first person voice of a character from one of her previous books experiencing an event that we can all relate to.

www.ingramcontent.com/pod-product-compliance
Lightning Source LLC
Chambersburg PA
CBHW051334250626
47155CB00007B/2589

* 9 7 8 1 9 4 0 7 3 8 3 9 0 *